# Praise for Mr. R

Looking for a great summer read? I loved *Mr. R – A Rock & Roll Romance* by Tracy Neis. This modern retelling of *Jane Eyre* surprised and delighted me. For me, I know a book is great when I don't want it to end, and can't stop thinking about it after I've finished. That's what happened when I read *Mr. R*.

—*Syrie James, bestselling author of
"The Secret Diaries of Charlotte Brontë"*

*Mr. R* kept me entertained; I'd certainly recommend this one to Brontëites.

—*Nicola Friar, author of
The Brontë Babe Blog*

The book was a page-turner for me. I was so invested in the story and wanted to know how all of the conflicts would resolve. And everything was wrapped up in a believable and emotional way. I thought this was a wonderful retelling—especially for its focus on the character of Rochester.

—*The Eyre Guide Blog*

The Rock and Roll Brontë Series

by Tracy Neis

♫ ♫ ♫

*Mr. R - A Rock and Roll Romance*

A modern reimagining of *Jane Eyre*

♫ ♫ ♫

*Restless Spirits*

An Alternate Take on

*Wuthering Heights* and *Agnes Grey*

♫ ♫ ♫

*Wildfell Summer*

A magical mystery trip through the pages of

*The Tenant of Wildfell Hall*

♫ ♫ ♫

*Nowhere Girl*

Inspired by an unfinished manuscript by Charlotte Brontë

# Mr. R

## A Rock and Roll Romance

### By Tracy Neis

Mr. R – A Rock and Roll Romance
by Tracy Neis

Previously published by
Mischievous Muse Publishing Alliance
Los Angeles County, California

All rights reserved.
Copyright © 2018 Tracy Neis
Second Edition, 2020

The characters in this book are fictitious.
Any similarity to actual persons, living or dead,
is purely coincidental and not intended by the author.

This book is protected under the copyright laws of the
United States of America. Any reproduction or other
unauthorized use of the material or artwork herein
is prohibited without the express written
permission of the publisher and author.

Cover artwork and author illustration
by Karen Neis

Library of Congress Cataloging-in-Publishing Data
Neis, Tracy
Mr. R / Tracy Neis

Neis Family Publications
Paperback ISBN: 978-1-7343600-3-5

*for Mike*

*My hope, my heart, my life*

# Prologue

"This is for you," she said, handing him the small wrapped package. "Happy birthday."

"Thank you, love," Eddie replied. He gave her a quick kiss, then slipped the ribbon off the gift and tore away the shiny red paper.

"Well, I'll be damned," he said as he ran his index finger over the gilt lettering on the brown leather cover. "'*Sonnets from the Portuguese.*' Your favorite book." He opened the cover to read the dedication and furrowed his brow. "This is yours, darling. Your dad gave it to you. I can't take it."

"No," she said, closing his fingers over the book. "I want you to have it."

He scanned the inscription once more and noted the date. "Your fifteenth birthday. This would have been one of the last things he—"

"Never mind that," she insisted, letting go of his hands. "I remember when he gave it to me. That's why it's dear. And that's why I want you to have it—because it's so very dear to me. Anyway, I don't need it anymore. I've memorized all the poems."

"Really?" Eddie laughed. He brought his hand to the nape of her neck and started playing with a loose tendril of hair that had slipped from her bun. "Prove it. Number twenty-five."

"A heavy heart, Belovèd, have I borne, from year to year until I saw thy face."

He opened the book to the proper page, read the opening lines, and shook his head. "All right, show-off. How about number thirty-five?"

She closed her eyes and cleared her throat. "Alas, I have grieved, so I am hard to love."

He skipped ahead a few pages and skimmed the sonnet. "Well, you're both right and wrong about that one, m'dear. That's the third-to-last line. But you are easy to love."

She leaned against his chest and wrapped her arms around his waist. He rested his head on top of hers and breathed in the sweet floral fragrance of her newly washed hair.

"You don't know me very well yet," she whispered. "If you did, you wouldn't say that."

"I know all I need to know," he replied. "I know that I'm madly in love with you."

"Love is fire," she said, withdrawing from his embrace. She took his hand in hers and started tracing the lines on his palm with her thumb. "And when I say at need, 'I love thee,' mark, 'I love thee!' And in thy sight I stand transfigured."

She gazed into his eyes and hardly blinked. He felt a tingling in his gut as a wave of heat started spreading through his body.

"That's from number ten," she added, curling her soft, plump lips into a smile.

"I'll trust you on that," he said, resting the book on a table so he could use both hands to unbutton her blouse.

"I read through that book so many times while you were on tour," she confessed, raising her hands to his shirt so she could undo his buttons as well. "I felt like Elizabeth Barrett Browning. An invalid, brought back to life through love."

"And I'm your Robert?" Eddie laughed, slipping the blouse from her shoulders and cupping her breasts with his hands.

"You are my 'most gracious singer of high poems'," she answered. She leaned forward and gave him a long, deep kiss, then stepped back and looked down. "I'm 'more like an out-of-tune worn viol, a good singer would be wroth to spoil his song with'."

Eddie put his hand to her chin and lifted her face to meet his once more. "Don't say that, love. That's your brother's voice you hear in your head. You have to stop listening when he puts you down like that, and start believing in me instead. I think you're perfect. I knew, from the very first moment I met you, that you were the most wonderful woman in the world."

He leaned forward and kissed the top of her head. "How do I love thee?" he whispered. "Let me count the ways." He lowered his lips to her cheek, her throat, her breast, her nipple, punctuating each kiss with another whisper—"You're brilliant. You're beautiful. You're sexy. And you're so goddamned mysterious."

# Book One

*"Great God! What sweet madness has seized me?"*

– Charlotte Brontë
*Jane Eyre*

# Chapter One

## *Munich, Federal Republic of Germany — 1971*

"Excuse me!" Eddie shouted, working his way through the crowd of drunken revelers. "'Scuse me. Just wanna say goodbye to the birthday boy before I leave!"

"You are going already?" a sultry voice protested. "The party is just beginning!"

Eddie looked down as a woman in a low-cut dress placed her hand on his shoulder. The satin fabric of her red halter dress slid partially open as she nuzzled closer, revealing the soft, fleshy tops of her breasts. She tilted her head to meet his eyes. "You like?" she asked, her voice barely audible over the din of the party.

"Very much," Eddie replied.

The woman brought her hand to Eddie's cheek and started stroking his sideburns with a long painted fingernail. "I like you too," she said in a thick German accent, bringing her face closer to his. "You have always been my favorite Pilot. I love your lyrics. They are so passionate."

"Mm-hmm," Eddie mumbled. He quickly sized up the woman's considerable attributes—nice tits, pretty face, lovely hair. Obviously willing. He stole a quick glance at his watch and debated whether he really needed to leave the party after all—or if he ought to leave it by himself, at any rate. He looked back at the woman's eyes. They were a gorgeous shade of blue. Sexy. Inviting. Dilated.

"All right everyone, shut up!" shouted Eli Deere, Eddie's bassist and the host of the party. "Time for the cake!" He switched off the lights. A scantily-clad woman worked her way across the room, parting the crowd with a serving trolley bearing a large cake covered in candles. The drunken guests fell into a chorus of song.

"Happy birthday, dear Gerr-eee, happy birthday to yoooo!"

Gerry Enis—the celebrated man of the hour—threw back his head to take a breath, knocking his crumpled paper hat to the floor. He blew out the candles and pitched the room back into darkness. The woman in the halter dress started massaging Eddie's thigh. After a few seconds of blind chaos, someone in the back of the room found a light switch. The crowd hailed the return of the light with a shower of whoops.

Eddie gazed once more into the luminous eyes of the woman by his side. Her enlarged pupils had barely registered a response to the changes in the room's brightness.

He took hold of her roving hand. Loosening her firm grip on his trousers, he brought her fingers to his lips. "Another time," he whispered, gently kissing her knuckles. He let her go and approached his drummer Gerry.

*He looks drunk, as usual,* Eddie thought as he watched Gerry sway unsteadily on his feet. *That didn't take long.* But he forced a smile and called out in a tone of practiced joviality, "Hey, mate! Wanted to say 'Happy Birthday' before I left!"

"What? You can't go yet!" Gerry protested. "You haven't even had a piece of my cake!"

" 'S'alright. I'm not hungry," Eddie said. "Have fun!"

"Like you need to tell me to do that?" Gerry laughed. The woman who had brought in the cake scooped a dollop of frosting off the top and brought her finger to his tongue. Gerry licked it greedily. Eddie turned and walked away.

"Hey Rochester! You leaving already?" yelled Eli. "The night's still young!"

Eddie sized up his bassist and couldn't decide if he looked more drunk or stoned. "I've got a date," Eddie lied. "Gotta go home and get ready to pick her up."

"A date with a book," laughed the shaggy-haired man standing behind Eli.

Eddie shared a knowing smile with his pianist and song-writing partner Jim McCudden. "Gotta go now, mate. I'm at the dirty part. Tess is just about to lose her virginity."

Jim smiled. "In grand Victorian style, no less. I remember reading that book in seventh form and not even realizing Tess and Alec had it off, and the next thing you know she'd given birth."

"You have to learn to read between the lines," Eddie replied, tapping the corner of his eyes. He glanced over Jim's shoulder and saw the woman in the red dress kissing his manager's younger brother Alan Poole. *That didn't take long either,* he thought with a fleeting wave of disappointment.

"You have to learn to stop looking for love in books," Jim said. "Someday you're gonna fall for a real woman, Eddie."

Eddie shrugged and sighed. "Hope so. Though probably not at this party." He looked back at Eli. "Where'd'ya put my coat?"

"Dunno. Threw it in a bedroom I think." Eli staggered towards Gerry. "You wanker, Enis! Save some cake for the rest of us!"

Eddie slipped out of the crowded living room and stepped into a long hallway. He opened the first door and saw his lead singer Tony Wright locked in a passionate embrace with a nearly-naked blonde. He shut the door, peeked in the opposite room, and saw two people snorting coke off a mirror. They looked up at him and laughed. He turned away and walked to the end of the hallway. Bracing himself for another awkward spectacle, he rested his fingertips on the last doorknob and slowly rotated the handle.

The door creaked open, revealing a floor covered in coats. Eddie stepped inside and removed a ladies' tweed overcoat from the top of the pile. He was just about to throw it onto a bed in the far corner of the room when he noticed a woman was sitting on top of the mattress. She had curled herself into a ball, with her knees drawn up to her chest. In her right hand she held a book.

"Oh, I'm sorry," Eddie said. "You were so quiet, I didn't even notice you."

The woman ignored him and continued to read her book.

Eddie examined her carefully while he waited for her to respond. Long, dark curls of raven-colored hair cascaded in luxurious waves around her silhouetted profile, shielding most of her face from view. The topmost strands of her untamed mane glowed like a halo in the soft light cast by the room's solitary lamp.

"I'm sorry, miss," he repeated.

She remained silent.

He took a step towards the bed and summoned his courage. "May I ask what you're reading?"

She drew her knees closer to her chest.

His curiosity piqued, Eddie stepped even closer to the bed. "I'm sorry if I'm bothering you. It's just that—well, I usually prefer books to parties too."

Without looking up, the woman began reading aloud from her book. Her voice was low and dusky and bore traces of a foreign accent Eddie couldn't place:

*"—Come and kiss me.*
*Never mind my bruises,*
*Hug me, kiss me, suck my juices*
*Squeezed from goblin fruits for you,*
*Goblin pulp and goblin dew.*
*Eat me, drink me, love me—"*

The woman marked her page and closed the book, then lifted her head and gazed at Eddie with an inscrutable expression.

Eddie stared at her face. Though the room was dim, the light from the bedside lamp accentuated her features with dramatic shadows. Her lips were soft and full. *And they're wet too,* he noticed as they reflected the glow of the lamp back at him. Without thinking, he ran his tongue over the surface of his own lips.

He started admiring her large, wide-set eyes, then realized with a jolt that she was staring back at him just as intently. *How does she expect me to respond to a passage like that?* he wondered in a panic. He tried to make sense of her cryptic invitation, but was too mesmerized by her face to think clearly. After a few seconds of embarrassed, painful silence, he managed a rambling reply.

"Kiss you? Suck your—goblin juices? Christ! I mean—um. Oh, wait. Goblins!—I know that poem! It's *Goblin Market* by Christina Rossetti. I read that at university."

The woman smiled, her lips parting ever so slightly. Eddie's heart started pounding.

"You like poetry too?" she asked in a husky whisper.

Her smile was dazzling. Bewitching. Eddie gazed at her longingly and grinned back.

"Could I—?" he asked, stepping towards her. "I mean, if you don't mind, could I see your book?"

She offered no reply, but continued to smile at him. *I'll take that as a 'yes',* he decided. He sat down on the edge of the mattress and took the book. He gazed into her eyes for a brief moment, then looked down at the cover and smiled. "This is the same anthology I used in my Victorian literature class at uni. Are you—um, going to school now?"

The woman said nothing, but reclaimed her book and started reading aloud once more:

"—*She gorged on bitterness without a name—*
*Ah, fool, to choose such part*
*Of Soul-consuming care!—*"

Eddie took a deep breath and rested his hand on top of hers. He felt a brief spark.

"I'm Eddie," he whispered. "That is, um, you probably knew that already, right? I'm Eddie Rochester? Of the Pilots?"

The woman fixed a steely gaze at him.

"You know? Gerry's group?" he floundered. "Gerry Enis! The birthday boy. And this is Eli's house. Eli Deere, our bassist."

The woman stared at him blankly, obviously unimpressed by his pop-music credentials.

"What's your name?" he asked.

She smiled at him again, even more radiantly than before, but said nothing.

"Would you like to come outside with me and join the party?" he asked.

"No!" she said, her voice finally rising above a whisper. "I can't."

Eddie furrowed his brow. "Why not?"

"Don't ask me!" she exclaimed, her eyes flashing. "Just go! You need to go now!"

"I don't understand," Eddie replied. "Please, just tell me your name."

She buried her face back in the book.

"Hey, I'm sorry," he apologized. "I didn't mean to upset you. If you don't want to join the party, then maybe we could just sit here and talk for a while."

She drew her legs more tightly towards her chest.

"Please, just tell me your name," Eddie pleaded.

"Who the hell are you?" a threatening voice called out from across the room.

Eddie looked up and saw a gaunt, dark-haired man approaching him. The stranger grabbed Eddie by the shoulder and shoved him off the bed.

"Get away from my sister, you asshole!"

"I'm not—I wasn't doing anything," Eddie protested. "I was just trying to talk to her."

"Well, don't!" the man shouted. "Nobody asked you to do that. Now get the fuck away from her. Fetch your coat, Roberta, I'm taking you home. Now!"

The woman turned her face towards Eddie once more. Her eyes seemed to be begging him for help. Imploring him to do something. Anything.

"Seriously, I didn't even touch her," Eddie insisted. "I was just—we were just reading poetry. Listen. I'm Eddie Rochester. I'm one of the Pilots! Who the hell are you?"

The man grabbed the tweed overcoat Eddie had discarded earlier and pushed it into the woman's hands. "Goddamned pop star! You only want one thing from the girls you meet at parties, and it's got nothing to do with reading fucking poetry. C'mon, Roberta. Let's get the hell out of here."

The woman said nothing, but as she reached for her book she met Eddie's eyes once more. He tried to read her expression but felt too confused to think clearly. She looked frightened, but angry too. *Is she mad at me, or at her brother?* he wondered.

"Goodbye," he said, holding her gaze. "Roberta."

"It's Birdie," she whispered as the dark-haired man dragged her out of the room.

Eddie took a few deep breaths and struggled to make sense of the last five minutes. He tried to imagine what circumstances might have prompted this gorgeous, well-read woman to appear at Gerry's birthday bacchanal. He cursed his luck for having lost the mysterious woman to an even more mysterious man. Then he steeled his resolve and decided to seek out Gerry or Eli for an answer. He found his coat on the floor and went back to the party.

He stepped out of the bedroom and was hit by a malodorous reek of incense. Covering his nose, he eased his way past a group of four strangers groping each other in an orgiastic huddle. He walked into the living room, found Gerry and shouted to him.

"Hey Ger! I need to ask you about a bird I just met!"

Gerry flashed Eddie a lopsided grin and beckoned him closer.

"This is the best fucking party ever!" he growled into Eddie's ear. "I feel *sooo* good."

Eddie's heart sank. He stared into Gerry's bloodshot eyes and knew his drummer was in no position to help him track down the woman. But then he remembered the last time Gerry had looked this high and felt a pang of worry. "What did you take?"

"Dunno. Don't care. But it was fucking wonderful!" Gerry let loose a throaty laugh.

Eddie sighed. *Stupid bastard,* he thought as he left Gerry and went to look for Eli. *I'm not going to stick around so I can take him to hospital once more.* He found his bassist sitting alone in the kitchen, staring intently at the inside of a large metal spoon.

"I'm upside down, man," he moaned.

*Christ!* Eddie cursed in his head. *I am surrounded by morons!* He cleared his throat and decided against all reason to try his luck one last time. "Hey, Eli, I just met this chick named Roberta. She was with some bloke who claimed to be her brother. He was kind of skinny with short, dark hair. She had long, wavy, black hair. Do you know anything about them?"

"I'm upside down, man!" Eli repeated, his voice beginning to quiver. "How the fuck did I get upside down?"

Eddie took the spoon away from Eli and flipped it from the concave to the convex side. "You're fine," he said, handing the utensil back. "Now listen, you invited the guests. What can you tell me about this bloke or this bird?"

"You're a genius, Rochester!" Eli exclaimed, panting in relief at the sight of his right-side-up reflection. "You're a fucking genius!"

"Eddie! You're still here!" Jim shouted. He walked into the kitchen, smiling broadly and dangling a hand-rolled cigarette between his fingers. "I thought you wanted to nip off so you could read."

"I did," Eddie replied. "But then I met this chick, and she—"

Jim offered Eddie the joint. "This is good shit. Take a hit. Christ, Eddie, just for once why don't you try to enjoy being a pop star?"

Eddie slipped his hands into the pockets of his coat. "Not tonight. I can't think straight when I'm stoned, and I'm trying to find out anything I can about this girl I just met."

"You found yourself a woman?" Jim laughed. "Well, good for you. Sex beats drugs in my book any day! Tell me about her."

Eddie started to relax for a brief moment. "She's a stunner! She has these incredible eyes! And her face—Christ, she was just bloody perfect! And she was reading this book—"

"Wait, did you just say 'book'?" Jim interrupted.

"Yes, this collection of Victorian poetry—"

Jim broke into a fit of giggles. Eddie's face fell. He started walking away.

"I'm sorry, mate!" Jim called after him. "Really, I am. It's just that—Oh, Christ, Eddie! Victorian poetry? You are such a tosser!" He brought the joint to his mouth and inhaled deeply.

Eddie stepped back into the living room. The Pilots' latest single was booming from the stereo's speaker. He felt every bass note reverberate in his gut. The woman in the red dress spied him and ran back to his side. "God, I want you!" she cried over the cacophonous roar of the drunken crowd. She licked Eddie's face and grabbed at his crotch.

"Get off of me!" he yelled, pushing her away.

He started walking to the door, but his manager's younger brother Alan blocked his way. "I'll take her if you don't want her!" he shouted into Eddie's face.

"She's yours," Eddie grumbled. He slipped into the crowd. A throng of inebriated dancers pressed hard against him, flailing their limbs and jostling him roughly as they gyrated to the pulsing beat echoing through the room. He snaked his way through the undulating mass of bodies. When he finally reached the exit, a topless girl with glazed eyes forced her way in front of him, dripping vomit in her wake.

*I am so fucking tired of this!* Eddie thought in disgust. *Why does every party have to end this way? It didn't used to be like this when we first started out.*

The half-naked girl pushed the door open and ran outside. A blast of cold air enveloped Eddie, calling him back to his senses. But as soon as he stepped out of the building, a cascade of bright lights rippled before his eyes.

"Damned paparazzi!" he muttered under his breath as he stumbled into the yard.

*"Halt! Das ist nur Eddie Rochester!"* shouted a frustrated photographer. He spat out Eddie's name contemptuously, then asked about the Pilots' more popular lead singer. *"Wo ist der Tony? Wann kommt er draußen?"*

Eddie ignored the questions and started sprinting towards his car. An aggressive Fleet Street journalist broke away from the crowd at the door and pursued him.

"So how was the party?" the man asked. Eddie tried to dodge

him, but the reporter ran ahead and forced a camera in front of his face. Without waiting for Eddie to respond, he released the shutter button. A flashbulb burst a few inches away from Eddie's eyes, blinding him.

He staggered away from the photographer and reached out his hands towards his car. Pulsing circles of intense white light danced painfully in front of his eyes. He groped the surface of the vehicle, trying to find the door handle, and wondered if he would ever see clearly again.

## Chapter Two

Eddie blinked a few times to block out the late afternoon sun. Then he climbed out of his car, stepped around the disheveled man sleeping by the pavement, and walked up to Eli's door. A teenage girl in a bright orange mini-dress jumped out from behind a bush by the entrance and grabbed his sleeve.

"*Ist Tony noch darin?*" she asked, her dark brown eyes sparkling with excitement.

"Sorry, love," Eddie replied. "I'm sure he's left by now."

He held off knocking for a few moments, waiting for the girl to ask for his autograph, but she simply pouted and walked away. He sighed and rapped the door. He let a minute pass, then banged on the door again. After another thirty seconds, he raised his fist to knock once more. The door opened.

"Put down your dukes, mate, it's just me," Gerry said. He opened the door wider and let Eddie step inside.

The sweet, smoky smell of stale marijuana lingered in the air. Eddie surveyed the living room, reviewing the detritus from last night's party. The chairs, tables and sofa were crowded in a haphazard arrangement in the far corner of the room. Half-empty cups and glasses littered the stained rug that had served as an impromptu dance floor. The trolley cart that had borne Gerry's cake lay knocked on its side by the stereo.

A loud snore caught Eddie's attention. He turned his head and saw Alan Poole lying supine on the sofa, his hand stretched out toward a spilled drink on the floor.

"Sleeping like a baby," Gerry noted.

Eddie shrugged and turned towards his drummer. "Where are your trousers?"

"Dunno. I've been looking for them. Can't remember where I

was when I took them off."

A clock on the wall chimed. Eddie glanced up. "Four in the afternoon. You're up early."

"Yeah. Couldn't help it. The goddamned phone kept ringing."

"That was me. I need to talk to Eli."

"Think he's in the bath. Wanna go check?"

"No," Eddie sighed. "I'll wait. But maybe you can help me. There was a chick here last night. Long, dark, curly hair. Gorgeous face. Her name's Roberta, and she left with her brother. I want to ring her up, but I don't know her last name."

"With her brother?" Gerry mused. "What'd he look like?"

"Tall, thin, kind of sallow bloke. His hair was dark and rather short."

Gerry scratched his face, then started scratching his arms furiously. "I think I might know the gent. But if he's who I think he is, you don't want to meet him. He's not really your type."

"What's that supposed to mean?" Eddie asked.

A knock on the door interrupted their exchange.

"Get that, would ya? I'm not decent," Gerry said. He lifted a cushion off a chair and threw it on the floor. "Where the hell are my goddamned trousers?"

Eddie opened the front door and broke into a smile. "It's you!"

"Fuck. Do you five all live together in this house like the Monkees?" the visitor asked.

"Dick!" Gerry cried out. "So lovely to see you again. Eddie was just asking about you. He wants to chat up your sister."

Dick Mason stepped into the house and closed the door behind him. "That's not a possibility. Where's Eli?"

"In the bath," Gerry answered. "Eddie says your sister's a real stunner. How come you never introduced her to me?"

"She's shy," Dick answered. "Please excuse me. I'll wait for Eli in the kitchen."

Eddie followed him out of the living room and took a seat at the cluttered table. "Listen," he began. "I'm sorry if I made a bad impression on you last night. I was just sitting on the bed beside her. We weren't doing anything. But I'd really like to—"

"Roberta is too young to date the likes of you. So just forget about it."

"But I—"

Eli stepped into the room, naked but for a towel tied at his

11

waist. Rivulets of water dripped from his long hair and beard. "Dick, my mate! There you are! Looks like you found Eddie without my help." He turned to his bandmate. "Dick was just telling me on the blower how his sister's been asking after you."

Eddie smiled. Dick frowned.

"Don't worry, Eddie. I did you proud. I told him how upright and respectable you are. Not like a real pop star at all." Eli turned to face Dick. "Honestly, mate, Eddie's as square as they come. I'd let my sister date him, though he'd probably bore her to tears, trying to woo her with bloody Victorian love poetry."

Eddie leaned closer to Dick. "Your sister likes Victorian poetry. She was reading a poem by Christina Rossetti last night."

"I fuckin' well know that my sister likes poetry!" Dick shouted. "But that doesn't mean I'm gonna let her go out with you."

Gerry continued his search for his missing pants. "Why not?" he asked as he opened up the cabinet over the sink. "Eddie's a nice lad. Most of the time, anyway. My folks like him a lot more than they like me. And he's got more sovs in the bank than the rest of us do. 'Cept for maybe Tony. He doesn't throw his dosh away on frivolous pursuits like Eli and I do."

Eli turned towards Dick. "Eddie's got nice flats in London and Germany, and he's set to inherit his grandpappy's estate in America any day now."

"No, I'm not," Eddie protested. "My grandfather still has a lot of life left in him."

"So he's out of hospital then, is he?" Gerry asked as he rifled through the pantry.

Eddie sighed.

"How big is your grandfather's estate?" Dick asked, arching an eyebrow.

"Bugger, Thornfield's huge, isn't it, Eddie?" Gerry replied. "I got lost in one of the cornfields the last time we played the Cincinnati Gardens. Almost missed the show."

A soft moaning drifted into the kitchen from the other room. "I believe our manager's little brother is awakening from his beauty rest," Gerry said. "I'll go see to him."

Eddie turned to Dick. "Listen, I'd just like to ask your sister to dinner, that's all. If you could give me your number—"

"I could give you his number," Eli offered.

Dick frowned. "Roberta's not feeling right today. She has a

migraine. But maybe when she's—well, when she's in a better frame of mind, then perhaps—"

Gerry stepped back in the kitchen. "Hey Eli, you got any sauerkraut? I wanna mix some up with milk for Alan. Best remedy for a hangover ever."

"That sounds manky," Eli grunted.

"Trust me, I know a thing or two about hangovers," Gerry replied. He opened the small refrigerator door and smiled. "My trousers! How the fuck did they get in there?"

## Chapter Three

"Let's sit outside," Eddie said, leading Roberta down the pavement and towards the restaurant's *Gartencafé*.
She glanced up at the sky. "But it looks like rain."
"It's just cloudy," Eddie insisted. "I don't think it'll rain. I want you to experience a European outdoor café for once in your life. I can't believe your brother's never taken you to one."
"He's very protective of me," Roberta replied.
"I'll say!" Eddie laughed. "I didn't think he was ever going to let us leave your flat."
"I like staying at home," Roberta said. "I feel comfortable there. Being outside with people I don't know makes me nervous."
Eddie wrapped his arm around her shoulder. "Don't worry, love. You're safe with me."
They reached the wrought iron gate that opened up to the restaurant's cobblestone courtyard. The maître d' escorted them through a maze of small tables covered in dark green cloths to a larger table near a whitewashed stucco wall.
"Won't your fans bother you?" Roberta asked, throwing an anxious glance at the pedestrians passing outside the fence.
"No," Eddie promised. "People don't usually recognize me unless I'm with Tony or Gerry. I've always been more of a second-tier player."
*"Möchten Sie eine Flasche Wein?"* the maître d' asked as Eddie and Roberta took their seats.
Eddie looked to Roberta for an answer. She shook her head. "I'm not supposed to drink alcohol with my new medicine."
Eddie nodded. *"Nur Wasser, bitte,"* he said. The waiter handed them menus and left to fetch their drinks.
"You speak German, right?" Eddie asked as he scanned the

laminated card.

"Not very well," Roberta answered. "But it doesn't matter. I'll just order *Weiner schnitzel*. I know that's safe. It seems like everything else comes smothered in vinegar."

"I don't much care for German food either," Eddie replied. "It's been a year since my manager Emmett moved us here to Munich, but I find myself pining for bad British pub food on a daily basis."

"But you're closer to your fans now that you're in Germany," Roberta pointed out.

"What fans we still have left," Eddie agreed. "Our last two records sold a lot better on the continent than they did in England or the States, and it's easier to tour Europe when we're right in the thick of things. But I'm getting tired of touring. I'm really looking forward to packing it all in and leaving the music scene behind."

"What would you do then?" she asked.

"Move to Ohio, probably. Help my grandfather with his farm. The land is going to pass to me when he dies, so I should probably figure out what I'm going to do there."

"Well, I'm glad I caught you while you were still in Germany," Roberta said, looking down at her menu. "We never would have met if you were living on a farm in Ohio."

Eddie's heart leapt. *Christ, I can't believe she said that!* he marveled. *How did I get so lucky?*

She rested her menu back on the table. "So how is it you have an American grandfather? I thought you were English."

"I'm both," Eddie explained. "My dad was an American pilot stationed in England during the war. He met my mum at the air base in Debden, and I born in the U.K. When the war ended, Dad took a job with TWA and moved us all stateside. We lived on his parents' farm in Ohio. But after he died in a plane crash, Mum took me back to England. I still visited my grandparents' farm most summers, though. Ohio has always felt like my true home."

Roberta nodded. "I'm American too. I'm from St. Croix."

"So that's where you get your accent!" Eddie exclaimed. "You're from the Virgin Islands!"

"Is my accent that strong?" she asked, her face betraying more than a hint of self-consciousness.

"No," he assured her. "It just gives you a hint of exoticism, that's all. It's very—alluring."

Roberta looked down and hid her eyes.

The waiter returned, carrying two glass bottles of sparkling water. Eddie tried to engage him in a half-English, half-German conversation about menu choices, but Roberta interrupted and ordered supper for both of them.

"Thanks," Eddie said after the waiter finished filling their wine glasses with water. He reached his hand across the table and touched her fingers. He immediately felt a spark.

Roberta slipped her fingers into his hand and smiled. Eddie felt himself growing weaker. Then she let go of his hand, picked up her water glass and clinked it against his. "Drink to me only with thine eyes, and I will pledge with mine," she said, holding his gaze.

He lifted his glass and smiled back at her. "Or leave a kiss but in the cup, and I'll not look for wine."

She laughed and took a sip of water. "I'm impressed," she said, resting her glass back on the table. "You don't just read poetry, you memorize it."

"I spend too much time reading poetry," Eddie confessed. "My bandmates are always having a go at me for it. They think I'm wasting my time curling up with books instead of going to parties."

"I like curling up with books," she replied.

Eddie raised an eyebrow. "What have you been reading lately?"

"I've just been skimming through some Shakespeare," she said.

Eddie's face brightened. He settled back in his chair and cleared his throat, trying to sound sexy as he spoke:

*"Shall I compare thee to a summer's day?*
*Thou art more lovely and more temperate."*

She rested her elbow on the table and cupped her chin in her hand. Focusing her hazel eyes on him, she replied in a sultry voice:

*"Past cure I am, now reason is past care,*
*And frantic-mad with evermore unrest.*
*My thoughts and my discourse as madmen's are,*
*At random from the truth vainly expressed."*

A warm feeling began to spread through Eddie's body. "Ah," he said, fighting the urge to grab her in his arms. "You prefer the Dark Lady sonnets."

"And you the Fair Youth," she replied.

They sat in silence for a long moment, locked in each other's eyes. Then the waiter approached with their salads, shattering the mood with the sharp clank of cutlery against china plates.

Eddie looked down at the table, reached for his fork, and mumbled, "Tuck in."

"So much vinegar," Roberta sighed. She held a soggy lettuce leaf aloft and watched the vinaigrette drip back onto her plate. "I miss Caribbean cooking so much."

Eddie stabbed at a sodden slice of cucumber. "Island cooking is spicy though, isn't it?"

"Sometimes, not always," she replied. "But the food was always fresh. My family's cook used to pick vegetables and herbs right out of our garden as she was preparing our meals."

"My grandma would do the same thing in Ohio," Eddie said. "Nothing's as good as sweet snap peas pulled right off the vine."

"Except for mangoes plucked right off the tree," she countered.

"Aren't mangoes stringy?" he asked.

Roberta shook her head. "You just have to know which tree to pick from. The best fruit is so juicy it bursts right in your mouth the moment you sink your teeth into it."

Eddie smiled. "She suck'd until her lips were sore, then flung the emptied rinds away."

Roberta smiled back. "*Goblin Market.* That's the poem I was reading the night we met."

"I pulled out my copy as soon as I got home and re-read it."

"It's not that great of a poem," she demurred.

"But it made me think of you," Eddie said. He gazed into her eyes for several seconds, then leaned across the table and gently kissed her mouth. "I hope I'm not being too forward," he said as he sank back into his seat.

Roberta rested her fork on her salad plate and gazed back at him. "You're fresh too," she purred. "Like a ripe mango."

The warm feeling in Eddie's body ebbed into his loins. He lowered his eyes and stared at his salad for a long moment, then reached for her hand and brought it to his lips for a kiss.

"My love is a fever," he said. "Longing still for that which longer nurseth the disease."

She smiled. "That's the first line of the sonnet I just quoted."

"I know," Eddie replied.

She looked away briefly, then turned back to him. "If love be blind, it best agrees with night," she whispered. "Or so says Juliet."

"If love be blind, love cannot hit the mark," Eddie replied. "So says Mercutio."

Roberta smirked at him. "My cherry lips have often kissed thy stones. Thisbee, from *A Midsummer Night's Dream*."

"Graze on my lips, and if those hills be dry, stray lower, where the pleasant fountains lie," Eddie replied. "*Venus and Adonis*."

Roberta reached across the table and took his other hand. "Kiss me as if you entered gay, my heart at some noonday. *In a Gondola*, by Robert Browning."

"And all her face was honey to my mouth," Eddie replied, bringing her hands to his lips. "And all her body pasture to mine eyes. *Love and Sleep*, by Swinburne."

Roberta inhaled deeply and released her breath slowly. "Let thy love in kisses rain on my lips and eyelids pale," she whispered. "*Indian Serenade*, by Percy Bysshe Shelley."

"And the sunlight clasps the earth, and the moonbeams kiss the sea," Eddie whispered back. "What are all these kissings worth, if thou kiss not me? *Love's Philosophy*. Also by Percy Bysshe."

She laughed and looked away for a moment, then turned back and gazed at him, her eyes sparkling. "Whoever loved, that loved not at first sight? Christopher Marlowe."

"License my roving hands, and let them go. Before, behind, between, above, below," Eddie replied. "John Donne."

Silence fell between them as they stared at each other across the table. Eddie's mind went blank, all thoughts of poetry pushed aside by his overwhelming desire to pull Roberta into his arms. He didn't notice the first raindrop that landed on his hand. Or the second that landed on his nose. But when a series of fat drops splashed into his water glass, he finally heard the rain.

"You were right about the weather," he said, breaking eye contact with her. "Maybe we should go inside."

"How far is your flat from here?" she asked. She slipped her hands out of his and tucked a loose tendril of hair behind her ear. "My brother doesn't expect me back for a few hours."

Eddie smiled. He pulled some mark notes from his wallet, left them under his salad plate, and stood up from the table. "It's not far," he said, taking Roberta's hand. "Come with me."

\* \* \*

"There," she purred. "Right there."

Eddie sucked on her neck for a few more seconds, then lowered his tongue to her throat. He slowly licked her breastbone, then worked his way over to her nipple and began sucking again.

She arched her back in pleasure and moaned. After a few exquisite moments had passed, she rolled to her side and started stroking him until he was hard. Then she swung her leg over his side and straddled him.

"I'm yours," she whispered. "Take me."

He worked his way into her slowly. Then she began to ride him. He met her every movement for as long as he could, then burst inside her with an ecstatic spasm.

She moaned again and rolled her head back and forth, letting her long hair brush over his face. Then she lifted her hips to let him slip out of her. He reached for her soft, silky shoulders, damp with perspiration, and drew her back to his side. She cuddled in his arms. They lay beside each other in silence while their breathing steadied, and listened to the rain pounding the rooftop above them.

After a few minutes, Eddie leaned his face towards hers and kissed her gently on the mouth. "God, you're magnificent," he said.

"You are too," she replied, snuggling in closer to the warmth of his embrace.

Eddie rubbed her back and felt himself falling asleep.

"Do you want a cigarette?" she asked.

He sighed and tried to force himself to stay awake. "Do you?"

"If you'll have one," she answered.

He reluctantly slipped his arm out from under her. "There are some in my nightstand," he said, rolling away and grabbing a lighter and pack of Marlboros from his bedside drawer.

She sat up and rested her back against the headboard while she waited. He slapped the pack against his palm a few times, extracted two cigarettes and offered her one. She placed it between her lips, let him light the tip, then took a small puff. He lit his own cigarette, drew in a deep drag and exhaled a cloud of smoke.

"Where's your ashtray?" she asked.

"Sorry," he replied. He pulled a ceramic bowl off the table by his bed and handed it to her.

"This is cute," she said, admiring the painting of a blue windmill in the middle of the bowl.

"I pinched it from a hotel in Rotterdam on our last tour." He took another deep drag on his cigarette and exhaled. "Christ. I'm going to be back in Rotterdam next week. Stupid, bloody tour."

"It's your job," she reminded him, turning her face towards his.

"I want to quit," he confessed. "Especially now. I want to kiss the whole goddamned world of concerts and touring goodbye."

"Then what would you do with your time?"

He cast her a wicked smile. "Be with you."

She laughed and tapped her cigarette against the bowl. "That would be nice."

"That would be very nice," he repeated. "God, Birdie, do you even know how incredible you are?"

She lowered her head. "I'm not incredible. When you get to know me better you might not like me so much."

"Like you?" he protested. "I'm well past that stage by now. I am thoroughly in love with you."

She rested her cigarette in the bowl and leaned against him. "I think I love you too," she said. "But I'm not sure. I've never been in love before."

*I've never been in love before either,* he wanted to tell her, though he was too embarrassed to admit it. *I've shagged more girls than I can count, but I've never had a serious girlfriend. So why is it now that I've finally found you, I have to leave?*

He kissed her gently and clasped her hand. "I'll ring you every day I'm on the road," he promised.

"Don't call me," she said. "I don't like talking on the telephone. But write to me. Write me long, beautiful love letters. And I'll send you letters back, at the hotels where your band is staying."

Eddie furrowed his brow. "Why don't you like the telephone?"

She turned away from him and picked up her smoldering cigarette. "I don't like listening to disembodied voices. I prefer seeing the faces of the people who speak to me. Or reading words on a paper."

"Okay," he said, unsure of how else to respond. "I'll write you every day."

She brought her eyes back to meet his. "Write me poems."

# Chapter Four

### *Graz, Austria*

Tony Wright stepped out of the recessed doorway and walked into the backstage dressing room of the *Eisstadion Liebenau*. "Christ, that was beautiful! Sing it again!"

"Shit, how long were you spying on me, you wanker?" Eddie blurted out, slipping his guitar strap off his shoulder.

"Just long enough to hear that final chorus," Tony replied. He hummed a few notes and sang out the words he remembered: *"I'm dreaming tonight of you—"*

Eddie rested his guitar on its stand. "Yeah, well, it's just something I'm messing around with. It's not fit for public consumption."

"But it's good!" Tony protested. "I only heard you singing for a moment there and I've already got the hook stuck in my head. That song has hit written all over it!"

"No it doesn't," Eddie reiterated. "It's just something private I'm working on."

"Private?" Tony repeated, pulling up a folding chair and straddling it from behind. "You mean you wrote that by yourself? Without Jimbo's help?"

"Yes," Eddie said, looking away. "It's not for the band. It's for—" He let his voice trail off.

Tony leaned forward against the back of his chair and leered ever so slightly. "It's for that new bird of yours, isn't it? Gerry was telling me about her. What's her name again? Rebecca?"

"Roberta."

"Fuck it, man, you're in love!" Tony laughed.

"Bugger off," Eddie countered. "I've only seen her a few times.

And now we're on the road, touring all of goddamned Europe, so it'll be nine fucking weeks before I can see her again."

Tony lowered his lip into a mock pout. "But you're ringing her up every night, aren't you?"

"No," Eddie grumbled. He looked up at Tony briefly, then faced the ground again. "She doesn't like talking on the phone. She says she has a hard time handling disembodied voices. But I'm writing her every night, and she's—well, I've given her the tour schedule, and she's writing me back at a couple of the hotels. I've just picked up her first set of letters."

"That's queer," Tony said. "What do you mean, 'she has a hard time handling disembodied voices'?"

"I dunno," Eddie said, his voice tinged with frustration. "It's just what she said. But it doesn't matter. I like writing letters. This way I can stop and think about what I want to say, and not just blurt out something stupid, as I'm wont to do."

Tony laughed. "Well, to each his own, mate. Figures you'd fall for a chick who likes reading and writing."

"Yes," Eddie replied. He looked up and smiled. "She writes poetry too. I just read through her first post. She didn't write proper letters at all—just poems, bursting with all these mad, beautiful images. She sees things I've never even noticed before!"

"How charming," Tony replied in a disinterested voice.

Eddie laughed. He picked up his guitar again and twiddled the pegs to adjust the tuning. "I've starting writing some songs for her—just for her—not for the band to record. I've written four already. They're just pouring out of me—the words and melodies together. It's like she's untapped a font of creativity inside me."

Tony shrugged. "That's cool. But maybe after you sing them for her, you can let us have a go at them. Honestly, if the others are as good as the one I just heard, why not share them with the world?"

"Because they're personal."

"Well, change up the lyrics a little then," Tony suggested. "Take out the private references and re-write the words into a more all-purpose love song that everyone can enjoy."

Eddie scowled. "By 'everyone', you mean, of course, your legions of adoring fans?"

"Why not? We could use another hit. Our last record tanked."

"You're a mercenary."

"No, I'm just telling it like it is." Tony stared into a dark corner of the cramped dressing room and sighed. "I don't dig living in Germany. I mean, I'm cool with touring the continent and reaching as many fans as we still have left. But I want to move back to London. Or maybe even Los Angeles. Someplace where they speak English. But we need a really big hit if we're ever gonna reclaim our old audience."

Eddie stared thoughtfully at his friend. "We're holding you back."

Tony started to argue, but Eddie cut him off. "You don't need to keep playing front man to a band whose best days are behind them. You could record a solo album of drippy love songs and take it to the top of the charts on both sides of the Atlantic. Gerry would hate it, and Jim and I would mock you mercilessly, but you'd have the last laugh, 'cause your record would actually sell."

"Hmm," Tony demurred, offering Eddie a weak smile of agreement. "Maybe someday. But I like being in this band. It's fun having you lot around me. But something tells me *you're* not so keen on being a Pilot anymore."

Eddie looked away. "What makes you say that?"

"Oh, c'mon, mate. Stop pissing about. You can't keep secrets in a group this tight. We all know you're set to inherit your granddad's farm in Ohio someday. And we all know your gramp's been in and out of hospital a lot lately too. Once you take title to that land you love so much, you're never gonna leave it. Your touring days are numbered already."

Eddie offered no denial.

"I can just see you, posing in front of a barn with a pitchfork in your hand, like that old bloke in the painting."

"Right, but the farmer in *American Gothic* had a woman by his side," Eddie pointed out.

"And now you've got a woman!" Tony laughed. "Or at least you've finally got yourself a girlfriend."

"I hope so," Eddie replied.

"So tell me about her! What's she look like?"

Eddie hugged his guitar to his chest and smiled. "She's gorgeous. She has the most incredible eyes I've ever seen. They're like of mix of amber and emerald all swirled up together. And she has long, wavy, black hair, and a deep, sexy voice, with a hint of a Caribbean accent. She's from St. Croix, in the U.S. Virgin Islands."

"Nice tits?"

"Fabulous."

"How old is she?"

"Twenty-one."

"You cradle-robber!"

"I am not! I'm only twenty-six. Well, okay, I'm almost twenty-seven, but—"

"But you're as innocent as a schoolboy when it comes to chicks."

Eddie glowered at Tony. "I've been with plenty of birds!"

"Groupies," Tony noted. "Cheap slappers who eat you up like you're the candy. Not that I'm criticizing, mind you. I prefer groupies to girlfriends most of the time, too. But I have been in a relationship here and there. And I grew up with three sisters too, so I know how to talk with chicks. But you, mate, Christ! I mean, you can write a damned beautiful love song, I'll grant you that. But you don't know much about being in love, now, do you?"

Eddie squared his shoulders. "Well, perhaps I do now."

Tony smiled. "Hope so, mate. You deserve a nice girlfriend."

"Mm-hmm," Eddie agreed, repositioning his guitar against his chest. "You wanna practice some harmonies before the other three get here? Emmett said we sounded off last night."

Tony glanced at his watch. "No. Let's just wait till they show up and run through the numbers together. I don't think Eli's bass was in tune last night. It kept throwing me off. Christ, I think he's the worst bassist we've had yet."

"Don't knock Eli!" Eddie scolded. "If it weren't for him, I wouldn't have met Birdie."

Tony furrowed his brow. "What d'ya mean by that?"

"Eli's friends with Birdie's brother Dick," Eddie explained. "He invited Birdie and Dick to Gerry's birthday party."

Tony scooted his chair closer to his friend. "Run that one by me again, Rochester. You said Roberta's brother is friends with Eli?"

"Yeah, what's wrong with that?"

"Well, Eli is—I mean—he runs with a rather dodgy set, don't you think? He's not the most sober individual I know."

Eddie scowled. "Dick's clean. He's a decent bloke."

"What's he doing in Germany? Why would anyone leave a tropical paradise like St. Croix and move to fuckin' Bavaria?"

"He did a stint in the Army ten years ago," Eddie recalled,

remembering what Birdie had told him. "Worked in medical supplies for an American military hospital. Afterwards, he stayed in Germany and became a travel agent. He helps English-speaking tourists plan their trips."

Tony snorted. "Did I just hear you right, mate? This friend of Eli helps people 'plan their trips'? Does that not set off bells and whistles? Let's get real here. I might not have gone to uni like you and Jimbo, but I'm not stupid."

"I'm not stupid either," Eddie said, his voice growing tenser by the second. "And Birdie's brother is not a drug pusher."

"All right! Okay!" Tony said, holding up his hands in a gesture of contrition. "Don't get your knickers in a twist! I just meant—well—it seems to me that this whole romance of yours has a veil of mystery hanging over it. I'm a bit concerned. That's all. I don't want you getting your heart broken."

"I don't intend to," Eddie replied. He turned his back to Tony and started tuning his guitar for the afternoon's sound check.

## Chapter Five

### *Munich, Federal Republic of Germany*

Roberta squeezed Eddie's hand and gazed up at him adoringly. "Thank you so much for taking me here. I've always wanted to visit the *Kunstareal*."

"How come Dick never took you?" Eddie asked.

She looked away. "I don't know. I guess he just doesn't like going to art museums very much. And he doesn't like me going places by myself."

*Your brother never wants to let you out of his sight,* Eddie thought. *I wonder why he's so protective.* Then he noticed Roberta's sad posture and decided the question could wait. "Well, there's something for everyone here," he said in a cheerful voice. "We can see the Dürers and Rembrandts in the *Alte Pinokothek*, or the Greek and Roman relics in the *Glyptothek*."

Roberta looked back at him and smiled. "And I can pretend you're a modern-day John Keats, wandering into the British museum and seeing the Elgin marbles for the first time. Maybe you'll be inspired to write an ode."

Eddie wrapped his arm around her shoulder and laughed. "I'm not sure I have what it takes to pen an ode. I'm much better at writing sappy love lyrics for Jim to set to music."

"I liked the poems you sent me while you were away," she said.

"I liked yours too," he replied. He considered mentioning the songs he had written for her, but decided that could wait as well. He still hadn't run them by his songwriting partner, and he wanted to make certain they sounded perfect before he sang them to her.

They stepped around a crowd of tourists who had gathered in front of a juggler, and strolled hand-in-hand down the walkway that traversed the large arts district. Roberta spied a poster advertising an exhibit of Alfred Kubin lithographs at the *Lenbachhaus* and pulled Eddie to a stop.

"Can we go see this?" she asked. "I've seen Kubin's drawings in a book. His work is amazing!"

"Your wish is my command," Eddie replied. He pulled his arts district map out of his jacket pocket, checked the location of the *Lenbachhaus*, and led her to the museum.

\* \* \*

Roberta's eyes grew wide as she admired the large, framed lithograph. "I love this! This is just how I feel some days. It's as if Kubin crawled into my head and saw exactly what I was thinking!"

Eddie examined the picture carefully. He tried to imagine why the artist had depicted his female subject in such a precarious position—balanced unsteadily on a two-wheeled contraption and plummeting down the hill of a steep roller coaster. The woman at the focus of the picture was naked, with long, white hair rising from her head like a pale, pointed dagger. Her hands were tied behind her back. The track she was soaring down had no discernible beginning or end—it simply plunged from the top of the drawing and faded into a distant, barren horizon.

He struggled for a response. "I suppose I have days when I feel like that too," he replied at length. "Like I'm stuck on a path to nowhere and can't for the life of me find a way out." He turned away from the picture and started reading the pamphlet he had picked up at the desk about the German Expressionist artist.

"It says here that Kubin died in 1959. That was twelve years ago, Birdie, so I don't think he could have crawled into your head. Though I, for one, would love to get inside of you."

He gazed at her longingly for a few moments, then realized with a pang of regret that she was too enraptured by the lithographs to pay him much mind. Disheartened, he started skimming through the booklet. "Hey, Birdie. This pamphlet says Kubin was also a novelist. I wonder if his books are as strange as his pictures."

"These pictures aren't strange, they're beautiful!" she snapped. She stepped away from Eddie and started admiring a lithograph of a fat, naked man sitting on top of a rock in the middle of the ocean.

Eddie inspected the picture and wondered why the artist had given the sad looking man a dog's head. He turned his attention back to the pamphlet and read that Kubin's best-known novel was an 'apocalyptic fantasy, with a Kafkaesque atmosphere of claustrophobic absurdity.' *Yup*, he decided. *This bloke's stories are just as barmy as his drawings.*

Looking back at the wall, he spied a picture of a leering skeleton climbing out from under a table in the middle of a cluttered room. "This reminds me of Gerry," he said with a laugh. "After he's had a few too many."

He took Roberta's hand in his. "I saw a sign in the lobby that said the museum was selling some limited edition prints of a few of the lithographs. I could buy one for you if you'd like."

Roberta returned her gaze to Eddie. "That would be wonderful!" she exclaimed. She stood up on her tiptoes and offered him a passionate kiss of gratitude.

Eddie's heart raced. A warm feeling rose from his loins and started spreading through his body. *She is so magnificent!* he thought. *How the hell did I ever find a woman like her?*

She ran her tongue down his neck, then released him and turned her attention back to the gallery wall. "Oh, I hope they have a copy of this one," she said, pointing to a picture of a naked pregnant woman marching in front of a row of skulls. The woman's arms were raised high above her head. A shower of dark droplets cascaded from her fingertips.

Eddie stepped closer to the picture. "Do you think those are seeds?"

"They look more like blood drops to me," Roberta replied. She walked across the room to examine the pictures on the other wall.

Eddie hovered close by her side. *I should just shut up,* he decided. *She obviously knows a lot more about modern art than I do, and I don't want to sound like a fool.*

Roberta stopped in front of a lithograph of a tall, thin woman dressed in black, standing at the bedside of an even taller, thinner woman dressed in white. The woman in white appeared to be praying. The woman in black was smothering her helpless companion with the palm of her splayed hand.

"Let's see if they have a print of this one!" Roberta exclaimed. She started running out of gallery.

Eddie chased after her. "Hey, Birdie, wait for me!"

"*Hallo, Sie da, halt!*" shouted the security guard at the doorway. "*Im Museum wird nicht so schnell gelaufen!*"

Eddie grabbed Roberta's arm and pulled her to a stop. "You shouldn't run like that in the museum!"

Roberta simply smiled in reply. She slipped her arms around Eddie and started to laugh.

The guard shook his head. "*Ach, diese Frau ist doch wahnsinnig,*" he muttered under his breath.

Roberta turned a glowering face at the guard. "Don't call me that!"

"What did he say, Birdie?" Eddie asked. "What does *wahnsinnig* mean?"

Roberta stared furiously at the guard and offered no reply.

The guard turned towards Eddie. "No run in museum," he stated in heavily-accented English. "To run *ist verboten.*"

"We're sorry," Eddie apologized. "We won't do it again."

The guard nodded. Eddie took Roberta's hand and led her away from the man. Just as they approached the exit, he heard the guard mutter the words "crazy woman" in a disdainful voice. Eddie fought back the urge to punch the man, and escorted Roberta to the gift shop instead.

\* \* \*

Roberta stood in the middle of Eddie's sitting room and turned in a slow circle so she could examine each corner and wall. "Where should we hang this?"

*Maybe in the bathroom?* Eddie thought. He cleared his throat and made a sincere effort to sound interested. "I'll trust your judgment, love. But it's your lithograph. Don't you want to hang it in your own flat?"

"Dick wouldn't like it," she said. "He'd rather I surround myself with pictures of bright pink flowers and sunny beaches."

"But wouldn't those remind you of your home in St. Croix?"

Roberta frowned. "It wasn't always sunny and perfect back there. A lot of my childhood was ugly."

He stepped closer to her and took her hand. "How do you mean?"

She slipped out of his grasp, rested her framed print against a table, and sat down on the sofa. She brought her legs to her chest and wrapped herself into a ball. "It's just that my mother, well—" She rested her head on top of her knees and closed her eyes. "I'm sorry. I don't want to talk about this just now."

Eddie sat down beside her. "That's all right. I'm sorry I brought it up. What would you like to talk about?"

"I don't know. Why don't you tell me about your tour?"

Eddie let loose a sad laugh. "It's over. That's all I want to say about it. Touring used to be fun back in the day—drinking and chatting up chicks after the shows. But the parties are getting out of hand now. I'm just not into the whole drug scene, and there's no other woman I'd rather spend time with than you."

She lifted her head and smiled. "You mean that? Really?"

"Of course I do." He draped his arm over her shoulder and drew her closer. "As a matter of fact, I love you so much that I'll let you hang that hideous lithograph anywhere you want in my house."

She pouted, then broke into a laugh. "You know, when I first met you, I thought it was funny that your name 'Rochester' sounded almost like 'rock star'. But now I think it's more ironic. You don't act like a rock star at all. You're too—responsible."

"Ouch," Eddie replied. "Do I act as old as that?"

She lifted her face to meet his and kissed him softly on the lips. "I don't mind. Either way, you're my 'Mr. R'."

## Chapter Six

"Well, *that's* an interesting picture," Jim said, contorting his face in disgust.

"It's an original Alfred Kubin lithograph," Eddie replied. "I bought it for Birdie at the *Lenbachhaus* a couple of days ago."

"So why is it hanging in your sitting room, not hers?"

"She didn't think her brother would approve of it. Actually I'm not so sure he approves of me either."

Jim laughed. "Well, he'd better start getting used to you. I've never seen you go so potty over a woman before."

"She's incredible," Eddie gushed. "She's smart and sexy and gorgeous and—" His voice trailed off.

"And?" Jim repeated.

"And gone. Her brother took her to Baden-Baden to try out a new treatment for her migraines. She gets them a lot, apparently, out of the blue."

Jim nodded sympathetically. "Hope it helps. I had an auntie who used to get them. Migraines can be wicked shit."

"Yes, I know," Eddie agreed. "I'm trying to be a supportive boyfriend. But I miss her so much."

Jim sat down and turned his chair away from the wall. "So fetch your guitar and play me those songs you were telling me about."

Eddie drew in a deep breath and sighed. "Okay. And promise you'll give me an honest appraisal. If these songs are crap, I don't want to play them for her."

"Don't worry," Jim assured him. "I'll be brutal."

\* \* \*

Eddie closed his eyes and held the last note of his final song until his voice gave out. He slipped his left index finger up the neck of the guitar and played a series of ascending bar chords. Then he took a deep breath and rested his elbow on top of the instrument. He opened his eyes and looked up at his erstwhile songwriting partner. Jim stared back at him blankly.

"You haven't said a damned thing," Eddie noted after several silent seconds had passed.

"I'm speechless," Jim whispered.

Eddie winced. "Are they that bad?"

Jim crossed his arms in front of his chest and smiled a wide, toothy grin. "Eddie, those are the most beautiful love songs I have ever heard. They are astoundingly good. Your lyrics fit the music so perfectly! It's as if the words and melodies were just meant to be together."

Eddie smiled in relief. "That's how they came out—together, in one seamless piece of music."

"But you've never composed melodies before," Jim said. "You've written the occasional middle eight by yourself, but you always relied on me for the bulk of the tune."

"I know," Eddie agreed. "I don't understand it either. But Birdie inspires me, Jim. Christ, she makes me feel like I'm an artist."

Jim shook his head and laughed. "You're gonna put me out of work. How the hell am I supposed to come up with songs for our next record, now that I know what you're capable of doing all by your lonesome?"

"No, no—that won't be a problem," Eddie assured him. "You're great at what you do. You have so much more musical talent and training than I have. That's why I wanted to run these songs by you first, before I sang them for her."

"You want my honest opinion?" Jim asked, holding Eddie's gaze. "Record them."

"No," Eddie replied, his tone emphatic. "These songs aren't for the group or the record-buying public. They're just for Birdie."

"That's not what I meant," Jim said. "I think you should go into a studio and put those songs onto a demo pressing for her. That way she could listen to them whenever she wanted, just like you kept re-reading those poems she wrote you on our tour."

Eddie ventured a half-smile. "Maybe I should. That way, I wouldn't be so nervous about singing them to her face."

"Why would you feel nervous?" Jim laughed, settling back in his chair. "If you love this bird enough to write music like that for her, why would you feel nervous singing those songs to her face?"

Eddie turned away and gazed at the Kubin print. "It's just that ever since I came home, she's been so moody. Sometimes she'll act all sweet—real shy and quiet—and she'll flash me these puppy dog looks like she utterly adores me. But other times—well, it's hard to describe. She starts talking to herself and becomes so—"

He remembered the way she ran through the museum, and frowned. "She recently told me how she lost her parents when she was fifteen," he added, looking back at Jim. "Her house caught fire, and she was trapped inside the building with her mum and dad. She managed to escape, but they didn't. She told me she saw her mother's body engulfed in flames, and heard her screaming in agony as she died. So she has a lot of fear and guilt bottled up inside her."

Jim's eyes grew wide. "Has she seen a doctor about that?"

Eddie shrugged. "I don't think so. I mentioned to her once that my old childhood friend Bob Carter was studying to be a psychiatrist, and she completely flew off the handle. I've never seen her so cross. So I gather she has no use for analysts."

Jim leaned back in his chair. "Well, why not take advantage of her being away in Baden-Baden? Book a day or two at the studio and lay down those tracks. Then when she gets back, you can give her the record as a welcome home present."

Eddie looked back at the lithograph, laughed at how out-of-place it seemed in his room, and returned his gaze to Jim. "That's a good idea. I'll ring up that engineer who worked on our last LP and see if he can fit me in. What was his name again?"

"Matthias Grieselhuber," Jim replied. "I know his home number. Let me write it down for you."

\* \* \*

Eddie rolled his head over the pillow and buried his face in Roberta's luxurious mane of hair. He nuzzled her neck, then cradled her body with his right arm while he cupped her breast with his left hand.

"You were absolutely magnificent," he whispered.

"Mmm," she purred, running her fingers through his shoulder-length hair. "You weren't so bad yourself."

Eddie squeezed her tightly for a few moments, then loosened his grip. "Next time, I want to do it with the lights on. You're just too gorgeous to be kept hidden under cover of darkness."

"I like the darkness," she replied. "Bright lights give me headaches." She repositioned herself in his arms and looked up. "Why are you so nice to me?"

"What kind of question is that?" he laughed. "Why wouldn't I be nice to you?"

"Most people aren't," she answered.

"Well, maybe most people don't know you like I do. You don't get out much, you know."

"You don't know me very well."

"I know all I need to know," he said. "I know that I love you."

Roberta eased herself out of Eddie's embrace and rolled over. She switched on the bedside lamp and picked up the book of Irish poetry she had left on the nightstand. "I like Yeats' interpretation of the story much more than Homer's," she said, resuming the conversation they had abandoned the previous hour.

Eddie smiled. *This is what I get for falling in love with a girl who likes poetry,* he thought. *So much for pillow talk.*

"Who would have thought a blarney-spewing Irishman could write more erotically than a hot-blooded Greek?" he joked. He gazed at Roberta's soft, round breasts and ran his index finger in a circle around her nipples. He let his finger drop and slowly traced a line between her sternum and navel.

Roberta pulled the sheet up to her neck, covering both her breasts and Eddie's wandering hand. She opened the book to the page they had been reading earlier and started reciting a stanza from *Leda and the Swan.*

When she finished reading, she clapped the book shut. "So the Trojan War was all Zeus' fault," she said. "If he hadn't raped Leda, then Helen would never have been conceived, and Paris would never have kidnapped her."

"And her face would never have launched a thousand ships," Eddie agreed.

Roberta slipped her hand under the covers and took hold of his roving fingers. "I once read another, older version of the story in which Helen spent the entire war living in Egypt, serving Artemis," she added. "The woman whom Paris abducted was an imposter, and the whole war was fought over an illusion."

Eddie leaned back against his pillow. "You're much better read than I am, love."

"Of course, Helen didn't like that poet's interpretation," Roberta continued. "So she invoked her father's wrath and blinded him."

"Ouch," Eddie replied, copping a wince. He rolled over and flashed Roberta a goofy grin. "But then again, I suppose there's a lesson in that as well. Never cheese off a really pretty girl."

Roberta cast Eddie a dubious look. He laughed and clasped her hand once more. "Homer was blind too," he said after kissing each of her fingertips one by one.

"Mmm," Roberta agreed. "What a funny coincidence."

Eddie took the book away and snuggled up against her. "No more poems tonight, my darling. Let's make love again."

She glanced at the clock. "Not now. I should be going home soon. Dick is probably worried about me."

"You're a big girl," Eddie chided. "You don't need a curfew."

Roberta frowned. "It's not a curfew. I live with Dick. He's taken care of me for the past six years, ever since our parents died, and he worries when I'm out late. I'm just showing him the respect he deserves, that's all."

"Sorry," Eddie replied. "I didn't mean to make you mad."

"Don't call me mad!" she shouted. "I don't like that word!"

Eddie released Roberta from his embrace and backed away to his side of the bed. "I'm sorry, love. I didn't mean anything by that." He took her hand back in his and brought it to his mouth for another kiss. "Do you have to leave right away? We could have a smoke first. Or maybe even listen to that record I made you. I kept a second copy for myself."

Roberta's fury dissipated as quickly as it had arrived. "Okay," she agreed. She sat upright against the headboard and repositioned the sheet over her chest while Eddie climbed out of bed and put the record on the turntable. When he returned, he pulled his Marlboros and lighter out of the nightstand drawer and lit cigarettes for them both. Roberta took two small puffs, then held her cigarette a few inches away from her face. She stared intently at the glowing embers as they slowly ate away at the paper.

"Which song is your favorite?" Eddie asked.

"*Dreaming Tonight*," she answered, her lips curling into a smile.

"But they're all lovely." She focused her attention on the cigarette for several seconds, then turned and faced Eddie. "You should release the record as an LP and sell it in stores."

Eddie frowned. "But I meant these songs just for you."

"But they're good. Other people should have a chance to hear them."

"But I don't want to release the album to the general public." He took a long drag on his cigarette while he chose his words.

"Music changes so much in the recording process," he offered at length. "So many people get involved, and everyone gets caught up in trying to make the record sound as commercial as possible. And anyway, I'm not even the lead singer of my band—Tony is. And I don't want him singing those songs. They're my gift for you."

"*You* should release the LP," Roberta clarified. "Just you, not the Pilots. You should release those songs on a solo album."

"But I don't want to leave the band," Eddie protested.

"That's not what you told me earlier," she argued. "You said you could hardly wait to stop touring and settle down on your grandpa's farm in Ohio."

"Yes, that's right. But I meant to retire from show business completely, not just branch off on my own and start a solo career."

"This record could sell. Then you'd have enough money to retire."

"I have money socked away already. I really don't need to—"

"This record could sell well," Roberta interrupted. "Dick thinks it's got the potential to really push you over the top."

Eddie lowered his head and sighed. He took another long drag on his cigarette before resting it in the ceramic bowl on his nightstand. "You played my record for Dick?"

"Of course I did," Roberta replied. "We share everything. He's the only family I've got. He takes care of me."

"Well, just because Dick thinks the record could sell well, that doesn't mean it will," Eddie countered.

"Yeats published his poetry. So did Homer."

"But my lyrics aren't that good," Eddie laughed. "You can't compare me with that lot!"

"Your songs are beautiful. You should share them with the world."

"But Birdie, I don't want—" Eddie started to reply, but then he noticed the ashes had fallen from Roberta's cigarette and were burning a small brown hole in the middle of the crisp white sheet.

"Christ!" he exclaimed. He leapt out of bed, tore off the sheet and threw it on the floor. After beating out the small fire, he turned to face Roberta. His voice crooned out of the speakers in the corner of the room:

*I stand before you like a vessel at the launch,*
*My last restraint is gone...*

She was watching him carefully, displaying no visible trace of emotion. Her smoldering cigarette dangled precariously between her fingers.

*Christ!* Eddie cursed in his head. *I would have thought she'd be having a flashback to the fire that killed her parents. But she's as cool as ice.*

He held her gaze for a long, awkward moment, then climbed back onto the bed and took away her cigarette. "I'm sorry, love," he apologized. "I should have given you the ashtray."

She offered no response.

He wrapped his arms around her and hugged her tightly. "I'm so sorry, darling," he repeated. "I hope you're not frightened."

"I'm not frightened," she said in a cool, flat voice. She extricated herself from his embrace and climbed off the bed. Turning her back to him, she stooped down to pick up her clothes. Eddie stared at her in bewilderment as she fastened the hook of her bra.

"You should get dressed too," she said as she slipped her arms through the sleeves of her blouse. "So you can take me home. Dick is probably wondering what's taking me so long."

## Chapter Seven

Gerry rested his sticks on the drum skin and leaned in towards the microphone. "Was that gentle enough for ya? Or should I play it even softer?"

"Come have a listen," replied Matthias Grieselhuber. "Tell me what you think."

Gerry tugged off his headphones and walked over to the glass-paneled isolation booth. He took a seat while the recording engineer pulled a few levers on the soundboard and started playing back the newly recorded track.

Gerry shook his head. "It's not right. I'll re-do it."

"No, let me play with it," Matthias said. "I can maybe bring up the tone *ein bisschen*. But I want the drums to stay *weich*."

"If they were any more *weich*, I'd fall asleep," Gerry groused. He leaned back in his chair. "If you ask me, this record's a real snoozer. All these pretty love songs, but where's the passion?"

"You would not say that if you saw Eddie this morning," Matthias joked as he scribbled down a few notes.

Gerry's eyes grew wide. "Damn it! What happened? I hate when I show up late for a session and miss out on all the fun!"

Matthias smiled. "Roberta came into the studio."

Gerry sank back in his chair, disappointed. "I thought that barmy bint was suffering another mysterious migraine this week."

"Well, *offensichtlich* she got better. She came here just after noon, and Eddie took her to lunch."

Gerry checked his watch. "It's three-thirty already! What kind of meal takes three-and-a-half fucking hours to eat?"

"Perhaps they stopped by Eddie's place afterwards for *Nachspeise*," Matthias suggested. "Or maybe they went there straight away from the studio—for a little *Vorspeise*."

Gerry scratched an itch on the side of his nose. "Dessert or starter, it doesn't matter. That bastard's getting more action than I am lately. S'pose I ought to be happy for him. Lord knows, Eddie deserves some real romance in his life after all those years of curling up with nothing but books of soppy poetry for comfort. Can't say I much care for his woman, though."

Matthias laughed. "I am happy for him also. And I hope he comes back to the studio feeling better. He was—*Scheiße!*—how do you say '*außer sich vor Wut*?'"

"Beside himself with rage? Our Eddie? I don't believe it! What the hell happened?"

"Eli showed up stoned again. So Eddie gave him sack. That is the right phrase, yes?"

"Close enough," Gerry replied. "So he's gotta find himself a new bassist now, huh?"

"No, no," Matthias answered. "Eli sent his friend to say good words for him. So now *alles ist gut.*"

Gerry arched his eyebrow. "His friend? Do you mean—?"

"Yes. Dick. Roberta's brother. You know him well?"

Gerry laughed. "I know him in a professional capacity, just like Eli does. Though I wouldn't exactly call him a friend."

"*Nun, ja.*" Matthias shrugged. "So Eddie makes good with Eli and Dick and leaves the studio with Roberta. He comes back soon, I am sure. I should be ready." He started rewinding the tape. "*Was macht* with your band now? I am confused. Are you still Pilots? Or is it now Eddie and the Pilots? Like Diana and the Supremes?"

"Bugger, I dunno," Gerry said, fumbling with his shirt pocket for a cigarette. He pulled out an empty pack and sighed. "Nobody's said anything about breaking up yet. Tony's still pressing Emmett to arrange another tour. But this record is Eddie's baby. He's just using us as studio musicians. Kind of weird."

"You are happy with this *Anordnung?*" Matthias asked.

Gerry shrugged. "Got naff all else to do at the moment. Ringo played on John Lennon and George Harrison's solo albums. And Neil Young can't decide if he wants to stay with Crosby, Stills and Nash or not. Maybe this is the new direction music's gonna take now that the Sixties have stopped swinging. Bands-in-flux. Welcome to the Seventies. It's all organic."

"You make no sense," Matthias laughed. He glanced at his watch. "I should not do much more work without Eddie. He wants to go over *alles* so carefully."

"Right," Gerry agreed. "Our mild-mannered rhythm-guitarist-slash-background-vocalist has evolved into a singer-song-writer-slash-record-producer-slash-pain-in-the-arse-*artiste*! Talk about your bands-in-flux!"

"*Sei nicht albern,*" Matthias chided. "He is not so *voll von sich* as that. I mean, not so full of self."

"Yeah," Gerry replied. "You're right. He's too full of Roberta to be full of himself. That woman has sucked up his soul like a fuckin' vampire. What does he see in her anyway?"

"She is beautiful," Matthias said. "And I think maybe she is hot in bed. She is also smart and likes to read poetry, just like Eddie."

"I know, but—" Gerry let his voice trail off and started drumming his fingers absent-mindedly against the soundboard. "It's just that I never would have pictured Eddie falling for a chick like her in a million years. She's so weird, and he's so—boring. Boring in a good way, mind you, like an indulgent big brother who's always there to get you out of scraps, but who's too busy setting a good example to have much fun himself."

"*Was für eine* scraps has Eddie gotten you out of?" Matthias asked with a sly smile.

Gerry rolled his eyes. "Don't get me started! I could go on for days, but it's Eddie I'm worried about now. Last week he showed me this book he was gonna give Roberta with pictures of all these exotic, tropical birds from the West Indies. But I'll tell you, Matt, what Eddie really needs is a little brown wren. Some Midwest farmer's daughter who can grow soybeans alongside him in Ohio and make him feel all right. But what could I say? I felt like Ringo trying to tell John that maybe he ought to consider ditching Yoko."

Matthias looked up. "Tell him now. *Er kommt herein.*"

Eddie opened the door to the sound booth and stepped inside. "Sorry I took so long."

"S'alright, mate," Gerry replied, leaning back in his seat and assuming a pose of nonchalance. "We were just playing back one of the songs with my new drum track."

"Give us a listen," Eddie said. He pulled up a chair between the two men and placed the earphones on his head. Matthias started playing the tape. Eddie grimaced, removed the earphones and switched off the machine.

"You need to redo the drums, Ger," he said. "Let's call up

Tony and have him lay down a new guitar solo too. I want it to sound more like 'Layla', where the instrument becomes the voice. I want to hear the longing in the guitar."

"Tony *ist nicht* Clapton," Matthias noted.

"Well, then call up someone else!" Eddie shouted. "Use your connections, Matt! Find me a guitarist who can make this record sound the way I want it to sound!"

Matthias threw a cool glance at Gerry and left the sound booth. Gerry kept a close eye on Eddie as he rewound the tape to play back another track.

"So how was lunch?" he asked.

Eddie smiled.

Gerry squinted. "What's that on your throat?"

Eddie covered the left side of his neck with his hand and started rubbing it. "I dunno. A hickey I s'pose."

"That's not a hickey," Gerry countered. "That's a fuckin' chomp. I saw scabs, mate. That woman drew blood."

Eddie laughed. "She's passionate." He reached for a knob to replay the music, but Gerry put his hand out and stopped him.

"I don't know how to say this, Eddie," he began. "I'm sure there's no right way. And you're probably just gonna hit me. But I can't let this sit any longer. I think you really ought to consider—"

Eddie glared at his drummer. Gerry held his gaze and crossed his arms in front of his chest defiantly. Silence fell between the old friends. Eddie leaned back in his chair and crossed his own arms to match Gerry's posture. A small trickle of blood ran down Eddie's neck. Gerry drew in a deep breath, then turned his head and stared at his drum kit through the glass walls of the booth.

"I only wanted to say—" Gerry fumbled. "Well, it's just that—I mean—Eddie, I know you're really into peacocks these days, but I just think you're more of a duck person."

\* \* \*

Eddie shifted his head to a more comfortable position on Roberta's lap and gazed up into her eyes. "Hey good lookin', whatcha got cookin'?" he crooned with an exaggerated twang.

She ran her fingers over his long sideburns and smiled down at him. "Nothing. I'm hopeless in the kitchen. I always burn everything."

"That's all right," he replied, stretching out his long legs across the sofa. "I'll get a chef to cook for both of us. And I'll hire a maid for you and a valet for me, and we'll all live happily ever after together in our very own palace."

"I thought you wanted to take me to your grandfather's farm in Ohio," she replied.

"I'll build a palace for you there. Or a mansion anyway."

"Better not put it too close to the cow pasture," she teased.

"I wouldn't dream of it. I'll build it right in front of a big cornfield. And in the autumn, all the stalks will turn gold and bow down to you each time you walk by."

"You are the most ridiculous man I've ever met," Roberta said with a shake of her head. A loose tendril of hair tumbled out of her bun, skimming her cheek.

"And you are the most beautiful woman I've ever seen," Eddie replied. He reached up and caressed her rogue curl.

Roberta repositioned her knees and offered him a pillow.

"No, don't move, love," he said. "I'm perfectly comfortable where I am. As a matter of fact, there's no place I'd rather be."

"Okay," she whispered, stroking his sideburns affectionately as she might pet a beloved dog.

"God, wasn't today just lovely?" he asked. "Everything was so absolutely, bloody perfect. Window-shopping in the *Altstadt* together, then riding out that sudden cloudburst in the *Frauenkirche*, and dodging raindrops under the sidewalk awnings all the way home. And then just hanging around my house all evening, eating chocolate and reading to each other—"

"You're pretty easy to please," she interrupted.

"And nobody pleases me like you do," he replied. "Especially on days like today."

Roberta stopped petting Eddie's sideburns and stiffened her back. "What's that supposed to mean?"

"Nothing," he answered quickly, regretting his last words and hoping he hadn't upset her. "It's just that, well, you know. You seem like you're in a really good mood today. That's all."

She relaxed her posture a bit. "I'm allowed to have a good day here and there."

Eddie laughed in relief. He rolled his head to the side and kissed her thigh. "Well, I'm glad I took today off from the studio and spent some time with you. 'Cause after all, what's the point of making an album of love songs for the woman I love if I can't spend any time making love to her?"

"You know, Eddie, you're a lot more poetic when you have a pen in your hands," she admonished him. "Your free association leaves a bit to be desired."

"All I desire is you," he said.

"Mmm," she mumbled.

He slipped a roving hand under her blouse. "Why can't every day be like this? Why can't every day be perfect?"

"Because if every day were perfect, then you'd never appreciate a perfect day, silly," she said. "It would be like living in Southern California, where it's sunny all the time. Who would want that?"

"Isn't it sunny all the time in St. Croix?"

"Of course not! It rains every day during the wet season." Relaxing her posture still more, she pulled out her hairpins, leaned her head over Eddie's face, and let her long, dark tresses tumble on top of him like a cascade of black silk. "An' it de storm cloud dat make de sun look so pretty," she whispered in a sing-song cadence.

Eddie laughed and swept a lock of her hair out of his eyes. "I love it when you use that accent, Birdie. You are my very own tropical island princess."

Roberta laughed back at him. "You smil' now, silly English boy. But maybe you not smile so bright when de hurricane come and blow you away."

## Chapter Eight

"So what's the word from London?" Eddie asked. He closed the door to his manager's office, slipped into a seat across from the desk, and pulled a pack of Marlboros out of his breast pocket.

Emmett Poole swiveled around in his brown leather chair, a broad smile sprawled across his face. "Tell me I'm the world's greatest manager!"

"You're the world's greatest manager," Eddie replied indifferently. He slapped the pack against his palm and removed a cigarette.

"No," Emmett insisted. "This occasion calls for a cigar."

"I prefer cigarettes," Eddie said, bringing a Marlboro to his lips and lighting it.

"Suit yourself," Emmett sighed. He opened his briefcase and laid a thick stack of clipped papers on top of the desk. "Get a load of all the zeros. Just count them!"

Eddie picked up the contract and scanned it briefly. His eyes displayed an undeniable look of surprise, but he held his smile in check.

Emmett furrowed his brow. "I worked hard to get you this."

"I worked hard on the album," Eddie replied. "I've never spent so many hours on a single project in my entire life. For the past three months I've hardly had a chance to see the woman I wrote these songs for. I feel like I've been living in the fucking studio."

"Well you can get out of the studio now," Emmett said. "I have everything planned out for you. I'm booking you on Carson in L.A. and Mike Douglas in Philadelphia, and I'm hammering out details for some radio interviews in New York as well. Then you'll be flying to London to make appearances on *Top of the Pops* and *Desert Island Discs*."

"Bollocks!" Eddie exclaimed, throwing the thick bundle of papers on the desk. "You can't expect me to punt the record already. I haven't even signed the bloody contract yet! And it'll be weeks before EMI sets a release date."

"They want it out by January, so they can plan a big Valentine's Day promotion," Emmett retorted. "But we'll release *Dreaming Tonight* in November, to start building interest. The studio thinks it could be the Number One Christmas Single."

"Wish you'd have told me that earlier. I would have added jingle bells," Eddie replied with a scowl. He took a deep drag on his cigarette and exhaled through his nose, sending a small cloud of smoke over his head like a lifting fog.

"EMI has never worked this fast for us before," Eddie added, tapping his cigarette against the ashtray on Emmett's desk. "They started dragging their feet on our projects years ago, then dropped us. Why the sudden turnaround?"

Emmett rested his hand on top of the contract and splayed his fingers. "Because this record is going to sell through the roof. Those songs you wrote are absolutely breathtaking. I cried the first time I heard them. Lew Grade stopped by the studio while I was playing your tapes for the big brass, and *he* got all weepy. This music you wrote goes right to the heart, and your vocals—Christ, when did you ever learn to sing like that? This album is magic! And everyone at EMI agrees with me. The label is prepared to bump all its other projects out of the way and just focus on this."

Eddie crushed out his cigarette. "Well, EMI doesn't generally release that many new records at the beginning of the year, now, do they?" he noted in a dismissive voice. "They usually just let the holiday albums play out their sales."

Emmett leaned back in his chair. "Why are you being so cynical, son? Aren't you even the least bit excited? Christ, Eddie, you are poised to become a superstar!"

Eddie rolled his eyes. "Oh, come off it, Emmett. I'm a lesser player in a lesser band that rode to a middling success for a few years on the coattails of the Beatles. EMI has never been that interested in me. Our own fans weren't even that interested in me—not like they were about Tony, or even Gerry."

He stood up from his chair and walked to the window. "I'm willing to release this record, Emmett, because Birdie says she wants me to. But I don't for a minute buy into all this shit you're shoveling at me—that the LP will go gold the moment it hits the stores and I'm gonna be the hottest new thing since Tang."

"Trust me, Eddie," Emmett replied in a calm, measured voice. "I know the business, and I know that this record is going to sell beyond your wildest dreams. Look this over." He handed the contract to Eddie and beckoned him to sit back down. "Carefully this time. Check out the advance against royalties they're willing to give you up front. The label believes in you."

Eddie sat back down and started reviewing the papers, then furrowed his brow. "This is a three-record deal, Emmett. I only want a contract for one record."

Emmett closed his eyes and took a deep breath. "Keep reading, lad. There are clauses for how you can get out of that. Don't worry so much about the future, Eddie. Think about the now."

Eddie turned a page and frowned. "What's this about renaming the album?"

"The boys in publicity don't like your title."

"That's not negotiable," Eddie said. *"A Vessel at the Launch* is a line from the poem Birdie was reading the night I met her. This album is for her. I'm giving it a name that means something to us."

Emmett drummed his fingers impatiently on his desktop. "Eddie, once this album is released, it's not going to be 'personal' anymore. It's going to belong to the world."

Eddie threw the contract back on the desk. "You think I don't know that? You think I didn't have huge reservations about even going to the studio to polish up the songs? I never intended to record a proper album. I just wanted to make a little demo pressing for Birdie. I meant this record as a gift for her—a token of my affection—to show her how much she means to me."

Emmett opened the top drawer of his desk and searched in vain for his own packet of cigarettes. "Can I bum a fag?"

Eddie tossed his pack across the desk. "So much for cigars."

Emmett lit a cigarette and took a few puffs while he collected his thoughts. "Eddie, there's no point in going back," he offered at length. "You've polished up the songs. They're ready for market. And EMI is prepared to promote them. I know you're getting tired of the business. I know you've been talking about retiring to Ohio for years now. But think for a few moments about the people around you. Think about the band. If this record sells well—and it *will* sell well—EMI is finally going to release that greatest hits LP they've been shelving for years. And I'm going to arrange a proper tour for you lads this time, in the States and the U.K. Big arenas again. And afterwards, if you decide to chuck it all and become a farmer, fine. Go plow your field. But this way you'll have a big nest egg to retire on. And you'll be going out on top."

Eddie closed his eyes and clenched his hands in and out of fists. "I don't want to go on tour again. I want to spend more time with Birdie!"

Emmett rested his smoldering cigarette on the ash tray and gave Eddie a look of concern. "How's she been feeling lately?"

"Not so good," Eddie mumbled. "Her migraines are back."

"She's seeing a doctor for that?"

"Yes. Dick took her back to Baden-Baden. They'll be there till the end of the week."

"You don't like him, do you, this 'Dick' fellow?" Emmett noted.

Eddie turned his head and stared out the window. "I'd better start liking him. It's important to get along with your in-laws."

Emmett's pensive face broke into a sly smile. "You dog! Why didn't you tell me you were getting married?"

"I'm not engaged yet. I'm just thinking about it." He turned his face back to meet his manager's.

"Well, ask the lucky lady already! What are you waiting for?"

"I'm waiting for her to get back from Baden-Baden." Eddie stood up from his chair and picked up the contract. "And I'm waiting to catch her in a good mood too. She's been awfully flighty lately." He walked to the door and started fiddling with the knob. "I'll look this over at home. I promise. I could use a break from reading poetry."

\* \* \*

The black Porsche slashed through a large puddle as it rounded the tight street corner, thrusting a wave of cold water onto the sidewalk and drenching Eddie's legs.

*Fuck it,* Eddie thought. *Fuck it all.* He kept walking down *Dachauer Straße*, rain pelting him from above and wind whipping through his soaked jacket. *Love is not supposed to feel like this!*

He couldn't understand Birdie. Why she was so passionate one moment and indifferent the next. Why she didn't call him from

Baden-Baden. And why the hell she felt the need to share all of the intimate details of their relationship with Dick.

*That contract is mind-blowing,* he reminded himself. *I shouldn't have been so rude to Emmett. If everything goes like he predicts, I can retire before I'm thirty!*

*If only Birdie were here,* he mused. *Then I could talk to her and see if she'd be willing to tag along on the tour.*

He tried to imagine Gerry's face when he discovered Birdie might be hitting the road with the band. *Christ, why does he hate her so? Why does nobody else seem to think she's right for me?*

A fast stream of rainwater spewed from an overhead gutter onto the sidewalk in front of him, forming a small, black pond that sparkled under the streetlamp. He dodged it and turned the corner onto Roberta's street. Lifting his face into the rain, he sought out her bedroom window. A soft, golden light glowed from within.

*She's back!* His heart immediately lifted. He ran down the block to her flat, splashing through puddles along the way and nearly slipping on the oil slick that sprouted from under Dick's rusty VW. He grabbed some ornamental pebbles from a potted plant on her doorstep and hurled them at her window. After the sixth throw, Roberta flung back the curtain and stood before him, a backlit shadow.

"What light through yonder window breaks?" Eddie shouted up to her. "It is the east, and Birdie is the sun!"

She put her finger to her lips and closed the curtain. Moments later, she slipped through the front door. She lingered under the shelter of the small awning but took a small step towards him.

"Don't yell, you'll wake Dick!" she scolded him as she closed the door behind her.

"She speaks! Oh, speak again bright angel!"

Roberta laughed. "You're soaked through. What are you doing, walking the streets this time of night?"

Eddie kissed her quickly, then put his cold, wet hands to her warm cheeks. "Marry me," he whispered. "Marry me and come on tour with me and never go away from me again. Say that you will."

She stepped back. "What are you talking about?"

"Emmett's arranging a giant tour for the band to punt the record," he said, his words tumbling out in a fevered rush, not at all the way he'd planned them. "Come with me. We'll see the Louvre in Paris and the Tate in London and the Met in New York and every night you can come to my concerts and I'll sing my songs for you for all the world to hear!"

She leaned her back against the door. "I just got home this evening. I haven't even unpacked yet! And now you want me to marry you?"

"Just say you will. Marry me and see the world with me!"

"Eddie, I—"

The front door opened. Dick Mason glowered at Eddie over his sister's shoulder.

"What the fuck, Rochester? The girl just got back from the hospital a couple of hours ago. Can't you let her rest for a single night without getting in her face? Give us a break!"

"I have big news," Eddie explained, water dripping in small rivulets from his wet hair onto his damp face. "Great news. Let me come in for a moment and I'll tell you."

Dick grabbed his sister's shoulder and pulled her back into the house. "Not now, asshole. You're wet as a drowned rat. Come back in the morning. No. Make that the afternoon. Let the poor kid get a good night's sleep."

"Birdie, I—" Eddie stretched out his hand towards Roberta just as Dick slammed the door in his face.

"I love you," he whispered. He stepped back from the shelter of the awning and let the rain pour down over him as he stared at Roberta's window, waiting for the amber light to be extinguished.

## Chapter Nine

"So you get all the royalties from your solo album, but only a quarter from that Greatest Hits record the studio's issuing, right?"

Eddie shook his head. "No, Dick, I'll get a *fifth* from the Greatest Hits record. The band shares everything equally."

"But only four of you have been in the group since the beginning. You keep switching out bassists."

"We'll divvy up the bassist's share between Joe, Pete and Eli. They've all been Pilots."

"Right," Dick said, scanning the pages of the contract. "But you'll get songwriting royalties too."

"Jim and I will share those from the Greatest Hits record. But not from my solo album."

Dick cast a nervous glance out the front window of his flat, then turned back to Eddie. "So what kind of numbers are we talking here?"

Eddie let out an exasperated sigh. "I have no idea. The LP hasn't even been released yet. How can you expect me to give you sales figures?"

Dick shrugged. "Well, maybe your man Emmett can estimate tour grosses. If you add up all the tickets from all the venues you'll be playing—"

"You're assuming we're going to sell out everything. I wouldn't. We left a lot of empty seats the last time we toured America."

"But this record should make a difference, shouldn't it?"

The telephone rang. Dick jumped from his seat before Eddie could answer his question.

"Right, I've got that. I can't really talk now," Dick mumbled into the phone. "Yes. Mm-hmm." He turned his back to Eddie and stepped as far away as the phone cord would stretch. "I'm in the middle of a conversation here. I'll call you back as soon as I can."

He hung up the phone and turned around. "Business," he said.

"Don't let me interrupt you," Eddie said curtly.

Dick walked to the window and looked down the street. "How many groceries did she say she was going to buy?"

Eddie laughed. "Christ, I don't know. Why are you so worried? She's a grown woman. She can walk to the store by herself."

Dick pulled up a chair, slicked back his short, greasy mop of black hair and faced Eddie. "Now your grandfather's land. You said it was the biggest farm in Southern Ohio."

"That's what he always said."

"So we're talking how many acres here?"

"Hell, I don't know! I don't have the title!"

"But you will, won't you? When your grandfather—"

"What the hell, Dick? When my grandfather pegs out? Are you really asking me this?"

"Hey, I'm Roberta's guardian. I've taken care of her since our parents died. I'm only asking you what our dad would have asked. I need to make sure my sister will be provided for if you marry her."

Eddie rolled his eyes. "I'm set to inherit the farm. But Grandpa could live another ten years. Or he might change his will and leave everything to the Shriners. You never know. He's given them a lot of money lately for the burns unit they're adding to their hospital in Cincinnati."

Dick frowned. "But he wouldn't do that, would he? The land's been in your family for generations, hasn't it?"

The front door opened and Roberta stepped in, carrying a large wicker basket of food.

Dick cut his eyes towards her. "Where the hell have you been?"

Eddie stood up from his chair and walked to her side. "Hello love," he whispered as leaned in to kiss her.

Roberta gave Eddie a long, wet kiss, then turned to face her brother. "I bought bananas and ice cream."

"That shouldn't have taken so long. Where have you been?"

"Lighten up, Dick, Christ!" Eddie interrupted. "She just bought ingredients for sundaes. She told you she wanted to make something special to celebrate our big news."

Dick glared at his sister. "I haven't given her permission yet."

"I'm not making sundaes," Roberta said, holding her brother's gaze with a steely glint. "My boyfriend has asked me to marry him, and I'm feeling festive. I'm going to make Bananas Foster."

"So you went to the off-license. That's what kept you." Eddie smiled, dug his hand into her basket and pulled out a bottle of rum. "Marvelous choice, love. I had Bananas Foster once in New Orleans. You light them up, just like Cherries Jubilee. Very festive." He leaned over to kiss Roberta's cheek, then noticed she was still glaring at her brother. He looked at Dick and realized their eyes were locked. "Is this some kind of inside joke?"

Dick's nostrils flared. *"Ce n'est pas un jeu, soeur,"* he hissed.

"Don't speak to me in French," she replied. "You know I don't like that."

A shrill ring pierced the air. Dick held Roberta's stare. The phone rang again.

"You should get that, Dick. It might be a client," Roberta said.

Dick took a step towards the phone. "Go ahead," he shouted over the ringing. "Make your festive bananas, *bébé*. But give the matches to your boyfriend. I don't want you igniting anything."

\* \* \*

Eddie stretched his legs out on the floor in front of his couch and wrapped his arm more tightly around Roberta's shoulder. "Are you comfortable, my love?" he whispered in her ear.

She tucked her head down and rested it against his heart. Then she adjusted the blanket at her feet and snuggled in closer.

"Hmm," she mumbled.

"Your brother said 'yes' to our engagement," he reminded her.

"I know," she agreed. "He gave you a reluctant 'yes'."

"So are you going to say 'yes' to me now too?" he asked.

"You know what I want."

"I want to hear you say, 'yes, Eddie, I'll marry you'."

"You're silly," she replied. She inched away from him. Light from a streetlamp poured in through a window and illuminated her face with a soft glow.

"You've been so quiet since we left your house," Eddie whispered. "And Dick was acting so—"

"He worries about me, like you do," she interrupted. "He just wants to make sure I'll be in good hands."

"You're in good hands," Eddie promised, clasping her hands with his own. "You're in very good hands." Then he noticed she was shaking. "You're trembling," he added.

"It's the medication."

"I think you should talk to your doctor about that. He must be giving you too strong a dose. It can't be good for you to take medicine that makes you shake like this."

"It's for my head. It helps a lot."

"But why does it make you quiver so?"

"A lot of things make me quiver. You make me quiver too, you know."

Eddie smiled and kissed the top of her head. "I adore you," he whispered.

"I can tell."

He laughed and ran his fingers through her hair. "Grow old along with me—the best is yet to be," he whispered.

Roberta gazed up at Eddie and kissed his cheek. "I love Robert Browning. He's always been one of my favorites."

"I thought you preferred Elizabeth Barrett Browning."

"I like them both," she said. "He's more passionate, but she has a better sense of form and structure. Don't you think?"

Eddie adjusted the blanket at her feet so that it covered both of their legs. "Something tells me we're going to be spending a lot of nights like this. Sitting on a floor together, me quoting you lines of romantic poetry, trying to get you to come to bed. And you wanting to discuss the merits of the poems instead."

"What tells you that?" she asked.

"I don't know," Eddie laughed. "Just a little voice in my head, I suppose."

Roberta's eyes grew wide. "You hear voices in your head?"

Eddie laughed more deeply. "No, no! That's not what I meant! I was just making a joke."

She turned her face away abruptly. "It wasn't funny."

"I'm sorry," he said. He took hold of her left hand and examined her long, thin ring finger in the soft lamplight. "Do you want a diamond engagement ring, or maybe something less traditional?"

"It doesn't matter. I've never much cared for jewelry."

"Well, how about the wedding?" he continued. "Do you want to get married in a church or at a registry office?"

"Whatever," she answered.

Eddie's heart sank, but he continued to press her. "Dick says he really wants us to be married by a Catholic priest. He says that would have been your parents' fondest wish."

Roberta smirked. "Maybe we should ask the pope."

Eddie laughed, elated by the shift in her mood. "I'll have Emmett contact the Vatican. Lord knows, he has every other aspect of my life planned out for the next few months. What's one more phone call? And if Paul VI can't make it, then maybe we could get the Archbishop of Canterbu—"

Roberta cut him off. "I want a small wedding. No fuss. No crowds. Just the two of us and our witnesses. And I want it to be absolutely private. No photographers. No press."

"They're a nuisance," Eddie agreed. He drew in a deep breath and let go of her hand. "I suppose Dick will be walking you down the aisle," he grumbled.

"Mm-hmm," she agreed.

"You don't want to invite any other relatives?"

"No. Dick and I don't keep in touch with anyone else from the family."

"Why not?"

"We just don't."

"Dick once mentioned your uncle in Martinique," he added. "Your mother's brother. Maybe he'd like the honor of giving you away."

"No!" Roberta exclaimed. Her body grew instantly rigid and she edged away from Eddie.

"What's wrong, love?" he asked.

"Nothing," she insisted.

He stroked her arm reassuringly. "Did you ever visit him in Martinique? I've heard it's very pretty there."

"A few times," she whispered, focusing her eyes squarely on the floor.

"They speak French there, right?"

"Yes. My uncle and mother both spoke French."

"Is that why your middle name is Antoinette?"

"I hate that name!" Roberta shouted. "It was *her* name!" She lifted her head and looked up at the window. Her eyes reflected the light from the street lamp and glowed brightly, like a cat's.

Eddie's mind started reeling. *I hate when she acts like this!* he thought. *I never know what to say to calm her down.*

He took a deep breath, then rested his hand on top of her leg and started tickling her kneecap. "My middle name is Llywelyn," he said after a few awkward moments had passed in silence. "My mum's half-Welsh. She named me after her father."

Roberta took a deep, calming breath, then faced Eddie once more. "What's your mother like?"

"She's rather quiet," Eddie said, encircling Roberta's hand with his fingers. "I'm sure the two of you will get along fine." He sighed and turned his face away. "Though I don't think you're going to like her husband, my stepfather Stan. He's such a tosser. I'd rather not invite him to the wedding at all. But I don't see how I can ask mum and their son, but not him."

"Then don't invite any of them," Roberta proposed. "We'll see your family in a few months when your tour stops in Manchester. You can introduce me to them then."

Eddie ventured a half-smile. "Yes, that might be the best thing to do." He slipped his hand under the blanket and started stroking her thigh. "I imagine it might be hard for you to see my mother at the wedding, when yours can't be there."

"I'm glad my mother won't be at the wedding," Roberta replied. She stiffened her back and stared blankly into space. "She was always mean to me. She used to hit me and yell at me and call me all sorts of horrible names."

Eddie brought his hand to Roberta's chin and made her look at him. "You never told me that."

"She was a witch. I hated her," Roberta continued in a hollow voice.

Eddie fumbled for an appropriate response. "I'm sorry. I didn't know. But still, losing her the way you did, it must have been so unspeakably awful—"

"That's why I don't speak about it," she said, turning her face away. "But I never meant—my father—"

"Hush, now," Eddie whispered. "Let's not talk about this now. What's over is over. Let's think about happier things, like planning our honeymoon."

Roberta closed her eyes and rested her head against Eddie's protective shoulder. She remained silent for several minutes while he stroked her hair. Then she bolted upright out of his comforting embrace. "We should elope to Italy!" she exclaimed. "Just like Robert and Elizabeth Barrett Browning did. Let's get married in Florence!"

# Chapter Ten

### *Tuscany, Italy - 1972*

Emmett Poole's mother Grace fluffed Roberta's long veil until it hung perfectly over her shoulders, then stood back from the gilt-edged, floor-length mirror to admire the bride. "You look lovely, dear," she cooed. "I'm so glad you chose the mantilla, and not that drapey old hood."

"But Margaret Trudeau looked so pretty in her wedding cape," Roberta protested.

"Tricia Nixon looked far more elegant in her veil," Grace replied, gently stroking the lace that edged the bottom of the gossamer-thin tulle. "Everyone said she was the prettiest bride in the world last year—but I think you'll take the title for 1972."

Roberta blushed. "I don't want to be in the running. I don't want my picture in the newspapers."

"Emmett has done everything he could to keep things under wraps," Grace assured her. "But he can't hold the entire world's press at bay. Ever since Eddie's record came out, you and he are too much the *cause célèbre*."

"I just wanted a simple, quiet wedding," Roberta whispered, tears forming at the corners of her eyes.

"It will be simple, and it will be quiet," Grace promised, pulling a handkerchief from her bag. "Emmett has posted guards at all the church doors, so nobody will bother you during the ceremony." She dabbed at Roberta's tears. "Now don't cry, lamb. We don't want to ruin your mascara. And don't you worry about the crowds. The guards will form a shield around us as we walk in and out of the limousine. You'll be safe."

Roberta rubbed her hands over the satiny surface of her gown and offered Grace a wan smile. "Thank you so much for your help. I never would have found such a pretty dress by myself."

"It's been my pleasure, lamb," Grace replied. "I've raised two sons, and played den-mother to your husband's band of minstrels for years now. But I never thought I'd get to play 'mother-of-the-bride'."

"Eddie's not my husband yet," Roberta pointed out.

Grace checked her watch. "He will be in less than an hour. So are you ready, Birdie? Shall we go to the car now?"

Roberta stole another quick glance at her reflection in the mirror, then looked back at Grace. "I'm as ready as I'll ever be," she whispered.

She bunched up her skirt in her hands and took a few steps towards the door. Her long organza train made a faint, whispering sound as it slipped over the polished tile floor, like dried leaves rustling in the breeze before a gathering storm. She stopped abruptly. "Oh, wait, I forgot to take my medicine this morning."

"I'll fetch it for you," Grace offered. "Is it in the bathroom, or at your bedside?"

"Dick has it," Roberta replied. "I'll have to remember to ask him for it at the wedding dinner."

\* \* \*

"You have the rings?" Eddie asked, clenching his hands in and out of fists.

"Yes, for the tenth time, I have the rings," Emmett answered. He checked his watch. "She should be here shortly. Let's walk a little closer to the altar."

"I should have stayed with her at the villa. I hate to think of her fighting her way through that crowd outside with just Grace and Dick beside her."

"She'll be fine," Emmett assured him. "The guards will escort her from the car to the church. Just relax. Take a deep breath."

Eddie inhaled. The tang of nine hundred years of incense tickled his nostrils as the musty air passed through his nose and filled his lungs. He felt a light-headed buzz coming on.

"I'm glad I picked this church," Emmett said. "*San Miniato al Monte* isn't as famous as some of the other churches in town, but it's away from the city's center. And that view—Christ! You can see all of Florence from the steps in front of the building."

"Don't swear, you're in a church," Eddie scolded him.

"I wasn't swearing, I was talking to the man," Emmett replied, pointing to the gold inlay mosaic of Jesus built into the curved ceiling above the altar. "That's seven hundred years old. The padre told me so."

Eddie glanced at the elderly priest kneeling before the crucifix, waiting for the bride to arrive so the service could commence. "He looks like he might have been around when the artist made it."

"Don't be cheeky," Emmett admonished him.

A noise arose from outside the church—a cacophonous blend of high-pitched screams and low male voices shouting in multiple languages for Roberta to look their way.

"Your bride has arrived," Emmett said.

Eddie turned to face the church's entrance. The priest made a quick sign of the cross and processed to the front of the altar. Grace dashed down the aisle to join the groom and best man by the first pew. A monk in a brown robe whom neither Emmett nor Eddie had noticed before started playing Bach's *Sheep May Safely Graze* on an organ tucked into a lofted alcove above the altar. Music echoed off the cavernous ceiling and marble floor, making the centuries-old church come alive with sound.

Roberta slipped her hand into the crook of her brother's arm and looked straight ahead. "My god, she's beautiful," Eddie whispered as he watched her walk up the aisle to him.

Roberta looked down at her bouquet of fragrant flowers—yellow, five-pointed Ginger Thomas from her native Virgin Islands, white roses from Eddie's England, and fresh daisies symbolizing the Ohio farm they hoped to make their home. She looked up at Eddie and smiled. His knees felt weak for a moment and he leaned against Emmett for support. But then he smiled back, took her by the arm, and led her away from her brother.

\* \* \*

Eddie brought Roberta's hand to his lips and kissed her knuckles. "I love you, Mrs. Rochester," he whispered.

Roberta slipped her hand away and stared at the canopy bed at the end of the room. "God, I'm tired," she said. "It's been a long day."

"Mmm-hmm," Eddie agreed. He ran his hand slowly down her bodice, luxuriating in the smooth, sensuous feel of the silk fabric against his fingertips. "I'll help you unbutton your dress."

She edged further away from him and continued to stare at the bed. "Who do you suppose pulled down our quilt?" she asked.

"The maid, I imagine," Eddie replied. "Maybe she placed some chocolates on our pillows. Why don't we go check?" He reached for her hand again, but she kept it defiantly by her side.

"I thought your manager was going to keep things quiet for us," she said. "How did all those fans and photographers find the church?"

Eddie shrugged. "Rumors fly. Emmett tried his best. It could have been much worse."

Roberta's eyes flashed. "There were so many people outside the church! They were all pushing and shouting our names!"

"Yes," Eddie agreed. "I suppose our wedding was more of a Richard Burton-Elizabeth Taylor sort of affair than a Robert Browning and Elizabeth Barrett elopement. But we managed to dodge the crowd quickly. Nobody followed us to the restaurant afterwards."

Roberta furrowed her brow. "My uncle did. I saw him in the piazza as we were leaving. He was outside the church too. My Uncle Jean and Aunt Louise were both there."

"Really?" Eddie asked incredulously. "Your mother's brother? I thought you told me you weren't in contact with him anymore."

"I'm not!" Roberta shouted. "I hate him. And I hate his wife too! They're horrible people! Why did they have to come to Italy and try to ruin my wedding?"

Eddie stared at her helplessly. Her exquisite features were distorted into a mask of such palpable rage that he hardly recognized her. "I don't know, love," he answered at length. "Maybe they read about us in the newspapers, and decided they wanted to see you on your wedding day. They are your family, after all. They probably discovered the location of the church the same way the journalists and fans did. All it takes is one registry clerk to spill the beans, and before you know it—"

"There are spies everywhere!" Roberta hissed. "We should have stayed in Munich! We never should have come here!"

Eddie rubbed her arm. "But we're here now, love. And we have this gorgeous Italian villa all to ourselves for a whole week. Don't worry. The photographers only wanted to take our picture for the newspapers, and the fans were just there to wish us well."

"My uncle wants to kill me," she countered, her dusky voice growing deeper.

"What? That's nonsense!" Eddie scoffed. "Why would your own uncle want to kill you?"

"He blames me for my mother's death. He thinks the fire was my fault."

"That's ridiculous! How could anyone think such a thing?"

Roberta offered no reply.

Eddie watched her nostrils flare in and out as her breathing became more rapid. "Darling, I think you're just overwhelmed," he suggested. "It's been crazy lately, what with planning this 'secret' wedding and dashing off to Florence. And I know you're still recovering from your last migraine. Your mind must be playing tricks on you. That man you saw was probably just some bloke who looked like your uncle."

"I know what I saw!" she yelled. "My uncle and aunt were there! They're stalking us!" She started shaking violently.

Eddie wrapped his arms around her and held her tightly. "Don't worry, love, don't worry," he said, his voice strong and deliberate. "If they try to visit us, I won't let them in. I just want you to relax and be happy." When she stopped shaking, he released her from his protective embrace and took a step back. He lowered his voice to a whisper. "It's our wedding night. Let's put all of this behind us now. Let's go to bed."

Roberta looked up into Eddie's eyes. He watched her face shift through a series of changing expressions. She looked frightened. Helpless. Vulnerable. And then she looked hungry. Wanton. Brazen. A shiver ran up his spine as he remembered the last time she had gazed at him like that. *I'm in for a wild night,* he realized.

"Do you need me to undo the buttons on your back?" he asked.

She brought her hands to the collar of his shirt and started loosening his tie. "Let's do it here on the floor," she replied.

\* \* \*

"Why is she staring at us like that?" Roberta asked.

Eddie gazed at his plate of linguini. "I'm sure she just wants to see if we're enjoying the meal. Eat, love. It's lunchtime. You need to eat. You've hardly touched any food for days now."

"She's slipped something into my dish. I know she has."

"This is ridiculous, Birdie. Stop talking like that! Nobody is trying to hurt you."

"She's working for my uncle. She has to be. Just look at her face," Roberta hissed. "She's waiting to see if I'll take a bite from the food that she's poisoned."

Eddie pounded the table with his fist. "Stop it, Birdie. Stop it right now!"

The cook scurried back into the kitchen. Roberta started to laugh.

"This isn't funny!" Eddie shouted. "Why are you acting like this? Nobody is trying to poison you! The cook is a member of the villa staff, just like the maid and chauffeur. She is working for *us*, not your uncle."

"How do you know for sure?" Roberta challenged, her eyes darting back and forth between him and the kitchen door. "You can't understand what they're saying any better than I can. You don't speak Italian."

"I've talked to the chauffeur," Eddie replied, trying and failing to hold her gaze. "He speaks a little English, and he's a perfectly nice chap. All of the people here are perfectly nice. I'm tired of the way you're acting."

"You're tired of me already?" Roberta shouted. "We've only been married for three days, and you're tired of me already?"

Eddie covered his face with his hands and groaned. "I don't understand why you're behaving like this, love. Ever since you came to Italy, you've been acting like a completely different person. I don't know what's gotten into you."

"Well, *you've* been getting into me an awful lot lately," Roberta answered. "In and out. In and out. God, it's like you think I'm some sort of fucking machine!"

"Be quiet!" he shouted. "Don't say things like that in front of the help!"

"The help's not here, Eddie," she pointed out, her voice dripping with scorn. "There's nobody in this goddamned room except you and me. The servants are all hiding in the kitchen. Perhaps you're starting to see imaginary people now too, my love."

Eddie threw his napkin on the table. "What the hell is that supposed to mean?"

She pushed away her plate and silverware, sending her fork and spoon clattering to the floor with a loud clang. "You don't believe anything I say! You think I just imagined my uncle and aunt were here. You think I'm just imagining that the staff is working for them. You think I'm just imagining everything! Well, maybe you're right! Maybe I just imagined that *you're* here. Maybe I just imagined that we got married. Maybe I just imagined that you promised to love me forever and ever, till death do us part."

"Birdie, what is wrong with you?" Eddie shouted. "If there's something you want to tell me, then say it. But say it politely, for Christ's sake!"

Roberta glowered at him, her face darkening to a deep shade of red. "You're an asshole."

Eddie pushed his plate away and brought his elbows to the table. Covering his face with the palms of his hands, he counted to five slowly and willed his anger to abate.

"You can't even stand to look at me anymore!" Roberta screamed. "You think I'm ugly now, don't you? All those pretty little poems you wrote for me—you've forgotten all about them, haven't you? You think I'm just some crazy bitch you picked up at your drunken drummer's birthday party! Another goddamned groupie who threw herself at you after a concert! And now you want to ditch me, just like you ditched those other sleazy whores the morning after you screwed them!"

Eddie looked away from his bride and focused his attention on his hands. They were shaking. He closed his eyes and made a sincere effort to speak in a measured, calm voice. "I think we should go back to Munich this afternoon. I need to talk to Dick."

"Why?" Roberta challenged. "You hate my brother! Just like you hate me!"

Eddie looked back up at her and sighed. "I don't hate you, Birdie. I love you with all my heart. But I'm worried sick about you. I think you must be having a bad reaction to that new medicine you're taking. It's making you paranoid."

"I'm not taking *any* medicine!" Roberta spat back at him. "Dick was carrying my pills in his bag, and he forgot to leave them with me when he went back to Germany. This is me, Eddie, without my medicine. This is the real me. How do you like what you see?"

Eddie gazed at her helplessly for several seconds, then stood up from the table and took a cautious step towards her. "Let's go back to Munich, Birdie. Right now. We'll pack our bags and ask the chauffeur to pull out the car. We could leave within the hour."

Roberta stared back at him with a scowl and remained firmly in her place.

Eddie closed his eyes tightly and took a deep breath. "Maybe you've been right all along, love," he added through clenched teeth. "Maybe the cook is working for your uncle. But that's all the more reason why we should go now. I don't want anything to happen to you. I want to take you away from all these prying eyes. I want to take you home."

Roberta's rage lifted in an instant. She cast Eddie a plaintive look of relief, then rested her head on top of the tablecloth and started to weep.

## Chapter Eleven

### *Munich, Federal Republic of Germany*

"She's asleep," Dick said in a hushed voice as he stepped out of Roberta's old bedroom. "We can talk now."

Eddie glowered at him from across the cluttered kitchen table. "It's about fucking time."

Dick tossed a pile of old newspapers off the seat of a chair and sat down across from Eddie. "Listen, I understand that you're angry at me," he began. "But I never forced you to marry her. I discouraged you from even going out with her in the first place. So don't go blaming me now that you're having regrets."

"I'm not having regrets," Eddie said. "I'm concerned. I'm very concerned. What is wrong with Birdie? She's sick, but I don't know how to help her. You've been keeping things from me. Both of you have. And I demand that you tell me now!"

Dick snorted. "Ooh, I'm scared! Such big talk from my little brother-in-law."

"Stop playing games with me!" Eddie shouted, thumping his fist on the table. "Tell me what's wrong with her!"

"Keep your voice down," Dick replied. "She's sleeping, remember?" He pushed his chair closer to the table and leaned in. "There's nothing you don't know. Or not much, anyway. Roberta was trapped in a burning building when she was fifteen, and almost died in the fire. She watched our mother burn to death. She was fuckin' traumatized! She's had recurring nightmares ever since. Sometimes she even dreams that she started the fire, or that she tried to stop our father from saving our mother.

"Now, you know as well as I do that that's not true. But she has all this guilt built up inside because she survived and our parents didn't, so she blames herself. I've taken her to see a lot of doctors. They all say she's suppressed her real memories and replaced them with fantasies, and that the whole experience has left her—well—kind of fucked up. She gets anxiety attacks. She gets depressed. She's got horrible agoraphobia too—she hates going anywhere she doesn't feel comfortable. So the doctors prescribe medicine to help with her symptoms. But the drugs give her headaches. So then they have to try out new drugs. We're still working on getting the right prescription. That's all. I forgot to leave Roberta's pills with her after the wedding. She must have experienced a withdrawal. I'm sorry. But she's gonna be okay now. Why don't you just let her rest here for a few days and—"

"Because she's my wife, dammit! She sleeps at my house now!"

Dick rolled his eyes. "Jesus, Eddie, grow up! Think about what's best for Roberta. She needs structure. It helps her deal with the stress. She's comfortable in my pad. She lived here for six years. Let her sleep in her old bedroom tonight."

"She feels comfortable at my house too. At our house. It's her home now."

Dick nodded begrudgingly. "Hey, we're brothers, remember? We've been brothers for, what, four days now? I know you've never liked me, Eddie, but I think it's about time you start trusting me."

Eddie leaned back in his chair and glowered at Dick. "What drugs is she taking?"

"I told you. Anti-anxiety pills and something for her migraines."

"What drugs? What are the medicines called?"

"Hell, I don't know. They've got Latin names. They're not exactly stop-at-the-chemist lozenges."

"Let me see the prescription bottles."

"I don't keep her medicine in prescription bottles. I put it in pill boxes marked for each day of the week. That way she knows if she's taken the right dose."

"Then let me see the empty bottles."

"I threw them away," Dick said, edging his chair away from the table. "Her prescriptions are done up at the chemist, and after he fills them, I put her pills into little boxes so she remembers to take them every day."

"So you have no record of the names of her medicines?" Eddie asked incredulously.

"Don't need to," Dick said. "Everything's on file with the chemist. But even if I could dig up an old bottle, it might not be the most current prescription. Her doctor in Baden-Baden started her on a new routine, but he keeps changing her dosage. And he's probably gonna want to change it again after he finds out how she behaved in Italy."

"What's this doctor's name?"

"Kurt."

"His last name, I meant," Eddie said with a scowl.

"Schmidt. Why is it you sound like you don't trust me?"

"Because I don't trust you," Eddie answered, his eyes focused on Dick's like a laser.

"Fine," Dick replied. "And for the record, Eddie, I don't much trust you either. I think you're a fucked-up cross between a romantic poet and sex-crazed rock star, without a single practical bone in your entire body. And I'm worried about how you're gonna take care of my sister. She's all the family I have left in this world."

Eddie fixed an angry stare at his brother-in-law. "You have other family. Your Uncle Jean and Aunt Louise from Martinique, remember? Birdie couldn't stop talking about them these past few days. She couldn't stop talking *to* them either, under her breath."

Dick tapped his fingers against the table. "Let me guess. She said she saw them?"

Eddie nodded.

Dick stood up and ran his hand over his newly cut hair. "You want a beer? I'm gonna have one."

"No."

"Suit yourself," Dick said, turning his back to Eddie and shuffling across the length of his kitchen. He pulled a bottle of pilsner from the refrigerator and started rummaging through a drawer by the sink for a bottle opener, sending the metal utensils clanking loudly against each other. After he found an opener and pulled off the bottle cap, he fetched a tall glass from a cabinet, tipped it at a precarious angle and slowly filled it with beer.

Eddie struggled to maintain his composure while his brother-in-law went about his drawn-out business.

When Dick finally sat back down at the table, he took a long drink from his beer, then stared Eddie right in the eye. "My uncle and aunt figure prominently in Roberta's nightmares," he explained. "They said some awful things to her at the funeral, and their words keep coming back to haunt her."

"You told me earlier that Birdie didn't go to your parents' funeral," Eddie replied. "You said she was in hospital, recovering from smoke inhalation."

"That's what I meant," Dick said. He turned his face and looked at the oven while he spoke. "They came to St. Croix for the funeral and visited Roberta in the hospital. Uncle Jean grilled Roberta about the fire. He wanted to know every last detail. And then Aunt Louise had the nerve to suggest Roberta should live with them until she finished high school, instead of with me."

Dick took another large sip of beer before he continued. "But I wouldn't have my sister living with that bastard and bitch. She would have felt lost on Martinique. She doesn't even speak French—just a little Patois slang. And besides, she wanted to stay with me. So I took her out of the country as fast as I could."

Dick turned his head back towards Eddie at last. "Listen. I know you're confused. My little sis can act kind of scary when her meds need adjusting. But you have to trust me. I have her best interests at heart. And, despite what I said earlier, I know that you do too. I also know that she really loves you. So I'll ask you once more—let her spend the night here. Maybe even tomorrow night. You can come visit her during the day. Read her some poetry. Shit, man, she really digs the way you do that. And after she starts feeling better, then you can take her back to your pad."

He reached his hand across the table and gently punched Eddie's bicep. "Enjoy the night off," he laughed. "After what you've been going through, you probably need some rest too."

Eddie eyed him warily.

"Listen, *brother*, you're starting rehearsals next week," Dick added. "Then you're leaving on a world tour. Something tells me you might need me to tag along to keep an eye on Roberta while you're at work. So we better start trying to be friends."

Eddie stood up from the table and looked down at his brother-in-law. He wanted to believe Dick's long-winded explanation, but knew there were holes in the story. "She can spend the night here," he agreed reluctantly, struggling to keep his voice calm. "But I'll be back first thing in the morning to bring her home."

\* \* \*

Eddie dug his hands into the pockets of his jacket and picked up his pace. A crowd of teenagers screamed as he passed them. "Eddie! Eddie Rochester! *Wir lieben dich!*" A girl in a bright yellow sweater broke away from her friends and ran up to him, begging for an autograph. He forced a smile and signed the paper she held out to him, then turned away as quickly as he could.

He sprinted up a dirt trail leading to a small copse of trees and cursed his newfound fame. *I never had to dodge fans before,* he groused in his head. *Not like Tony did. I used to take long walks through the Englischer Garten all the time, and nobody ever bothered me.*

The long, winding paths of Munich's enormous park were like a second home to him. Since moving to Germany, he'd regularly taken refuge in the garden whenever he felt lonely. Its mish-mash of old-growth trees and crumbling neo-classical statues used to delight him. And though the park was often crowded, he could always blend right in alongside the locals and tourists, as if he had magically melted into the overgrown scenery.

But now everywhere he went, the ground seemed to be tilting towards him. Fans and photographers never left him alone. He was almost starting to wonder if there might be some truth in his wife's ravings about there being 'spies everywhere.'

He wondered if he had done the right thing, leaving her at home while he took a walk to clear his mind. Someone might be bothering her right now.

*She seemed fine when I left the house,* he reminded himself as he slackened his pace. He hadn't wanted to leave her alone, but she'd urged him to go out for a long walk, assuring him that she felt better than she had in weeks.

The medicine Dick had given her appeared to be working. Roberta was acting like she had when he first met her—coy, clever, eager to please him, and only occasionally given to short fits of anger. He remained furious at his brother-in-law for keeping him in the dark about Birdie's condition, but was so delighted by the change in her disposition that he was almost willing to forgive Dick his sins of omission.

Birdie was adjusting to married life much better now that she was back on familiar ground, he reminded himself. She'd even scoured his well-stocked library and pulled out a huge stack of books to bring along with her on the upcoming world tour, to keep her occupied while he was busy with his sound checks and concerts.

Eddie had hoped he'd be able to take her sightseeing once the tour commenced. But after his experience in Italy, he was worried about her ability to cope with the vagaries of travel. He hesitated to take Dick up on his offer to join them on the road, but he knew he probably should. Birdie had even told him she wanted her brother to come along.

*God, if only I didn't hate that bastard so much,* he thought. *My life would be so much easier if I actually got along with him.*

He crossed a stone bridge and looked at his feet to avoid the stares of the patrons at a nearby *Biergarten*. Then a bright light exploded in front of his face. He lifted his head and was met with the long lens of a photojournalist's camera. He turned around and broke into a jog, cursing as he fled.

*Birdie won't be able to handle the press once we hit the road,* he realized with regret. *Hell, I can hardly handle them anymore!* He spied a parked taxi in the distance and ran towards it.

"Eddie Rochester!" a teenager screamed as he passed. *"Mein Gott! Ich kann es nicht glauben! Das ist der Eddie Rochester!"*

He dodged the fan and jumped into the cab, then gave the driver directions to his house and told him to hurry.

\* \* \*

"I'm back!" Eddie shouted as he opened the front door. He threw a quick glance at the sitting room. Roberta had turned off the lights and closed the curtains. He switched on the hall light, glanced at the couch and saw her poetry book lying on top of a cushion, its pages splayed open.

He walked to the kitchen. It was empty. He stopped outside the bathroom and knocked. Hearing no response, he opened the door. She wasn't there.

"Birdie?" he called up the stairwell. He bit his lip. *She might be sleeping,* he thought. *Maybe I shouldn't make so much noise.*

He checked the bedrooms and found them both unoccupied. His hopes started to fade. "Birdie?" he called out once more, his voice tinged with alarm. "Where are you, love?"

The bathroom door in the hallway was closed. He leaned against it. "Darling? Are you in there?" He tried the knob. The door was locked.

"Birdie!" he yelled, banging loudly on the wooden door. "What's wrong? Answer me!"

He ran to his bedroom, grabbed a hairpin off his wife's dresser and hurried back down the hall. He jammed the pin into the bathroom's keyhole and fiddled with the lock. As soon as he heard a loud click, he threw the door open and switched on the light.

Roberta lay prostrate on the bathroom floor. Her eyes were closed. Her wild mane of raven hair tumbled sumptuously over the soft, plush bath rug. The pale white skin on both of her arms was streaked with lines of bright red blood.

## Chapter Twelve

Eddie pulled his chair closer to Roberta's hospital bed. Her face looked angelic in repose. Her long dark hair spread across her pillow like a sable cloud. Her arms were wrapped in gauze. "Is she going to be okay?" he asked in a hoarse whisper.

"The wounds were not deep. She did not lose much blood," replied her doctor, Heinrich Müller. "It does not appear that she was attempting suicide. More likely she was just cutting herself and fainted. It is a disturbing behavior, but not uncommon."

Eddie sighed in relief. "When can I take her home?"

"We need to speak," Dr. Müller answered. "Come. Follow me."

Eddie remained in his chair.

"She is sedated," the doctor added in a gentler tone. "She will be fine. Come. We must now talk."

Eddie kissed Roberta's forehead gently, then stood up and followed the doctor out of the hospital room and into a small office. Dr. Müller closed the door behind them, sat down at a desk and gestured to a stiff-backed chair. "How much do you know about your wife's condition?" he asked as Eddie took a seat.

A wave of embarrassment swept through Eddie, momentarily pushing aside his fear. "Not much," he admitted. "Just what I told you before. Oh, and she started seeing a doctor in Baden-Baden for an experimental treatment."

Dr. Müller looked directly into Eddie's eyes. "Do you know what medicine she is taking?"

"No," Eddie confessed, his cheeks flushing with shame. "Her brother just gives it to her in a pill box marked for each day of the week."

"Her brother Richard Maurer?"

"Richard Mason," Eddie corrected him.

Dr. Müller curled his lips into an almost imperceptible smile and tapped his finger against the top of his desk. "'Maurer' is the German word for 'mason'."

"Yes, but my wife's maiden name is Mason, not Maurer."

"And her middle name is Antoinette?"

"Yes, but she never uses that name. She hates it."

The doctor nodded and repositioned himself more comfortably in his chair. "She has been in this hospital once before, four years ago. I was her attending physician. Her hair was shorter then and she looked much younger, but I recognized her face the moment I saw her and pulled out her file. She had been admitted under the name 'Antoinette Maurer.' Her brother Richard brought her in."

Eddie's heart pounded rapidly in his chest.

The doctor fixed his gaze at Eddie. "Did she ever behave in a peculiar manner before today? Has she ever experienced hallucinations, or displayed symptoms of paranoia? Does she have sudden mood swings, or speak inappropriately at times?"

Eddie's stomach lurched. "A few times," he admitted. "She acted kind of strange on our honeymoon. But she wasn't feeling well, so we left Italy early. She's been doing much better since we came back to Munich and she started taking her medicine again."

"How long has that been?"

"About a week now."

"I see," the doctor said. He made a tent with his splayed fingers, then focused a piercing look at Eddie. "Mr. Rochester, there are some things I need to tell you about your wife."

Eddie swallowed hard, then looked up at the doctor with a plaintive stare and nodded.

Dr. Müller met his gaze and held it. "The last time your wife was admitted here, she was experiencing uncontrollable hallucinations. I kept her under observation. After careful examination and analysis, I felt quite certain in my diagnosis." He paused briefly before adding in a calm, clear voice, "Mr. Rochester, your wife suffers from schizophrenia."

Eddie blanched. The room started spinning and his mind went blank.

"I put her on a regimen of Thorazine," Dr. Müller continued. "The medicine had an immediate, positive effect. After a week of treatment, I released her into her brother's care, with instructions to bring her back for a follow-up visit within seventy-two hours, or before that if she displayed any more symptoms of psychosis. Unfortunately, that was the last time I saw your wife until today. Her brother never brought her back."

Dr. Müller fell silent for a few moments, allowing Eddie time to process his revelation, then he continued his speech. "Schizophrenics have a very unique sense of self. They often appear to withdraw from the world and fold completely into their own minds. During these instances, they are prone to hearing voices in their heads. Voices they cannot control, which may encourage them to behave in unpredictable ways."

"I see," Eddie mumbled almost inaudibly.

"Your wife does not need to be institutionalized," Dr. Müller assured Eddie. "She can live an active and relatively normal life. With proper care, of course."

"I see," Eddie repeated. He stared at his shoes, but saw nothing but the scuffmarks on the linoleum floor. Then he closed his eyes tightly and drew in a deep breath. "Did you give my wife some more of this thor-a-zone? This medicine? Will she be okay?"

"This is a matter of some concern," Dr. Müller continued. "Thorazine is the most common medicine used to treat the psychosis. And your wife has responded positively to it in the past. But it may not be the best drug for her to use at the moment."

Eddie lifted his face and met the doctor's eyes. "Why not?"

"She is pregnant," Dr. Müller said. "I estimate that she is two months along. I suggest we transfer her to a private hospital and keep her there for a few weeks while we assess her condition and decide what drug and dosage would be best for her and the child."

\* \* \*

The first thing Roberta felt when she awoke was the needle in her arm. *Why am I hooked up to a tube?* she asked herself. Then she remembered what she had done. *I must be in the hospital.*

The second thing she felt was Eddie's hand, entwined with her own. It felt dry and rough and strong.

She opened her eyes slowly and examined his face.

"Hello, love," he whispered. He leaned closer to the bed. His voice was even. His posture was solid and steady. His eyes looked terrified.

*He knows,* she realized, her stomach lurching. *Now he knows.*

## Chapter Thirteen

"Divorce is an entirely reasonable option!" Emmett shouted. "I'd even say an annulment might be in order. This is not the gig you signed up for!"

"I promised to care for her in sickness as well as in health. For worse, not just for better," Eddie replied in a hollow voice.

"But you didn't know what you were getting into," Emmett countered. "Dick and Roberta lied to you. You can't be held accountable for promises you made under false pretenses."

Eddie gazed at his manager with a pitiful expression. "I can't blame them for not telling me the truth. I should have known. The symptoms were all there. I was just blind. I was so in love with her that I refused to see the obvious."

Emmett threw a quick glance at one of the bookshelves that lined the walls of Eddie's sitting room. "Thine eyes were made the fools o' the other senses," he noted with a mirthless laugh.

"Don't be quoting Shakespeare at me, Emmett. I have far too much on my mind right now to deal with any more poetry." Eddie stared at his feet and dug his heels into the plush nap of the Persian carpet Emmett had just given him as a wedding present. *He probably bought it with money he made off my new record,* Eddie thought with a twinge of bitterness.

Emmett walked to the front window. The curtains were drawn, shielding him from the photographers lurking behind the glass. "So what do you want to do now? Those bastards outside were asking me why Roberta didn't come home with you earlier tonight. They'll soon find out that she's in hospital."

"I don't know," Eddie said. "I was hoping you could think of a good lie."

Emmett turned to face Eddie and considered his proposal.

"They don't know which wing of the hospital she's in," he pointed out after several seconds had passed. "I could drop hints that she's suffered a miscarriage. That way, if they find out she's in the psychiatric ward, they'll assume she's suffering from depression."

"You can't say that!" Eddie protested. "Our child is still alive!"

Emmett's eyes widened with incredulity. "Christ, Eddie, you can't be thinking of keeping it! For God's sake, do you really want a child that might inherit her condition? And what if Roberta's medicine causes birth defects? She has to have an abortion!"

"No," Eddie said. "That's not a possibility. It's not even legal."

"I'm sure I could find you a sympathetic doctor," Emmett replied. "Just give me a few days to ask around."

"I said no, and that's the end of it," Eddie insisted. "She's suffered enough losses already. I can't take this baby away from her too. And I won't take the life of my own child."

Emmett sat down and pulled a packet of Benson & Hedges out of his shirt pocket. He took out a cigarette and rolled it between his fingers, then shook his head and placed it in the ashtray on the coffee table. "So what about the tour? How are we going to handle this—complication?"

Eddie hunched his shoulders. "I think we should cancel it."

"We can't, Eddie. We just can't," Emmett said. "Everything is sold out—in Europe, in the U.K., even in America! It would be career suicide to back out at this point. Not just for you personally, but for the rest of the band. It wouldn't be fair to them."

"I don't want to go on a fucking tour!" Eddie yelled, hitting his fist against the table. "I never did! I only agreed to go because Birdie said she wanted me to. But I can't leave her like I did on the last tour, stuck in Munich with that fuckwit of a brother looking after her. And I can't take her with me either! How could I possibly keep an eye on her?"

Emmett thought for a long moment. "I'll call my mum. She and Roberta got along famously at the wedding. Mum'll be here at the drop of a hat once she learns about this. You know how she dotes on you boys. You're like a second set of sons to her."

Eddie eyed the discarded cigarette greedily, then looked back at his shoes. "I do not want to go on tour," he repeated. "I do not want to promote this fucking album. Christ, I don't even need to. It's already number one in every fucking country in the known universe. And that goddamned Greatest Hits album the label rushed to market is sitting right behind it on all the charts. We don't have to hit the road to sell any more fucking records."

Emmett reached across the coffee table and patted Eddie's knee. "Listen to me, lad. If you want to stay married to Roberta, and you don't plan to keep slogging your way through the muck and mire of the music business, then you need to make as much money as you can right now. This is your golden opportunity to make a shit-load of cash, so that you can retire and take care of your sick wife for the rest of your life on a quiet little farm in Ohio. Don't walk out on this tour."

Eddie looked up and held Emmett's gaze. "Are you saying that because you really mean it, or because you don't want to go through the legwork of canceling the concerts?"

"I have your best interests at heart, Eddie," Emmett insisted. "I always have. Trust me."

Eddie hung his head. "I don't know what to do anymore. I can't think straight. I can hardly even feel anything. The moment that doctor said the word 'schizophrenia,' my insides turned to jelly. And now I feel like that jelly has hardened into a tough lump of Indian rubber, and I barely have one sentient point left inside me."

"You're in shock, Eddie," Emmett said. "That's to be expected. But you'll learn how to cope with this. You trust this Dr. Müller, don't you? He seems like a good man?"

Eddie shrugged his shoulders and stood up from the couch. "I don't want to talk anymore. My mind is reeling. I'm going to bed."

"Would you like me to spend the night on your sofa?" Emmett offered. "So you won't be alone just now?"

"No," Eddie said. "I don't want company. I just need some quiet time to think."

Emmett nodded. He watched Eddie walk up the stairs and listened for the sound of the bedroom door closing. Then he braced himself for the onslaught of popping flashbulbs sure to greet him the moment he stepped outside the house.

\* \* \*

"So now you know everything," Dick said, staring defiantly into his brother-in-law's eyes.

"The only thing I don't know is why you kept me in the dark for so long," Eddie replied. He kicked a crumpled magazine away from his feet and slipped his finger into a fresh rip in the stained couch. "I take that back. I also don't know why you can't so much as pick up a dirty napkin by yourself. This flat is turning into a pigsty."

"Roberta used to do the cleaning," Dick said.

Eddie glowered at him. "I'm waiting for a proper answer."

Dick held his gaze. "Would you have married her if I'd told you? Would you have even gone out with her? She liked you, Eddie, right from the very start, and I wanted her to be happy. And you liked her too. Hell, you were fucking obsessed with her! So I let you come to my parlor and play court to her, just like a gentleman caller in one of those stupid Victorian novels you both dig so much. I figured you'd put two and two together eventually and notice she was nuts. After a while, I just assumed you didn't care."

"She said at the hospital that you forbade her from telling me," Eddie replied with a scowl.

Dick shrugged. "I just wanted to give her the chance to experience a romance for once in her life, and see where it led."

Eddie rolled his eyes. "I'm not falling for this. You had obligations."

"And I still do. Now that you're gonna dump her, I'll have to mind her again."

"I am not going to dump her. I intend to take care of her."

Dick snorted. "Where? In that madhouse you shipped her to?"

Eddie's nostrils flared. "She is not in a madhouse. I've transferred her to a convalescent home just outside of town while her doctors adjust her medicine. Her condition is delicate and—"

"Has she been asking for me?" Dick interrupted.

"No," Eddie fibbed. "She hasn't."

"Now you're the one who's lying, Rochester. I can see it in your eyes."

"I don't think it would be wise for her to see you at the moment," Eddie retorted, holding his gaze. "My manager's mother will be joining us on the tour to keep an eye on Birdie, and it's important that the two of them start building a relationship. A visit from you just now might simply confuse her."

"I'm her brother!" Dick protested. "I've been working my ass off these past six years, taking care of her day in and day out! She needs me. I'm all the fucking family she has!"

"She has me now, and Grace," Eddie replied. "And we will be taking care of her from this point forward."

Dick sneered. "So why did you come here? To say goodbye?"

Eddie continued to glare at him. "I came to collect Birdie's things. Right now she only has the clothing she packed for our honeymoon. She wants her books and diaries too."

Dick eyed him warily for a few quiet moments, then spoke in a disinterested voice. "Her clothes are in her bedroom. So's her bookcase. Help yourself."

"Are her diaries in her bedroom too?"

"Hell, I don't know. I guess so," Dick said. "Where else would she have left them?"

"She told me you took some of them to Baden-Baden to show her doctor. She said he wanted to see the journals she kept right after she moved here from St. Croix."

"Yeah, but I brought them back. They should be in her room."

Eddie stood up from the dirty couch. "All right then. I'll fetch some boxes from my car and start packing."

"Right," Dick said, standing up from his chair. "Go ahead. I'll be in my bedroom. I need to make a couple of phone calls."

\* \* \*

"You couldn't find my diaries?" Roberta asked as Eddie stroked her hand. "You looked under my bed? In all my drawers?"

"They weren't there, but Dick promised to look for them. His place is such a mess now, they could be anywhere." He brought her hand to his lips. "Don't worry, love. They'll turn up. Right now, we just have to concentrate on getting you well again. The new medication seems to be doing its job. Your tremors are gone."

She pulled back her hand. "I'm just so embarrassed. I feel so stupid, and mean, and—"

"What's done is done," Eddie whispered reassuringly. "I understand why you didn't tell me. I was angry at first, but not anymore. I love you no matter what."

"I'll be better in time for the tour," Roberta promised. "The new drugs make me sleepy, but then I won't be such a bother."

"You're not a bother," he said with a smile. "You just focus on getting stronger now, and I'll get on with the show."

She wrapped her fingers back around his hand. "Play thy part of chief musician," she whispered. "Poor, tired, wandering singer, singing through the dark."

Eddie smiled. "*Sonnets from the Portuguese?*" he asked.

Roberta nodded. "Number three. The chrism is on thine head—on mine, the dew."

# Chapter Fourteen

### *Millcote, Ohio*

Eddie watched the wind cut a serpentine path through the rows of dark green cornstalks. The hot, muggy air bore down on him like a wet blanket. Overhead, a cluster of black rainclouds circled slowly in the gunmetal-grey sky. A distant roll of thunder signaled the approach of a summer storm.

"Rain'll be here in about ten minutes," predicted Eddie's grandfather Rocky. "See how those clouds are turning tighter over there by those hills? That's where a funnel might be forming."

Eddie looked to the southeast. "I didn't hear any tornado warnings on the radio."

Rocky laughed. "There's a standing tornado watch in Butler County from April through August, m'boy. You should know that. You spent enough summers here when you were young."

Eddie smiled. "I remember riding out storms in the basement when I used to come here for my summer vacations. But I never saw an actual cyclone."

"Count your blessings," Rocky replied. "Remember that old barn on the north edge of the property where I used to store my broken tractors? Twister finally took it down last May."

"I can't believe that crappy old building lasted so long!" Eddie laughed. "It's been on the verge of collapse for as long as I can remember."

Rocky nodded. "For years it looked like a disaster just waiting to happen. A man from the insurance company stopped by a few summers back to inspect the property, and ordered me to tear it down. Said it was a fire hazard. But I was too busy to do anything about it at the time. I kind of hoped the termites might raze it and save me the trouble."

"Why didn't you bulldoze it in the fall, when you had the chance?"

"My grandpa built it. I didn't have the heart."

Eddie smiled. "Well, I see then. That makes sense."

"You're a sentimental fool," Rocky said, clapping his grandson's back. "Just like me. You always see glimmers of hope in places where everyone else just turns their backs."

A ripple of light passed through a far-off cloud. A few seconds later, thunder rumbled in the distance.

"Did you count the seconds?" Eddie asked, gazing thoughtfully at the sky. "To see how far away the storm is?"

"Don't need to," his grandfather answered. "I know it's coming soon, but we're close enough to the house to rush back inside as soon as the rain hits."

"Maybe I should go inside now and check on Birdie," Eddie said. "A sudden thunderclap might wake her up."

"She's fine on the couch," Rocky replied. "And Grace is there if she wakes up. Don't you worry."

Eddie looked back at his grandfather. "What do you think of her?" he asked nervously.

"Grace Poole? Lovely woman. Wish she'd move to Ohio. Maybe I'd marry her. God rest your poor grandmother's soul."

Eddie rolled his eyes. "I meant Birdie."

Rocky looked away from Eddie and watched the clouds trace their circle in the sky. "She's lovely too. I don't think I've ever seen a more beautiful woman. But she's pretty damned quiet."

"She's shy in front of strangers," Eddie said.

"But I'm not a stranger. I'm part of her family now."

"But she doesn't know you yet, and she's been—" Eddie hesitated. "Sick."

"Hmm," Rocky sighed. "Sorry to hear it. But if she makes you happy, son, then I'm happy. That's all I ask for in a granddaughter-in-law. That she makes you happy."

"I'm happy," Eddie replied in a sad voice.

Rocky bit his lip and looked back at the cornfield. The wind picked up, carrying with it the scent of rain. The tassels on the ears started dancing wildly in the breeze. "Storm'll be here soon," he said. "It's moving faster than I thought."

"I wish I could stay here tonight and not drive back to

Cincinnati," Eddie said. "But I have to do an interview with the *Enquirer* first thing in the morning." He cast a sidelong glance at his grandfather. "Any chance you'll come to my show?"

"Sorry, but I'm not interested in any rock and roll concert," Rocky blustered. "You boys play your music too loud for an old geezer like me to enjoy. But pull out your guitar before you drive back to town and sing me a song. I like that new album of yours, son. And I know your grandma would have loved it too."

"Thanks," Eddie said, lowering his gaze. "The songs meant a lot to me when I wrote them. It's been weird singing them to crowds of screaming fans. That's not how I intended them to be heard."

Rocky nodded. "You wrote them for Birdie."

"Yes," Eddie agreed. A pause settled between them.

"When's she due?"

Eddie winced.

Rocky laughed. "I'm a farmer, m'boy! I know a pregnant female when I see one. Birdie might not be showing yet, but I can tell."

"She's four months along," Eddie confessed.

"And you've been married to her for how long now, two months?"

"Almost three."

Rocky chuckled. "I'll let you in on a secret. My ma was pregnant with me when she married Dad. So my folks had a real short engagement too, just like you and Birdie did."

Eddie smiled. *He can think that if he wants,* he decided. He turned his gaze toward the rippling cornfield. "I'm nervous."

"All new fathers are nervous," Rocky replied. "Heck, I was scared to even hold your daddy when he was first born. But I got used to it. You will too."

"It's not just the baby I'm worried about," Eddie confessed. He closed his eyes and considered telling his grandfather the whole story. But after several seconds of painful deliberation, he couldn't find the words.

"Is there something you want to tell me, son?" Rocky asked in a gentle voice.

Eddie turned and faced his grandfather once more. He gazed into the kind eyes of the man who had comforted him when his father died. He had struggled to speak on that occasion too, but it hadn't mattered, because he simply knew that the old man understood what he was going through. But now he just felt lost. No words seemed adequate to convey the gut-wrenching rollercoaster his life had become.

He looked past his grandfather's penetrating eyes and stared at the old farmhouse that featured so prominently in his happiest childhood memories. A fat drop of rain fell squarely on his forehead, followed by several more drops in rapid succession. The sky grew suddenly darker. Thunder rumbled overhead.

"I'll tell you later, Grandpa," Eddie promised. "Let's get inside now."

### *Philadelphia, Pennsylvania*

"It's horrible!" Roberta sobbed. "It will give me nightmares."

"It's just a wallpaper pattern," Eddie said, stroking her hair and drawing her closer to his chest.

"I want to change rooms now!" she protested.

"There, there," Eddie cooed, cradling her in his arms. "Close your eyes and imagine you're lying in a bedroom papered in a yellow daisy pattern. It's bright and cheery and looks like spring."

"I can't!" she cried. "All I can see are those horrible orange and red swirls. They make the room look like it's on fire!"

"Hush now, they're just paisleys. They look like paramecium to me. Did you ever look through a microscope in science class?"

She took a few shallow breaths and coughed. "Yes. We looked at cheek cells," she whispered. "They didn't look anything like paramecium."

"What did they look like?" Eddie asked gently, dabbing her wet cheeks with a handkerchief.

"Like floppy breasts with dark nipples," she answered.

"Ah, the nuclei," Eddie murmured.

"Uh-huh," she agreed, swallowing a sob.

"Well, close your eyes and imagine you're lying in a bedroom papered with a floppy breast pattern. It's calm and soothing."

"No it's not."

"Yes it is," he assured her. "Now just cuddle close, and I'll hold you until you fall asleep."

\* \* \*

Eddie stepped into the sitting area of his hotel suite and collapsed on the sofa besides Grace.

"She's sleeping now?" Grace asked.

He glanced at his watch. "Yes. And it's only—what—three in the morning? Christ! It's getting harder to settle her down every night! She says the wallpaper is giving her nightmares. In Denver she didn't like the way the toilet flushed. The pattern on the curtains in Chicago gave her the willies. I had to take them down and hang them back up inside out."

"I remember," Grace said, resting her hand on Eddie's knee. She drew in a deep breath. "Birdie's not well enough to keep on traveling, Eddie. I know you have two more cities to play in the States, but after that, I want to take her back to Germany. I'll stay with her at your house. I promise I won't let her out of my sight."

"I've been thinking the same thing," Eddie confessed. "Though I was hoping I could take her to Manchester first, so I could introduce her to Mum."

"Your mum can fly to Germany after the tour is over and meet her there," Grace proposed. "Have you told her about Birdie's condition yet?"

"Which one?" Eddie answered with a sardonic laugh.

"Either. Or both. Which condition worries you the most?"

"I dunno," Eddie replied. "I really and truly don't know."

Grace scooted closer to Eddie and wrapped her arm around his shoulder. "Let me bring her back to Germany. I'll take her to see that Dr. Müller again, and her obstetrician too. She must be due for another check-up. And if she misses you too much, then the two of us can always fly back and join you for the rest of the tour."

Eddie squeezed his eyes shut and brought his hands to his throbbing temples. "Okay. I think she'd be happier back home. And I'll fly in and visit her on the nights I don't have a show."

"Good," Grace said. "I'll ask Emmett to rearrange the flights tomorrow. Or rather, this morning."

Eddie rested his head on Grace's shoulder. "Okay," he agreed. "But whatever you do, don't let her see Dick. I don't trust that bastard any further than I can throw him."

# Chapter Fifteen

*Amsterdam, The Netherlands*

Eddie bowed to the screaming fans, then extended his hand to acknowledge his bandmates. The crowd whooped and cheered as the other members of the Pilots took their bows one by one and left the stage. Then holding his Fender Stratocaster high over his head, he ran off to join them. A deafening roar followed him into the wings.

Gerry flashed him a lopsided grin. "God, it's great to be back on top!" he bellowed, his scratchy voice barely audible over the noise of the crowd.

Jim cracked his knuckles and flexed his fingers in preparation for the encore. Eli handed his bass to the closest roadie and shouted, "Tune the fucking E string! Now!" The roadie leaned in closer and asked if he said 'E' or 'D'. Tony crossed his arms in front of his chest and smiled enviously at Eddie. Eddie shrugged his shoulders and smiled back.

Emmett's brother Alan peeked through the backstage curtain and watched the darkened arena fill up with flickering dots of light as the fans held their cigarette lighters aloft and swayed to the unsteady rhythm of their pounding feet. He threw a quick glance at his wristwatch and watched the second hand rise in an arc. "Let 'em cheer a bit more!" he yelled.

Emmett took a few cautious steps towards the band, then stopped. Eddie looked so happy for once—basking in the glow of the audience's adulation and enjoying the camaraderie of his old and trusted friends. Emmett didn't have the heart to tell him about the dozen, frantic, operator-assisted phone calls Roberta had placed over the last hour-and-a-half. He caught Eddie's eye and gave him a half-hearted 'thumbs up' sign instead.

Eddie waved and took a quick swig of water. He wiped his mouth, handed the empty glass to Alan and shouted, "Thanks," though his words were drowned out by the rising chants of "Ed-die! Ed-die!" spilling into the wings from the auditorium.

Eli grabbed his bass back from the roadie, yelling, "That's good enough! Nobody can bloody hear it anyway!" Alan raised the empty glass as a signal for the Pilots to start their encore. Gerry led the band onto the stage, followed by Jim and Eli. Eddie fell into place behind the bassist, but Tony held him back.

"You go last, remember?" he shouted. "When are you going to learn that, you wanker? *You're* the star now, not me."

Tony ran onto the stage and pulled his electric guitar out of its stand. Eddie waited until Tony positioned the strap over his shoulder, then stepped out of the wings. The audience erupted into a thunderous roar. Eddie started playing the opening chords of his newest hit song. The crowd's cheer rose to a deafening crescendo that echoed back from the rafters like a shockwave.

### *Munich, Federal Republic of Germany*

Eddie handed the cabdriver a twenty-mark note and hurried up the front steps of his house. "I'm sorry I'm so late," he told Grace as he stepped through the front door. "There was a heavy fog over *Schiphol*, and all the flights out of Holland were delayed. Christ, what time is it now, anyway? Three o'clock? Four?"

"It doesn't matter," Grace said, taking Eddie's jacket. "You're here now. Try to calm down. She's all right at the moment. I checked in on her about ten minutes ago. She was sound asleep."

"Christ, she sounded like such a wreck on the phone!" Eddie exclaimed. "I wish I could have been with her for the doctor's appointment, but I can spend a couple of days here now. I don't have to be in Brussels until Thursday."

"Relax, Eddie. Try to keep your perspective," Grace said. "Just because Birdie tells you something awful on the phone, that doesn't mean it's true. The obstetrician said everything seems normal, as far as he can tell."

"But she was flipping out!" Eddie protested. "She said the baby was turning into a horse! What the hell did she mean by that?"

"Fetal heartbeats are very fast," Grace explained. "I was sitting right beside Birdie throughout the entire exam, and I heard the doctor say everything was fine. But that damned fool of a nurse insisted on turning up the volume so Birdie could hear the fetal monitor. Birdie thought the baby sounded like a galloping horse, and she—well, she just got a little bit confused."

"A little bit? She said she was pregnant with a centaur!"

"She was confused," Grace reiterated. "That poor girl doesn't have a strong grip on reality. You know that better than anyone, Eddie. Don't worry—this too shall pass. Now why don't you go upstairs and cuddle with her? You could both use a little comforting tonight."

Eddie sighed and hugged Grace tightly. "Christ, I can't wait for this goddamned tour to be over."

Grace gave him a quick squeeze, then stepped back. "Go to her now," she whispered. "You need some rest."

Eddie nodded and walked up the stairs. When he entered his bedroom, he found Roberta resting peacefully. A dim light from the hallway shone softly upon her face. *Christ, she looks like an angel,* Eddie thought. *How could an angel cause me such worries?* He stripped out of his clothes and climbed under the covers beside her.

"Mmm," she murmured as he wrapped his arms around her. "You're back."

"Yes, love," he whispered. "I'm back. And everything is going to be okay now."

\* \* \*

"Alice is a lovely name," Eddie said, resting his hand gently on Roberta's rounded abdomen. "I've always liked it."

"And we can decorate her nursery with drawings of white rabbits and caterpillars," Roberta suggested.

Eddie took the book from her and rested it on the nightstand. "Let's just stick with drawings of rabbits," he said. "I don't want any pictures of hookah-smoking larvae hanging on my daughter's wall."

Roberta laughed. "Fair enough," she agreed. "And how about 'Lewis' for a boy?"

"No," Eddie replied. "I don't like the sound of it. And anyway, 'Lewis Carroll' wasn't even his real name."

"Well, we could name the baby Charles or Ludwidge," Roberta

proposed. "Or maybe even 'Dodgson.'"

"Dodgson Rochester," Eddie proclaimed in tone of mock formality. "Rather posh, don't you think? But I'm afraid we'd have to ship him off to boarding school with a moniker like that."

Roberta laughed again and kissed Eddie's hand. "What was your father's name?"

"Thomas, but I don't want to name our son after him," Eddie said. "There was already one Tommy Rochester who grew up at Thornfield. This child deserves a name of his own."

"Then how about 'Paul Thomas,' after both our dads?"

Eddie smiled and rubbed her tummy. "I like that. Paul Thomas if it's a boy, and Alice Carol if it's a girl."

Roberta rested her hand on top of his. "No 'Dodgson' then?"

"We'll name the dog Dodgson," Eddie laughed. He wrapped his arms around his wife and cuddled her more tightly. "I'm glad you're feeling better."

"I'm glad you're home," she replied. "I missed you."

"The tour's almost over," he said. "And then I'll be home all the time. You'll probably grow tired of me before long."

"Never," she promised. "I'll never grow tired of you."

"And I'll never tire of you, love," he said, stifling a yawn. "But I am exhausted. It's been a long day, and I hardly slept last night."

"Then close your eyes, and sleep soft," she whispered.

"I will," he replied. He brought his lips to hers for a gentle kiss, then turned his head on the pillow and drifted into a deep, dreamless slumber.

\* \* \*

"Grace! Wake up!" Eddie yelled, knocking on the door of her bedroom. "Have you seen Birdie? She's gone!"

Grace was at the door in an instant. "What do you mean?" she asked. "How could she be gone? I didn't hear her leave."

"I don't know," Eddie moaned. "She wasn't in bed when I woke up this morning, so I searched for her in every room of the house. Then I checked the hall closet. Her coat is missing."

"Oh Lord," Grace sighed. "I can only think of one place where she'd go at this time of day."

Eddie's face blanched. "Please don't say 'Dick's flat'."

Grace frowned. "He's been ringing her up ever since the two of us came back to Munich. He said he had something he wanted to show her."

"Bugger! Why did I ever encourage her to start using the telephone?"

"Because you wanted to chat with her while you were finishing up your tour," Grace answered. "Now stop dilly-dallying. Change out of your pajamas and go collect her. It's still early in the morning. He can't have had enough time yet to say or do anything too damaging."

* * *

Eddie knocked on Dick's front door and waited impatiently under the awning for half a minute. Then he pounded on the door. Hearing no response, he tried the knob. The door opened. He let himself in. "Birdie, it's me!" he shouted. "I know you're here!"

He stepped into the foyer and noticed that the living room was uncharacteristically bright. All of the overhead lights and table lamps had been turned on. The harsh illumination threw stark patterns of overlapping shadows into the recesses of the room. "Birdie?" he called out warily.

"You bastard!" screamed a voice at the far end of the flat.

Eddie turned around and saw Roberta rushing towards him, her eyes wild with fury, her untamed hair flying in her wake like a black thundercloud racing across the sky. In her right hand she held a long carving knife.

"Birdie, no!" Eddie shouted. "What the hell are you doing?"

Roberta thrust the knife at him, but he grabbed her arm before she could stab him and forced it high over her head. He pried the weapon from her fingers. It dropped to the floor with a clang. She howled in frustration and struggled to break free. Thwarted by his powerful grip, she lunged at him with her face and bit his left hand, piercing the skin on his thumb.

"Christ!" Eddie yelled. He tore his hand away from her and seized her other arm. With both of her hands restrained, she started kicking him.

"I hate you!" she screamed. "You're a liar! You never loved me!" She punched him with her elbows and knees, nearly knocking him off balance. He shifted his weight and wrapped his arms tightly around her, constraining her back securely against his chest. She let loose a torrent of piercing wails, then broke down into tears. Moved by pity, Eddie loosened his grip on her body.

"I saw the picture," she sobbed. "You were kissing another woman." She slipped out of his arms and collapsed into a heap at his feet. As she fell, she hit her head against the corner of the coffee table and cut the skin by her eyebrow.

Eddie bent down to examine her bleeding head. "What picture?" he whispered. "What are you talking about?" As he cradled her limp body in his arms, he became aware of another person's presence in the room.

Looking up, he saw a movie camera aimed squarely at his face. Glancing frantically to the right and left, he saw Dick standing a few feet behind the unknown photographer.

"What the hell are you doing?" Eddie yelled, his face contorted into a mask of uncontrollable rage. "Get that fucking camera away from me, you bastard!"

Dick didn't move. Eddie grabbed the knife off the floor and pointed it directly at his brother-in-law. Fighting an overwhelming desire to thrust the blade into Dick's heart, he tightened his grip on the handle and slowly raised his arm. "I said put it away," he repeated, repositioning the knife towards the lens. The photographer took a large step backwards, but kept his camera focused squarely at Eddie.

Panting heavily, Eddie looked back and forth between Dick and the cameraman. With a crushing blow, he realized he had been set up for this shot. He glanced back down at Roberta's face.

A trickle of bright red blood streamed over her closed eyelid and dripped onto her cheek. Tears began filling her other eye as she gazed up at him.

Eddie looked back at Dick. "You bastard," he hissed between clenched teeth. "You goddamned, fucking bastard."

He scooped Roberta into his arms and stood up. He stared directly into Dick's eyes and held his gaze.

"You stay away from us," Eddie warned him. "From both of us! If you ever come near Birdie or me again, I'll use that goddamned knife to slice your fucking throat!"

Birdie clung to his neck, sobbing. "I'm so sorry," she whispered. "I'm so sorry."

He carried his new bride over the threshold of her old home and ran with her to his car.

# Chapter Sixteen

### *Zurich, Switzerland*

Eddie placed his hand on Roberta's swelling belly and pressed down gently.

"I can't feel anything," he said.

"It's kicking," Roberta insisted. "It feels like someone's popping popcorn inside of me."

Eddie laughed. "Maybe he wants to watch a movie."

"Maybe *she* wants to watch a movie," Roberta countered.

"Maybe she does," Eddie agreed, giving her a kiss. "Things are going to be okay now," he promised. "Only two shows left. Then we can go back home and forget I was ever famous. We'll curl up in bed like this every night and read poetry to each other, and the baby will take it all in and come out reciting Keats."

Roberta snuggled her head against Eddie's shoulder and ran her fingers through his wiry chest hair. "I'm so sorry for what I did in Munich," she whispered.

"Shh," Eddie replied. "It's all forgotten. It wasn't your fault. Dick was egging you on. He made you do that."

"But I should have known those photos he showed me weren't taken when you were in England last month. Your hair was so much shorter than it is now."

"Shh," Eddie repeated. "It's all over now. We're both okay, and the baby's okay. Your new medicine is starting to do its trick too. You seemed better today than you have in weeks."

"I didn't hear any voices this afternoon," she said.

"Good," Eddie replied. He kissed her cheek, then yawned and rubbed his head against the pillow. "I'm absolutely knackered. When this tour is over, I'm going to sleep for a solid month."

"I thought we were going to recite poetry together."

"You can take the first shift. My voice is too hoarse after all these concerts." He slid his hand off Roberta's tummy and whispered, "Goodnight, love."

"Eddie?" Roberta asked as he turned his head away from her. "Why do you love me?"

Eddie chuckled softly. "I don't know, darling. I simply know how I love you." He rolled his face back towards hers and whispered, "I love thee with the breath, smiles and tears of all my life." He kissed her forehead, then closed his eyes.

\* \* \*

Roberta listened to Eddie's breathing grow deeper and more rhythmic. After a few minutes, he began to snore. She repositioned her head and looked up at his face. Though she couldn't make out his features in the dark hotel bedroom, she had committed them to memory and recalled them fondly. His dark brown eyes and shoulder-length dark hair. His aquiline nose and square jaw. His broad shoulders and strong arms. The funny pattern of moles on his chest that looked like a crescent-moon.

*He's so handsome,* she thought. *And so kind. So good to me. He's a much better husband than I deserve.*

A bittersweet pang of recognition flooded over her. *He's so much like my dad.*

Roberta closed her eyes and tried to fall asleep, but cherished memories of her father sprang into her head. She remembered how he used to shield her from her mother's violent rages. How he used to assure her that her own wild impulses were signs of originality and artistic talent, and not symptoms of an inherited madness. She called to mind his warm laugh and sparkling eyes. His receding hairline and funny mustache.

And then another image flashed in front of her—the look of terror on his face when he tried to pull his wife from her burning bed, and flames engulfed his body.

She squeezed her eyelids shut and blinked back a tear. She'd never meant for him to die. That was the last thing she'd wanted.

Roberta stroked the hairs on Eddie's chest and breathed in his familiar, masculine scent. It made her feel safe again.

She thought about the many times Eddie had promised to

protect her. She used to doubt him when he said that. But after he forgave her for that horrible misunderstanding at Dick's flat, she finally accepted that he was a man of his word. He would take care of her for the rest of her life, just as her father had always taken care of her mother. Eddie would never abandon her.

Roberta slipped her hand down the length of his arm and encircled his fingers with her own. She ran her thumb over his thumb and felt the small scar she had left behind with her teeth. She recoiled and withdrew from his embrace.

Eddie let loose a loud snore as she lifted her weight off his outstretched arm. He repositioned his elbow and rolled over, turning his back to her completely.

Roberta stared into the blackness overhead and heard a voice—a quiet, gentle whisper.

She couldn't place it at first. It didn't belong to the rude, foulmouthed speaker who usually taunted her. Nor was it the barking, snarling voice that had risen from the darkest recesses of her mind and urged her to stab Eddie the morning Dick had shown her those photographs of him kissing another woman. No, this was an almost imperceptible voice. She closed her eyes and concentrated on the muted, muffled sound.

And then she recognized it. It was a familiar voice she had heard many times before, but had always tried to block out. "Divorce her now, Eddie," the voice said. "You have grounds."

She felt the sting of the quiet rebuke like a sharp blow. But then another whisper pushed the first voice aside.

"It's only going to get harder after the baby comes, Eddie. You can't take care of both of them all by yourself."

More hushed voices forced their way into her mind and started spilling over on top of each other:

"You're too young to burden yourself like this. Divorce her before you're trapped forever."

"Put her in a home, Eddie. That's what she needs. And get on with your own life."

"Don't be embarrassed to ditch her. We all make mistakes."

"I know a doctor who does abortions up to six months. He's good. You can trust him."

The floodgates of her memories broke open, and more voices tumbled into her mind. At first she could distinguish the speakers. She recognized the familiar clipped inflections of Emmett Poole.

Gerry's gruff growl. Tony's sweet tenor voice. Jim's squeaky peal. Eli's charming brogue. And with a clarity that surprised her, she even remembered the circumstances that surrounded the memories, when Eddie's friends deliberately lowered their voices to address him when they thought she was sleeping.

After a few minutes, she could no longer identify the individual voices. The hushed murmurs piled on top of each other and formed a single, loud, buzzing drone. Her hands started to shake.

Then suddenly, like a clap of thunder, another voice burst through the cacophony in her head. *"Elle est aliénée!"* shouted the terrifying voice of her Uncle Jean. "Lock her up! She is a dangerous lunatic! A threat to all decent people!"

Roberta lifted her trembling hands to her ears and tried to block out the voice. Eddie rolled over again and released a powerful, rumbling snore that instantly silenced the dissonance. She placed her quivering hand on his cheek and petted his sideburns in relief. Then she lifted up the sheet and quietly slipped out of bed.

She walked to the hotel bathroom, turned on the light and started rummaging through her medicine bag. She pulled out her bottle of neuroleptics and swallowed a pill with a large drink of water. Then she rested the glass back down on the sink and stared at her reflection in the medicine cabinet's mirrored door.

Her heart still pounding frantically, she tried to summon up a memory of Eddie's reassuring voice—his deep, full-bodied speaking voice, or his throaty, seductive singing voice—but her mind drew a blank. All she could remember was his hoarse, tired-sounding voice whispering Elizabeth Barrett Browning's famous line to her before he drifted off to sleep.

She took a deep breath and closed her eyes, hoping to calm her racing heart. Then she opened her eyes and gazed once more at her reflection in the mirror.

The face of a hideous specter stared back at her—its nose dripping foul, green snot; its mouth twisted into a lascivious snarl; its eyes sunken and oozing rust-colored tears; its hair a mass of leaping flames.

She flung the cabinet's door wide open to banish the horrifying ghoul from view. Panting heavily, she stared at the bright, white shelves now facing her, empty but for a few bars of hotel soap wrapped in shiny green paper. Struggling desperately to focus her attention on a solid object, she looked down at the sink and gazed into her open medicine bag.

After a few minutes, her heart ceased its rapid pounding and her hands no longer shook. She closed the cabinet door and cast a wary glance at the mirror. Her own familiar, hollow-eyed reflection stared back at her once more. Sighing in relief, she looked back at the open medicine bag and started to absent-mindedly finger the bottles inside. Her neuroleptics. Her migraine tablets. The sleeping pills Emmett had lent Eddie.

"Don't, Birdie!" Eddie shouted from the doorwell. "Stop it now!"

She trembled at the sound of his voice and cast a shameful glance over her shoulder. With a disconcerting shock, she realized he was not there.

Leaving the light on over the sink, she walked back to the dark bedroom to see if Eddie had called her. He was asleep in bed, just where she had left him. The soft light from the bathroom bathed his profile in an angelic glow. She sat down on the edge of the mattress and rested her hand on top of his chest. It rose and fell steadily, along with his calm, reassuring breaths.

The baby kicked.

She shifted her hand to her own abdomen. She felt another brief flutter in her womb, and started wondering what the baby would look like when it was born. But before she could picture her son or daughter's face, the restless musings of her imagination took off like wildfire, and she envisioned the baby growing into a child who would kill Eddie, just as she had inadvertently killed her own father.

Overwhelmed by fear, Roberta started kneading the surface of her abdomen—softly at first, but then with increasing strength, until her skin started to hurt from the rough pinching.

The baby kicked again. She pulled her hands back to her side.

Steeling her resolve, she stood up from the bed and felt her way through the darkness to the desk by the television set in the far corner of the room. She opened the top drawer, pulled out a pen and a sheet of hotel stationery, and returned to Eddie's side. Her hands now strong and steady in their purpose, she scribbled down the last line of the sonnet he had quoted before falling asleep:

"*And, if God choose, I shall but love thee better after death.*"

She left the paper on the table by his bedside and walked back to the bathroom.

Silently, and with a steady sense of purpose, she pulled each of the bottles out of the medicine bag and lined them up in a row. Then she poured herself a tall glass of water, opened up the vials, and began swallowing pills, three at a time.

## Chapter Seventeen

"If only I'd woken up one goddamned hour earlier!" Eddie moaned. He leaned forward in his chair and buried his head in the palms of his hands. "Or even a half-hour earlier. Christ! Just a few fucking minutes might have made all the difference in the world!"

Emmett stopped pacing the floor of the hospital's private waiting room and rested his hand on Eddie's shoulder. "I'm so sorry. I don't know what to say."

"The doctors don't know if she'll ever speak again," Eddie continued in a hoarse whisper. "Or walk. Or, Christ—she might never be anything more than a hopeless vegetable."

"She's breathing, though, right?" Emmett asked.

Eddie nodded. "Yes, she's breathing on her own, and her heartbeat is strong. But one of her pupils isn't responding to light. A nurse told me that's a bad sign. There might be brain damage."

Eddie stood up from the stifling chair and walked across the room to a rain-streaked window. Long rivulets of water dripped over the glass, obscuring his view of the dark, grey clouds outside. He focused his attention on a single, rogue raindrop forging a jagged path across the pane. It vibrated frantically as it snaked its way over the glass. But then a fast-flowing stream of water sucked it in and carried it away.

He shifted his gaze and noticed a small throng of reporters gathered under an awning by the building's entrance. "They're clamoring outside, aren't they?" he scoffed.

"A few called out to me when I walked by them," Emmett replied. "Though they had the good grace to keep their distance."

"They're fucking bastards, the lot of them," Eddie said.

Emmett sighed. "You do realize that I have to issue some sort of statement. If we don't say something soon, the papers will start speculating, and God only knows what they'll print."

"Fuck 'em all," Eddie replied. "They can write whatever they please. I don't give a damn."

Emmett sighed, but offered no argument.

Eddie looked back up at the sky. "The baby's dead," he said.

"I figured as much," Emmett replied. "I'm so sorry."

Eddie swallowed hard. "Birdie will be devastated when she finds out—when she wakes up from her coma. If she wakes up from her coma."

"I'm here for you, Eddie. I'll do everything I can to help you get through this," Emmett said.

"I know. Thanks. But right now, I think I just want to be alone."

Emmett patted Eddie's shoulder, then left him to his private thoughts.

\* \* \*

"Hey there," Jim said, pulling up a chair beside Roberta's hospital bed and sitting down next to Eddie. He watched the slow drip of clear fluid work its way through the tube in her arm, then rested his hand on Eddie's knee. "How are you doing?"

"How do you think I'm doing?" Eddie grumbled.

"I don't know. You kind of look like shit. When was the last time you showered?"

"Haven't a clue."

Jim withdrew his hand and stared at Roberta's lovely face, her eyes closed in seemingly restful slumber. "Do the doctors have any idea when she'll come to?"

"No," Eddie said. "We're all just waiting to see what happens."

Jim took a deep breath. "Eddie, Emmett asked me to come here because he can't seem to get through to you. You must issue some sort of statement to the press."

"No," Eddie said. "This is nobody's business but Birdie's and mine."

Jim sighed. "You don't need to feel ashamed, you know. Roberta's sick, and people who are sick like she is do things like this all the time. It happens every day."

"I'm not ashamed of Birdie's being sick," Eddie replied. "I'm ashamed of myself for being so stupid. I left all those medicine bottles right on the sink where she could reach them. Even her gobshite brother knew enough to put her pills into little boxes so she never had access to more than a few at a time."

Jim looked back at the drip line. "He's here. You know that, right? Dick's been hanging around the hospital for a couple of days now."

"I know," Eddie said. "And I've told the nurses not to let him near this room."

"Eddie," Jim sighed. "Dick is talking to the press. He's planting stories. And what he's saying is not good. You have to do something."

"I don't care what Dick says. He's a fucking liar."

"I know. But you can't let him dictate the terms of this story to the press. You must release some sort of statement."

Eddie grunted. "The truth will come out eventually. There's no need for me to get involved. I have better things to do."

Jim rolled his eyes. "Like what? She's in a *coma*, Eddie. You can't do anything for her at the moment."

"I'm reading to her," Eddie replied.

"Right," Jim said. He stared at Roberta's blank face and shook his head. "Do you think she can hear you?"

"Maybe," Eddie answered.

Jim stood up from his chair. "Well, do what you need to do. But think about issuing some sort of statement, please. I'm gonna go downstairs and see if I can get a cuppa. Do you want to take a break and join me?"

Eddie shook his head. After Jim left, he brought his chair closer to the bed and pulled a slim volume of poetry from his jacket pocket. He paged through the short introduction and stopped at the first poem.

"*Sonnets from the Portuguese*," he read aloud. "Number One."

He cleared his throat and quietly read the first eleven lines to his wife. Then he swallowed hard and recited the poem's concluding stanza:

*"And a voice said in mastery while I strove,*
*'Guess now who holds thee?'* — *'Death,' I said. But, there,*
*The silver answer rang. 'Not Death, but Love.' "*

\* \* \*

A loud, incessant pounding on the door of his hotel room roused Eddie from a restless sleep. He staggered out of bed and yelled, "Fuck off!" at his unwelcome visitor through the door.

"Fuck off, yourself," replied the voice in the hallway.

*Shit,* Eddie cursed in his head. *Why won't they leave me alone?* He opened the door and reluctantly ushered Tony into his room.

Tony strode in with a purposeful gait, rested a guitar case on Eddie's bed, and tossed a large pile of dirty clothes off a chair so he could sit down. "Hello, mate, haven't seen you in a while. Thought I'd stop by and see if you wanted to jam."

"What part of 'fuck off' didn't you understand?" Eddie asked. He shoved Tony's guitar case to the side of the bed and lay back down on the mattress.

"I brought you an English newspaper," Tony answered. "I know how you like doing the cryptic crossword."

"Go away," Eddie groused, pulling his blanket over his face.

"Get your arse out of bed, Rochester. You need to hold a press conference."

Eddie rolled to his side, away from Tony. "Don't forget to take your guitar when you leave," he added.

Tony got up and started switching on all the lamps in the hotel room. "I said, get up!" he barked.

Eddie rolled over and stared bleary-eyed at his visitor. "What is your problem?"

"My problem? I don't have a problem." Tony walked to the bed, opened his guitar case and pulled out the newspaper he'd packed with the instrument. He tossed it at Eddie and sat back down. "You're the one with a problem. Your fuckwit brother-in-law has given an interview with *The London Eyewitness* in which he claims Roberta is dead."

Eddie sat up. He read the headline and stared at the photograph of Roberta lying lifelessly on her hospital bed. "What the fuck? I don't understand."

"I don't either, mate. I don't know why he's spreading this lie, or what he hopes to accomplish. But I do know how he got the photograph."

Eddie skimmed the article, then put down the paper and turned towards Tony with a broken look. "I hate to say this, but if everyone thought she'd died, then maybe they'd finally leave us alone," he murmured.

Tony scowled at Eddie. "Dick's not going to leave you two alone. He has contacts inside this hospital. You may not know this, but your brother-in-law is a drug pusher."

Eddie sighed loudly. "I know. He specializes in pharmaceutical-grade painkillers, but can get his hands on just about anything his clients covet. He's been doing it ever since he was discharged from an Army medical supply unit in Germany a decade ago. Birdie told me after I brought her back on the tour."

"Well I'm glad you're not completely out of the loop," Tony said.

"What's that supposed to mean?"

"I dunno. It's just that your world seems to be falling apart, and as far as all of your friends can tell, you're just standing still in the eye of a hurricane, waiting for it to suck you in too."

Eddie rolled his eyes. "Just because I'm ignoring the press, that doesn't mean I'm standing still. I sit with Birdie for hours every day, and talk to her doctors all the time. She's out of her coma, for Chrissake! She looked straight at me yesterday and started to cry."

"Good," Tony said. "I'm glad she's doing better. But what the hell are you going to do about Dick?"

Eddie threw off his blanket and climbed out of bed. He dug a pair of jeans out of the pile of dirty clothes and slipped them on over his undershorts. "Nothing," he said as he rummaged through the heap for a clean shirt.

"I hate to tell you this, chap, but Dick seems to have other tricks up his sleeve too," Tony added. He selected a shirt from the top of the pile, sniffed the armpit and threw it back on the floor.

Eddie retrieved the shirt and slipped his arms into the sleeves. "This one's not so bad. I've only worn it twice, I think."

Tony shook his head. "Listen, I'm relying on Eli for news here, since he knows some blokes in Dick's inner circle, so I realize our informant is of dubious merit. But Dick's been talking about selling Roberta's diaries to the highest bidder. God knows what's in them. Poetry, I suppose."

"I can't imagine he's going to make much of a fortune off those," Eddie said. He walked to an opened suitcase in the corner of the room and pulled out a clean pair of socks.

"Dick has also mentioned some sort of movie he has of you," Tony added. "Any idea what that might be about?"

"Christ," Eddie cursed. He dropped his socks on the floor and walked back to the bed. He looked at Tony and started to laugh.

"That is not a happy laugh," Tony said. "I've heard you snicker and giggle before when something tickled your fancy. Even chortle. But that definitely sounded like a sardonic bit of laughter."

Eddie fell back on the bed and spread his arms out wide.

"A home movie of the wedding, perhaps?" Tony suggested. "Super 8 footage of you and your bride frolicking in Florence?"

"More like a horror film," Eddie said, his voice grim. "Dick showed Birdie a few grainy old snaps of me kissing some bird in England to rile her up, then handed her a knife and had her charge at me while a friend of his rolled a camera."

Tony stared blankly at Eddie for a few moments before speaking. "Well that's unexpected. Dare I ask, was blood drawn?"

"Not exactly. I wrestled the knife away from her, but she fell and hit her head on a table and cut her forehead. So she had blood dripping all over her face."

"While you were still holding the weapon," Tony surmised.

"Well, I dropped it at first. But then I picked it back up."

"How big a blade are we talking about here?"

Eddie sat up and held his two index fingers about eight inches apart. "It wasn't exactly a cutlass. More like a large carving knife."

"Bollocks," Tony swore and cleared his throat. "Well then. I imagine such a film might indeed fetch a princely sum at auction."

"Right," Eddie agreed. He stood back up and retrieved his socks.

Tony got out of the chair and walked over to his guitar case. "Leave off with the socks and shoes for now, Eddie. Let's jam."

"Are you mad? I'm going to the hospital to see Birdie."

Tony tuned his E-string. "She can wait a few minutes. I see your Alvarez over there in the corner. C'mon, pick it up. Play with me."

"I don't have time for this," Eddie scoffed.

"Yes you do," Tony said. "You need to sing or scream or just strum very, very loudly and break a few strings. The guitar's your refuge, mate. You told me that you started playing after your dad died. And you wrote all those amazing songs for Roberta because you missed her and couldn't get a hold of her."

"No," Eddie replied.

"Yes," Tony insisted. "Roy Orbison should do the trick." He

started strumming a D chord and sang the opening line to *Crying*.

Eddie stared at his bare feet for a long moment, then cut off Tony mid-verse. "No. *Pretty Woman*. I'm going to see my girl."

Tony stopped playing and rested his right arm over the body of his acoustic guitar. "*Only the Lonely*."

"*In Dreams*," Eddie countered.

"*Blue Bayou*," Tony proposed.

Eddie closed his eyes and sucked in a deep breath. "Remember that night in New Orleans when we all got legless on Hurricanes, and Gerry started singing that song to the barmaid?"

"I do. Just barely."

Eddie opened his eyes. "Birdie made Bananas Foster to celebrate our engagement. They tasted like New Orleans."

Tony smiled. "Fetch your guitar, mate. Let's sing a verse about looking forward to happier times."

## Chapter Eighteen

### *Andermatt, Switzerland — 1973*

"Stop it, Birdie!" Eddie yelled. He grabbed her wrists and forced her arms down to the surface of the table.

"Kandoot!" she shouted. "Dwontoot!"

Eddie held her hands in place until she settled down, then released her and picked up a pencil from the box on the corner of the table. "C'mon, love. You have to try. This is so important. I need to be able to know what you're thinking."

He closed her fingers around the pencil, but as soon as he took his hand away, she dropped it.

"Let me try," said the woman sitting on Roberta's other side. She slid a clean piece of paper in front of Roberta and guided her hand towards the box so she could try to pick up her own pencil. Roberta managed to lift one, but almost immediately dropped it.

Eddie exchanged a sad smile with the other woman. "Well, that's an improvement anyway."

Roberta growled and whacked the box to the floor.

"Christ, Birdie, don't do that," Eddie grumbled.

"I vill pick zemmup," said the other woman. She got down on her hands and knees and started collecting the pencils.

"Look who's here!" boomed a gruff voice from the doorway. Gerry bounded into the room with a laugh. He stopped and watched the woman in the tight skirt scooping pencils off the floor for just a moment, then clapped Eddie on the back. "Hey, mate! Hey, Birdie! How's everyone doing?"

"Wonderful," Eddie groaned. "Where's Emmett?"

"Parking the car. Sorry we're late. We had a hard time finding this place. And we almost hit a few goats along the way."

The woman in the tight skirt stood back up and Eddie offered introductions.

"This is Birdie's therapist, Gretel. This is my old drummer—"

"*Hansel. Ich heiße Hansel,*" Gerry interrupted. "*Wie gehts?*"

Eddie scowled. "Gerry. This is my old drummer, Gerry Enis."

"It iz pleasure to meet you," Gretel said, extending her hand.

Instead of shaking her hand, Gerry kissed it. "*Das Vergnügen gehört mir,*" he replied, arching his eyebrows and smiling. Gretel laughed.

Gerry grabbed a chair and pulled it up to the table. "So we're working on writing now, are we?" he asked, examining the mess of crumbled papers covered in chicken scratches.

"Trying to," Eddie replied.

Gerry picked up two pencils from the box Gretel had just placed back on the table. "Try holding them like this, Birdie," he said, resting them in his fingers like drumsticks. He handed them to Roberta and tried to position them properly. "There are a lot of different grips that work. You just have to find the one you like."

Birdie wrapped her fingers around the ends of the pencils.

"Not so tight," Gerry said. "You need to find the balance point against your thumb."

"Gerry, this is not helping," Eddie chided.

Gretel laughed. "You two get coffee. I vill stay und help Birrtee."

"Thanks, you're an angel," Eddie said. He stood up and kissed the top of Roberta's head, then started leading Gerry out of the room. A pencil came soaring after them, pointy side first. Eddie turned around quickly. "Birdie! No!"

Roberta had already turned her head away from him.

"I think she's attempting Keith Moon's signature grip," Gerry said. "It often results in projectile stick throwing."

Eddie frowned. "Let's go to the lobby and look for Emmett."

\* \* \*

Eddie sifted through the architectural drawings Emmett had spread across the table in the nursing home's dining area. "I'm gobsmacked! I can hardly imagine living in a mansion like this."

"It'll be a good for you to be near a city again too," Gerry said. "Even if it's only Cincinnati. Can't have been too much fun for you this past year kipping in Heidi's old cottage while Birdie's been learning how to walk again."

"Andermatt is a beautiful old town," Emmett said. "Out of reach of reporters, and home to a marvelous convalescent facility."

"Right," Eddie agreed half-heartedly. He started stacking the drawings back into a neat pile.

"And how is she?" Emmett asked.

Eddie shrugged. "Well, you know. It's been a slow process. She's walking okay now and can feed herself most of the time, though her grip on her utensils leaves a lot to be desired. But she can't talk. At least not clearly. And as Gerry just witnessed, she can't write anymore either. So she can't communicate what she's feeling. Which makes it almost impossible for the doctors to figure out the correct dosage of neuroleptics to give her. If it's too high, she gets lethargic and can't do anything for herself. If it's too low, she starts seeing hallucinations, and then, God help us all."

"How is she doing today?" Emmett asked.

"I dunno. I told her I was flying to Ohio for a few weeks to get Grandpa's estate in order, and start the paperwork for the two of us to move to America. She didn't seem very happy about it."

"Maybe she was just cheesed off 'cause you were ogling that pretty nurse in the tight skirt," Gerry suggested.

Eddie glowered at him. "I was not. *You* were ogling her."

"I saw you checking out her bum when she bent over to pick up those pencils. It wasn't just me."

"Bugger," Eddie cursed. "A man can look. That doesn't mean anything."

"It might mean something to Birdie," Gerry countered. "'Specially if you ain't checking out her bum anymore."

Eddie started clenching his fists. "I am taking care of my wife. I am trying to help her recover. She is not in a position—"

"To try a new position," Gerry interrupted. "Probably can't even manage the missionary anymore."

"Fuck you!" Eddie swore. He stood up from the table.

Emmett grabbed Eddie's arm. "Sit down. And shut up, Gerry. You're being an arse." He picked up the drawings and placed them in a large folder. "These should make her happy, don't you think? Imagining what her new home will look like?"

Eddie sat back down reluctantly. "I guess so. I promised Birdie I'd build her a mansion. But I'm starting to think she might prefer the old farmhouse. She found it quite charming when we visited Grandpa on the tour. She liked how cozy the small rooms felt."

"We'll see," said Emmett. "You should like the mansion, in any case. Did you see the architect's plans for the recording studio?"

"Yes, they're great," Eddie said, managing a half smile. "By the way, how's Alan?"

Emmett's face grew long. "Better. The methadone seems to be working. His doctors say he should be cured in a few months, though you never know. It's hard to beat heroin. Mum's looking forward to having him come home so she can take care of him herself. Or at least keep an eye on him."

"She's a saint," Eddie said. "She was such a big help, getting Birdie back on her feet when we first moved her out here from Zurich. I hated to see her leave."

"I know she wants to come out to Ohio with you after the new house is built, and help Roberta settle in," Emmett said. "Assuming Alan is in a position to look after himself by then."

"Right," Eddie said. He turned to Gerry and eyed him warily. "So what brings *you* here? I thought you were laying down drum tracks for Tony's new solo album."

"Better gig came up," Gerry answered, puffing his cheeks with pride. "I'm taking M.C. Monty's place for the rest of The Whimsy Lords' world tour. I'm meeting them in Geneva for a couple of days of rehearsals, then it's off to Paris to play for the fans. Figured I'd say hello to you and your missus while I was *in der Schweiz*."

"What happened to M.C.?" Eddie asked.

"Fell out of a tree after a party in Interlaken and broke both his arms. Can't drum worth shit."

"What was he doing in a tree?" Emmett asked.

"Something to do with a marmot. I thought it best not to ask."

Emmett laughed. "I'm going to miss being your manager, Gerry. You always kept me on my toes."

"We all did," Eddie said.

"Yes. Though I never would have thought you'd be the one who gave me the biggest worries, Eddie," Emmett replied, his voice growing sadder.

"What is it now? Is my brother-in-law making waves again?"

"No," Emmett said. "The last I heard he was still in Amsterdam, sleeping rough on houseboats and hiding from Interpol.

Eddie sucked in a deep breath and tapped his fingers against the table. "He's not trying to hawk that film of his anymore?"

"Not that I've heard of. He's just laying low. I'm sure he regrets the notoriety he received from giving that interview with *The Eyewitness*. It's hard to run an illicit pill peddling operation when your face has been plastered on newspapers all over the world."

"Well, I don't exactly pity the man," Eddie said.

"You shouldn't," Emmett replied. "Though I must admit, his lie has worked in your favor. The press has left you alone ever since you brought Roberta up to this facility. They all think she's dead."

"Either that, or they don't want to risk life or limb on the hairpin turns that line the road from Zurich to Andermatt," Gerry suggested. "Or maybe they're just afraid of the goats."

"The goats are dead fierce," Eddie agreed.

"They miss Heidi," Gerry said. "They've grown mean."

Emmett put his hand to his brow and chuckled softly. "Right. Let's go check on Roberta, shall we?" He stood up from the table, then threw a quick glance out the window. "I almost forgot. Mum crocheted her an afghan as a belated wedding present, and I left it in the boot of the car. Take these drawings, Eddie, while I go collect it. I won't be a minute."

Eddie took the folder and started leading Gerry to the lobby.

"You know if Gretel's single?" Gerry asked.

"I've never asked her. But she doesn't wear a ring."

"Ah. So you looked," Gerry said.

"One notices these things," Eddie replied nonchalantly.

"The world is full of beautiful women, Eddie. You don't need to tie yourself down for the rest of your life to one who can't love you back anymore."

"Birdie loves me. She might not be able to say so anymore, but she loves me."

Gerry frowned. "What would it take to make you consider calling this marriage a day and looking for happiness elsewhere?"

Eddie sighed. "Oh hell, Gerry. I don't know." He thought for a long moment before offering a wistful response.

"Find me another woman with beautiful eyes and a sexy smile, who arouses both my passions and my protective instincts. A woman who prefers my solitary company to parties and society, and harbors an unhealthy appetite for Victorian literature. Oh—

and give her nice breasts too. Find me another woman like that, Ger, and maybe I'll take a second look."

Gerry stroked his shaggy beard. "How nice of breasts?"

"Exquisite breasts," Eddie said, holding Gerry's steely gaze.

"Damn, you're one hell of a picky man."

"Once you've found true love, then you'll be picky too," Eddie replied.

Gerry looked out the lobby window and watched Emmett walk towards the building, carrying a colorful blanket in his arms.

"Suit yourself, mate," Gerry said with a smile. "But for now, I think I'll just ask Gretel for her phone number."

# Book Two

*After a youth and manhood passed half in
unutterable misery and half in dreary solitude, I have found for the first
time what I can truly love — I have found you.*

— Charlotte Brontë
*Jane Eyre*

## Chapter One

### *Munich, Federal Republic of Germany — 1988*

Eddie lay back against his pillow and closed his eyes. He'd drunk enough whiskey to loosen his conscience, but not enough to entirely blot out the pangs of guilt that stirred in his gut.

Inge straddled him and rested her weight against his crotch. "Take off your trousers," she purred, the words slipping softly from her lips, sounding more like a plea than a command.

"I can't," he replied. "You're sitting on my zipper."

She laughed and rolled off. As Eddie reached for his fly, she stroked the dark, wiry hairs on his bare chest and whispered in his ear, "I still cannot believe I am here in your bed. I have dreamt about screwing you since I was a teenager."

Eddie rolled his eyes and reached for the lamp on the bedside table, hoping the darkness would mask the exasperated look on his face. "I hope I won't disappoint you."

"You could not," she said. "Just being with you is a dream come true. And I am *dreaming tonight!*"

He fumbled in the dark for the condom he'd left on the nightstand. *It's all right,* he assured himself. *I'm at Gerry's house in Germany. And when I fly back to Ohio next week I'll be in a much better mood to cope with Birdie.*

He tore off the edge of the wrapper and was just about to pull out the sheath when the door to the bedroom burst open.

"Herr Rochester!" cried a small voice. *"Kommen Sie schnell! Papa ist krank!"*

"Christ!" Eddie shouted, throwing the unused condom on the floor and grabbing at his pants. "You need to learn to knock, Gisela!"

The child ignored his reprimand and continued her plea. *"Bitte, Herr Rochester! Papa ist krank! Er braucht seine Hilfe!"*

Inge draped the sheet over her breasts. "See to the girl. I will come *gleich.*"

Eddie offered Inge a quick kiss, then zipped his fly and followed Gerry's young daughter out of the room and down the hallway. Outside the bathroom, his former drummer lay sprawled across the floor, a trickle of vomit dribbling from his mouth, an unlabeled bottle of pills resting beside his open palm.

Eddie crouched down to make certain Gerry's chest was still rising and falling. "Well, you're breathing, but just barely," he muttered. He glanced at the open vial and shook his head. "What the fuck did you just swallow, you arsehole?"

*"Was ist los mit ihnem?"* Gisela sobbed.

*"Ich weiß nicht, liebchen,"* Eddie replied. *"Ich weiß nur daß er ein Doktor braucht."*

Inge stepped out of the bedroom, wrapped loosely in Eddie's oversized shirt, and joined them by the bathroom door. *"Mein Gott!"* she exclaimed. "I will call for help!"

Eddie nodded and watched her hurry away to find a telephone. The tail of his shirt flapped back and forth as she ran, grazing the soft, white mounds of her buttocks and offering him one last tantalizing glimpse of the guilty pleasures he would not be enjoying this evening. He turned back to the child and tried to reassure her. *"Sei nicht ängstlich, meine kleines. Er wird sich erholen,"* he said, but then he glared at Gerry and silently cursed his old friend for forcing him into this awkward situation.

*Why didn't you ever teach your daughter to speak English, you wanker? And why did you take these pills, after all the whiskey you drank tonight? What happened to that woman you brought to your bedroom? And where the fuck is Gisela's nanny?*

He glanced back at Gisela. *"Wo ist deine Kinderfrau?"*

*"Sie ist weg,"* she cried. She rubbed her damp cheek and explained that she'd awakened to the sound of the front door slamming, and run to her nanny's bedroom for comfort. It was empty, so she'd gone searching for her father instead.

Eddie stood up and stole a quick glance at Gerry's open bedroom door. He saw no sign of the woman Gerry had been partying with earlier that night.

*"Wo ist dien Papa's Freundin?"* he asked, dreading the answer he'd

already guessed.

"*Meine Kinderfrau ist Papa's Freundin,*" she replied softly.

Eddie threw a dirty look at Gerry's blood-drained face. *You bastard,* he thought. *How could you be shagging your kid's nanny? You have all the scruples of a rutting pig.*

A small, weak moan escaped from Gerry's mouth.

*Right,* Eddie thought, the sickening pangs of guilt returning to his gut. *Who am I to cast stones?*

Inge returned to the hallway, dressed in her own clothes. *"Der Krankenwagen kommt,"* she said. She cast a sad glance at Eddie. "I think I should go."

He looked away from her and attempted to comfort Gerry's sobbing daughter. "It's okay, *liebchen,*" he murmured unconvincingly. *"Dein Papa hat nur Bauchschmerzen."*

"Some stomachache," Inge muttered. Then she turned to Eddie and spoke more distinctly. "I will call a taxi. You stay with your friend."

Eddie started to nod, but then a wave of panic hit him. "No, wait!" he exclaimed. "Gisela will need someone to stay with her while I take this pillock to the hospital!"

Inge crossed her arms in front of her ample chest. "That is not the kind of night I planned."

*"Bitte,"* he pleaded. "I can't just leave her here by herself."

"I must be at work in the morning," Inge grumbled.

"I'll be back before dawn," he promised. "As soon as I get Gerry checked in with a doctor, I'll come home to watch the girl."

"Where is her nanny?" Inge asked with a smirk.

"I don't know," Eddie sighed. He glanced back and forth between the child and her father. *She could have been mine,* he reminded himself. *If she had been born just a few months earlier, she could have been mine.*

"Be back by six," Inge said, her words sounding distinctly like a command and not the least bit like a plea. "I must go home to change my clothes before work."

Eddie nodded and squeezed Gisela's hand. The cry of a siren pierced the air. It grew louder as it approached the house, then whined to a stop. A loud knocking echoed up the stairs from the front door. "I'll let them in," he said, offering the child a quick kiss. *"Geh mit Fraulein Inge.* She'll tuck you back into bed."

## Millcote, Ohio

Eddie sat on the edge of the mattress and leaned towards the pillow. Gisela wrapped her skinny arms around his neck and drew him towards her with all the strength she could muster. She rubbed her damp face against his bristly cheek.

"*Warum nicht?*" she sobbed. "*Ich verstehe nicht!*"

Eddie extricated himself from the hug and stared hopelessly at the child's tear-stained face. *I know you don't understand,* he wanted to say. *But I'm not going to tell you why you're not allowed to visit the old farmhouse. It's simply for your own good.*

"*Ich kann nicht sagen,*" he answered instead—I cannot say.

He pulled the covers up over the girl's shoulders and promised to have breakfast with her the following morning before he flew back to Germany. He assured her that his housekeeper would find her a good nanny straight away.

Gisela continued to weep. Eddie's heart sank. *Lord, why did I agree to take care of her?* he thought. *I am so out of my depth!*

He reached out his hand and stroked Gisela's long brown hair until her sobs receded into deep, hiccoughing sighs. He whispered her name to make certain she was sleeping, then stood up from the bed and left the room as quietly as he could. His golden retriever Pancho was waiting for him on the floor outside the door, lying exactly where he had left her.

"Good girl," he whispered. She stood up and followed him down the hallway and into the large sitting room in the back of the mansion.

Eddie's housekeeper Sally Fairfax called out to him the moment he reached the bottom step. "Is the girl asleep?"

"Yes," he answered. "She's had a long day. I imagine she'll be out like a log for the next twelve hours."

"Oh, I don't know about that," Sally replied. "A small child in a strange house? She'll probably sleep pretty lightly tonight."

Eddie sighed. *Christ, she's right,* he thought. *Whatever made me think I could take care of this girl? I know absolutely nothing about childrearing!*

"She'll need a nanny," he said in an emphatic tone, hoping that he sounded like a confident guardian and not like a clueless single man. "Straight away."

"So Gisela will be staying here for a while then?" Sally

surmised.

"Yes," Eddie replied.

"How long?"

"A while then," Eddie mumbled. He turned towards the large window that lined the back wall and stared at his grandfather's old farmhouse across the yard. A full moon shone brightly upon the building, bathing its steep roof in a pale, eerie glow and casting long shadows from its gabled windows and overhanging porch. The front entrance to the house was masked in a veil of black.

He started walking to the back door. "I'm going to bring Pancho back to the farmhouse and say hello to Alan and Grace. I need to discuss a few things with them before I return to Europe."

Sally knotted her forehead. "You're going back already?"

"Yes," he replied, turning to face her. "I have to help Gerry find a good place to dry out."

"Gerry Enis? Dry out?" Sally laughed. "That's going to take some time!"

"Yes," Eddie agreed with a sigh. "It will probably take a while." He took a few more steps towards the back door, then turned and faced Sally again. "I need you to find a nanny for Gisela. Someone who can teach her to speak English."

"I can try," Sally said hesitantly. "But I'm not quite sure where to look."

"I trust you, Sally," Eddie said. "You know a lot more about taking care of children than I do. I'm sure you'll find someone good." He reached for the door knob.

"What should I tell her?" Sally called out. "I'm sure she'll have a lot of questions. How much are you willing to pay? How long will the position last?"

Eddie glanced back at Sally with a hopeless expression. "I don't know. Offer her a good salary. Whatever is customary, plus something extra. And I don't know how long the position will last. Until Gerry's ready to collect his daughter. A few months, maybe?"

He turned to the door again and opened it. Pancho dashed in front of him and ran to the large elm tree in the middle of the yard. He took another deep breath.

"Offer her whatever you think is fair," he said before leaving the room. "And work out whatever sort of schedule she wants. I don't care. Just make sure to tell her—tell her to never bother the Pooles in the old farmhouse." He closed the door behind him, called to his dog, and walked across the yard to the house sheathed in shadows.

## Chapter Two

### *Munich, Federal Republic of Germany*

"This place is no good," Gerry whined, his ruddy cheeks blushing a deeper shade of red. "You gotta spring me from this joint. Take me home now, and tomorrow I'll check into that other clinic we visited. The one with the nice curtains. I promise."

"The curtains don't matter, Gerry," Eddie replied, casting a cursory glance at the drapes that had been pulled shut to block out the late afternoon sunlight. "What matters is the type of care you'll be receiving. And everyone here seems very nice."

"They're just acting nice 'cause you're with me!" Gerry protested, stretching his legs out over the top of his mattress and kicking the blanket askew. "Everyone likes you! You're a fuckin', tragic, romantic hero! All these nurses are just itchin' to doff their uniforms and offer you a little tender loving care. But as soon as you leave, they're gonna start bein' mean to me. I can see it in their eyes. They think I'm just a stupid, drunken drummer."

"You are a stupid, drunken drummer," Eddie replied. "That's why you're in hospital. So you can mend your wicked ways. You need their help."

Gerry slumped his shoulders, then looked up at Eddie with a hopeful expression. "Tell you what," he proposed. "How 'bout I blow this joint and give a concert for the blind instead, like Keith Richards did? I'd be doing a greater service for humanity."

Eddie rolled his eyes. "But you wouldn't be doing much of a service to yourself. You need to learn how to stop drinking."

"But I'm not an alcoholic!" Gerry protested. "I only drink when I'm taking a breather from my pills. Or when my nose starts hurtin' from the coke."

Eddie covered his eyes with his hand to hide his irritation. "Relax, Ger. Try to think of this place as a sort of holiday camp, like Butlins."

"Like Butlins with a staff full of *Krankenschwestern* and bloody pastel colored walls," Gerry groused.

Eddie smiled. "Exactly. That's the spirit. Just think of all the fun, new things you're going to learn while you're here."

"What, like archery? Or canoeing?"

"You can paddle a boat much better if you're sober," Eddie said. "Trust me. Being sober is a wonderful thing. You might even enjoy it once you start getting used to it."

Gerry shuddered and turned his face away in disgust. "That's what you think! But you never really enjoyed having fun."

"Right," Eddie replied. He started to get out of his chair. Gerry turned and grabbed his arm.

"Don't leave me!" he begged. "I'm not ready to be alone yet!"

"You won't be alone," Eddie reminded him. "The nice nurses will tend to your every need."

"Bloody hell," Gerry grumbled, running his fingers through his mop of spiked, brown hair. "Why are you in such a hurry to leave? You planning to ring up Inge before you fly back to the States?"

Eddie turned his head away. "No."

"But why not?" Gerry asked. "She's pretty, and she digs you. Her English is really good too."

"What does that matter?" Eddie said. "My German is passable."

"But it's nice having a chick you can actually talk to," Gerry said.

Eddie scowled.

Gerry immediately apologized. "Don't get your knickers in a twist! I didn't mean anything. I'm just upset about being here."

"Well, I'm not too keen on your being here either," Eddie replied. "I mean that sincerely. I want you to check out of this clinic as soon as you possibly can, so you can fly to Ohio and collect your daughter. I'm really not in a position to take care of a small child. I do have other responsibilities." He looked down at his left hand and stared at his wedding ring.

"But Zellie likes you," Gerry said softly, calling Eddie out of his reverie. "You're like a second father to her. Every time you come to Munich, you dote on her as if she were your own little girl."

Eddie turned his head away. "Well, she could have been. There but for the grace of God. And for the fact that I passed her mother along to you as soon as I had my fill of her."

"Yeah, thanks again for that, mate," Gerry replied. "I do appreciate how you always send your romantic conquests my way when you're done with them."

"You liked Bettina a lot more than I ever did," Eddie countered. "To me, she was just another brief diversion to help me through those long Ohio winters. But you lived with her for five years."

"Mm-hmm," Gerry agreed. "Until she ran off with that right midfielder from F.C. Bayern and left me with the kid."

"And why did she leave you?" Eddie asked pointedly.

"Don't ask stupid questions," Gerry replied, resting a hand on his belly and staring at his pale, bare feet. "You know perfectly well why. She didn't like living with a drunk."

Eddie scooted his chair closer to the bed. "Gerry, you need to clean up your act. You can't just keep sending Gisela to Bettina's mum, or passing her off to those silly tarts you pick up at parties. You have to get sober so you can become a real father to her."

"Yeah, I know," Gerry sighed. He cast Eddie a look of regret. "So how is she, anyway? Have you heard from your housekeeper?"

"I spoke with Sally this morning," Eddie said. "She's found a nanny who speaks German, and Gisela seems to like her."

"That was quick."

"Yes," Eddie agreed. "Sally told me she rang up an old friend of hers who used to run a Catholic boarding school in Indiana, to see if she knew anyone who could help. And by a stroke of luck, there was a former student still living at the convent who spoke German almost fluently. Alan drove out to Indiana to collect her."

"Are you kidding me?" Gerry laughed. "You have a nun living at your house now?"

Eddie shook his head. "No. I don't believe the young lady is a nun. Sally said she's just a former student who didn't have a place to live, so the Mother Superior allowed her to stay at the convent. Apparently she's an orphan."

"God, this sounds suspiciously like *The Sound of Music* to me," Gerry said with a leer. "You'd better watch out, mate, or you'll be falling for this chick, just like Christopher Plummer went to town for Julie Andrews."

"That won't be a problem, I assure you," Eddie said. "I am, as you are no doubt well aware, already taken."

"Right," Gerry laughed. "Like that's stopped you from boffing the likes of Bettina and Inge on your little 'vacations' from home."

"This is different," Eddie insisted. "I would never get involved with a woman when I was at Thornfield with Birdie. And besides, Sally told me this nanny is quite young."

Gerry arched his eyebrow. "How young?"

"I'm not sure. But under twenty-one, I believe."

"Over sixteen?"

"Probably."

"Well that's all that matters then, no?" Gerry laughed.

Eddie glared at his friend. "I am not the sort of bloke who preys on young women. I make no claim to be a man of high moral standards. But I am not a dirty old goat!"

"Oh, come off it!" Gerry exclaimed. "I'm just having a bit of a laugh! I'm not saying you're a cradle snatcher, or that there's anything wrong with your having the occasional how's-your-father when you're on holiday. I mean, it's not as if your missus is keeping the home fires burning for you back in Ohio."

Eddie looked down at the floor. "I'm not proud of my proclivities."

Gerry frowned. "Bugger, Eddie, why is it whenever I spend time with you, I feel like I need a dictionary?"

Eddie looked back up at his friend. "You know what I mean."

"So how is Birdie these days, anyway?" Gerry asked.

Eddie stood up from his chair and walked to the window. "Same as she's been for the past fifteen years. She has her good days."

"Really? What's a good day for her?"

Eddie tugged open the curtain and stared at the tree across the lot. "Well, this past spring she seemed to perk up when I read her the collected works of Coleridge."

Gerry sighed. "Remind me again. Which one is he? The tosser with the daffodils?"

"No, the genius who wrote *The Rime of the Ancient Mariner*."

"It's not ringing a bell."

Eddie turned, stretched out his arms to mime holding a tray, and called out in his best imitation of John Cleese's voice, "Albatross! Albatross!"

Gerry broke into a wide smile. "Two choc-ices, please."

"I haven't got choc-ices!" Eddie shouted. "I've only got the albatross! And don't you be asking for any bloody wafers with it!"

They both started laughing. Eddie returned to Gerry's side and pulled his jacket off the back of the chair. "Thank God for Monty Python. Otherwise you would be living in a cultural vacuum."

Gerry's smile faded. "No. I'm not living in any bloody vacuum. I'm living in a goddamned sobriety clinic."

Eddie put his arm through a sleeve of his jacket. "Well, listen to your doctors and do what they say so you can leave. The sooner you get out of here, the better. I can't watch your daughter forever."

"I know," Gerry said. He stood up from the bed and offered Eddie a brief hug. "Thanks for minding Zellie."

"You're welcome," Eddie replied. He reached for the door.

"Enjoy your albatross," Gerry added.

Eddie scowled at him and left the room.

### *London, England*

Philip Randall tore a sheet out of his typewriter and called to his assistant June. "Be a doll and take this to typesetting, would you?" He offered her the page with one hand and pulled a pack of cigarettes out of his shirt pocket with the other.

"I'll give it to Elsie to proofread first," June replied.

Philip lit a cigarette and inhaled deeply. "Dammit, June, just take it to the girls in typesetting, would you?" he asked, blowing out a cloud of smoke. "I don't want to deal with that bitch this afternoon. I've had a long enough day as it is."

June scanned the article. "There's only one 'N' in Munich," she noted. "And someone who speaks German should double-check the spelling on this clinic's name. It doesn't look right to me."

"I copied the name straight off the newswire," Philip said. "Don't you trust me?"

June offered him a weak smile. "Phil, nobody at *The Eyewitness* trusts you. The Editor-in-Chief doesn't even trust you. That's why he assigned me and Elsie to look after you."

"Bugger Elsie," Philip scoffed, searching through the clutter of papers on his desk for the tear sheet he had referenced. "Just look over my article and tell me if you see any obvious typos. And don't give me that crap about Roger Silvia not trusting me. He knows

*Randall's Scandals* is one of the paper's biggest draws."

June pushed aside a pile of folders and sat down on the edge of Philip's desk. As she read through the story, her eyes started to twinkle. "That's so nice of Eddie Rochester to help out his old friend. I wish he'd come out of retirement one of these days and put out another album."

"Gerry Enis needs all the help he can get," Philip snorted. "What is it with drummers, anyway? You'd think they would have learned from Keith Moon's example."

"Right, just like every guitar player learned from Jimi Hendrix's example, and every singer learned from Elvis," June said dismissively.

Philip rested his cigarette on an ash tray and smiled. "Just between you and me, Junie, I've heard rumors that Ringo might be checking into a clinic soon too. He's become quite the boozer."

June rolled her eyes. "Well, double-check your sources before you print that. *The Eyewitness* can't afford to have the Beatles' lawyers suing us for libel."

Philip cracked his knuckles and leaned back in his chair. "But that's what you're here for, isn't it, love? To help me with research and keep me out of trouble? Now I tell you what, after you hand this to typesetting, how 'bout you go down to the archives and find me a photo of Gerry Enis looking spectacularly pissed? I'm sure we must have a few dozen of them on file. And I'll talk to Roger about running the picture on the front page to punt my column."

"You'd be better off re-writing this piece and focusing on how Eddie Rochester checked Gerry into that clinic," June replied, handing the paper back to Philip. "And run a photo of Eddie on the front page. *That'll* sell some papers."

Philip let the page fall to his desktop and frowned. "Rochester hasn't put out a record since 1972! That bastard's been moping over his dead wife for sixteen fucking years! Who the hell wants to read about a boring old fart like him?"

June reached for a clean sheet of paper. "I would," she said, slipping the page into Philip's typewriter and hitting the return key twice. "And so would Elsie. And so would every other woman our age who grew up listening to *Dreaming Tonight* on the radio and wondering how it would feel to have a poet like Eddie Rochester write a song like that for her."

She took a few steps away from the desk and straightened out her skirt. "Rewrite your column, Phil, and concentrate on how Eddie's helping out his old bandmate. And while you're typing, I'll nip down to the archives and find a photo of Eddie looking all dark and brooding and handsome to run by Roger. *That* will sell some papers."

## Chapter Three

### *Millcote, Ohio*

Eddie eased his MG off the highway exit ramp and turned onto the state route that led into Millcote. The thunderstorm that had delayed his plane's landing had dissipated, but rain drops continued to sprinkle his windshield.

*Please God,* he prayed in his head, casting a quick glance at the grey clouds above him. *I'm too tired to drive in bad weather. A break in the rain would be much appreciated. How about sending me a little present, if you haven't forgotten what day this is?*

His favorite radio station broke for a commercial, so he switched the dial down to an oldies channel. His own voice starting serenading him from the speaker, crooning *Dreaming Tonight.* He shut off the radio and cursed in his head. *Jesus fucking Christ! Why did I ever release that goddamned record?*

He drove through the town of Millcote in a foul mood, and didn't notice that the rain had stopped until his wipers started squeaking as they brushed the dry windshield. He switched off the wipers and turned onto the country lane that led into Thornfield.

The road wound a serpentine path through a series of rolling hills. He took the curves slowly, then turned onto an unmarked driveway on the eastern edge of his property. Spying the gabled rooftop of his grandfather's old farmhouse in the distance, he put his foot to the accelerator and began to race home. A bright shaft of sunlight burst through the clouds and momentarily blinded him. He blinked only briefly, but when he opened his eyes, he saw a dark, hooded figure on a bicycle heading directly towards his car.

"Christ!" he yelled. He slammed his foot on the brake just as his car was passing over a slick patch of pavement. The MG started spiraling out of control. Thinking quickly, he turned the steering wheel into the direction of the spin, but he accidently pressed his foot against the accelerator and sent the car whirling off the side of the road and down an embankment. The back bumper slammed into an old oak tree. The impact sent Eddie's right hand crashing into the steering wheel. His left knee hit the bottom of the dashboard with a fierce blow.

"Fuck! Fuck! *Fuck!*" he bellowed. Spasms of pain radiated from his wrist. He took a few deep breaths to remind himself that he was still alive, then remembered the cyclist and checked the road for signs of carnage. Seeing nothing out the front windshield, he turned his head and looked out the driver's-side window.

A shapeless figure stood directly in front of him, peering down at him through the glass. Eddie flinched. He noticed an old, three-speed Huffy leaning against a tall maple tree and realized that his mysterious visitor was the cyclist, come to check on *him*. He took another quick breath to calm his shaken nerves and examined the stranger.

At first glance, he couldn't tell if the cyclist was male or female. A loose-fitting cloak enveloped the stranger's head and torso, and a pair of oversized, horn-rimmed spectacles covered much of the inscrutable face. A rogue shaft of sunlight broke through the clouds and shone brightly upon his unknown companion like a theatre spotlight. It reflected off the stranger's large glasses, creating the unearthly illusion of glowing, white eyes. Swallowing hard, Eddie brought his left hand to the door handle and pushed a button to lower the window.

"Are you all right, sir?" the hooded figure asked in a frightened, high-pitched voice.

*It's a girl,* Eddie realized. *She sounds young. And terrified. I should be nice to her.* But then his right wrist began throbbing again and the pain pushed aside his good intentions.

"Dammit!" he cursed. "What the hell were you doing up there? Don't you know which goddamned lane to ride your bike in?"

"Are you all right, sir?" the cyclist repeated. "Should I go look for help?"

Eddie hung his head in embarrassment and used his left hand to open the door. Hoping to dispatch the bug-eyed stranger quickly, he said, "No, I'm okay. Just let me check the damage." As soon as he attempted to stand, his left knee buckled. "Shit," he cursed again, shifting his weight to his right foot.

"I can ride home and make a call for you," the girl offered. "Do you think you might need an ambulance?"

"I said I'm okay!" he shouted. He edged his way around to the back of the MG, leaning heavily against the vehicle for support and struggling to keep his footing on the carpet of wet leaves. "Ah, Christ," he sighed as he examined the large dent in the fender. He looked back at the cyclist. "I'm fine! You can go now!"

"I can't leave until I know you're all right," she replied.

He shook his head. "You're as persistent as you are dangerous," he grumbled, feeling his way back around the car and into the driver's seat. Reminding himself to be nice to this well-meaning stranger, he addressed her with all the politeness he could summon. "It's not as bad as it could have been. I can drive home now. Just leave me alone."

The girl stood her ground and continued to watch him. Eddie ignored her as best as he could and turned the key in the ignition. The engine started, but when he tried to move the car forward, the back wheels spun wildly in a slick pile of leaves and mud. He killed the engine and hit his hands against the steering wheel in frustration, wincing again as his wrist slapped the hard surface.

"Would you like me to ride back home and call for a tow truck?" the girl asked. The fear he had previously detected in her voice seemed to have been replaced by a growing layer of impatience.

Eddie glowered at her. "Where do you live? I don't remember anyone who looks like you from these parts."

"I live right up the road, at Thornfield," she answered, pointing to the roof of the old farmhouse.

"Thornfield?" he exclaimed. "What the hell are you doing at Thornfield?"

"I'm the nanny," she replied.

*Oh, hell!* Eddie thought, overcome by another wave of humiliation. *So much for making a good first impression!* He examined the girl a little more carefully and noticed a lock of light brown hair escaping from the inside of her hood, curling up over her freckled cheek. She reached her hand up to her face and tucked it back behind her ear. As she moved her arm, Eddie noticed she had a sizable hole in the elbow of her jacket.

"I don't think I'm going to need a tow truck," he said, more gently this time. "I just need to get the tires out of the slick spot. You get in and steer. I'll push."

"What? You want me to drive your car?" the girl asked. Her eyes grew wide with trepidation. They were green, Eddie realized. A remarkably vibrant shade of green.

"Can you drive a stick?" he asked. Forcing himself to look away from her eyes, he glanced down at her sneakers and noticed that her shoelaces didn't match.

"No," she answered. "I don't have my license. Nobody ever taught me how to drive."

*Christ! What the hell kind of girl did Sally hire?* Eddie worried. He stared blankly at the frayed hems of the girl's jeans and realized that he ought to introduce himself, but felt too embarrassed to say anything personal, so he forced a laugh instead.

"Well, I guess it's about time you learned," he said. He started the engine again, adjusted the gear shift and hand brake, and stepped out of the car.

"I've put it into neutral. Now look at the pedals first before you get in. The left one is the clutch. The middle one is the brake. The right one is the accelerator. Got that?"

"Umm, yes—?" she answered.

"Point to them and show me," he replied. She correctly identified the three pedals.

"Good girl. Now get in the car," he said.

She climbed onto the seat.

"Put your right foot on the brake, then release the parking brake with your right hand," Eddie directed her.

"Huh?" she asked. "How many brakes does this car have?"

Eddie sighed. "Here, I'll do it," he offered. "Just keep your foot on the brake pedal. Don't worry. The car's not going to roll backwards over the tree." He leaned across the girl's lap and eased the parking brake to the floor. She squirmed noticeably as he rested his body against her legs. He immediately raised his torso.

"Now, keep your right foot on the brake, and put your left foot on the clutch. Push it all the way to the floor," he said. He glanced at her feet to make certain she was following his instructions.

"That's right. Now I'm putting it into first," he said, adjusting the gear shift. "Keep both of your feet where they are. Now when I tell you to drive, take your right foot off the brake and move it to the accelerator. Then very slowly, push the accelerator down to the ground while you lift your left foot off the clutch. Got that?"

She gripped the steering wheel tightly in her hands and threw him an exasperated look. "Seriously, sir? I just told you I can't drive, and you expect me to remember all that?"

Eddie held her gaze. *Well, all right then,* he realized as he locked eyes with her. *The girl's got some spunk.* He once again considered introducing himself, but his longing to extricate himself from the predicament overpowered his desire to be courteous. He offered her a sly smile, repeated his instructions more slowly, and added with a laugh that he hoped sounded friendly, "Try not to kill me." He limped back to the rear of the car, leaned against the trunk with the full strength of his left arm and supported the brunt of his weight on his right leg.

*This is not going to work,* he thought. But he nevertheless called out to the girl in an authoritative shout, "Now drive!"

The engine roared and the wheels spun furiously as she stepped on the accelerator, but then the vehicle stalled.

"Oops!" she called back to him. "I think your clutch is broken!"

Eddied returned to the driver's side window. "Get out," he grumbled, his voice hoarse with frustration. He edged himself back into the seat as soon as she climbed out.

"I'm going to try to rock the car out of this myself," he said without meeting her eyes. "If I can't manage, then you ride your bike back to Thornfield and get help. But let me try this first."

The girl stepped out of his way. Eddie started the car and began inching it forwards and backwards. The wheels spun wildly on his first attempts, but finally, in one great thrust, he succeeded in driving the car back onto the street. He stopped a couple of yards away from the girl and called out the window, "Go now!" Then he took off quickly around a bend in the road.

*Well, that went extraordinarily well,* he thought, berating himself for once again acting like a complete idiot in the presence of a female. But then he remembered the girl's exquisite green eyes and suddenly couldn't think of anything else. He drove the MG up to the security gate and stopped. Reaching for the remote control, he felt another spasm of pain in his right hand.

*Christ!* he cursed in his head, casting an angry glance at an emergent patch of bright blue sky. *What a way to celebrate turning forty-five! Thanks for the nice birthday present, God.*

## Chapter Four

Pancho barked and ran up to Eddie the moment he stepped into the old farmhouse.

"Hey there, girl," he said in a tired voice. He bent down to pet her and felt a spasm of pain in his left leg. "God, I'm getting old," he moaned. Clenching his teeth and clinging to the door frame for support, he performed a sloppy knee bend and allowed the dog to lick his face.

Alan Poole stood up and greeted him with a laugh. "Of course you're getting old, Eddie. That's what birthdays are all about."

Eddie reached out his left hand. "Help me up," he begged in a pitiful whisper.

Alan's eyes grew wide with shock as he noticed Eddie's mud-splattered clothes. "Jesus, what the hell happened to you?"

"I had a little accident on the drive up here," Eddie said. "I hit the brakes too fast on a wet patch of road, spun out of control, and went skidding into that old oak tree on the edge of the farm."

Alan offered Eddie a supportive hand. "You all right, mate?"

"Yes, I'll be fine," Eddie said. "But you'll need to take the car to the shop for me. There's a big dent in the back fender, and the boot'll probably need some bodywork."

"Looks like you could use some bodywork yourself," Alan joked as he watched Eddie limp to the sofa.

"Couldn't we all," Eddie replied. "Where is everyone?"

"Mum's in the kitchen, baking you a cake. I told her you wouldn't want one, but she insisted. Birdie's upstairs, having a lie-down."

"How's she been?"

"Fine. Bit of a cough, but it doesn't seem too serious."

"Good," Eddie said. He patted the couch with his good hand

and motioned for Pancho to sit beside him. She scrambled to the top of the cushion and rested her head on his lap.

Grace walked into the living room, wiping her hands on a tea towel and smiling at Eddie. "Welcome back! And Happy Birthd— dear Lord, boy, what did you do to yourself? You have mud all over your trousers. And on your jacket too."

Eddie offered Grace the same explanation he had given Alan.

"But how did your clothes get so dirty?" she asked.

"It's a long story," Eddie answered, looking away from her penetrating gaze.

Grace eyed him suspiciously and waited for him to elaborate. After a few seconds of awkward silence, she clucked her tongue. "Well, isn't that just the way things go? You travel halfway around the world safely, then get into a scrap a stone's throw from your own house! Now what hurts, son? Tell me the truth. Don't pretend that you're fine with me."

Eddie sighed. "My right wrist, and my left knee."

Grace shooed the dog off the couch and sat down beside Eddie to examine his injuries. "It's not broken," she said, turning his right hand gently with her own. "That bruise looks a bit angry, but there's no swelling."

"But it hurts," he groused.

She offered him a sympathetic smile and asked him to try stretching out his bad leg. He did so begrudgingly and allowed her to massage his kneecap.

"I'll fetch you some aspirin," she said, standing up from the couch. "I'll pull out some bandages too, though you should probably take a bath before I wrap you up. You look like you could use a good long soak."

"I will in a minute," Eddie replied. "Let me just sit for a bit. My mind's still reeling from the crash."

"How's Gerry?" Alan asked.

Eddie snorted. "As well as can be expected. He's not happy to be at the clinic, but he promised to keep his nose to the grindstone."

Grace threw a glance at the clock and turned towards her son. "Is this your day to collect Gisela from school?"

"Nah, I drove her yesterday," he replied. "It's Sally's turn."

Grace nodded and walked upstairs to fetch the pills and bandages.

"How's Gisela doing?" Eddie asked.

"Dunno," Alan answered. "I only see her on the days I take her to kindergarten. She'll sit in the back seat and talk to me like I'm her best friend in the world, but I can't make out a bloody word she says besides *danke* and *auf weidersehen*. I never did pick up much German those years we lived in Munich. Hope that nanny teaches her to speak English soon."

Eddie nodded. "How's the nanny working out, then?"

"Fine, I suppose," Alan said. "'Cept she can't drive."

"What else can you tell me about her?"

"Not much." Alan leaned forward and picked up the newspaper's entertainment section from the coffee table.

"You've met then, have you?" Eddie continued. "The nanny?"

"Yeah, I drove her here from the convent," Alan replied. He flipped through the paper and found the day's television listings. "You wanna watch a movie? *To Sir with Love* just started about fifteen minutes ago, but I think we both know how it begins."

"No, I don't want to watch the telly just now," Eddie answered impatiently. "She's fitting in nicely here? The nanny?"

"I wouldn't know. I never talk to her," Alan replied. He dropped the newspaper in his lap and gazed at Eddie with a puzzled expression. "When would I ever get the chance? She's over at the mansion, with Sally and Gerry's brat. I live here with Mum and Birdie. And never the twains shall meet. Isn't that right, mate?"

"Well, yes, I know that," Eddie agreed, repositioning his sore leg. "But I thought you might have seen her in passing, you know. Here and there?"

"Nah, not really," Alan said. "I'll walk through the mansion on the days I take the kid to school. But I never speak to the nanny."

"You drove her here from the convent," Eddie pointed out. "Didn't you talk to her then?"

"Just a little," Alan said. "I mean, I had to say hello to her, you know. Just to be polite. And she wanted to bring her bike along, so we had to puzzle out a way to get it here. I ended up shoving the damned thing into the back seat of the Beemer, and got some grease stains on the upholstery. But don't you worry. I took it to the shop the next day, and they cleaned up everything real nice."

"I'm not worried about the BMW!" Eddie exclaimed. "I'm worried about the nanny!"

Grace stepped back into the room and offered Eddie some

aspirin and a glass of water. "Take these," she said. "They'll help with the pain." She eyed him carefully while he swallowed his pills, then took back the glass. "Happy birthday, by the way."

"Don't remind me," Eddie said gruffly. He stared into space for a moment and wondered if the nanny's glasses had somehow distorted her eyes and made them look greener than they actually were. Then he blinked and stood up from the couch. "I suppose I should take that bath now," he said, grimacing as he placed his weight on his bad leg.

"Will you be having tea with us tonight?" Grace asked as Eddie headed towards the steps. "Or do you want to catch up with your young ward this evening?"

"I should eat with Gisela," he answered. "Just to make sure she's doing okay."

"And then you can chat up the nanny yourself," Alan pointed out with a smug smile.

Eddie hobbled to the stairs, looking at his feet and remembering the nanny's mismatched shoelaces and frayed jeans. He wondered if she was truly poor, or just had a bohemian sense of style. He reached his good hand towards the railing and flinched. Roberta was standing on the bottom step, looking at him.

A wave of guilt washed over him. *I shouldn't be thinking about the nanny*, he chided himself. *I should be happy to be home.*

"Hello, love," he said in a forced bright voice. "I'm back from Germany. Did you miss me?"

She held his eyes for a few seconds, then grunted.

*Why does she always look like she can read my mind?* he wondered. He tried to banish the nanny from his thoughts, but then an image of Inge's bouncing breasts flashed before his eyes.

Grace joined them at the foot of the stairs. "I'm glad you're up, lamb. But you were so quiet! I didn't hear you on the steps."

Roberta coughed and wiped her runny nose with the back of her sleeve. Eddie kissed her cheek, then stepped aside to let her pass. She brushed against his chest with her elbow cocked at a sharp angle and stepped off the bottom stair.

"I'll be down in a bit," he called to her. "I'm just going to soak in the bath for a while."

She offered no response and walked to the couch. Pancho climbed up beside her. "Ponsh," she murmured as she petted the dog's head. "Sweedockee."

Eddie sighed. *At least she's glad to see someone,* he thought. He gazed sadly at his wife for a few seconds more, then noticed Alan reaching for the remote and turning on the TV.

"Here we go," Alan said. *"To Sir with Love.* What d'ya think, Mum? You suppose Sidney Portier can hold off that teenage schoolgirl? Looks to me like he's met his match."

Eddie sighed and limped up the stairs.

## Chapter Five

Eddie stood outside the back door to the mansion and gritted his teeth. He'd spent the better part of the afternoon trying to think of the best way to introduce himself to the nanny after their awkward meeting, but had drawn no inspiration. *Enough already!* he decided at last. *This is my house and I'm her boss! I have every right to go inside and say whatever I damn well please!*

Pancho looked up at him with a pleading expression, then jumped against the door and started pawing at the wood. "All right, girl," he grumbled. "Let's go inside."

He turned the knob and let Pancho push her way into the home. She bounded into the spacious sitting room and found Gisela waiting a few feet away from the door.

"*Grüß Gott, Herr Rochester!*" Gisela exclaimed, ignoring the dog and running directly into Eddie's sore knee. "*Wie gehts mit meinem Papa?*"

Eddie grimaced. Before he could catch his breath, the nanny interrupted. "*Achtung, meine kleines. Herr Rochester hat heute schon einmal verletzt worden!*" she said, warning the child not to injure her guardian for a second time in one day.

Gisela whispered an apology and gazed up at Eddie with the same pitiful expression Gerry had used when Eddie left him behind at the clinic. Eddie leaned forward and kissed the child's forehead, wincing as he bent his left knee. He stole a glance at the nanny. She was looking away from him and petting the dog.

Gisela began peppering him with more questions about her father, but he ignored them and examined the nanny instead. Without her oversized coat she appeared quite small—almost waiflike. Her face was round and freckled, her nose rather broad. Light brown hair fell messily from her crooked part and grazed her shoulders. Thick-lensed, tortoise-shell glasses obscured her eyes and gave her profile a slightly lopsided appearance.

After a few seconds of awkward silence, she stood up and introduced herself. "Hi. I'm Jenny Ayr," she said.

He cleared his throat. "I'm Eddie Rochester."

"Yeah, I kind of figured that out," she said with a smirk.

Sally Fairfax barged into the room, shouting out a welcome. "You're here at last, Eddie! I saw your car in the driveway. What happened?"

Jenny looked down at her feet and started to blush. Eddie quickly surmised that she hadn't told anyone about their previous encounter.

"Nothing serious," he said. "I was taking a turn too fast on the wet pavement and skidded off the road. But I'm okay."

"Thank goodness for that," Sally said. "Will you be joining us for dinner?"

"Yes. I want to catch up with Gisela."

"I'll set another place at the table," she said. "Though I wish you would have called first to let me know you'd be coming. I would have grilled you up a steak. As it is, I've just put a tray of fish sticks into the oven to go with the macaroni and cheese."

"That sounds delightful," Eddie said. He looked back to Gisela and ruffled her hair. *"Dein Papa schickt seine Liebe. Es geht gut mit ihnem."*

Gisela smiled, relieved to hear that her father was missing her and doing well. She turned to Pancho and started petting her.

"I'll set the table, Mrs. F," Jenny said, making a quick escape.

Eddie watched her leave and sensed a heavy weight falling off his shoulders. *She doesn't sound angry with me,* he realized with a wave of relief. *Though she ought to be. I was pretty rude to her.*

He looked down at Gisela. *"Magst du deine Kinderfrau?"* he asked, hoping to hear a good report on his new employee.

"She is *sehr* nice," Gisela answered. "I have her much *gern.*"

Eddie smiled at the child's convoluted English, but stopped short of laughing.

*'Jenny,'* he mused as he limped towards his favorite leather chair. *Every young woman her age seems to be called 'Jenny.' She's just a common girl. Nothing to get excited about.* He sat down and waited to be called into the dining room for supper.

\*\*\*

Eddie closed the oversized book of animal photographs and congratulated Gisela for pronouncing each creature's name correctly. "Your English is coming along beautifully," he said. "I dare say, at this rate you'll be more articulate than your father by Christmastime."

Gisela scrunched up her brow. *"Ich verstehe nicht."*

Eddie chuckled. "It was a joke. *Ein Witz.*"

Gisela pouted, so he pouted back. She giggled. But then Eddie scooped her off his lap. *"Das war genügend Lesen für heute Abend. Gehst du jetzt schlafen."*

Gisela whined that she wanted to read one more story, but Jenny took her by the hand and guided her towards the stairs. "You heard Herr Rochester," she said. "It's bedtime."

*"Aber ich bin nicht müde!"* the girl protested.

*"Das macht nicht aus,"* Jenny replied. "Tired or no, it's bedtime."

Eddie called after them. "When you're done putting the child to bed, Miss Ayr, come back downstairs so we can talk."

Jenny nodded, but then Gisela tugged at Jenny's arm and whispered into her ear.

*"Ja, ich weiß, daß er nicht den sagte,"* Jenny replied.

"What do you know that I didn't say?" Eddie shouted.

Gisela turned to face him. "You did not say 'please'!"

Eddie rolled his eyes. *"Zum Bett!"* he barked. "Now!"

Gisela giggled and started running up the stairs. Jenny chased after her. Eddie looked down at Pancho, who was lying contentedly by his side on the floor.

"I don't say 'please' to you, girl," he grumbled.

Pancho scratched her ear with her hind leg and yawned.

Eddie started paging through the picture book while he waited for Jenny's return. He stretched out his sore leg on an ottoman and tried to make himself comfortable. A short time later, Jenny re-entered the room and took a seat on a chair by the steps.

"No, Miss Ayr," he said without looking up from the book. "Sit down where you were before. Pancho doesn't bite, and I usually don't either."

She got up from her seat and moved closer to him. He put down the book and smiled. "You're an obedient girl," he said.

"You're a cranky boss," she replied.

Eddie laughed. *She doesn't act at all like I assumed a convent school girl would behave,* he thought with relief.

"I'm sorry, Miss Ayr, but I'm not at my best. I'm tired from my flight and sore from the car crash and feeling rather old today."

"You don't look that old," she said.

"But I am. I feel like quite the old man today," he countered.

"What are you, like fifty or something?" she asked.

He glowered at her. "No, I'm forty-four. I mean, forty-five."

Jenny giggled. "I'm sorry. I guess I was wrong. If you can't even remember your own age, then maybe you are old."

Eddie cleared his throat. "And dare I ask how old you are, Miss Ayr?"

"I'm nineteen," she replied. "But I'll be twenty soon."

"How soon?"

"November twenty-second."

Eddie repositioned himself in his seat. "Ah, so you were born on the day Kennedy died."

"Actually, I was born on the fifth anniversary of his assassination," she corrected him. "So you can't ask me that question everyone your age always wants to know: 'Where were you when you heard that Kennedy had been killed'?"

"You make too many assumptions about people my age, Miss Ayr," Eddie retorted. "I've never asked anyone that question."

"Really?" Jenny scooted up to the edge of her seat. "Why not?"

"Because then I would have to admit that I don't remember where I was when I first heard about the murder." Eddie looked away from her and stared at his sore knee. "I was at university, and a delicious-looking girl by the name of Laura had just given me the brush, so I went on a bender and spent two weeks staggering around the campus in a state of complete inebriation. By the time I sobered up, the funeral was already over." He looked back at Jenny and smiled. "But then again, I was in England at the time, so perhaps I ought not to be held to the same patriotic standards as an American man of forty-four-or-forty-five."

Jenny giggled again. "I read in a book that you were half English and half American."

Eddie's smile vanished. "You read a book about me?"

"No, just a few paragraphs," she clarified. "I asked Mrs. F to take me to the library one afternoon while Gisela was in kindergarten, and I found a book about rock groups from the sixties. It had two pages about your band."

"Ah," Eddie said. "So you've been researching me."

"No," she insisted. "I just wanted to know who I was working for. I'd never heard of your band before I came here."

He laughed. "I suppose you're more into George Michael or Madonna."

She shrugged. "Well, I know a lot about Madonnas. There's a beautiful one hanging in the library at the convent."

Eddie rolled his eyes. "I meant the singer from Detroit. You know, *Like a Virgin*?"

"Madonnas are always virgins," Jenny replied. "Mary conceived Christ through the power of the Holy Spirit. Not by Joseph."

"Right," Eddie agreed. *I suppose she is a sheltered convent schoolgirl after all,* he realized. "So what did you learn about my band in that book you read?"

"That your group came from Manchester, England, and had a couple of big hits that I'd never heard of, and then you had a big solo album that I also never heard of. And then your singer Tony Wright had an even bigger hit song called *Your Face in the Morning,* which my old friend Eileen once said was the worst song ever written. But I've never heard your friend's recording. Just Eileen's version of it, and she changed the words a bit to be rude."

Eddie laughed. *I've never heard my life summarized quite like that before,* he thought. "Well, I agree with your old friend," he said, his eyes twinkling. "Tony's song was crap. So I guess you know everything there is to know about my musical career."

Jenny scooted off her chair, sat on the floor and started petting the dog. "I don't know why your band was called the Pilots."

"That was my idea," Eddie replied, repositioning himself more comfortably in his chair. "We went through a series of names at first, but then I noticed the 'Pilot' connection. My dad was a pilot, and he named me after Eddie Rickenbacker. Our lead singer Tony shares a surname with Orville and Wilbur Wright. Our pianist Jim shares *both* his names with James McCudden, one of England's most distinguished World War I flying aces. And Gerry's middle name is Albrecht, which also happens to be the middle name of Rittmeister Manfred Albrecht Freiherr von Richthofen."

"The Red Baron!" Jenny exclaimed.

"The one and only," Eddie laughed. "I don't think they're related. But then again, with Gerry, one can never be quite sure."

"He's Gisela's dad, right?"

Eddie nodded.

"Why didn't he teach his daughter to speak English?"

Eddie shrugged. "He speaks fluent German. He learned it from his maternal grandparents, who escaped to England during the Great War. Gisela was mostly raised by her mother and grandmother in Munich. Gerry was probably too drunk to notice that she only spoke *Deutsch* with him when he played with her."

"Will he be coming to get her anytime soon?"

"I don't know. He's spent the past twenty-five years cultivating his bad habits. I imagine it will take him at least a few months to kick them."

Jenny lowered her eyes and gazed at the dog. "Well, I'm sorry for Gisela's sake that he'll be gone for so long. But for my sake, I hope he doesn't hurry back. I like working here. Thornfield is so beautiful."

"It is, isn't it?" Eddie replied with a smile.

She looked up at him and smiled back. Eddie observed her more carefully and realized she wasn't as skinny as he first thought she was. She actually had rather nice breasts.

*Stop it!* he scolded himself. *Don't even think that!* He turned his face to the dog and redirected the conversation. "Sally told me you've been living at the boarding school she used to attend when she was a child."

Jenny nodded.

"You don't have a family?" he continued.

She looked back at the dog. "None that will claim me. Or that I want to claim."

Eddie waited briefly for her to elaborate, then nudged her on. "Dare I ask why?"

"My parents are dead. My aunt's a drunk, and my cousin John's a jerk," she said, shuffling her feet back and forth against the carpet. "He was always really mean to me. The nuns didn't think I'd be safe if I moved back home, so they kind of adopted me."

Eddie nodded. "So you consider the nuns your family now?"

She shrugged. "I suppose so."

"Do you miss them?"

"Sometimes," she said. "But Sister Claire told me to think of this job as a practice run for going away to college someday."

Eddie laughed. "I can't quite imagine how teaching a five-year-old to say her colors and numbers will prepare you for university life. College is a bit of an academic leap from kindergarten."

Jenny looked back at him and flashed a naughty smile. "There's more to university life than academics. You just told me you spent your college years wandering around in a drunken stupor, mooning over some girl named Laura who dumped you."

*"Touché,"* Eddie said, his eyes sparkling. "Though that was only for a fortnight. The rest of the time I was hitting the books religiously."

Jenny glanced over at a large bookshelf. "Yeah, I suppose you probably were. Or at least hitting the book stores. You sure do have a lot of books."

"I like to read," he said. He cast her an anxious look. "Do you?"

"I'm working my way through your Trollopes," she answered, then started to blush. "I mean, your Anthony Trollope novels. I'm a few chapters into *The Prime Minister* right now."

His face brightened. "Well, that sounds thoroughly academic to me, Miss Ayr. You're quite a clever girl."

"No, I'm not," Jenny said. "The only subject I'm any good at is art. I couldn't get accepted into any college worth attending."

"Don't be ridiculous, Miss Ayr," Eddie replied, pulling a face. "A girl who works her way through Trollopes in her spare time ought to have a leg up on the competition when applying to universities."

Jenny rolled her eyes. "Trust me. I'm not college material."

Eddie offered her a kind smile. "Maybe you should put down your Trollope and try reading some Jane Austen instead. Most girls seem to like her books."

"Is that a reading assignment?" she asked, eyeing him suspiciously.

"No, no!" Eddie insisted. "You're the English teacher. I'm just your cranky old boss. But I like talking about books, so maybe we could try reading the same novel and discussing it."

"Okay, Mr. Rochester," she agreed reluctantly. "As long as you don't make me write an essay on it."

"I promise," he replied. His voice softened. "Why don't you call me 'Eddie'? 'Mr. Rochester' sounds so formal."

She looked down at the floor and blushed again. "But you're so old. It would feel really weird calling you by your first name."

The words stung like a slap and completely dispelled his

flirtatious mood. He clenched the armrests of his chair in frustration. A fresh stab of pain coursed through his right wrist.

Jenny looked back up at him. "I'm sorry. That was kind of rude, wasn't it?"

"No, it wasn't," he replied in a sad voice. "I'm old enough to be your father. Don't ever be afraid to remind me of that."

She smiled shyly. "How 'bout I call you, 'Mr. R'?"

Eddie closed his eyes and remembered the time Birdie had called him that; so many years ago—back when she could talk. *It's just a coincidence,* he tried to convince himself. *Nothing more.*

Pancho looked up at him and yawned, then curled herself into a large ball by his feet.

"So why did you name your dog 'Poncho'?" Jenny asked. "Is it because she's so soft and warm?"

Eddie chuckled, relieved to change the conversation topic again. "No. She's Pancho with an 'a', not an 'o'. I named her after Pancho Barnes, the aviatrix who founded the Movie Stunt Pilots Union."

"So Pancho shares a name with a pilot!" Jenny giggled. "She could join your band if she learned to play the guitar."

"No, my band has long since broken up," he said. "No guitarists—human or canine—need apply. The Pilots have landed."

"That sounds pretty final," she remarked.

Eddie nodded and held her gaze. She stared back at him, then looked away self-consciously and brushed a stray lock of hair behind her ear. As she did so, Eddie noticed a small pimple on her cheek.

*She still has spots!* he realized. *She's just a kid! Why can't I stop looking at her?* He felt a sudden need to extricate himself from her presence.

"Give me your hand," he said, shifting his injured leg from the ottoman to the floor. "I need help getting up."

Jenny reached out her hand and took hold of his sprained wrist.

"Jesus, woman!" he cried out, the pain pushing aside the last remnants of his civility. "What is it with you? What part of my poor old body do you plan to injure next?"

"I'm sorry," she apologized. She took hold of his other hand and supported him while he stood.

As Eddie leaned on her, he felt a tingle rush through his body like an electric current. He gazed directly at her face, peering past her large glasses and staring into her vibrant green eyes.

"Thank you, Jenny," he said at length. He released her hand and started limping towards the staircase.

\* \* \*

He collapsed on top of his king-sized bed. Pancho jumped onto the mattress and lay down beside him. He considered shooing her away, but decided he needed company for the time being, and stroked the dog's long fur.

Jumbled memories of the past twenty-four hours raced through his mind. The long flight. The disconcerting accident. The half-hearted kiss he had given Birdie. The spark that coursed through his arm when Jenny held his hand.

*What is wrong with me?* he scolded himself. *Jenny is not my type. I only sleep with sluts. And she's so young. Young enough to be my daughter.*

He took a deep breath and tried to remember the names of the lovers he had taken over the past seven years. He drew a blank, so he tried to remember their faces instead. That didn't work much better—they all looked too much alike. And none of them had looked a thing like Jenny.

He clenched his fists in frustration. His right wrist began hurting again. The pain ran up his arm and into his heart, reminding him of how horrible he'd felt the first time he had cheated on Birdie. Until that otherwise unremarkable day seven years ago, when he finally succumbed to the easy charms of a dimwitted blonde and cast aside his marital vows, he hadn't realized he was the sort of man who was capable of leading a duplicitous life.

But the second time he cheated hadn't been nearly as hard. And the third time had been easier still. Eventually he'd been able to distance himself almost completely from his nagging conscience when he was in the company of a willing and beautiful woman in a far-off land, and lose himself in a delirious weekend of passion.

Yet he always came home to Birdie afterwards and resumed his place by her side—reading to her, caring for her, doting on her with all the love he still had in his heart.

*It just doesn't seem like my heart is capable of producing much love anymore,* he thought. *Not for Birdie. Not for the other people I care about. Not even for myself.*

A powerful wave of fatigue enveloped him. He closed his eyes and let his mind start drifting off. But then he heard a noise down the hallway and realized Jenny was walking into her bedroom. He opened his eyes and looked out the window at the old house across the lawn. He saw the shadow of a woman behind a curtain on the top floor. He drew in a deep breath and started kneading Pancho's long golden fur more roughly with his good hand.

"What the hell is happening to me?" he asked her.

Pancho turned her face towards him. She yawned widely, then rolled over to her side so he could pet her belly.

He gave her a few strokes, then rolled over and closed his eyes.

*She likes to read,* he thought as he started drifting off to sleep. *Jenny likes to read.*

## Chapter Six

"Well, it's about time you stopped by," Grace called out from the farmhouse kitchen.

Eddie ignored her remark and limped over to the couch where Roberta sat, curled up under her colorful crocheted afghan. "Hello, Birdie," he whispered, kissing the top of her head. She looked up at him briefly and sniffled, then turned her attention back to the television.

"*Wheel of Fortune?*" he said, throwing a cursory glance at the clock on the mantle. "I thought that didn't come on until seven."

"It's a tape," Alan said without looking away from the screen. "We just finished watching *The King and I,* and this was at the end of the cassette. It's funny, I must have seen this episode a half-dozen times, but I can't remember the puzzle."

Eddie examined the block letters and announced, "It's 'May-December Romance'."

"Oh, right," Alan agreed. "It's coming back to me now. She'll get it after she buys the 'E'." He turned to Eddie and smiled. "I must be too dazzled by Vanna White's gleaming teeth to think clearly."

"A pretty girl's smile will do that to you," Eddie laughed. He nestled up closer to Roberta and wrapped his arm around her shoulder. "How are you today, love?"

She looked back at him. Her eyes were puffy and moist, and the skin above her mouth was raw and red, as if she'd been wiping her nose excessively. She coughed to clear her throat, then turned her face back to the television screen. Eddie sighed.

"Could you help me in the kitchen, Eddie?" Grace called out. "I could use a hand chopping onions for tonight's pot roast."

Eddie curled his fingers around a tendril of his wife's grey-streaked hair, then hobbled out of the room and took a seat at the kitchen table. Grace placed a cutting board, knife and two onions in front of him. Eddie picked up the heavy knife with his sore right hand and sighed. "Maybe I should use my left hand to cut."

Grace rolled her eyes and pushed the board to the other side of the table. "Give me the knife. I'll chop," she said, taking a seat across from him. "I just wanted to talk to you in private for a bit." She peeled a layer of dried skin off the largest onion and picked up the knife. "So how do you like that governess Sally hired?"

"I like her very much," Eddie replied. "I think she's going to work out just fine."

"Good then," Grace said crisply. "So now you can stay here and help me and Alan with Birdie."

Eddie's face fell. "Right," he mumbled in agreement.

Grace noticed Eddie's slumping shoulders. Laying her knife on the cutting board, she reached across the table and gently touched his injured wrist. "So how's your hand feel today?"

"Better," he answered with a shrug. "I mean, I hadn't really noticed any pain until just now. It didn't seem to hurt very much this morning when I was talking to—" He let his voice trail off and turned his head towards the window that faced the mansion.

Grace sighed. "So, tell me about the nanny," she said, picking the knife back up and cutting through the onion.

Eddie's smile returned. "Her name is Jenny Ayr," he said. "She was born on an ashram in California. But her parents died when she was a baby, so her uncle collected her and brought her to live with him in a posh part of Cincinnati."

"Ooh, so she's an Ayr from Mount Airy?" Grace said in an affected, snooty voice. "How la-di-dah!"

Eddie scowled. "No. She was raised by her mother's family. The Reeds of Indian Hill."

Grace shrugged. "So she's rich, then."

"No," Eddie said. "Her uncle died in a car crash when she was six, and after that, the rest of the family treated her like a poor relation. Her aunt turned to drink and her cousin John started bullying her. So a friend of her uncle arranged for her to go to boarding school when she was eight."

"I hadn't realized there were boarding schools in America that catered to such small children," Grace said.

"Well, this school was pretty singular," Eddie agreed. "Jenny said most of the girls came from military families. But the nuns took in a few hard-luck cases like her too."

Grace finished chopping the second onion and walked to the refrigerator to pull out the meat. "I can't decide if I should use a dash of Tabasco sauce, or just stick with the Worcester. Are you in the mood for spicy?"

"Oh, don't plan around me," Eddie replied. "I'm eating supper with Gisela again tonight. Sally said she'd broil me up a steak, to make up for the fish fingers she served me yesterday."

"Did she now?" Grace replied, resting the raw meat on the counter and crossing her arms in front of her chest.

Eddie met her gaze with a defiant stare. "It's important that I spend some time with Gisela. She hasn't made any friends yet in kindergarten. I feel bad for her."

Grace clucked her tongue. "I see," she said, pulling a Dutch oven out of the cupboard. "You just want to spend some time with a lonely little girl. You haven't the slightest interest in spending time with a lonely little nanny."

"Don't be ridiculous," Eddie said. He looked out the window at the mansion again and stood up. "I'll sit with Birdie for a while first. Don't worry. I know where my responsibilities lie."

"Yes, you do that," Grace huffed. She scooped up the board full of chopped onions and carried it over to the stovetop.

Eddie glanced at the bookshelf in the hallway beside the kitchen. "Have you seen my *Annotated Austen* lately?" he asked. "It's a large, red book with a leather cover."

"What would I be doing with a book like that?" she retorted.

"Well, I usually keep it on the top shelf of this bookcase here," he said. "Oh, wait. I remember. I left it in Birdie's room. I was reading her *Mansfield Park* this past summer."

Grace offered him an apologetic smile. "I understand now. You want to read Birdie another one of Miss Austen's novels."

"Yes," Eddie agreed. "I thought I'd read her *Sense and Sensibility*. Girls like Jane Austen, you know." He went upstairs to find the book and left Grace to her dinner preparations.

### *Athens, Ohio*

John Reed dug his hands deeper into the pockets of his bomber jacket and walked past the abandoned gas station. Since his last arrest for selling pot on Ohio University's campus, he'd been using the deserted building as a rendezvous point to meet his clients. But today he made a point of not looking at the graffiti-laden plywood sheets that covered the broken windows, and stared at the sidewalk instead. He noticed an empty beer bottle wedged inside a deep crack in the pavement and kicked it out of his way towards a rusty gas pump.

A loud thumping of bass notes approached from behind. John turned and watched a blue Chrysler sedan pull up to the curb beside him.

"Hey there, Johnny!" shouted a young man in the passenger seat, his voice barely audible over the blare of the car's radio. "Whatcha got for me today?"

"Can't fuckin' hear you!" John shouted back. "Turn that damned thing down."

The driver twiddled the volume knob while the passenger leaned out the open window. "Party at Zeta Lambda this Saturday. We need your help with some refreshments."

"Prices have gone up," John replied. "Back-to-school sale's over."

"You're an asshole," the young man protested. "That pot you sold me last week wasn't worth shit. You gonna cut your weed like that, you better cut your prices too."

John stepped closer to the car. "Buy your pot someplace else then. I'm getting out of the business. I've found a more lucrative line of work."

The driver shut off the radio and turned towards John. "And what might that be, my dear Mr. Reed?"

John placed his hand on the roof of the car and leaned towards the open window. "Pharmaceuticals. Medicinal grade. They'll blow you away."

The two young men in the car exchanged glances and started laughing. "Sounds good," said the passenger. "Whatcha got?"

"I'm meeting my dealer now," John replied. "Come to my place tonight around seven. I'll show you then."

"Fuck, your dealer lives here?" the driver asked. "In this shit-hole part of town?"

John stepped away from the car and squared his shoulders. "Just temporarily. He needs to keep a low profile for a while, until some heat blows off him, if you know what I mean."

"Right," laughed the passenger. "Anything you say, Johnny boy. You go score your shit, while we send out some invites to Saturday's festivities. See you at seven."

The driver revved the engine and drove off like a bullet. John flinched at the shrill screech as the car peeled around a corner. Then he resumed his march across the littered sidewalk to the seedy motel where he had an appointment to meet Dick Mason.

# Chapter Seven

### *Millcote, Ohio*

*I've tried,* Eddie reassured himself. *I've sincerely tried.*

He'd spent the past three days at the old farmhouse, venturing back to the mansion only to have dinner with Gisela and read her a bedtime story. He'd lain beside Birdie while she was falling asleep each evening, then slipped into his own bedroom across the hallway to read, just as he'd done countless nights before. But the hollow feeling inside his gut just kept growing.

He tried to convince himself that it was Birdie's cold that had come between them. The cough medicine Grace was giving her was making her uncommonly sleepy. She'd shown little interest when he tried to read her *Sense and Sensibility*, and barely perked up when Alan slipped a Gene Kelly videotape into the VCR.

But now he sat in his brown leather chair in the sitting room of the mansion, still smiling from playing a silly game of Mousetrap with Jenny and Gisela after supper.

*Who could blame me for wanting to spend an evening in the company of people who make me laugh?* he thought. *Birdie's so tired, she probably won't even notice I'm gone.*

Jenny came down the staircase with a smile on her face.

"She's asleep," she said. "And you're still here."

"How could I tear myself away from such a sparkling conversationalist as yourself?" he asked.

She took a seat in the chair across from him and blushed. "I'm not much of a conversationalist," she demurred.

"But you are *sparkling*," he replied. "There's something on your cheek that keeps catching the light. It was driving me crazy the whole time we were building that damned mousetrap."

She put her hand to her face and wiped away a tiny square of silver foil. "Oh, this is just glitter. Gisela and I were working on an art project this afternoon when she got back from school. Some of the sparkles must have stuck to my skin."

Eddie sighed. "So my hopes are dashed. You're not a fairy."

"Don't be ridiculous, Mr. R," she scolded him.

"You know, when I first met you I thought you were a Jawa."

Jenny knitted her brow. "What's a Jawa?"

"You know, one of those creatures from *Star Wars*," he replied. "That big hooded jacket you were wearing looked like the robes that they wore. And the way the sun reflected off your glasses, your eyes seemed to be glowing."

Jenny continued to stare at him in complete bewilderment.

"You have seen *Star Wars*, haven't you?" he asked hesitantly.

She shook her head and lowered her gaze. "I haven't been to a movie theatre since I moved to the convent."

Eddie gaped at her in disbelief. "Not even when you used to go home for the holidays?"

"No, my aunt never brought me along when she took her own children. And I stopped going home after I turned twelve."

"You never left the convent grounds after you turned twelve?" he asked incredulously.

"Well, I used to go on long bike rides sometimes," she replied. "By myself, or with my friend Eileen."

He nodded in recognition. "The girl who wrote the parody of Tony's wretched single. What's she up to these days?"

Jenny lowered her voice to a whisper. "She's dead. She caught chicken pox, and this stupid old doctor who looked after everyone at the convent told the nuns to give her aspirin to break her fever. So she got something called Reyes Syndrome and died."

"Oh," Eddie mumbled. "I'm so sorry." *God, she's suffered so many blows, but still seems cheerful most of the time,* he marveled. *Why do I keep feeling sorry for myself?*

Jenny looked back up at him. "You would have liked her. You remind me of her even. She read a lot. And she used a bunch of ridiculously big words too, just like you do."

"I don't use ridiculously big words," he protested.

"You called Gisela 'obstreperous' today at dinner time."

"That was the proper word to describe her. The child simply wouldn't shut up!" Eddie exclaimed. He noticed Jenny was making a face at him. "I was just being 'waggish'," he apologized.

"You were just being 'supercilious'," she replied, then broke into another smile. "But that's okay. Gisela couldn't understand you."

Eddie scooted to the edge of his seat and returned her smile. "So what have you been up to these past few days? I wasn't able to speak to you properly over dinner with Gisela chattering on."

"I rode my bike to the library while she was at school, to see if I could learn anything more about you."

Eddie folded his arms and leaned back in his chair. "Any luck?"

She shook her head. "Not really. It's a pretty small library. I think you have more books on your shelves here at Thornfield. But I did find an article about Gisela's father in a copy of *People*."

"Really?" Eddie said. "How big of a spread?"

"Just one page. It talked about how he was in rehab now, and mentioned some of his drunken exploits from the past. And it ran this funny picture of him wearing a kilt and posing with a monkey and toucan. That was very strange."

Eddie laughed. "That was from an advert he did last year for a tropical wine cooler. I think the ad agency was aiming for 'delightfully unexpected,' but you're right, it just looked strange."

"The article also mentioned how you helped him check into the hospital. It ran a picture of you too."

Eddie winced. "A recent shot?"

"No. It was you at your wedding, standing outside the church with your wife." Her eyes sparkled. "I recognized the building. You were married at *San Miniato al Monte* in Florence."

Memories began flooding Eddie's mind. The heaving crowd of photographers gathered outside the church. The security guards shouting in Italian as they tried to clear a path to the waiting limo. Birdie clinging to his arm so tightly she left bruises on his skin.

"I wrote a report on him once," Jenny said, breaking his reverie.

He tried to focus his attention back on the conversation. "A report on whom?"

"*San Miniato al Monte*," she replied. "He's one of my favorite saints. Do you know his story?"

Eddie shook his head.

"He was an early Christian martyr," she said. "The Roman Emperor threw him to the wild beasts in an amphitheater outside Florence, but the animals refused to eat him, so the soldiers beheaded him. But then San Miniato scooped up his head and carried it across the Arno and up the hillside. The church you were married at was built over his grave."

Eddie's eyes widened. "He carried his own head up the hill?"

"Yeah. It was his first miracle."

"I see," he said, swallowing back a laugh. "I never knew that."

"I've seen pictures of the inside of the church," she continued. "There's a golden mosaic over the altar, with Christ in the middle, and Mary and San Miniato standing on either side of him."

Eddie closed his eyes. "I remember," he said in a soft voice. "Though I thought the bloke to the right of Jesus was holding a crown, not a head."

"Well, you know artists. Always using ambiguous symbols in their work."

Eddie opened his eyes and chuckled. "Right. So you've taught me something new today."

Jenny smiled. "There's something else I wanted to tell you. On my way home, I rode my bike down this old path on the edge of the farm and saw what looked like a crop circle. I thought you might want to check it out."

"Are you serious?" Eddie asked, his cheerful mood immediately dissolving. "A crop circle? On my land?"

"Well, it looked like one to me. I wrote a report on them once too. I think a flying saucer must have landed in your cornfield."

Eddie scowled. "You are joking, aren't you?"

"Yes," Jenny laughed. "Crop circles aren't caused by aliens, they're caused by sudden bursts of electricity in the atmosphere. Or something like that. I've forgotten what I wrote in my report."

"They are caused by pranksters who want to draw attention to themselves," Eddie said, standing up from his chair. "The neighbor's kids must have made that. Jesus Christ, I do not need a swarm of reporters descending upon Thornfield!" He started walking towards the back door.

"I'm sorry, I didn't mean to upset you," she said. "If you'd like, I can show you where I saw it tomorrow while Gisela's at school."

Eddie took a deep breath and ran his hand through his hair. "Yes, I would appreciate that." He glanced at the back door, then turned and faced her again. "I'll drive you."

"The path I took wasn't very wide. And the pavement was all torn up and crumbly. Do you have a bike you could ride instead?"

He closed his eyes and remembered the pair of bikes he had purchased when he first moved to Thornfield. Birdie had balked at riding hers, so he'd covered them both up with a tarp and left them in the corner of his garage. *I'll need to dust off the cobwebs,* he thought. *And oil the chain and tighten the gears and pump some air into the tires. Maybe even scrape some rust off the frame.*

He opened his eyes. "Yes, but I'll have to work on it a bit first. I'll sleep here tonight so I can get up early tomorrow morning without waking the Pooles and start getting it back into shape."

"That'll be great!" she exclaimed. "It will be so much fun to have someone to go bike-riding with again."

He noticed another rogue square of glitter sparkling on her forehead. He couldn't stop staring at it. "Yes," he agreed. "It will."

\* \* \*

"He's cheating on you, you know he is."

Roberta put her hands to her ears and tried to block out her brother's voice.

"Who could blame him? You're so fat now!" Dick's voice continued, rising in pitch until it sounded like a sneer. "You can't even fucking talk to him anymore about your precious poetry!"

*Stop it,* she told the voice in her head. *Go away.*

"He's a bastard. Always has been," the voice taunted. "Too bad you missed your chance to slice his balls off. But you couldn't even hold onto that goddamned knife I gave you."

Her heart beat faster. *I said go away!* she pleaded.

The harangue in her head refused to let up. "You know why he didn't come to bed with you last night. He found out what you did to Mom and Dad. I didn't even have to tell him. He read your old diaries. He knows what kind of person you really are."

A moan escaped from her lips.

*"Meurtrière!"* shouted the voice of her Uncle Jean. *"Tu as tué ma sœur!"* His face flashed before her. His eyes were filled with hatred. The veins on his neck were bulging. "You killed her!"

"No!" Roberta shouted. "Noooo!"

Grace threw open the bedroom door. "What's wrong, lamb? Were you having a nightmare?"

Roberta looked up at Grace's face and started panting. Grace's white hair glowed like a halo in the bright morning sunshine flooding through the window. Her eyes were calm and reassuring.

*It wasn't a dream!* Roberta wanted to say. *They were here! I heard them!* She struggled to form words, then broke down crying. "Dik," she whimpered between sobs. "Dikenzhonwherheeer."

"Were you dreaming about your brother Dick?" Grace asked.

Roberta buried her face in her hands and continued to weep until a fit of coughing overcame her.

Grace sat down on the edge of the bed and stroked Roberta's long hair. "Let's get you dressed, lamb. It's so late. You've slept through breakfast. I'm going to call Dr. Bob today and see if he can stop by to look you over. That cough medicine I'm giving you doesn't seem to be helping much."

She took Roberta's hand and helped her sit up. Roberta sniffled and turned her head towards her nightstand. "Klux."

Grace looked at the empty Kleenex box on the bedside table. "You've used up all your tissues, love. Come with me to the toilet. I'll help you freshen up." She helped Roberta stand and started leading her out of the bedroom.

Roberta coughed a few more times and stopped walking for a moment to catch her breath. A bright ray of sunlight shone through the window pane onto her face, forcing her to blink. She reached out her hand to pull back the curtain and saw Eddie standing by the garage. She looked down and watched him. He was pumping air into the tire of a bicycle.

\* \* \*

"Bugger," Eddie cursed under his breath as he stepped into the large crop circle. "Damn those Pembauer boys."

"Who are the Pembauer boys?" Jenny asked.

"Two college-age kids who live on the neighbor's farm. They probably bribed a group of their friends with a couple of six-packs to slip over here one night and help them make this."

"I don't know," Jenny said. "Look at that swirling pattern the stalks form as they twist into the center. It's so elaborate. A group of drunken boys couldn't have made such a perfect spiral."

Eddie examined the coil. "You have a point," he said, a sense of frustration creeping into his voice. "Tell me what you learned about crop circles when you wrote your paper."

"I don't remember much," Jenny admitted. "Just something

about electrical storms forming tiny tornadoes that flatten the crops."

"Hmm," Eddie mumbled. "There used to be an old barn near here when I was a little. My grandpa stored his tractors in it. A twister took it down about twenty years ago."

"Is that why there was a road leading up here?"

"Yes, but nobody's driven on it since the barn came down, so I've never bothered to repave or repair it. Maybe there's something about this patch of land that calls down twisters."

Jenny walked to the middle of the flattened circle of corn stalks. "Do you think if I spin fast enough, I can summon another tornado and make the circle bigger?"

Eddie rolled his eyes and offered no reply. He squatted down to inspect the broken stalks on the perimeter of the circle.

"What are you looking for?" she called to him.

"Signs of fungus. Some types of mushrooms grow in circular patterns. I'm wondering if they might have killed the corn."

Jenny flung out her arms and started twirling in a circle. "I'm in a fairy ring!" she giggled.

Eddie looked away from the clump of corn he'd been examining and watched her spin. With each rotation she made, his fears that the crop circle would call down an invasion of paparazzi receded further, replaced by the simple joy of watching her. *When was the last time I was just spontaneously silly like that?* he asked himself. He walked to the center of the circle to join her.

Jenny stopped spinning and smiled at him. "That was a stupid thing to do. Now I feel dizzy!"

Eddie smiled back at her. "You're giving me a flashback to a time when Gerry stumbled upon a fairy ring in a field in Yorkshire. He started twirling around inside it too."

"Really? You're having a flashback? Does that mean—?"

He hesitated a moment before answering her question. "Canny observation. Gerry was in fact tripping on acid on that particular day, but I was not. I should choose my words more carefully."

Jenny grew serious. "Did you use to take drugs, Mr. R?"

Eddie laughed. "Of course I did! It was part of my job description!" But then he noticed her sad expression. *Her parents were hippies who died on an ashram,* he remembered. *Drugs aren't a joke to her.*

"I smoked pot and took prellies," he confessed, meeting her

157

eyes. "But mostly I just drank. I dropped acid a few times, but it scared the hell out of me. After that I shied away from parties."

Jenny nodded. "But Gisela's dad took a lot of drugs, didn't he?"

Eddie sighed. "Oh yes. He could write a book. Though I suspect it would be rather incoherent."

Jenny fell quiet and started walking to the edge of the circle.

Eddie watched her in silence for a few moments before venturing a question. "Is something wrong?"

She turned back to him. "I was just thinking about my parents. When Uncle Henry flew to California to collect my mother's body, he didn't wait around for the coroner's report to see what drugs were in her system. He just wanted to get me out of the ashram so I'd be safe. He told me the guru gave him the creeps."

"Some of the people who claimed to be enlightened back in the sixties were just stoned out of their minds," Eddie said in a sympathetic voice. "It wasn't all just groovy peace and love."

Jenny nodded. She sat down on top of a row of fallen stalks.

Eddie walked to the edge of the circle and sat down beside her. "Did your dad die from a drug overdose too?"

"Yeah, on the same day as my mom. My uncle suspected they shared some tainted drugs. And that's all I know about my father. That and his name—Cory Ayr."

"And your mother's name was—?"

"Charlotte. And my real name is Sajani. But my uncle thought kids in Ohio would tease me, so he nicknamed me 'Jenny'."

Eddie smiled. "Sajani's a beautiful name. It's Hindu for—"

"Beloved. Yeah, I know."

"Well, that's one more thing you know about your parents," Eddie said, resting a hand on her knee. "They loved you."

"Hmm," she replied with a sad laugh. "I suppose so."

"Accidents happen," Eddie added, squeezing her knee in a gentle grasp. "My manager died from taking too many sleeping pills one night when he was drunk. It's ironic. His brother Alan was a heroin addict, but he survived. I imagine Emmett's death probably inspired him to stay clean."

Jenny nodded. "Mrs. F told me you invited your manager's mother and brother to live on your farm with you after he died."

"That's right," Eddie agreed.

"I don't see much of them," she continued. "They hardly ever seem to leave their house."

Eddie took his hand off her leg and considered his response. "They're a quiet lot," he offered at length. "They like to keep to themselves."

An awkward silence fell between them. Eddie re-examined the spiral of broken cornstalks and wondered how it had formed—and how long it would take his estate manager to clear the field.

"I read in that issue of *People* that you've been living on this farm ever since your wife died," Jenny said softly.

Eddie's shoulders stiffened. The hairs on the back of his neck stood up. *I should tell her,* he realized. *There's no reason for me to hide the truth from her. And she's just confided in me.*

He turned to face her. Her expression was kind. Her eyes were full of sympathy. Her lips looked wonderfully soft.

"Since she overdosed," Eddie whispered, turning his face away.

He let a few quiet moments pass, then stood up and offered her his hand. "Let's go. Gisela should be back from school soon."

Jenny took his hand and let him pull her up. A spark coursed through Eddie's fingers at her touch. She smiled at him.

"Maybe there is some weird kind of electrical current in this part of your farm," she said. "It's so staticky. Did you feel that charge?"

## Chapter Eight

"That's a good girl, keep your eyes open and look down," Bob Carter directed his patient.

Roberta groaned in protest as the doctor shone the light into her pupils, but followed his instructions.

He switched off his pen-sized flashlight and rested it on the table beside her, then brought his fingertips to her neck and gently examined her glands.

"Everything looks normal," he said, taking a step backwards. "You've just caught a bug. But you're still awfully congested."

Roberta grumbled a nonsensical reply.

Bob pulled a prescription pad and pen from his jacket pocket. "I'm going to give you something for your cold that shouldn't interfere with your neuroleptics. It should make you feel a bit more alert. But if your mind starts playing tricks on you, I need you to tell someone right away—the moment the hallucinations start. What sign can you give us, Birdie?"

She stared at him blankly.

"Come on, Birdie. I know you understand me," he said. "Think for a minute. What can you do to let us know things are starting to go wrong?"

She turned her face towards the table, picked up the penlight and switched it on and off.

"Brilliant," Eddie said, squeezing Roberta's free hand. "Just shine a bright light at us if you see or hear anything that makes you feel uncomfortable."

Roberta acknowledged his remark with a weak smile.

Bob took the penlight from her and slipped it back into his pocket. "You know, Birdie, you are my favorite patient. I realize you can't speak, but you always find a way to express yourself."

Eddie kissed the top of her head, then handed the prescription to Alan. "Could you drive into town for me and pick this up?"

"Sure," Alan said, glancing at his watch. "It's my day to fetch the imp at school anyway."

"Thanks for dropping by, Dr. Bob," Grace said. "Would you like a cup of coffee before you drive home?"

"How 'bout we step outside for a smoke instead?" Eddie suggested. "Alan, can I bum some fags?"

Alan laughed and tossed him a pack of Camels. "I thought you gave up smoking five years ago."

"Just this once," Eddie insisted. "I need your lighter too."

Roberta grunted her disapproval. Eddie kissed her forehead once more before he left the room. "I'll just be a minute, love," he promised as he followed Alan and Bob out of the farmhouse.

Eddie hit the packet against his hand and extricated a cigarette. He lit it, then offered Bob the Camels and lighter.

"I feel like we're thirteen again, sneaking outside for a smoke while your grandma isn't looking," Bob said with a smile.

"Well, I'm feeling a lot younger these days," Eddie replied.

"Don't smoke 'em all!" Alan called from the open car window as he pulled out of the driveway. "They're my one remaining vice!"

Bob waved to him and lit his cigarette.

Eddie took a long drag, then exhaled slowly as he leaned against the porch. "I wanted to ask your professional opinion on a matter that's been bothering me."

Bob puffed on his cigarette. "Ask away."

"It's about the nanny I hired to watch Gerry's daughter."

"Grace was telling me about her," Bob said. "She said the girl's been living in a convent ever since her boarding school closed."

"Right," Eddie said. "She confessed to me last night that she hasn't earned her high school diploma yet. The nuns have been trying to tutor her, but she seems to have a hard time concentrating on her assignments. For instance, she was supposed to write a report on agriculture in Indiana, but zeroed in on a photo of a crop circle in her text book and wrote about that instead. Same thing with her art history report on Romanesque architecture. She ended up researching this weird headless saint they named a church after in Florence and did a paper on him."

"*San Miniato al Monte,* perchance?" Bob asked.

Eddie cocked his eyebrow. "You've heard of him?"

Bob laughed, exhaling a pale cloud of smoke. "He's the patron saint of that church you were married at, you idiot! Anne and I visited *San Miniato's* when we went to Italy last year and learned all about him. Didn't you read the literature in the vestibule?"

Eddie scowled. "I had other things on my mind that day."

Bob laughed again. He took a slow drag on his Camel. "So—you hired a girl with a learning disability to teach Gerry's kid English."

"She doesn't have a learning disability!" Eddie protested. "She's just, I don't know, a little unfocused. And I want to help her. She had a shite childhood. Her parents died of drug overdoses when she was a baby. She had a kind uncle who took her in, but then he died in a car crash, and she was left to the clutches of an alcoholic auntie. Her best friend at the convent died a few years back too."

"Rotten luck," Bob said. He puffed on his cigarette again before offering a reply. "There could be any number of reasons why she can't focus on her studies. She might be depressed. She might have cognitive problems from being exposed to drugs as a baby. Or she might just not give a damn about Romanesque architecture or Indiana agriculture. I can't diagnose a person I've never met."

Eddie took a long drag on his cigarette and stared at the mansion across the lawn. "Yes, I realize that. I'm just worried. The more I get to know her, the more I care about what happens to her. I want her to be able to leave the convent and go to college. Have a real future. I want to help her somehow."

"That's kind of you," Bob noted.

Eddie hung his head low. "Maybe. I don't know."

Bob observed his friend carefully for several seconds before speaking again. "How old is she?"

"Nineteen. Nearly twenty."

"Has she ever had a boyfriend?"

Eddie smirked. "She's been living in a fuckin' convent!"

Bob dropped his cigarette in the dirt and ground it out with the toe of his shoe. "I could recommend some school psychologists who might be able to help her, though she's old enough to decide for herself if she wants to seek their services. She's too old to enroll in to a regular high school. You might want to buy her some study guides so she could practice for the GED exam."

Eddie took a last drag on his cigarette and dropped it to his feet. "What's that?"

"It's a high school equivalency diploma. If she earns a GED, she could go to almost any college. And I don't think there are too many questions on the test about medieval architecture or subspecies of hybrid corn."

Eddie smiled. "That's a great idea, Bob. I'll get her some books and help her study."

Bob threw him a look of warning as he walked to his car. "Fine, Eddie. But be careful. You just want to help her graduate. Not take her to the prom."

\* \* \*

"C'mon, Mr. R!" Jenny exclaimed. "Anyone can twist!"

Eddie dug his hands deeper into the pockets of his trousers and leaned against a bookcase in his spacious library, watching Jenny gyrate to the music.

"You're not listening to the singer!" she shouted as she twisted her arms back and forth in front of her chest. "He's telling you to 'do the twist'!"

"I have extraordinarily deep wells of self-restraint," he replied as the song came to an end. He walked to the record player and picked up the tonearm just as the stylus was slipping into the final large groove. "Though I must compliment you on your twisting technique. Wherever did you learn that 'funky chicken' style?"

"From watching *The Uncle Al Show* on TV," she replied, panting as she caught her breath. "He used to play *The Twist* sometimes before Captain Windy handed out the marshmallow cones, and all the children would dance along."

"Good Lord, we have something in common!" Eddie laughed. "I remember watching *The Uncle Al Show* when I was a small boy living my grandparents. That show is a Cincinnati institution! Tell me, did he play *The Twist* on his accordion?"

"No, he played a recording. But I think it was a different version than the one you just played for me."

"Hank Ballard's original is much better than Chubby Checker's cover," Eddie said. He pulled another single from his stack of 45's. "And speaking of covers, let me play you the original *Hound Dog*. Elvis' version doesn't even compare."

He placed the record on the turntable. Jenny's eyes lit up the moment the singer opened the song with a drawn-out, raunchy 'yooou'. Eddie laughed and swayed as he mimed the guitar lick.

A knock on the door interrupted them.

"You have a visitor, Eddie," Sally yelled into the room. Eddie looked up and smiled at his old bandmate Jim.

"Big Mama Thornton!" Jim shouted. "Damn, that woman could sing like nobody's business!"

Eddie lifted the tonearm and switched off the turntable. "It's great to see you Jim, but what the hell are you doing here?"

"I wanted to glimpse your crop circle before the teeming masses arrived," he replied. "Alan told me all about it."

Eddie walked over to Jim and gave him a brief hug. "Let me introduce you to Jenny. She's the nanny I hired to watch Gisela. Jenny, this is Jim McCudden, my old songwriting partner."

"I'm not that old," Jim said, offering Jenny his hand.

She hunched her shoulders and shook his hand shyly. "Hi."

"Jenny, why don't you come with me to pick up Gisela at kindergarten?" Sally suggested. "We'll let these two catch up."

"Okay. It was nice to meet you, Mr. McCudden," Jenny said as she slipped out of the room.

Jim watched her leave. "She's a quiet one," he noted.

"Not once you get to know her," Eddie replied, his eyes lingering on the door. He took a deep breath, then turned to face Jim. "So seriously, what brings you here? Why didn't you call?"

"I did call," Jim said. "Twice. Alan told me you're spending all your time at the mansion these days, ignoring the folk in the farmhouse whilst you tutor your new governess in the principles of elementary biology."

Eddie glowered at him. "I'm helping her with geometry."

"What, no chemistry?" Jim replied. "Pity, she's kind of cute."

"There is nothing going on between us," Eddie insisted, his voice growing testy.

"I should hope not," Jim said. "How old is she, anyway?"

"She's nearly twenty," Eddie answered.

"Ah, here I thought she was just seventeen," Jim said, pulling a face. "And you know what I mean."

Eddie took a deep breath and exhaled slowly. "I said there is nothing going on between us. I am simply helping her prepare for her high school equivalency exam."

"What, they have questions about Leiber and Stoller songs on the test?" Jim laughed.

Eddie sighed and collapsed on a sofa in the corner of the room. "No. I was playing Q102 on the radio as I was quizzing her on isosceles triangles, because I want her to become familiar with contemporary pop music," he explained. "It's important. When she goes off to college, she'll need to fit in with her peers. But she started asking me what music I listened to when I was her age, and the next thing you know, I was playing her my old records."

Jim took a seat in a chair across from Eddie and smiled. "Some girls will do anything to get out of studying maths."

Eddie rolled his eyes. "Well, the funny thing is, even though she didn't recognize the new hits on the Top 40 radio, she knew the words to a lot of the old songs. When she was little, she had a housekeeper who listened to R&B classics when she cleaned, and Jenny used to dance along to them while she helped her."

"Maybe she's an old soul," Jim suggested, his eyes twinkling.

"Perhaps. She likes the same music as I do, anyway."

"And how does she feel about Victorian literature?" Jim teased.

Eddie smiled. "She prefers Dickens to Trollope, though Lewis Carroll is her real favorite. She would rather read novels than poetry, but she harbors a soft spot for 'The Bells' and 'Annabelle Lee,' because her best friend used to like Poe."

Jim cleared his throat. "I see. So you've quizzed her on the most important topic, and she has passed the test with flying colors."

Eddie shrugged and looked down at the rug. "Right now we're both reading *Sense and Sensibility* so we can discuss it together. Though of course Jane Austen pre-dates the Victorian era."

"You wouldn't happen to be pre-dating this chick, would you?"

"Of course not!" Eddie insisted, his lighthearted mood instantly falling away. "She's young enough to be my daughter. I am quite aware of that, you needn't remind me." He fell silent for a few moments before continuing in a sadder voice. "It's just nice to have a person to talk to, who has similar interests as me. That's all. She's nothing like the tarts I shag when I'm on holiday."

"Good," Jim said. He stood up from his chair and walked to the piano in the opposite corner of the room. "And now that I'm done interrogating you, I'll answer your original question. I'm doing some session work in Nashville later this week, and thought I'd drop by Cincinnati first to see you. I left two messages with Alan and Grace yesterday. But apparently you haven't been visiting them much lately. Not even to take Pancho for her walkies."

Eddie ignored the rebuke. "Nashville? That's a bit of a change."

Jim cracked his knuckles and lifted the cover from the keys. "I've developed a new affection for country music. It hasn't embraced synthesizers the way that that rock music has. Rosamond Oliver has asked me to play piano on her new record."

"Ever the purist," Eddie laughed. "The honkytonk beckons."

Jim smiled. "Pull out your guitar. You have all the makings of a great country song right here that's just begging to be written. You have your farm. Your faithful dog. Your little girl whose daddy is drunk and asleep at the bar. You've even got a love triangle."

"I am not in a love triangle," Eddie protested.

Jim ignored him. "All you're missing is a broken truck. Though Alan told me you smashed up your MG the moment you set eyes on Jenny. Maybe we can write that into the lyric somehow." He set his fingers to the keys and started pounding.

## Chapter Nine

*"Ein Pferd!"* Gisela squealed in delight. She raced past two cow pens and nearly crashed into the horse stall. Jenny ran after her and quickly grabbed her hand.

Eddie watched them from the front of the barn. "I hope you don't mind the company," he told his estate manager Ron Hayworth. "The child wanted to see some animals, so I thought she might have a look while we spoke about that crop circle."

Ron cast Gisela an indulgent smile. "She's a cutie. I'm guessing she looks more like her mother than Gerry."

"I can see a bit of both of them in her face," Eddie said.

"Oh, you knew her mother?" Ron asked.

Eddie cleared his throat. "Yes. Now about that crop circle—"

"It's a big one," Ron said. "Very intricate pattern woven into the spiral. Almost hate to plow it over."

"I don't want any reporters coming round to see it."

"I understand. I'll get rid of it," Ron promised. "But there's this professor at Purdue who wants to drive out and study it first."

"A professor!" Eddie barked. "How in hell did he hear about it?"

"I told him," Ron confessed. "Or rather, my daughter did. Angie happened to call home the day you told me about the circle, and I mentioned it to her. She said her horticulture teacher was always going on about them. Apparently, he's some sort of expert. So she told him, and he called me and begged me not to plow over it until he checked it out. We made an appointment for him to stop by next week. But don't worry. He promised to be discreet."

"All right," Eddie sighed. He looked back at Jenny and watched her guide Gisela's hand over the horse's long nose.

Jenny turned and noticed the men were looking at them.

"Could Gisela feed a carrot to the horse?" she asked Ron.

"He prefers apples," Ron answered. "I can fetch you a few. But first, get a load of these little angels!" He directed their attention to a ewe and her three newborn lambs in a stall at the opposite corner of the barn.

Gisela bounded over to the sheep, crying, "*Lämmchen!*"

"Can she pet them?" Jenny asked.

Ron shook his head. "Not yet, they're too little. But come back in a week and I'll let her. Would she like to see the chickens now?"

Jenny nodded and took Gisela's hand. They followed Ron and Eddie out of the barn.

"Make sure you tell me what that professor says about the crop circle," Eddie said as they stepped into the chicken coop. "If he thinks it was just a prank, we might need to install a better surveillance system around the edge of the farm."

"But that would only stop unwanted visitors from coming in by land," Ron protested. "It might have been space aliens who created the pattern, and they fly down from the sky." He walked over to Gisela and picked up a downy, yellow chick. "Let me show you how to hold this little critter."

Eddie lingered by the gate and watched Jenny scoop up a tawny chick. She smiled in childlike delight as she rubbed it against her cheek. Soft rays of afternoon sunlight poked through the autumn leaves on the trees just outside the fence and shone upon her light brown hair, lending it an almost golden radiance.

Jenny looked up at him.

*Damn,* Eddie cursed in his head. *She caught me staring again. I have to stop doing that!* He cleared his throat and walked over to Ron. "Think you could put a saddle on that horse? I'll tie a rope to his halter and give the child a ride around the yard."

\* \* \*

"Hello!" Eddie called out as he stepped into the farmhouse. Pancho jumped off the couch and bounded towards him. Eddie smiled and bent down so she could lick his face.

He turned towards the couch and saw Roberta watching him. He scrutinized her expression, but couldn't tell if she was excited or angry. He sat down beside her and kissed the top of her head.

"Hey there, love, how's your cold?"

She held his gaze and coughed without covering her mouth.

Eddie sighed. "Well, it sounds like it's not as deep in your chest anymore. That medicine Dr. Bob gave you must be working."

She looked back at the television and started petting the dog.

"You came just in time, Eddie," Grace called out to him. "I want to pull some boxes of winter clothes out of the cellar. The paper said we might be getting the first frost later this week. Could you lend me a hand?"

Eddie stood up and walked to the basement door.

"We'll just be a minute, lamb," Grace told Roberta. "I'll leave the door open. Flick the light switch if you need us."

Eddie followed Grace down the stairs and over to a set of wooden shelves sagging with large boxes. "I thought the weather forecast called for more sun through Saturday," he said.

"It did," Grace agreed. "I just wanted to scold you in private."

Eddie sighed. "Listen, I'm sorry I'm not coming round so much, but I'm busy. Jenny can't get any studying done while Gisela's at home, so I'm sticking around in the afternoons to help her with maths and science. And then I'm trying to teach Gisela some English too. She can't make friends in kindergarten if the other children can't understand her."

"So why did you borrow Alan's set of *Star Wars* videos?"

"Jenny hadn't seen them. She'll never fit in at college unless she understands the cultural references."

"Jim said you were playing old records for her."

Eddie shrugged. "We were taking a break from geometry. Her mind was going numb from the figures. Nothing gets the juices flowing like the crackle and hiss of old vinyl."

"I'll give you some crackle and hiss if you don't start spending more time here with Birdie," Grace huffed. "This poor girl needs you too. She misses you when you're gone."

"Really?" Eddie replied. "She didn't show much emotion the other day when I was here with Jim. She hardly even looked at me."

"Perhaps that's because you were talking to Jim the whole time and not to her. You haven't read her any chapters of that Jane Austen book for days now. And I can't even remember the last time you pulled your guitar out to play for her."

Eddie felt the tug of guilt pulling at his conscience. He'd already finished his copy of the book at the other house. *Does this count as cheating?* he asked himself. *Reading a book aloud to Birdie so I can discuss it later with Jenny?*

He ran his eyes over the rack of shelves. "Which box should I pull down for you?"

"The one in the very back of the top corner that's the hardest to reach," Grace answered. She started walking to the steps. "I'll wait for you upstairs. We shouldn't leave Birdie alone for too long."

## Chapter Ten

"That's enough maths for today," Eddie said, closing the practice book and reaching for his cup of coffee.

"There's no 's' in math," Jenny pointed out.

"There is in England," he retorted. He sipped his coffee, opened the book to another section, and held it at arm's length so he could read it. "Here we go. American History and Government. Let's see if I can pronounce these questions properly."

"How about we watch *Return of the Jedi* instead?" Jenny asked. "You promised we could finish seeing the trilogy this week."

"First things first," Eddie insisted, running his finger down the page. "Now, the highest court of authority is called the—?"

"College of Cardinals?" Jenny guessed.

Eddie clucked his tongue. "Not even close. The Supreme Court. Next question. The head of the executive branch of the government is called—?"

"The President," Jenny said. "See? I'm not a complete moron."

"Glad to hear it. So tell me, who are you planning to vote for in the upcoming election?"

"There's an upcoming election?" she asked.

"Yes. In just a few weeks. Vice President Bush is running against Governor Dukakis of Massachusetts. You're nineteen. Are you registered to vote?"

"Umm—" Jenny mumbled.

Eddie laughed. "That's all right. I'm not sure I want to vote for either man myself. But I do know which candidate is a Democrat and which is Republican. Do you?"

She frowned. "I don't know anything about this upcoming election, but I know a lot about historical Presidents."

"Really?" Eddie said, closing the book and looking into her

eyes. "Which ones? Thomas Jefferson? Franklin Roosevelt?"

"I know a lot about John Tyler."

"Who the hell was John Tyler?"

"He came right after William Henry Harrison."

"I'm sorry," Eddie said, resting the book on the table. "I went to high school in England, so I didn't study very much American history. I'm not familiar with either man."

"See, now who's clueless?" Jenny teased. She scooted forward in her chair and smiled. "I once had to write a paper about a President. I chose William Henry Harrison, since he died a month into his term, so I figured I could write a really short report. But he didn't do anything besides catch pneumonia, so I started researching John Tyler, who took his place. His wife died right after he took office, and he started dating this chick thirty years younger than him. Then he ran off and eloped with her, while he was still President! When his term ended, he retired from politics and hunkered down with his young bride. They had seven children. I called my report, 'America's Happiest Ex-President'."

Eddie tried to suppress a grin. "But you said you were supposed to write a paper on President Harrison, not President Tyler."

"Yeah, the nuns docked my grade for that," she admitted.

Eddie brought the workbook to his face to hide his smile. "Well, I see some questions here about Abraham Lincoln and George Washington, but I don't see any about 'America's Happiest Ex-President'."

"I'm doomed," Jenny moaned.

Eddie closed the book again and fixed his eyes back on her. "Where there's life, there's hope. You just have to believe in yourself, Jenny. You can pass this test."

She smiled at him. "Thank you, Mr. R. I'm not so sure about that. But if I do, it's because of you."

### London, England

Philip Randall leaned over June's shoulder and watched her scan the BBC wire service headlines on her desktop computer. He swallowed the last dregs of his cold tea and rested his cup on top of her stack of unproofed typeset sheets. All around him, the newsroom of the *London Eyewitness* buzzed with the cacophonous sounds of clicking keyboards, muted phone conversations and cursing reporters.

June took her finger off the scroll button and turned to him. "Perhaps you could sit down and read these yourself. Then I could get up and fix myself a cuppa."

"No, June, I need two sets of eyes to sort through these leads," he replied. "I don't want to miss out on any more big scoops, like I did with that Rob Lowe scandal."

"You're a vile man, you know?" June said, turning her face back to the computer. She hit the curser and sent a large block of green type rolling to the top of the screen. "I can't see why you don't just write another piece about the 'Spycatcher' case. It's not only salacious; it's actually real news."

"I've beaten that dead horse into two columns already. My readers deserve something fresh."

"Ooh, you want 'fresh' now, do you?" giggled Elsie, Philip's proofreader. She walked up behind her co-workers, placed a Styrofoam cup of hot tea on the table next to the keyboard, and pinched Philip's bottom with her left hand.

"Don't be cheeky," Philip said as he picked up the new cup.

"Hey, that was for June!" Elsie exclaimed.

"Fetch her another cup!" Philip barked. "We're both too busy to leave our desks."

"My desk," June corrected him.

"Scroll back for a second," Philip said. "What was that bit about Fergie and Prince Andrew?"

"Nothing," June replied. "Just some speculation about who will be Princess Beatrice's godparents."

"Fuck 'em," Philip cursed under his breath. "They should baptize that kid today and post photos. Royal pictures always sell papers. Keep scrolling. Let's see what Diana's up to."

"We've already passed that," June said. "She cut a ribbon at a power plant near Leeds."

"What was she wearing?" Philip asked testily.

"The same dress she wore last May when she went to see those ballet students from Chelsea," June answered.

"Bloody hell! Did Charles cut her shopping budget again?" Philip shouted.

"I think she's just trying to show her common touch," Elsie said. "You know? If she's photographed wearing the same outfit a few times, then maybe she'll seem more down to earth."

"Nobody wants a down to earth princess!" Philip bellowed.

"Well, I thought it was a pretty dress," June said. "If I had nice frocks like Diana, I'd wear them over and over again too."

"Nobody's asking you," Philip huffed. "Try the AP Wire service."

June switched over to the next screen menu, typed in the word 'Gossip' and hit 'Search'.

Philip sipped his tea and continued to read over June's shoulder. "Bugger, this has to be the slowest news day ever. Nothing is happening out there!"

"I'll try Reuters," June said, transferring to the next service.

"Why don't you go stalk a celebrity yourself, Phil?" Elsie suggested. "Prove your own meddle as an investigative journalist!"

"Why don't you go fetch June a cup of tea?" Philip retorted.

"Don't bother, I'll get my own in a sec," June said as she skimmed through the Reuters reports. "Ooh! Look here, Phil! Great human interest story! A woman in Ipswich claims her cat has been giving her stock tips for three years. Together they've earned £16,000."

"Next," Philip replied without looking at the screen.

"Hmm. Well, how about a foray into the occult?" June proposed. "There have been three new crop circles reported this past week. Two in Eastern Wales and one in Surrey, just a few miles north of Eric Clapton's estate."

"Damn, you're really scraping the bottom of the barrel now, aren't you, Junie?" Philip said, taking another sip of tea.

"No, don't scroll up!" Elsie said, leaning in front of Philip so she could examine the screen herself. "I want to read that! My mum once saw one being formed, you know. A crop circle. It was right before sunset, at the bottom of a steep hill. She said she felt a sudden rush of static in the air, and then there was a loud pop and a bright blue flash of light!"

"And she was abducted by Martians on the spot," Philip said with a dismissive snort.

"No!" Elsie protested, flashing him an evil look. "My mum's not barmy. She's a perfectly level-headed woman from Kent."

Philip rolled his eyes. "Right. She just happened to be in the same neighborhood as the Martians."

"Actually, Mum said she found the whole experience rather mystical," Elsie added. "She thought the spirits of the ancient

Druids might have been somehow involved."

"Lord, save me from level-headed women from Kent," Philip moaned.

June continued to examine the screen. "Don't be so patronizing, Phil. It says here that a meteorologist from Wiltshire is teaming up with an American professor from Indiana to complete a worldwide study on the crop circle phenomenon. They're working on a theory that the circles are created by 'plasma vortexes'."

"Ooh, that sounds very erudite," Elsie laughed. "Why don't you follow up on this story, Phil? You might even win some sort of award for scientific journalism!"

Philip scowled. "You realize, don't you, Elsie, that scientists from around the world are presently developing 'spell-checker' programs for these brand-new word processor machines that will soon render your job obsolete?"

"As long as there are reporters like you, Phil, who don't know the difference between the three spellings of 'two', there will be work for proofreaders like me," she replied smugly. "And I'll always have the last word on everything you write."

"Stop the presses!" June interrupted. "This sounds like suitable column fodder. Yoko Ono is threatening to sue Albert Goldman's publishers over his new biography of John Lennon. It says here that she's been contemplating suicide ever since the book came out!"

"Print that article!" Philip exclaimed with a smile. "I'll rework it into a reader poll. Should she or shouldn't she? That is the question."

# Chapter Eleven

### *Millcote, Ohio*

"I can't believe this!" Jenny exclaimed, her eyes bright with excitement. "I finally get to listen to the unpalatable mediocrity of the Pilots' oeuvre!" She picked up the top album from the stack of LP's and examined the cover art.

Eddie smirked. "Perhaps I misspoke. We had a few good songs."

"You are your own worst critic, Mr. R," she noted. She picked up a second record and compared the two covers. "You were so cute back then. You looked like one of the Monkees."

"We were trying to project a 'Beatlesque' image," he replied. "Our debut album pre-dated the Monkees' by several years."

Jenny giggled, then examined the album covers more closely. "You look older than the other guys in your band."

"I'm a little older than Tony and Gerry," he agreed. "But Jim's a few months older than I am, and our bassist on this first record, Joe Sullivan, was an old man of twenty-six."

"And you were—?"

"I'd just turned twenty-one when Emmett signed us to our contract."

Jenny laid the records gently on the floor, then noticed the title of the next LP. "I think I detect a pattern here. *The Pilots Lift Off. Gaining Altitude. High Velocity—*"

"That was Emmett's idea," Eddie laughed.

She fanned the remaining albums out and read the names. "Oh, no! *Drop in Pressure. Turbulence.* This doesn't portend well."

"Check out the second-to-last LP," Eddie said, pulling it out of the pile and handing it to her.

"*Down in Smoke!?* Uh-oh! This definitely sounds ominous!"

"Emmett only agreed to use that title if we promised to name our next record *Smooth Landing*. So that's what we called our greatest hits album." Eddie handed her the bottom record from the pile. "Though Gerry insisted the art department make the liner sleeve look like an airsickness bag."

Jenny scanned the album covers once more. "Who's this guy?" she asked, pointing to a blonde man with a mustache on the cover of *Drop in Pressure*.

"He was our second bassist, Pete Cooper. Joe Sullivan got tired of touring and wanted to settle down, so he collected his earnings and went off to business school. He's one of my accountants now. Pete took his place, but he didn't last long. We replaced him with our third bassist, Eli Deere." Eddie pointed to a thin man on the cover of *Turbulence* with a scraggly beard and a far-away look in his eyes.

"He looks kind of grungy," Jenny said. "Like maybe he was stoned in this picture."

"He probably was. That was his usual *modus operandi*."

Jenny examined Eli's face more carefully. "Actually, he looks kind of like my dad in the one picture I have of him."

Eddie smiled. "Really? Can I see that photo?"

"Sure," she replied. "But not yet. I've been trying to get you to play me these records for weeks. I'm not gonna let you off the hook now while I go upstairs and fetch my box of photos."

"Fair enough," Eddie said. He slipped *The Pilots Lift Off!* out of its jacket and placed it on the turntable.

\* \* \*

Jenny opened the lid of a blue shoebox and flipped through her small stack of pictures. "I guess I should start with the photos you're least likely to make fun of." She handed Eddie a snapshot. "This is me and my Uncle Henry at the Pogue's Ice Cream Bridge in downtown Cincinnati. He took me there every year for my birthday. It's always been one of my favorite places."

Eddie smiled. "You had such long hair when you were little! It looks like it goes all the way down to your waist."

"Yeah, it did," she replied. She put the picture back in the box and handed Eddie a photo of a large Black woman with a broad, crooked smile. "This is Hannah, my old housekeeper. She's the nicest person in the whole world."

"She looks nice," Eddie agreed. "Do you still keep in touch with her?"

"We exchange letters. And every year at Christmas she mails me a box of hand-me-downs from my cousins Gigi and Lisa, and tucks in some cash and a little note to tell me what the family is up to."

"God bless her," Eddie said, handing the photograph back to Jenny. "She can't have it easy, living with your aunt."

"I know," Jenny agreed. "She told me she would have left years ago, but she wants to keep an eye on Lisa. She's anorexic."

"How about your other cousins?"

"Gigi's going to Case Western. Hannah says she hardly ever comes home any more. She spends her summers working at Cedar Point, and her Christmases with her boyfriend's family. I mean, her fiancé's family. She's engaged now. John flunked out of Ohio University, but he's still living in Athens. He was busted twice for selling pot last year, but my aunt hired a lawyer who got him off."

She slipped the picture back into her box and picked up a sepia-tinged photo of a girl wearing a dirndl. "This is Sister Waltrude, my German teacher. She gave me this picture a few years ago when she saw how few family photos I had. But she doesn't look like this anymore. She's seventy-six years old now."

"Well, she did a good job teaching you German," Eddie said. "You're practically fluent."

"Yeah, we used to spend at least an hour every day speaking to each other. She said she was trying to help me become proficient in German, but I think she was just homesick and wanted someone to talk to *auf Deutsch*."

Eddie smiled at her indulgently. "It was good of you to spend so much time with an old woman."

"Not really. I just kind of gravitate towards other lonely people. I can't help myself." She offered Eddie another picture. "This is my parents and me. Don't laugh."

He inspected the photo. On the left stood a long-haired, bearded man with three strands of lovebeads roped around his neck. Beside him stood a frizzy-haired woman in a loose-fitting, embroidered sundress and a large, floppy hat. In her arms she held a bald, naked infant.

"You're right. Your dad does bear a remarkable resemblance to my old bassist, Eli," Eddie said, suppressing a smile. "This is absolutely darling. You had a lovely family."

Jenny scrutinized his face. "No jokes? No snide remarks?"

"Absolutely none," he insisted as the corners of his eyes began crinkling up. "And now I won't have to lose any more sleep at night wondering if you have any birthmarks."

Jenny smirked. "Have you really been wondering that?"

"No," he fibbed. "That was a joke." He turned the photograph over and read the handwriting on the back. "'Cory, me and S.A.B.' What does that mean?"

"My mom wrote that on the back before she mailed this picture to my uncle," Jenny said. "Those are my initials."

"The 'S' is for Sanjani, but what do the 'A' and 'B' stand for?"

She grabbed the picture away from him and slipped it back in her box. "Take a guess."

"Hmm, Alice Barbara? Anna Beatrice?"

"Think 'hippie'," Jenny hinted.

Eddie laughed. "Oh hell, I don't know—Aquarius Butterfly?"

"Not even close," she said.

"I give up. Tell me."

"What's your middle name?" she asked instead.

"Oh, I see, this is a game now," Eddie replied. "Well, you try to guess. I'll give you a hint. It's Welsh."

Jenny crossed her arms in front of her chest. "That's no help. Give me another clue."

"It has no vowels."

Jenny giggled. "That's impossible!"

"Well, okay, it has one," Eddie admitted. "But you'd be hard-pressed to find it amidst the clutter of consonants."

She smiled and shook her head.

"I tell you what, let's come back to that later," he said. "Show me your next picture."

She took a deep breath. "It's of Eileen and me."

"Give us a look," Eddie said, scooting closer to her side.

She hesitated, then handed him her last picture. "No jokes," she insisted.

Eddie examined the snapshot. Two girls scowled rudely at the camera. Each wore a torn black t-shirt, stabbed with safety pins, and sported a short, spiked hairstyle. The smaller girl, whom Eddie just barely recognized as Jenny, had garish pink stripes in her hair.

The other girl's hair was streaked in green and blue. They sat cross-legged on the floor in front of a white-washed plaster wall, flanked by a crooked crucifix.

He eyed Jenny quizzically. "Please explain."

"This was Eileen's idea," she said.

"Please explain," Eddie repeated.

She took the snapshot away from him and gazed at it fondly. "We took this picture on New Year's Day, 1981. The night before—"

She rested the photo on the floor in front of her and stared at it quietly for a few moments. Then she cleared her throat and continued her explanation in a hoarse whisper.

"I'd gone home for the holidays. On New Year's Eve, I was by myself. Gigi and Lisa had gone to a sleepover, and Hannah was spending the night at her sister's. John was out with his friends, and my aunt was passed out drunk in her bedroom. I was sitting on the couch in the family room, cutting paper snowflakes while I waited for the ball to drop on TV, but I fell asleep before midnight. Then John came home. He was really drunk."

She took a deep breath and closed her eyes. "He—he pulled me off the couch and started groping me. He shoved his tongue in my mouth. I tried to fight him off. Then he grabbed the scissors I'd dropped on the floor and he—he cut off a big hunk of my hair. I started running away, but he caught me and cut off most of the rest before I was able to break free and lock myself in my room.

"When Hannah came home the next morning, I ran into her arms and cried and cried. She drove me back to the convent right away, and had a long talk with the nuns while I cried all over Eileen. After she left, Eileen made me dry my tears and put on a coat so we could ride our bikes to the nearest town. She found the house of the lady who ran the beauty shop, and told her to cut her hair just like mine. I tried to stop her. She had long, pretty red hair. But she said, no, this way when the other girls got back, we could just tell them we decided to do something impulsive together, and nobody would ask me any stupid questions.

"After that, we rode our bikes to a King Kwik that was open for the holiday, and Eileen bought all this junk—makeup and spray-on hair dye left over from Halloween. And two black T-shirts and a disposable camera. After we rode home, she made us up to look like this. She modeled us off some pictures she'd seen in a magazine of punk kids in England. Then we walked over to the gardener's cottage and asked him to take our picture. I kept this print. Eileen sent the others to her dad and stepmom. They'd gone to France for Christmas and left her behind."

Jenny looked up from the floor and gazed at Eddie. Her eyes were still dry. His were glistening with tears.

He swallowed hard and struggled to find his voice. "Don't let the bastards get you down," he whispered.

Jenny managed a weak smile. "That's exactly what Eileen told me that day. It was kind of her motto."

"It's a good motto," Eddie replied.

Jenny slipped the picture back in her box. "Yeah," she agreed. "I've kept my hair pretty short since then. It's kind of a tribute to Eileen, I suppose."

"Your bob becomes you," Eddie said. "Though I dare say, you carried off the pink streak and gelled spikes with aplomb."

She smiled at him more brightly. "How about we go for another bike ride before Gisela gets home? We can see if Mr. Hayworth mowed over your crop circle yet."

\* \* \*

"Domestic happiness is out of the question," Eddie recited. "If, however, I am allowed to think that you and yours feel an interest in my fate and actions—it may be something to live for."

"Ooh, that Willoughby is a rotter!" Grace chimed in. She put down the scarf she was crocheting and looked across the farmhouse's small sitting room at Eddie. "How do you suppose Jane Austen learned about men like him? You'd think growing up in a country parsonage, she'd have been sheltered from such scoundrels."

Eddie rested the book on his lap. "I imagine even young, innocent girls living in remote religious settings might occasionally glimpse some of the ugliness of the world."

"I'm sorry, Eddie. I didn't mean to interrupt," Grace apologized. "Please go on with the story."

"Actually, I wanted to take a break. My throat's a little dry from reading."

"I'll put a kettle on for tea," Grace offered.

"No, I'll make it," Eddie said. "I need to stretch my legs. Why don't you keep Birdie company for a bit?" He turned to face his wife, who was sitting beside him on the couch. He twisted one of her curly tendrils of hair around his index finger and smiled.

Roberta grunted loudly and grabbed the book off Eddie's lap. She slammed it down hard on the table beside the couch, threw off the afghan resting over their knees, and marched to the stairs. Pancho jumped up from the floor and followed her up the steps.

Eddie and Grace exchanged nervous glances.

"I'll see if I can figure out what's bothering her," Grace offered.

Eddie sighed. "Good luck with that," he replied. He watched Grace climb the stairs, then took off his reading glasses and walked into the kitchen. He found Alan sitting at the table, paging through a magazine and listening to music on his Walkman. Eddie took a seat across from him.

Alan took off his headset. "You finished that bloody book yet?"

"Almost," Eddie answered. "Just two chapters left."

"Christ, I never thought I'd hear myself say this, but I wish you'd go back to reading her poems. At least those are short. That fuckin' novel you're reciting is interminable!"

Eddie smiled. "Sorry to bother you."

"'S'alright," Alan replied. "I ought to be used to it by now."

Eddie glanced at the magazine cover, then turned back to Alan. "Do you think Birdie's having a bad reaction to that cold medicine Bob gave her? She's so short-tempered these days."

"No," Alan said. "I'd say she's more cheesed off than tetched."

"Why do you suppose that is?" Eddie asked.

Alan frowned. "Don't be stupid, Romeo. She misses you."

"Why? I come to see her every day. Well, almost every day."

"You're spending most of your time in the mansion now."

"But Alan, I—" Eddie looked down at the tablecloth and started tracing his index finger absent-mindedly against its striped pattern. He lowered his voice to a whisper. "I feel like I'm needed there too. Jenny is—Christ, that poor girl. She's lived such an awful life. I want to try to help her get a fresh start, and learn to face the world outside the walls of that sheltered convent."

"Yeah, like you're the one to teach her that," Alan laughed. "You've been hiding from the world for the past sixteen years!"

"I'm not hiding from the world," Eddie protested. "I'm rejecting it. That's different. But you don't get my point. Alan, this poor kid—Christ! We just had this really long talk, and she told me her cousin John molested her when she was twelve."

"Her cousin?" Alan replied. "Fuck, man, that's disgusting."

"I know," Eddie said. "She hasn't been able to go home since."

"Well, I s'pose she's been better off living at that convent then, hasn't she?"

"But she can't go on living there forever," Eddie said. "She needs to move on. But she doesn't know how."

Alan sighed. "Listen, mate. I'm sure the kid needs help. But you have a wife who needs you more."

"But Birdie has you and Grace to look after her, and she's not going anywhere," Eddie protested. "Jenny's only staying here until Gerry comes to collect Gisela. Then she'll probably go back to Indiana and bury herself alive in that convent again. I want to help her while I can."

Alan picked up his headphones. "Does she know that Birdie's still alive?" he asked. "Have you told her why you split your life between two houses? Or does she just think you're coming to chat with Mum and me in the afternoons?"

Eddie stood up from the table and grabbed the tea kettle off the stove. "The topic's never come up," he mumbled as he filled the kettle with water at the sink.

### *Athens, Ohio*

"You're forty-two dollars short," Dick Mason snapped as he counted the last dollar bill. He folded the wad of rumpled cash in half and slipped it into his wallet.

"I'm good for it," John Reed insisted. "You know I am. Don't I always come through with enough money for you to pay back your suppliers?"

Dick opened an unmarked pill bottle and started removing Vicodin capsules. "That's the problem, Johnny. You always come through eventually, but you never seem to have the amount you promised me on the day that it's due."

The young man looked on anxiously as Dick shorted his stash. "Listen, I have a great connection," John pleaded. "A trust fund kid with money to burn. He'll pay me double for anything I can get him. I'll have your forty-two-fuckin' dollars and then some as soon as I see him tonight."

"I thought *you* used to be a trust fund kid," Dick scoffed as he screwed the top back on the bottle. He tossed the pills at John with a sneer. "Word of advice. See if your connection can give you an advance. Looks like you could use some cash yourself."

John adjusted his scarf to cover the hole in the collar of his bomber jacket. "I'm coming in for a big windfall," he said, slipping the vial into his jacket pocket. "You'll see."

Dick laughed and patted the faded comforter on his motel room bed. "Take a seat, Mr. Reed," he said with a condescending sneer. He leaned back in his wobbly wooden chair. "I have nothing else to do at the moment. Tell me your big plan."

John remained standing on the worn grey carpet. "Fuck you," he snarled.

"Fuck you too," Dick replied nonchalantly. "Now sit down. I've taken a shine to you, boy. You know that, don't you? I see a bit of my own young self in you. And I'm interested in hearing about your impending good fortune. So tell me—will your ship be coming in on any sort of pre-arranged schedule, or are you just planning to drag a sinking boat into harbor?"

John brushed the comforter with the palm of his hand and sat down on the edge of the mattress. He fingered the vial of pills in his jacket pocket with his other hand. "I'm gonna hit up my sister's boyfriend. He's rich, and famous too. Well, sort of famous."

Dick snorted. "Oh, Christ, Johnny boy—you never cease to amuse me! It's like I have a twin."

John flashed him a dirty look. Dick laughed again.

"Oh, get off your high horse," Dick scolded. "I'm intrigued by your financial prospects. Honestly. I do have a professional interest in you, after all."

John relaxed his stiff posture. "Right. Well. It's like this. My sister Gigi got engaged this past summer to this dude from Cleveland. His dad's a Congressman who's thinking of running for Governor in '90. Gigi's an officer in her College Republican Club and she's real pretty, so this old geezer is always toting her along with the rest of his family when he's making public appearances, trying to court the youth vote.

"But here's the catch. A couple of years back, Gigi dated this real greaseball, and he took some skanky pictures of her one night when she was drunk. I overheard her mentioning them to my maid last summer when she came home to show off her diamond ring. She's worried those photos might fall into the wrong hands."

Dick's lips curled into a lascivious smile. "Oh my. Your poor baby sister! I do hope her gallant big brother can help her find a way out of this dire situation with her reputation intact."

John smiled back. "Yeah, I drove up to Cleveland as soon as I heard about the pictures and tracked down her scuz-bucket ex. Didn't even have to pay the bastard for the photos and negatives. He just traded them for some weed."

Dick arched his eyebrow. "Did you cut it first?"

"Don't worry, I never give away quality shit for free," John replied, visibly relaxing. "Now I'm just working out the kinks in my plan. I can't threaten to expose Gigi myself, since I'm family. But I met some frat boys who put together an annual 'Girls of Case Western' calendar, and I'm thinking of using them as a front. I just have to figure out how to approach Gigi and her rich fiancé with the bad news."

"Don't wait too long," Dick warned. "Jump while the fire's hot."

"But I could probably make more money if I held out till she's married into the family and the Governor's election is closer."

Dick cracked his knuckles. "Listen up, Johnny. I have some advice for you. Don't think so much. You can't outthink this politician. If he's a serious contender for Governor, then he's smarter than you are. He'll figure out a way to trump your card if you give him the chance. And don't underestimate the stupidity of the general public either. If some reporter gets hold of this story and presents it in the right light, everyone will sympathize with your poor little sis, and those pictures won't be worth shit."

John stood up from the bed. "What the hell do you know? You're just a two-bit drug pusher selling low-grade meds out of a fleabag motel room."

Dick ignored the insult and lit a cigarette. "Sit down, college boy," he said as he shut the lid on his plastic lighter. "I want to tell you a little story. It's all about a shit-for-brains older brother who thought he could make a fortune off a dicey film of his baby sister, and how his stupid-ass brother-in-law foiled him by changing the rules of the game."

# Chapter Twelve

### *Millcote, Ohio*

Jenny walked into the mansion's large sitting room after tucking Gisela into bed and flopped down on the couch next to Eddie. "I finished reading *Sense and Sensibility* last night," she announced. "I'm so glad Marianne ended up with Colonel Brandon."

Eddie closed the book he had been paging through and rested it on the table beside him. "Did you ever doubt that she would?"

"No," Jenny said, picking up a pillow and squeezing it to her chest. "He's her soulmate. Willoughby was just toying with her."

Eddie leaned back against the couch and examined her face. "Tell me honestly, Jenny. Do you really think Marianne could be happy with an old man like Brandon, whose love for her is mixed with an almost paternal devotion?"

"Of course!" Jenny said. "Brandon might see his lost youth in Marianne, but she makes him feel younger too. And he'll be all the nicer to her after they're married, since he's had to endure all those long years of heartbreak and loneliness."

Eddie smiled. "Perhaps you're right. But what about Elinor? How could she ever really trust Edward after she discovered he'd been courting her under false pretenses and keeping secrets from her about his personal obligations?"

Jenny shrugged. "She forgave him. And why wouldn't she? Edward was young and inexperienced when he proposed to Lucy Steele. And he remained true to his original promise, even after he fell in love with another woman who suited him better. How could any woman fault a guy with such a deep sense of honor?"

*Christ, why did I pick this book?* he asked himself. *I hadn't thought it would hit so close to the bone.*

"I'm so glad you suggested this book," she said, drawing him from his reverie. "I liked it a lot more than *Pride and Prejudice*."

"Really?" Eddie replied, taken aback by her remark. "*Pride and Prejudice* is considered one of the world's greatest novels."

"I don't like how everyone's happiness depends upon Lydia marrying that jerk Wickham," Jenny said. "She's only a teenager, for goodness sake, and she's gonna be stuck in a miserable marriage for the rest of her life! Why couldn't the older characters have written off her elopement as a youthful indiscretion? I mean, it's not like there's even any suggestion that she was pregnant."

"Well, things were different in the early 1800s," he replied.

"Right," she said dismissively. "Like nobody ever had premarital affairs back then."

"Well, of course they did, but that's not the novel's point," Eddie said. "And in any case, the story is about Elizabeth and Darcy."

"Darcy's a jerk most of the time too," she continued. "And after Elizabeth marries him, she'll have to spend the rest of her life kowtowing to his unspeakably rude aunt."

"I somehow don't imagine Lizzy's lot will be that bad," Eddie replied. "After all, she'll get to live in Pemberley."

"Trust me," Jenny countered. "I know what it's like to live with a mean-spirited, rich aunt. Lady Catherine will never let Lizzy forget that she doesn't belong in the family."

Eddie chuckled. "Well, I don't know that I agree with your interpretations of Miss Austen's work, Jenny, but I enjoy hearing your opinions. It's been a long time since I've been able to have a conversation with anyone about literature."

"Maybe you should go back to college, Mr. R," she suggested. "We could enroll at the same university, and meet up every Tuesday for coffee to see who's fitting in worse."

He closed his eyes and rested his head on his hand. *God, wouldn't that be lovely?* he thought. *Turning back the clock and being a carefree university student once more, with a running date already lined up with a sweet young thing like her?*

"What are you thinking about?" Jenny asked.

He opened his eyes. "Nothing. I was just daydreaming." He looked away and spied the GED practice book resting open-spined on the floor in front of the television. "Well Jenny, I believe you have what it takes to pass the English portion of any college entrance exam. You should concentrate on another subject now."

"Like Social Studies?" she whined.

He started to nod, but then he remembered their earlier conversation about President John Tyler and his teenage bride. "How about science?" he suggested.

"Biology or chemistry?"

Eddie turned his face back to Jenny. She looked vaguely terrified. "I take it those weren't your best subjects in school."

She frowned. "Couldn't we just watch *Star Wars* again? That's science fiction."

Eddie laughed. He turned his face to the window and realized he'd forgotten to draw the curtains. The back yard was completely dark, except for the soft yellow lights shining from the windows of the old farmhouse.

Jenny noticed that he had redirected his gaze. She stood up and walked to the window. As she reached for the cord to close the drapes, she stole a last glance at the yard. "The moon hasn't risen yet. If it weren't so cold, we could go stargazing."

Eddie looked back at her and smiled. "I used to do that with my dad when I was little. He knew all the constellations."

"Do you remember them?" she asked. "Maybe you could teach me some astronomy."

"I'll think about it," he replied. He stood up from the couch and started walking towards the stairs. But then he hesitated and returned to Jenny's side. He picked up the book he had left on the end table and offered it to her. "I want you to have this."

"Is this another reading assignment?"

"No, it's a collection of Indian poetry," he said. He cleared his throat and looked down at the floor. "When you told me your real name, I—well, it somehow reminded me of this book."

Jenny opened the cover and looked at the illustration on the frontispiece. A blue-skinned man was playing a flute. At his side stood a beautiful woman in an elaborate sari. "Who's this blue guy?" she asked.

"That's the Hindu god Krishna. The woman beside him is named Radha."

"Was she a goddess?"

"No," Eddie replied. "She was quite human. A simple shepherdess. But she was—his beloved. His *sajani*."

"Oh," Jenny mumbled. She closed the book and looked up at

Eddie. "Thank you."

"You're welcome," he whispered. He held her gaze for a long moment, then turned and walked back to the stairs.

\* \* \*

"That's Cassiopeia," Eddie said, pointing to a pattern in the sky. "Those five stars that look like a 'W', right by the North Star."

Jenny tilted her glasses askew to adjust the focus. "Right. I think I see it. It's actually brighter than the Little Dipper, isn't it?"

"I think so," he agreed. "Though not as bright as the Big Dipper."

"When will Orion start appearing?" she asked, tucking her hands behind her head to warm her fingers.

"Soon," he replied. "It'll be winter soon. You can almost see the tip of it down by Auriga. That's the bull constellation, over there by the farmhouse roof."

Jenny turned her face towards the sky above the dark building. "Is Orion the Hunter trying to kill the bull?"

"I'm not sure. But maybe. That makes sense anyway."

She laughed. "I don't think any of these patterns make sense. I recognize the basic shapes—the boxes and triangles and jagged lines—but I don't understand how anyone can see the outline of an animal in them."

"Well, you have to use your imagination," Eddie said. Noticing Jenny was shivering, he rolled off the afghan they were lying on and draped his side of the blanket over Jenny's legs. "Is that better?"

"Yes, thank you," she replied.

He lay back down on the cold grass beside her. "I suppose you're right. Some of the shapes are a bit of a stretch." He searched the sky for another bright constellation, then turned to look at her again. "Are you cold? Should we go back inside now?"

"We can stay a little longer. The moon's supposed to rise soon."

"Okay," he agreed, rolling his head away and looking back at the sky. "Look to the south of the Little Dipper. See that really bright star? Now follow it to the west. There's a line of smaller stars right behind it. And branching out perpendicularly from the second brightest star is another line. That's Cygnus the Swan."

She tilted her glasses again. "I think I see it, but the elm tree's blocking some of the view."

"Right. Maybe we should move the blanket," he suggested.

"No, I can still see most of the sky from here."

Turning his head, Eddie saw the moon make its first appearance on the horizon. He poked Jenny and pointed to it.

"I love how it's so yellow when it first rises," she said. Her teeth started to chatter.

"Me too," Eddie agreed. "Once when I was playing the Hollywood Bowl, there was a wildfire just outside of L.A., and the ash in the sky made the moon look orange all night long."

"That's scary!"

"No, it was cool. Or rather, it looked cool from my hotel balcony. It probably would have terrified me if I'd been closer to the fire!"

Jenny smiled and lay silently by Eddie's side as the moon rose.

"If you're cold, we could go back inside and make some tea," he suggested.

"In a minute," she said. "Let's just watch the moon a bit longer."

As the moon rose, a sudden flash of green light burst across the sky, then plummeted down to earth like a falling arrow.

"Wow! D'you see that?" Jenny exclaimed.

"Yes! That was brilliant! I didn't expect to see any falling stars tonight!"

"I usually only see them in August."

"Right. When the earth passes through the asteroid belt. I love lying in the backyard then and watching for meteors in the sky."

"One night this past summer I counted six of them," Jenny said.

Eddie rolled his head over on the grass and gazed at her tenderly. The moon bathed her face in the softest of illuminations. "Were you in the habit of lying out in the field behind the convent in the middle of the night?" he asked with a slight chuckle.

"Only sometimes," she said. "The nuns thought it was dangerous for me to be out by myself after dark, so they discouraged me. But some nights in August, the convent would get so hot that I couldn't sleep. So I'd sneak out of the building and lie down on the grass under the stars until dawn."

"And did you wish on the falling ones?" he asked.

"Of course, I always do. Well—I didn't wish on this one just now. I wasn't expecting it. But I used to wish on falling stars whenever I'd see them in the sky by the convent." She rolled over to face Eddie. "Do you make wishes on them too?"

"Yes," he confessed.

"What do you wish for?" she asked.

"I probably shouldn't say," he replied. "Isn't that bad luck?"

"Well, I think it's supposed to be," she agreed, rolling away from his gaze. "But I don't think it would matter for me anymore, since my wish has already come true."

"Is that so?" Eddie asked. "That's funny, mine has too. What did you use to wish for?"

She laughed. "Maybe we should answer that together, at the same time."

"Okay," he agreed. "On the count of three. One, two, three—"

"I wished I had someone to watch the stars with," Jenny blurted out. She immediately stiffened her back in embarrassment. "Hey, you were supposed to speak too," she scolded.

"I was trying to think of the right way to say it," he replied.

She inched away from him. "Well, what did you use to wish for?"

He rolled back towards her and smiled. "The same thing," he whispered.

He reached for her hand and clasped it. She gazed back at him and returned his smile. He stared at her for as long as he could bear, fighting the maddening impulse rising inside him to take her into his arms and cover her with kisses. She said nothing, but continued to gaze at him adoringly. He squeezed her hand.

"Your fingers are like ice," he said at last.

"Really?" she replied. "They don't feel so cold anymore."

He released her hand reluctantly and sat upright. "Let's go inside," he said. "The moon's too high in the sky now for us to star gaze. I'll make you some tea before you turn in."

She stood up and helped him fold the afghan. They took a few steps towards the house, but then Eddie stopped, unfolded the blanket and wrapped it over Jenny's shoulders. He draped his arm around her as well, and led her across the yard. As he opened the back door to the building, he cast a cursory glance at the dark farmhouse, then followed Jenny inside.

\* \* \*

Through the open window of her bedroom, Roberta heard the mansion's backdoor shut. She brought her hand to her face and tucked a stray lock of hair behind her ear. Nestled securely in her chair behind the windowsill, she fixed her gaze across the lawn.

Just a few hours before, she had watched Eddie pull her afghan off the couch, roll it into a tube, and carry it out of the house. She had spent all evening wondering why he took her favorite blanket. But now she knew.

The moon rose higher in the sky and shone brightly upon the field where Eddie had just held Jenny's hand. Roberta stood up from her chair and closed the curtain to block out the light.

## Chapter Thirteen

"Grab your coat, Gisela," Sally said as she collected the dirty breakfast dishes. "It's almost time for school."

Gisela stabbed her last bite of pancake with a fork. "*Mein* tummy hurts," she whined as she brought the syrupy morsel to her mouth.

"That's not going to work," Eddie chided her. "If your stomach really hurt, you wouldn't be eating that fourth pancake."

"Maybe it's the fourth pancake that's making her tummy hurt," Jenny suggested. She turned towards Sally. "I can load the dishwasher, Mrs. F. Just leave everything. I'll clean up."

"Thank you," Sally replied. "Though I still have a few minutes before we have to leave."

Eddie stood up from his chair. "I'll take Gisela into town, Sally. I want to drive into Hamilton to pick up something for Alan's birthday at the off-license. I'll drop her at school along the way."

Sally grabbed Gisela's dishes and chuckled. "I think someone's going to be enjoying a little single malt whiskey this evening."

Eddie smiled. "Well, I ought to at least raise a glass or two with him. I'd hate to think of the poor bloke drinking alone."

Gisela leapt out of her seat. "I will my teacher you show much *gern*," she squealed.

Eddie shook his head. "Well, your pronunciation and vocabulary are improving by the minute, *liebchen*, but I'm afraid we still need to work on your word order."

While Gisela ran to the hallway to fetch her coat, Eddie turned to Jenny. "Will you take a practice GED test while I'm gone?"

"I want to take a bike ride first before the rain comes," Jenny answered. "The paper is predicting thunderstorms this afternoon. I'll pull out my workbook then."

"Do me a favor and wait until I get safely on the road before you take off," Eddie teased.

Jenny scrunched up her nose and made a face at him.

Sally gazed out the kitchen window. "Funny how it's overcast all of a sudden. It's been so clear lately."

"Yes, there wasn't a cloud in the sky last night," Jenny replied.

Eddie glanced at her and met her eyes, then walked to the hall closet to fetch his jacket. *"Also, meine kleines,"* he directed Gisela. *"Gehen wir!"* He held the front door open and let the child run out ahead of him to the car.

Jenny stared at Eddie's empty coffee cup and sighed. Sally started rinsing the mixing bowl. "Oh, just ignore him," she said. "You go ahead and ride your bike. I'll wash up."

"Thanks, Mrs. F," Jenny replied. "You're so kind."

Sally threw a glance out the window at the old farmhouse and stiffened her shoulders. "Word of warning, dear," she added in a hesitant voice. "Don't be surprised if you hear some funny noises tonight. That Grace Poole can't handle her drink. She's been known to holler like a banshee when she's had too much."

"Okay," Jenny promised. "Though maybe the thunder might drown her out." She stepped into the hallway, fetched her hooded jacket and left the house.

\* \* \*

Pancho ran across the yard to greet Eddie the moment he stepped out of his car.

"She was anxious to see you," Grace called from the front door of the farmhouse. "Thought I'd let her out to welcome you in."

"Thanks," Eddie called back. "I'll be right there!"

*Damn, who needs a conscience?* he asked himself as he bent down to pet the dog. *I've got Grace to remind me where I'm supposed to be at all times.*

He stood up and let Pancho run around the lawn while he collected his sack of whiskey bottles. As soon as he picked up the bag, he noticed Jenny pulling up the driveway on her bike. He put the bottles back in the car and walked towards her.

"Eddie," Grace called out to him. "Could you help me for a moment in the kitchen?"

"Give me a minute," he replied, turning his back to her and

walking towards Jenny. He noticed she looked flushed.

"You must have worked up quite a sweat," he said. "Your cheeks are all rosy."

She looked away from him and walked her bike into the garage. "No. I'm just a little upset, that's all."

He draped an arm over her shoulder. "What's wrong? Tell me."

Jenny's face flushed a deeper shade of red. "It's nothing. I just—I rode for a long time and started feeling kind of winded, so I stopped to rest for a while, near that place where we saw the crop circle. And I saw some mice scurrying around. They looked so cute, like the animals in Gisela's Beatrix Potter books. But then out of nowhere, this hawk swooped out of the sky and grabbed one of them in her talons, and took off with it."

Eddie drew her closer to him. "Poor thing," he said gently. "The food chain looks pretty harmless on paper, but it's no fun to witness in the flesh."

"Yeah," Jenny agreed, cuddling against him and hanging her head low. "I know I'm just being stupid."

"C'mon," Eddie said. He led her across the yard to the elm tree that stood between the two houses. Pancho ran up to him. "I think she's hungry, Grace," he called across the yard. "Could you please feed her? I'll be right in."

Eddie could almost feel the daggers Grace was shooting at him with her look, but he held his ground. After a few seconds, Grace called to the dog. Pancho bounded back into the farmhouse. Grace closed the door behind her with a loud slam.

Eddie turned towards Jenny. "Why don't we sit outside for a while, before the rain comes? Winter's almost here. There won't be many more days like this. Let's enjoy them while we can." As he spoke, a ray of sunlight burst through a dark cloud and shone brightly upon the yard.

"Wow, how'd you do that?" Jenny laughed. "Are you magic?"

"No," he said. "You're the one who brings the sun with her everywhere she goes."

She blushed again and looked away from him. He sat down in a pile of dead leaves beneath the tree. As Jenny took a seat by his side, Eddie began to speak in an exaggerated Scottish accent:

*"Wee, sleekit, cow'rin, tim'rous beastie'*
*what a panic's in thy breastie?"*

Jenny giggled and looked back at him. "What does that mean?"

"It's Robert Burns' *To a Mouse*," he said. "Darling little poem. It ends with that famous line, 'the best laid plans of mice and men gang oft astray'."

"Hmm," she mumbled, stretching out her legs in the dry leaves with a crunching sound. "I've never heard of him. I liked your accent, though. Did he write anything else?"

Eddie cleared his throat and started to sing:

*"We twa hae run about the braes,*
*And pou'd the gowans fine;*
*We've wander'd mony a weary fit,*
*Sin' auld lang syne."*

Jenny laughed louder. "I've heard that song before, but I never understood the words!"

"It's a pretty indecipherable dialect," Eddie agreed. He wrapped his arm around her shoulders once more and spoke in a soft, sing-song voice:

*"As fair art thou, my bonnie lass,*
*So deep in luve am I;*
*And I will luve thee still, my dear,*
*Till a' the seas gang dry . . ."*

Jenny rested her head against his chest. "Thanks for making me feel better," she said.

"You're welcome," he replied. He pointed to a long tree limb overhead. "You see that branch? When I was little, my grandfather hung a swing over it for me. I spent a good part of my childhood in this very spot, swinging back and forth and watching the world."

Jenny smiled at him. "It's hard to imagine you being little."

"Yes," he agreed. "That was a long time ago. When the construction workers built the mansion in 1973, they wanted to cut this tree down, but I wouldn't let them."

Jenny looked up. "The tree does look old. A lot of the branches look dead, though maybe that's just because they're bare."

"Some of the higher branches are dead," he agreed. "And the rest of them shed their leaves early this fall. It's starting to dry out."

*Just like me,* he thought with a brief wave of melancholy. He squeezed her shoulder a little more tightly, then released her.

She stood up. "We should probably go. My butt's getting cold sitting here in this pile of leaves."

"Oh, by all means, we wouldn't want that," Eddie teased. He stood up and started brushing the dead leaves off the seat of her pants.

"Watch it," Jenny warned Eddie with a teasing smile.

"All right," he laughed. He rubbed his hands together to shake off the crumbled leaves and started walking back to his car to fetch the whiskey. She walked alongside him and opened the car door.

"I'm going to stay with the Pooles today, and help Alan finish off one or two of these after dinner," he said. "But I'll be back before midnight if you want to stay up and talk."

"Okay," Jenny replied. "I'll wait for you downstairs."

He scooped up the bag in his arms and started walking backwards towards the farmhouse. "Till then," he called out, his face alight with happiness.

"Till then," she repeated with a warm smile.

He turned around and walked towards the old farmhouse, looking straight ahead at Grace's reproachful face as she watched him from the downstairs window.

Jenny kept her eyes glued squarely on Eddie's back until he stepped into the building and closed the door behind him. Then she turned around and walked into the mansion.

Roberta stood in the top upstairs window and watched them both enter the two buildings, then pulled the curtains shut in front of her with a quick jerk.

\* \* \*

Roberta reached for Eddie's whiskey glass.

"No, Birdie!" Eddie scolded. "You can't drink this with your medicine. They don't mix."

"Yrunk!" she grunted. "Yrall yrunk."

Alan grinned. "Damn, I must be pissed. I could have sworn I just heard her say 'you're all drunk'."

"You are drunk," Eddie replied. Roberta attempted to take his glass again, but Eddie clutched her wrist. "No, darling. You're not allowed to drink. Those are Dr. Bob's orders."

She smacked his glass off the table with her free hand, spilling whiskey all over the floor. Pancho stood up and barked sharply.

"That's enough!" Eddie shouted. "I'm taking you to bed!" He stood up from the table and started leading Roberta to the stairs.

Grace blocked his way. "I'll go upstairs with her. You don't seem like you're in a very good mood just now, Eddie." She slipped her boney fingers into Roberta's free hand. "C'mon, lamb. Let's not ruin Alan's little party. I'll read to you tonight, and we'll let the menfolk clean up the mess for a change. I think I heard Eddie reading you *The Love Song of J. Alfred Prufrock* earlier this afternoon. Would you like to hear a little more Elliot?"

Roberta grunted and glowered at Eddie as he released her hand.

"Now, now, Birdie, none of that," Grace scolded. "Tell you what, how about we have Pancho sleep in your room tonight to keep you company? You'd like that, wouldn't you?"

Eddie signaled for the dog. Pancho obediently followed the women up the stairs. Eddie turned around and saw Alan on his knees, picking up pieces of broken glass.

"Careful," Alan warned him. "There might still be some slivers on the floor." He stood up, threw a handful of shards into the rubbish can and started rinsing a tea towel under the sink.

"Give me that," Eddie said. "I'll wipe the floor."

"Happy to," Alan replied. He pulled a clean glass out of the cupboard and filled it to the brim with whiskey. "This enough?"

Eddie shook his head. "I'm gonna regret this in the morning. Top off your own glass too, while you're at it."

"That's what I was planning to do," Alan laughed.

Eddie joined him at the table as soon as he finished swabbing the floor. "So, how's it feel to be forty?"

"Right now, I'd say it's feeling pretty damn good!" Alan said. "We should have done this on your birthday, mate. Put the demons of that car crash behind you. To hell with your banged-up wrist and knee. You would have felt no pain."

Eddie took a large swig from his glass. "Yes, but then I wouldn't have been able to exchange smoldering glances with Jenny over fish fingers and macaroni."

Alan snorted. "What is it with you, anyway? That girl is half your age! Less than half your age. And she's not even pretty."

"She damn well is pretty!" Eddie shouted. "She has gorgeous eyes."

"Behind her specs," Alan countered.

"She can't help it if she's myopic!"

"Keep your voice down, for fuck's sake," Alan said. "Mum's trying to put Birdie to bed."

"Fuck it all," Eddie moaned, feeling his drink. "I should divorce her and marry Jenny."

Alan rested his glass on the table and looked at Eddie. "That's an interesting new development. I thought you just wanted to help her get into college."

"I'd miss her if she went away to uni," Eddie whined. He looked up at Alan with a pitiful puppy-dog expression.

"You're pathetic," Alan said, picking up the bottle and refilling the glasses. "She can't stay at Thornfield. Once Gerry gets out of the clinic and collects his little brat, she has to go. Off to uni or back to the convent. Makes no difference. She has to go."

"But I like her," Eddie protested. "And she likes me."

"She wouldn't like you so much if she found out you've been lying to her," Alan said.

"I'm not lying to her! I just—haven't told her everything yet."

Alan shook his head and lifted his drink. "Bottoms up," he said, tipping the glass back quickly and swallowing its contents in a single gulp. "Damn, this is good Scotch. Too bad Gerry can't enjoy it anymore."

"Hmm," Eddie mumbled. "I wonder how he's doing."

Grace returned to the kitchen and took a seat at the table. "My guess is that he's hidden bottles in every corner of the clinic, and is shagging at least two of the nurses."

"I thought you were going to read to Birdie," Eddie said.

"She didn't want me to," Grace replied. "She just climbed into bed and hid her face under the covers."

Eddie sighed. "Well, with any luck she'll be asleep soon." He glanced up at the clock on the wall. "Ten-thirty. I'll stay here for another hour, but I told Jenny I'd be back by twelve."

Alan snorted. "Christ, Eddie, is she settin' curfews for you now? You're her fuckin' boss! You don't need to report home to her before midnight."

"I know I don't have to," Eddie said, glowering at Alan. "I just want to, that's all." He looked down at his drink. "I like seeing her face before I turn in each night."

"You're hopeless," Grace scoffed. "The sooner Gerry picks up his daughter, the better."

"She could have been mine, you know," Eddie said. "Gisela, that is. If she'd been born two months earlier, I could have been her father."

"Well, she wasn't and you aren't," Alan replied. "You passed her mum along to Gerry."

Eddie slammed his fist on the table. "Why is it I can screw some tart like Bettina, and you two just look the other way. But when I show the slightest interest in a nice girl like Jenny, then you're all over me like I'm some sort of child molester?"

"Because Jenny is still a child," Grace replied. "Or barely out of her childhood, anyway. She's not a girl to be trifled with, like that German *fräulein* you shared with Gerry."

"I didn't share her," Eddie protested. "It's not as if the three of us had a *ménage à trois*. I simply passed her along to the next available has-been pop star after I'd had my fill of her."

"Jesus, Eddie, that somehow sounds even more disgusting," Alan said, knotting his face into a scowl. "I used to think you were more of a decent bloke."

"I used to be a decent bloke," Eddie said, reaching for the whiskey bottle. "But now I'm just a dirty old man."

"Stop being so morose," Grace scolded. "This is Alan's birthday. We should be celebrating." She stood up from the table and picked up the half-eaten cake from the kitchen counter. "Who wants another slice?"

Alan stared at the turquoise-colored frosting that edged the side of the cake and belched loudly. "Oh, Christ. I don't think I should eat any more blue food. That suddenly looks very unappetizing."

"Fine," Grace replied. "I'll put it away then." She removed the two red candles shaped like a '4' and a '0' from the top layer of icing, rested them on the counter, and covered the remaining cake with cling film.

"Maybe I should have some soda crackers to settle my stomach," Alan said. "I'm starting to feel that Scotch."

Eddie reached for the bottle. "Not me. I feel like getting drunk." He refilled his glass and threw an impish grin at Grace. "Would you care for a wee dram, Mrs. Poole?" he asked in an exaggerated Scottish accent.

She rolled her eyes but smiled back. "Oh, perhaps just a drop. Even an old girl like me likes a little tipple every once in a while."

## Chapter Fourteen

Eddie stumbled across the grass towards the mansion. He stepped under the large elm tree where he'd sat with Jenny earlier that day, and remembered how lovely it had felt to hold her in his arms. Lost in thought, he tripped over an exposed root and fell into a large pile of dry leaves.

"Goddamn, fucking tree!" he cursed. "Somebody ought to get rid of this!"

He rose to his feet with considerable difficulty and staggered towards the house. Above him, dark clouds pulsed with brief, menacing flashes of light. But the rain that had been threatening all afternoon and evening remained stubbornly at bay. When he reached the back of the house, he tried turning the knob, then banged on the door. "I'm back! Let me in!" he called out.

He rested his head against the door and listened as someone fumbled with the lock. When Jenny opened the door, he fell towards her. "Hello, love," he said. "I'm back! D'ya miss me?"

"Shh!" Jenny scolded. "Keep your voice down. You'll wake up Gisela and Mrs. F."

"I can speak as loud as I want to in my own goddamned house!" he shouted. "Why is everyone trying to tell me what I can and can't do in my own goddamned house?"

"Please be quiet, Mr. R, it's after midnight," she pleaded.

He stared at her. She had turned off the lights in the back room, but left the light on over the stairwell. Her hair was tinged by a halo of backlight.

"You look like an angel," he murmured in awe.

"Pity I don't act like one," she replied.

"You turned off the lights," he groused. "I thought you were going to wait up for me."

"You said you'd be back before midnight," she said. "It's twelve-thirty. I figured I might as well go to bed."

Eddie's eyes brightened. "Hey, that's a great idea! I'm going to bed too. Let's go together! No. Wait. That's not what I meant."

Jenny tilted her head and furrowed her brow. "You're drunk, Mr. R."

"No I'm not," he replied. He tried to step forward, but ended up falling against his brown leather chair. "At least I'm not as pissed as Alan is. He's completely legless. I'm only shit-faced."

"Well, I'm glad to hear that," Jenny said. "Here. Lean on me and I'll help you up the stairs."

Eddie smiled and collapsed against her. The stink of tobacco smoke wafted up from his clothes.

"You smell like cigarettes," she said. "You told me you didn't smoke anymore."

"I only smoked this evening to cover up the smell of the whiskey. See?" He exhaled into her face. "You can't smell any alcohol, can you?"

Jenny coughed. "If you say so," she replied. "Hold my hand. I'll lead you to the staircase."

Eddie took her hand and let her guide him. A pulse of heat lightning flashed outside, flooding the room with a bright rectangle of light through the open doorway.

"I forgot to close the back door," Jenny said.

"Leave it," Eddie replied. "Just take me upstairs." He squeezed her hand tightly. Thunder rumbled in the distance.

She squeezed his hand back. Another ripple of lightning coursed through the sky and lit the room. The light in the stairwell flickered and went off, pitching the room into complete darkness.

"Let's feel our way to the steps," Jenny suggested. She extended her free hand in front of her and worked her way through the maze of furniture, pulling Eddie along behind her. As soon as they reached the stairs, the overhead lamp flickered back on.

Eddie laughed. "Damn, girl, you do bring light with you everywhere you go, don't you?"

Jenny offered no reply. "Watch the step," she said instead. "Put your hand on the railing and lean your other arm on me."

Eddie leaned against Jenny with more weight than he was putting on the railing. "You're so nice, Jenny. Did I ever tell you that?"

"I'm not sure. Be careful, now. Here comes the landing. Try to keep your voice down. Mrs. F and Gisela are sleeping."

She led Eddie up the final flight of stairs, then turned down the hall that led to his bedroom. She opened the door, switched on the light and guided him to the large bed set against the wall.

He pulled her towards him. "Are you going to bed with me Jenny?" he asked in an eager voice.

"I'm helping you to your bed. You're drunk, remember?" She pulled back the covers while he continued to gaze into her eyes.

"Oh, right. I am," he agreed. "Thanks for reminding me." He glanced at the bed. "Look, you've turned down the sheets. How did you manage that so quickly?"

"I'm magic," she answered. "You told me so this afternoon." She shifted his weight off her shoulder and pushed him towards the bed. He plopped onto the edge of the mattress.

"That's right, I did, didn't I?" he said with a loopy grin. He reached out his hand and started stroking her arm. "You're so pretty, Jenny. Did I ever tell you how pretty you are?"

"No," she answered, her cheeks starting to blush. "I think you'd be more comfortable if you took off your sweater."

"Right. I'll do that." He started pulling at his sleeve but got his elbow stuck.

"Here, let me help you," Jenny laughed. She put her arms around Eddie's waist and grabbed the bottom of his sweater.

"Hmm, this is nice," he said, leaning his face against her chest and nuzzling her breasts. "I like you Jenny. You're very pretty."

Jenny pulled Eddie's sweater up over his head. As it popped off, his shirt became untucked and rode halfway up his chest.

"You're taking my clothes off, Jenny!" he laughed.

"I'm helping you get ready for bed," she replied in an exasperated voice. She pulled his shirt back down and plucked a lighter and crumpled package of cigarettes out of his breast pocket. She laid them on his nightstand.

"So that's where they were," he said as he watched her. "I was looking for those. I remember now—I put them in my pocket to hide them from you."

"How very clever you are," she replied. She turned her face towards the pair of glasses sitting on his nightstand. "Do you wear contacts, Mr. R? Do you need to take them out before you go to sleep?"

"No, I have perfect vision," he answered with a scoff. "Whatever made you think I wear contacts?"

"I saw the glasses on your table."

"Oh. Those are reading glasses," he replied, his voice growing sadder. "I wear them sometimes, because I'm old. I'm very, very old, Jenny."

"You're not so terribly old yet," she reassured him.

He became aware of the fact that his head was pounding. A wave of melancholy enveloped him and the words of a familiar poem started echoing through his mind: "I grow old . . . I grow old . . . I shall wear the bottoms of my trousers rolled."

Then he felt even sadder because he couldn't remember where the line came from. A fuzzy sensation of numbness started to encroach upon him, and he looked up at Jenny in dismay. But then he saw her smile and forgot all about the poem.

"Hey, did I ever show you my moon blot?" he asked. He lifted his shirt back up and pointed to the splash of moles on his chest that formed a crescent shape.

Jenny laughed. "That's very nice, Mr. R. Now, why don't you try to sleep?" She put her finger to his sternum and gently pushed him down. He fell against the pillows with a soft thunk.

Eddie closed his eyes briefly, then rolled over on the mattress and faced her. He reached out his hand and stared at her pitifully. She offered him her hand in return. He clasped it and brought it to his lips for a kiss before releasing his grip.

She smiled at him again. "Try to sleep now," she whispered.

"Okay," he agreed, rolling onto his back and looking away from her. "Oh bugger. The ceiling's spinning."

"No, it's not," she replied.

"Yes it is. Look, Jenny. It's spinning like a spinning top." He pointed upwards. "I hate when that happens. It always means I'm gonna be sick."

Jenny leapt off the bed, ran to his bathroom and fetched a small garbage can. "Barf in here," she commanded him when she returned to his side.

"No," he grunted. "I feel fine. I'm much better now. Oh, Christ. Yes."

She deftly pulled him back to a sitting position so he could lean over the can. She supported his head with one hand as he retched, and held the can steady with her other arm. When he finished, she moved the can to the floor and helped him rest his head back against the pillow. She smoothed down his hair with her hand.

"Are you done throwing up, Mr. R?" she asked softly.

"Uh-huh," he moaned.

"Then I'll go get a cloth to wash you with," she replied. She climbed off the bed and carried the can back to the bathroom. Then she came back to Eddie's side and started wiping his face with a damp towel.

"You're so pretty, Jenny," he whispered as he drifted off to sleep.

\* \* \*

Jenny sat on the edge of his bed and watched him breathe. After a few minutes, he started to snore. Summoning her courage, she brushed aside the damp grey hair at his temples and kissed him gently on his forehead. He snored a bit louder in response. She repositioned her head and kissed him even more softly on his lips.

Eddie snorted and mumbled an incoherent series of noises in response. Jenny climbed off the bed. She noticed that the old afghan they had shared the night before was crumpled on the floor, so she picked it up and draped it across his body. Then she leaned over him and kissed him goodnight one last time before going to her own room.

## Chapter Fifteen

Roberta slipped out of her bedroom so silently that Pancho didn't even hear her leave. She crept through the upstairs hallway, following the glow of the nightlight that hung by the top of the steps. She hesitated for a few moments outside Alan and Grace's bedrooms to listen for the familiar sounds of their snoring. Then she stole down the stairs and into the kitchen.

The room was almost black, lit only by the glowing light of the oven clock. She waited for her eyes to adjust to the darkness, then surveyed the mess. The two numeral-shaped birthday candles that had topped Alan's cake lay on the countertop. She fingered them absentmindedly, remembering Eddie's boorish behavior at the dinner party. Then she slipped them into the right pocket of her dressing gown and proceeded into the living room.

The curtains were drawn, but periodic flashes of light shone through the gap between the drapes, illuminating the room in pulsating fits and starts. Thunder rumbled in the distance. She put her hand to the doorknob and hesitated. She had never left the confines of this building by herself. But the sights she had seen over the past two days empowered her with a newfound courage to embark into the world outside at last.

She opened the front door and breathed in the cool night air. It tasted familiar—with the same metallic tang that used to saturate the winds before the hurricanes struck St. Croix. She stepped onto the porch, closed the door behind her and strode across the yard, wind whipping her hair around her face.

The back door to the mansion stood wide open. She stepped into the house and surveyed the dark sitting room, lit only by the faint glow of a ceiling lamp hanging over the recessed staircase. Breathing more rapidly, she walked across the carpet.

A sharp pain stabbed at her foot and jolted her to a halt. She bent down and picked up the object she had stepped on. Fingering it carefully, she made out the shape of a small man. She ran her hand over the carpet and felt two similar toys lying close by. A flash of lightning illuminated the room, and she saw the three plastic dolls were shaped like a miniature mommy, daddy and little girl. She slipped the toys into the left pocket of her dressing gown and continued on her way.

Roberta climbed the steps carefully, one by one, lifting the hem of her nightgown to keep herself from tripping. When she reached the top floor she stopped and listened for the sound of her husband's snoring. She turned and headed towards the noise.

She put her hand on the knob of a heavy wooden door. The hinges squeaked slightly as she pushed the door open, but the rumble of Eddie's snores quickly drowned out the faint noise.

Her husband's bedroom looked dark and unfamiliar, but she was able to make out Eddie's shape by the soft light drifting in from the adjoining bathroom. He was sprawled diagonally across a large bed, his arm draped over his face.

The foul stink of vomit permeated the room. She followed the stench into the bathroom and saw a garbage can filled with puke and discarded papers. Wrinkling her nose in distaste, she started to turn away, but then she recognized Eddie's distinctive handwriting peeking out from behind the rancid stains. She lifted up the top sheet by its cleanest corner and realized she was holding the first draft of a poem, with cross-outs and arrows delineating the page. She brought the paper closer to her face, breathing rapidly through her mouth to mask the sour odor.

She saw the name 'Jenny' spelled out—two times, three times, four times! Grunting softly, she threw the paper back in the garbage can, then returned to her husband's bedside.

Eddie had rolled over while she was in the bathroom and moved his arm, so his face was now visible. She stared at him for a full minute while a jumble of emotions coursed through her head.

She sat down on the edge of the mattress and brought her free hand to his chest. She let it rise and fall along with his steady, rhythmic snoring. After a few minutes, their breathing became as one, and she felt calmer. Then she felt the familiar zig-zag pattern of her favorite afghan beneath her fingertips. She looked down and saw the blanket Grace had crocheted for her.

She ran her fingers gently over the yarn, remembering the many times Eddie had climbed under the afghan and cuddled with her in their home across the yard. Then she remembered how he had stolen the blanket from the house last night, so he could cuddle with that other girl in the field underneath the stars.

Standing up from the bed, she stared at the blanket in contempt, and peeled it off of Eddie. He shivered and let loose a loud snore, then rolled his head away from her and settled back into his deep sleep.

She watched him for a few seconds, fighting the urge to strike his face. Then she noticed a cigarette lighter lying on his nightstand. She stared at it dumbly for a few seconds.

A noxious voice in the back of her head started to snarl. *Do it!* the voice commanded her.

Roberta slipped her hand into her right pocket, pulled out the candle shaped like a '4', and lit its wick with the cigarette lighter. She held the candle a few inches away from Eddie's face. His skin glowed golden in the light of the flame.

She took a step back and watched her husband breathe.

*Those pillows will catch fire right away,* the voice taunted her. *Just like the pillows on your mother's bed did. Go ahead. Do it!*

Trembling, she took another step backwards and pushed her shaking free hand into the left pocket of her dressing gown. She nervously fingered the three toys she had pilfered and felt a small rush of relief. She pulled out the small male figurine and stared at it for a long moment by the light of the small candle. Then she tilted the candle over the doll until its face was covered with drips of red wax. She rested the toy on Eddie's nightstand, and dropped the lighter into her pocket.

*Kill him!* shouted the voice in her head. *Do it now!*

She hesitated by the bedside, fighting back the voice until she was at last able to silence it.

Gathering her resolve, she returned to the bathroom and plucked her husband's offensive poem out of the garbage can. Holding the paper carefully by the top edge, she put her candle to the bottom corner and set the page afire. The flame rapidly engulfed the lower half of the sheet. She threw the paper into the sink, where it curled up into a blackened crisp of ash. Then she returned to Eddie's side, collected her afghan off the floor, and slipped out of his bedroom as quietly as she had come in. She reached for the wooden door to close it, but it started to squeak once more, so she left it open and crept down the hallway.

She walked down the stairs, holding her candle aloft. Then she lingered in the large sitting room for a few minutes while she considered her next move.

A blinding flash of light burst through the open doorway, accompanied by a loud bang that sounded like a crack and a deep rumble of thunder that reverberated in her gut. She approached the back door cautiously and looked outside. The top bough of the elm tree was split cleanly in two. Its highest branches were aglow with sizzling yellow flames.

Roberta stared at the spectacle for a few seconds in silent awe, then smiled to herself.

She stepped out of the mansion, leaving the door open as she had found it, and crossed the lawn. When she reached the burning tree, she stopped at the spot where she had seen her husband sitting beside the girl with the glasses earlier that day.

*Jenny,* she thought irritably.

She tossed her afghan aside and put her candle to the pile of dry leaves and twigs by the exposed root. Then she stepped back and watched the kindling catch fire. The flames quickly grew into a small blaze that started creeping up the dried bark at the base of the tree. She blew out her candle and slipped it back into her pocket. Then she picked her blanket back up, repositioned it on the grass a few yards away from the tree, and returned to her home across the lawn.

\* \* \*

Pancho bounded out of the farmhouse as soon as Roberta opened the front door. Roberta tried to grab one of her long tufts of fur, but the dog evaded her grasp and dashed away. Pancho stopped for a brief moment by the burning tree to sniff the ground, then continued her race across the yard.

Bursting through the mansion's open back door, she dashed up the steps and ran into Eddie's bedroom. She leapt onto his mattress and barked in his face.

"Shut up!" Eddie howled at her through clenched teeth. "I'm sleeping!"

Pancho stopped barking long enough to lick his cheek with her sloppy, wet tongue. Then she grabbed his shirt with her teeth and growled. She pulled at the fabric until the top button snapped off, then licked his face again and gently nipped at his nose and chin.

"Bad dog!" Eddie shouted, finally opening his eyes. "Get off the bed. Off! Now!"

Pancho ignored his command and pawed at him, barking into his ear.

"What the fuck is wrong with you?" he cursed.

The dog jumped off the bed and ran to the window. Then she ran back to the bed and barked two more times before returning to the window.

Eddie slowly sat up. An excruciating current of pain rippled through his head. He tried to move his legs to the side of the bed, but his stomach lurched and he curled up into a ball instead. The inside of his cheeks felt like someone had scraped them raw with sandpaper. He felt a powerful craving for a drink of water.

Barking more emphatically, Pancho jumped back to his side. She sunk her teeth into his shirt and tried to drag him off the bed.

"I'm coming, I'm coming!" he protested. "Jesus Christ, girl, what the hell is wrong with you tonight?" Stumbling out of bed, he reluctantly followed the dog to the window. As he drew closer to the wall, he noticed a strange glow pouring in through the glass.

He stared at his back yard for just a moment in wide-eyed disbelief. Then he ran out of the bedroom and flew down the steps. Pancho followed at his heels and passed him as soon as he stepped outside. She ran to the middle of the yard and let out a loud howl.

"Holy fucking mother of god!" Eddie cursed.

Tongues of fire leapt from the top and bottom of the old elm tree. A wall of heat surged towards him, forcing him to keep his distance as he stared at the rapidly growing pillar of flames.

He gazed at it in terror for a few moments before flinging out his right arm and gesturing towards the farmhouse. "Go!" he yelled at the dog. "Wake up the others! Fetch Alan! Go! Go! Run!"

Pancho tore across the grass to her second home.

Eddie surveyed the yard frantically to make certain the fire hadn't spread beyond the tree. Then he looked back at the elm and tried to gather his wits about him. *How the fuck did it catch fire at both the base and the top?* he asked himself.

The sound of voices behind him made him turn his head. Jenny and Gisela were calling to him as they uncurled the garden hose that hung by the mansion's back door.

"Mrs. F is calling the fire department!" Jenny yelled. "Get the hose from the other house! I'll start spraying from this side!"

Jenny's composed voice forced Eddie back to his senses. "Right!" he yelled back. His heart pounding, he backed away from the tree and turned towards the farmhouse. Then he saw an object on the ground that made him catch his breath again. Roberta's afghan was lying on the grass in front of him, rolled up and bent into the shape of an arrow. He stared at it for a moment, then let his eyes follow the direction of the point.

A familiar throaty grunt rippled through the air above him, causing his stomach to lurch. He looked up and saw a small light shining from the window of his wife's bedroom. Roberta stood behind the open window pane, holding a glowing candle close to her face. She stared down at him defiantly, and curved her lips into a twisted smile.

# Book Three

*You think me an unfeeling, loose-principled rake, don't you?*

— Charlotte Brontë
*Jane Eyre*

## Chapter One

### *New York City, New York*

"I'm as clean as a whistle!" Gerry said, turning in a circle to let Eddie inspect him from all sides. "Never felt better, either. You were right all along. Sobriety suits me. So thank God you sprang me from that clinic early. There was nothing else for me to learn."

Eddie raised an eyebrow. "Let's hope you're right. Now, sit down and I'll tell you my plans for the next week or so. But first, I have to fill you in on what's been happening at Thornfield."

"No need," Gerry said, claiming the most comfortable seat in Eddie's luxurious hotel suite. "I spoke with Alan. He told me all about the fire—how the lightning struck the top of the tree, and your missus took care of the trunk. And he assured me that my daughter was unharmed and your better half is now safely sedated."

"Right," Eddie sighed. He wondered afresh if he was making the right decision in keeping Roberta at the farmhouse. *She hasn't harmed anyone or anything for sixteen years,* he reminded himself. *She's only dangerous when she's provoked. And I'm the one who provoked her this time. I just have to set things to rights.*

Gerry leaned back in his chair and coughed, calling Eddie out of his reverie. "The men from the fire department didn't ask how the tree caught fire in two places?"

"No," Eddie replied, focusing his attention back to the matter at hand. "They just blamed the lightning. There'd been several other strikes in the area that evening. And then the rain started pissing down shortly after they arrived. The fire was out in no time."

"So all is well at Thornfield again," Gerry surmised.

"Not quite," Eddie said, walking to the window to avoid

Gerry's penetrating gaze. "There's still the matter of the nanny."

Gerry broke into a hearty laugh. "I knew it! You fell for her, just like Captain Von Trapp got all hot and bothered over Maria!"

Eddie closed his eyes for a moment and remembered the look on Jenny's face when he told her he'd be flying to New York. *I can't keep deceiving her and leading her on,* he reminded himself. *She needs to see what kind of man I really am.*

"No," Eddie said. He looked back at Gerry and sighed. "Oh bugger, yes. I like her, and she likes me too. But I don't want her pining for me after she leaves. She needs to move past her infatuation and get on with her life. So I've come up with a plan. I will show her the way I've been treating women for the past several years, so she'll be able to leave Thornfield with no lingering regrets. And I need you to support me in this endeavor."

Gerry cocked his eyebrows and leered at his friend suggestively. "What, you want me to dress up in drag and pretend to be one of your mistresses?"

Eddie covered his face in exasperation. "No. I've arranged for two women to travel with us to Thornfield. We're going to flaunt them in front of Jenny and behave very badly."

"Hell, Eddie, your timing's a little off," Gerry pointed out. "I've just spent the past two months learning how to behave well."

"Sober or not, I'm sure you can still act like a rock star."

"Well, of course I can," Gerry huffed. "But *you* never acted like a rock star, even back when you were one." He offered Eddie a look of brotherly concern. "Do you need a few pointers?"

"I am perfectly capable of acting like an arse, Gerry, all by myself, with nobody's help!" Eddie exclaimed. He took a deep breath to calm his nerves before continuing. "I just need you to play along and, whenever an opportunity presents itself, show me off in the worst possible light."

Gerry shrugged his shoulders. "Well, sure, Eddie. I can do that. What are friends for?" He picked up the room service menu from the table at his side and started thumbing through the options. "So who are our mystery dates?"

Eddie hung his head in shame. "Belinda Graham and her sister," he mumbled.

Gerry dropped the menu onto his lap. "Jesus Christ! Are you serious? *The* Belinda Graham?"

Eddie looked back at Gerry and sighed. "In the flesh."

"Well, I claim her," Gerry said. "You can have the sister."

"Sorry. Belinda's taken. The two of us—share a bit of a past."

Gerry's eyes widened in disbelief. "You're having me on! When did you ever find time to date a *Sports Illustrated* cover girl?"

"We didn't date. We just fucked," Eddie said, his guilty conscience kicking in with an alarming ferocity. "Belle was the first woman I slept with after Birdie's overdose."

Gerry smirked. "You sure about that? I thought you told me you first slid down the slippery slope of adultery with Maria Mesrour, that Belgian skier with the Olympian tits."

"No, I didn't meet Maria until after the Sarajevo games," Eddie said, covering his eyes and swallowing back a fresh wave of shame. "I met Belinda in 1981, back when she was just one of the Bengals' cheerleaders. I rented a suite in the Netherland Hilton in Cincinnati so I could hide her from Birdie's roving eyes, and fucked her frantically for a fortnight. Then I gave her the brush. I told her I was still too in love with Birdie to pursue a new relationship, and went back to Thornfield."

"I see," Gerry said. "You played the tragic romantic hero card."

Eddie nodded. "I wasn't precisely lying."

Gerry cleared his throat. "Good move. I wish I had that trick up my sleeve. I'd use it more often than you do."

Eddie let loose a derisive snort. "We're a sorry lot, aren't we?"

"Speak for yourself," Gerry said. "So tell me more about Belinda Graham. Why'd you look her up?"

"I didn't," Eddie said. "I came to New York to look up Jim. He was backing Rosamond Oliver at her concert at the Lone Star Café. He knows what's been going on at Thornfield lately, and I wanted his advice. So I met him after the show and saw Belle and her sister backstage. Apparently, Belle and Rosamond are friends."

"Rosamond Oliver—she sang that song about rivers, no?"

"*Drowning in Rivers of Love,* that's right," Eddie agreed. "So anyway, the group of us went out for drinks—Jim, Rosamond, the Graham girls and me. Belle told me she'd be flying back to Cincinnati later this week to perform in a Ben-Gals reunion halftime show. And while the women were in the ladies fixing their hair and make-up, Jim and I hatched up the idea of bringing Belle and her sister to Thornfield."

Gerry snorted in laughter. "I see now why you and Jim were college boys. You're definitely the brain trust of the band."

Eddie threw Gerry an icy stare. "Well, it's the only plan I could think of. So put away that room service menu and shine your shoes. We're picking up our dinner dates in half an hour."

\* \* \*

"Oh, God!" Eddie groaned. He thrust deeper into Belinda. She spread her legs and moaned. The familiar ecstasy began to wash over him. He plunged into her again and again as the tension built and crested, then burst inside her with pulsing spasms of release.

He lay on top of her hot, moist body, waiting for his pounding heart to stop racing, then slowly rolled to his side.

She cuddled up next to him. "I've missed you," she whispered.

He said nothing for several seconds, glad that the darkness was hiding his face. *God, I am a bastard,* he thought. The mad passion that had consumed him after three Manhattans, two gin-and-tonics and one sexy, private strip tease had dissipated completely. He felt as drained as his spent, flaccid cock.

Belinda ran the tip of her impeccably manicured fingernail through his wiry chest hair in a figure eight pattern. "It's just like old times, isn't it? You and me, together again?"

Eddie sighed. "Yes," he mumbled. "Imagine that." He took a deep breath. "I don't suppose you have any cigarettes?"

"No, I gave up smoking. It's bad for your skin."

"For your lungs too," Eddie said as he extricated her hand from his chest. He sat up and started peeling off his condom, then stopped. "I'm gonna toss this in the rubbish. I'll be right back."

He stepped over the piles of clothing they had left on the carpet and walked into the hotel bathroom. He turned on the light and looked at his face in the mirror over the sink. *You are the world's biggest wanker,* he told his reflection. He tossed his condom, washed his hands and called out to Belinda.

"I'm gonna shower. I'm all sweaty." He scanned the lotions, gels, mousses and moisturizers lined up along the countertop, searching for a simple bar of hotel soap. Failing, he grabbed a bottle that looked like a cleansing product and turned on the shower. He plucked a small wash cloth from the pile of folded towels, then noticed Belinda leaning in the door frame, her huge, perfect breasts seemingly standing at attention.

"Mind if I join you? I can scrub your back," she purred.

Eddie looked away from her breasts. His eyes fell on her patch of perfectly trimmed pubic hair. *Any man in the world would be jealous of me right now*, he knew. *A gorgeous swimsuit model is standing naked not two feet in front of me, begging for more sex.*

He felt his cock start hardening again and closed his eyes. He tried to remember how beautiful Roberta had looked the first time he saw her naked. *But I don't feel like I'm cheating on Birdie now,* he thought. *I feel like I'm cheating on Jenny.*

Eddie opened his eyes and smiled at Belinda. He tried to imagine Jenny making such an offer to him. *She's an innocent convent school girl,* he reminded himself. *Nothing will ever happen between us unless I make the first move, and I'm not going to do that. I need to let her go. This will help me do that.*

"Such an enticing offer," he said to Belinda. He held out his hand and pulled her towards him.

### London, England

"Look, Junie, your dream lover is back amongst the living!"

Philip Randall handed the copy of the wire service photo to his assistant and smiled. "You conjured him up from the great beyond with that teaser you made Roger run on the front page."

June examined the picture and sighed. "If only he were in London and not New York."

Elsie stole the photo away from her. "He's aged well. The grey hair at his temples makes him look so distinguished."

"Can't say the same for Jim McCudden," Philip said, grabbing the picture back. "At the rate he's losing his hair, he'll be bald by next Easter." He pointed to the three women in the shot. "Looker, stunner, bit-of-alright."

"Is that how you'll be identifying the ladies in the caption?" June asked.

"Might as well," Philip said. "From what you two have told me, none of our female readers will care about any other person in this photograph besides Eddie Rochester. Though I believe our male readers will probably recognize Belinda Graham."

"The woman on the far left is Rosamond Oliver, the country singer," Elsie noted. "My mum likes her."

"Would you be speaking of that level-headed Kentish woman who once witnessed a crop circle being formed?" Philip asked.

"I only have one mum," Elsie replied.

"Who's that woman standing between Belinda and Jim?" June asked. "I don't recognize her."

"Doesn't matter. I'm going to crop her and Jim out of the photo and just show Eddie standing between Belinda and Rosamond," Philip said. "And I'll write a piece about how he's splitting his love between two women."

June glared at him. "You don't know if he's actually seeing either one of them, Phil. You're just making that up."

Philip shrugged. "All's fair in love, war and tabloids. I'll just run the column and see if he cares to comment afterwards."

## Chapter Two

### *Millcote, Ohio*

Eddie clenched his teeth into a forced smile and opened the front door to his mansion. "After you," he said politely, extending his arm to welcome the Graham sisters.

"Wow!" JoJo exclaimed as she stepped into the airy foyer. "This place is huge! That chandelier is as big as my whole kitchen!"

"Ladies first," Gerry said, gesturing for Belinda to follow her sister into the house.

"You go ahead," Belinda insisted, locking her hand in the crook of Eddie's elbow. "I'll walk in with Ed."

Gerry glanced over at Eddie and snorted. "Fine. You tend to your woman now, *Ed.*"

Eddie rolled his eyes and tried to extricate himself from Belinda's tight grip as Gerry stepped through the door. "I hope Thornfield doesn't disappoint you," he said to Belinda.

"Are you kidding?" she replied. "After all these years you're finally inviting me into your home. I'm already ecstatic!"

*Bugger!* Eddie cursed in his head. *This has to be the stupidest idea I've ever had.* He led Belinda into the house and looked frantically for Jenny. He found her standing at the end of the long hallway, holding Gisela's hand and looking crestfallen.

Gisela let go of Jenny's hand and bounded into Gerry's arms. "Papa!" she cried. *"Ich habe dich so viel vermisst!"*

*"Nicht auf Deutsch,"* Gerry replied as he gathered his daughter into a bear hug, "Herr Rochester told me you speak English now."

Gisela rubbed noses with him. "I have you missed, Papa."

*"Wunderbar!"* he exclaimed proudly. "Now introduce me to your English teacher."

Gisela clasped Gerry's hand and led him down the hallway.

"You must be Jenny," he said, holding out his hand in greeting. "Eddie's told me so many wonderful things about you. But he never mentioned that you had such spectacular tits."

Jenny blushed. "I guess I should say thank you?" she replied.

Gerry stood back and admired her outfit—a vibrantly patterned green and orange minidress with a scoop neck and bell sleeves. "God, you are an absolute vision!" he said enthusiastically.

Jenny crossed her arms in front of her chest in a futile attempt to hide the low neckline of her outdated gown. "Mrs. F told me to wear my nicest dress," she apologized.

"Is that an Ossie Clarke?" Gerry asked.

"I don't know what you mean," she said, her cheeks blushing a deeper shade of red.

"You don't know Ossie?" Gerry scoffed. "Why, he was the swingingest designer in all of swinging London, back in the day! Hell, I'm sure I must have seen Twiggy modeling that very same dress on the cover of *Vogue*. Back me up here, Eddie. Doesn't that dress look like one of Ossie's frocks?"

Eddie stared at Jenny and swallowed hard. *I'll bet she picked that up at a church jumble sale,* he thought. *It looks like something Birdie might have worn twenty years ago.* He walked towards Gerry and Jenny and shrugged. "You know I've never paid much attention to fashion, Ger."

Belinda stepped forward and extended her hand. "So nice to meet you," she said in a disinterested voice. "I'm Belinda Graham. And this is my sister JoJo."

Jenny pushed back her glasses and shook their hands. "Hi," she mumbled. "I'm Jenny Ayr."

Gerry continued smiling at Jenny. "Just look at you, love. If you had only walked into a party in 1968 wearing a dress like that, you would have saved Eddie a hell of a lot of heartbreak, you know what I mean?"

Jenny stared at him in bewilderment. "I have no idea what you mean."

Gerry took her hand and led her to the table of *hors devours* Sally had set out for the guests. "It doesn't matter," he said, his eyes twinkling mischievously. "All that matters is that you're here now. Let me get you a glass of wine."

"I don't drink," she whispered shyly.

Gerry laughed. "Hell, I nearly forgot. Neither do I! Whad'ya say I fetch us both some ginger ales?"

Belinda cast an anxious glance at Eddie and caught him staring at Jenny. She clutched his forearm and whispered into his ear. "My dress is a Versace. After dinner you could help me take it off and check the label yourself."

Eddie turned his face towards her and managed a sad half-smile. "Let's just see where the evening leads us, shall we? Here, let me pour you some wine while we wait for the Carters to arrive. Then we can all sit down for dinner together." He broke away from her vicelike grip and unconsciously wiped the sleeve of his jacket where she had just touched him.

\* \* \*

"Well, I always thought Eddie would fall for a writer someday," Bob Carter laughed. "But I never imagined she would look quite like you!"

Belinda smiled seductively. "I'll take that as a compliment."

"It's her looks that got her the contract with Simon and Schuster," JoJo pointed out. "It's a beauty tips book."

Belinda glared at her sister. "It's a lifestyle guide."

"Whatever the topic, I'm impressed," Eddie said, taking Belinda's hand in his and bringing it to his lips for a kiss. "Signing a book deal with a major publisher is a remarkable achievement." He glanced at Jenny to see if she had noticed his gesture, but saw she was looking down, cutting Gisela's meat into small pieces.

"When will it be coming out?" asked Bob's wife Anne.

"Not for several months," Belinda said. "I still have to proof the gallows."

"The galleys," Eddie corrected her. He felt her hand flinch inside his grasp.

"Yes, that's what I meant," she laughed. "Silly slip."

"So how long did it take you to write your book?" Bob asked.

"Oh, Belle didn't write it," JoJo piped in. "The ghostwriter did. She just posed for the pictures."

"That's not true," Belinda said, releasing Eddie's hand and picking up her wine glass. "Jacob just helped me organize my thoughts. But all the words on the pages are my own."

Eddie watched Belinda's eyes flash at her sister. Her cheeks streaked with a blush of bright color. "I believe most first-time authors use an editorial assistant," he said in a soothing voice.

Belinda turned back to him and sighed in relief. "Yes, Jacob was just my editorial assistant."

"A guidebook guider," Gerry suggested.

Belinda forced a smile.

Eddie looked down the table and noticed Jenny was smiling too. *Christ, this dinner conversation is painful,* he thought.

"Could you pass the wine please, Eddie?" Bob asked, breaking his reverie.

"Sure," Eddie said, picking up the bottle. "But let me top off JoJo's glass first. It's almost empty."

"Thanks!" JoJo exclaimed. "I love this stuff! Most guys just offer me beer."

Bob took the wine from Eddie, then turned to Jenny. "So Eddie told me you're looking into going to college."

"Not yet," she answered in a quiet voice. "I still have to finish up some things first."

"What would you like to study?" Anne Carter asked gently.

Jenny shrugged and started playing with her food.

"You could study German," Gerry suggested. "Hell, you could teach German! And Zellie tells me you're quite an artist too."

"Do you have a portfolio you could show to an art school?" Bob asked. "I think that's part of the application process."

"No," Jenny said, not meeting his eyes. "I just keep my pictures in a folder."

"Keith Richards went to art college," Gerry continued. "John Lennon and Pete Townshend too. Maybe if Jenny goes to an art school, she could meet some nice blokes like them."

Jenny raised her head at last and smiled at Gerry. Eddie noticed her eyes were twinkling. *Or maybe that's just her glasses,* he thought. *Damn, why can't I stop looking at her?*

"I have a portfolio," JoJo interjected. "Belle keeps telling me she's gonna show it to some agents she knows and maybe get me a modeling contract."

"And what are you doing till then?" Anne Carter asked.

"Right now I wait tables at the Howard Johnson's in Hamilton," JoJo answered. "But I'm hoping to become a Hooters Girl."

Gerry beamed at her. "Damn, JoJo, you're my kind of woman!"

She smiled at him gamely. He winked back and mouthed the word, "Later."

Eddie coughed loudly. "Maybe I should ask Sally to bring in the dessert."

"But the ladies have hardly touched their food!" Gerry protested. "Eddie, pass me down Belinda's plate. I can't let a perfectly good steak like that go to waste." He grabbed the dish, tore Belinda's dinner roll in half, and handed the two pieces of bread to Jenny and Gisela. "Eat up, *Mädchen*. A man likes a woman with a hearty appetite. It's a sign of sensuality."

Belinda glowered at Gerry. JoJo started cutting her meat.

Belinda stiffened her back. "I'm not in the mood for dessert, Ed. Let's go to the other room. Everyone else can join us there after they've had their coffee."

Eddie sighed. "Your wish is my command," he said, standing up from the table. "Bob, could you take over the hosting duties? Belle and I will pick out some records we can listen to after dinner."

\* \* \*

Eddie stood behind Belinda at the base of the front staircase and wrapped his arms around her waist, hiding his face in her cloud of golden hair so he wouldn't have to look at his guests. His insides had been churning with shame all evening. He had tried so hard to make a show of his interest in his former flame, yet each time he gazed into her face, she looked more and more like a freakishly sculpted mannequin. And each time he stole a quick glance at Jenny, she appeared so much more beautiful by contrast.

His charade was doomed, he knew. He could tell Jenny saw through him. All he wanted to do now was escape from the mansion and run through the rolling hills of Thornfield like he used to when he was a carefree teenage boy.

"Dinner was wonderful, Eddie," Bob said, bringing him back to earth. "Thanks so much for inviting Anne and me."

"I should have you over more often," Eddie replied.

"You should," Gerry agreed. "You really need to start being more social, Eddie, and stop living like a bloody hermit."

"I like how he's quiet," Belinda said. She clasped Eddie's hand and lifted his fingers up ever so slightly so that they grazed the bottom of her protruding breast.

"I think we should go now," Anne said, rolling her eyes at her host. Eddie released Belinda and opened the front door for them.

After the Carters left, Gerry turned to Jenny. "You said Zellie's asleep?"

"Yes. I just checked," Jenny answered. "She's out like a light."

"Good," Gerry said, squeezing JoJo's hand. "Then maybe I can tuck you in tonight." He turned towards Eddie. "Which room did ya put me in?"

"The one next to mine," Eddie replied. "Turn right at the top of the stairs."

"Gotcha," Gerry said. He started leading JoJo up the steps.

Jenny began climbing the stairs after them.

"Where are you going?" Eddie called after her.

"To bed," she answered without facing him.

"I need you to show Belinda to her room," he said. "She and her sister will be staying in the suite across the hall from you. Sally put their suitcases in there already."

"But Ed," Belinda protested. "I thought we would—"

Eddie leaned down and whispered in her ear. "Perhaps I'll knock on your door later and give you another goodnight kiss."

"Oh, but darling—" she whined.

He kissed her cheek, then started walking to the back of the house. "I'm going to say hello to the Pooles before I turn in for the night, and retrieve my retriever. I haven't seen Pancho in almost two weeks now."

Gerry stood on the landing and chuckled. "Yup. It's time for him to say hello to the bitch."

Eddie sighed and stood by the back door in the dark sitting room, twiddling the knob and listening to his guests' awkward conversation, bracing himself for an even more awkward reunion with his wife and her caretakers.

"Don't worry, Belle," JoJo called down to her sister. "You can have the room to yourself. I'm gonna cuddle with my own rock star tonight!"

Eddie heard the clip of her high heels and the thump of Gerry heavy feet climbing the stairs.

He listened for Jenny's voice, wondering if she would bother to address Belinda or just lead her away.

"Come this way," she said at last, her voice arch with a clipped politeness. "I think you'll like your room. It's where Mr. R hangs his gold records."

Belinda's response sounded chilly. "I suspect you like to sneak in there and gaze at them in your free moments."

"No," Jenny answered. "They're kind of boring to look at. I prefer it when he plays his real records for me on the stereo."

*Good girl,* Eddie thought with an unexpected surge of pride. He tried to imagine what Belinda's face had looked like when Jenny spoke to her, then pictured Jenny's most likely expression—a charming mix of innocence and snark. *Your old school chum would be proud of you,* he told his vision. *You won't let the bastards get you down. Even when the biggest bastard is me.*

He waited by the door, listening to both women's footfalls on the staircase, then slipped into the night.

## Chapter Three

### *London, England*

"C'mere Junie, I need you!" Philip Randall shouted from his desk. He pulled a sheet of paper from his battered IBM Selectric and handed it to June as soon as she stepped into his office. "Be a love and look this over. It's for next week's edition."

June scanned the article and furrowed her brow. "Prince Richard of Gloucester? What's going on, Phil? Are you trying to bring in the toff set by dropping Shakespearean references in your gossip column?"

"This story isn't about Richard the fucking Third!" Philip cursed, reaching for his pack of cigarettes. "It's about all the lesser royals who are leeching millions off the civil list. You know, the Queen's first and second cousins. That lot."

June rolled her eyes. "Why are you giving me next week's column already? It's only Monday."

"I'm taking a business trip." Philip dug through the piles of papers on his desk and handed June a black and white photograph marked with a grease pencil. "I pulled this off Sunday's wire. Have a look!"

June tucked Philip's article under her arm and examined the picture. "Well, what do you know? Gerry Enis is out of the clinic."

"And partying in New York with his old bandmates Jim and Eddie."

June's face lit up. "Cor! Are the Pilots getting back together?"

"Doubt it," Philip replied, leaning back in his chair and exhaling a cloud of smoke. "I can't see Tony Wright wanting to share his spotlight with Eddie Rochester anymore."

"So what's your plan?" June asked, handing the photo back to

Philip. "Are you going to badger Gerry and see if you can set him on the piss again?"

Philip snorted. "I don't give two shits about that boozer. I'm going after Eddie Rochester. My sources tell me he was last seen boarding a plane to Cincinnati with Belinda Graham tucked under his arm."

"Ooh, lucky you!" June teased. "You get to dodge boring old Manhattan and visit Eddie's farm in Ohio instead. Maybe you can talk to his estate manager about this year's cabbage harvest." She laughed and carried Philip's story back to her desk to edit.

Philip crushed out his cigarette stub, then lifted the ashtray and picked up the print-out he had hidden beneath it. He read through it one more time and laughed quietly. "Bloody crop circles," he mumbled to himself. "They're poppin' up everywhere these days."

## *Millcote, Ohio*

Eddie pulled Roberta closer to him and nuzzled her hair. "Good morning, darling," he whispered, kissing her forehead.

Roberta opened her eyes and mumbled an incoherent reply, then rolled away to her side of the bed. Eddie folded his arms behind his head and yawned. He lay beside his wife a few minutes more, listening to her steady, rhythmic breathing and trying to remember the last time he'd enjoyed her company.

*Do I still love her?* he asked himself. *And if I don't, when did I stop?* As far as he could recall, there had been no single turning point—just a gradual decline of affection as his frustration with her slowly grew.

He sighed and climbed out of bed.

When he walked into the kitchen, he found Grace hunched over the newspaper crossword puzzle. "Coffee ready?" he asked.

"Help yourself," she answered. "What's the French word for 'wife'? Five letters."

"I think it's *'femme'*," Eddie answered as he poured himself a cup. "But I'm not sure. It's *'Ehefrau'* in German. An English synonym might be 'somnolent'. Though that's nine letters."

Grace looked up. "Dr. Bob put her on some pretty strong meds. And after what she did the night of Alan's birthday, I can't say I blame him."

Eddie took a sip from his cup and glanced out the window.

"Looks like Ron cleared away what was left of the tree."

"He had a whole crew of workers helping him. With all the buzz saws and grinding machines they had blasting away, it's a good thing Birdie was heavily sedated. You know how she usually responds to loud noises."

Eddie nodded and took a seat at the kitchen table.

"So how's Gerry?" Grace asked, looking back at her paper.

"So far, so good," Eddie replied. "He drank nothing but juice and water when were in New York, and last night he kept to fizzy drinks and coffee."

"So he can collect his daughter then," Grace noted.

Eddie sighed. "I'd like to watch him for a few more days, just to be safe. I'm planning to take him to some restaurants and clubs this week and see how he handles the temptations."

Grace threw him a stern glance. "Dare I ask how *you* are handling your temptations?"

"I slept here last night, didn't I?" he replied, looking into his coffee cup and not meeting her eyes. "I spent the whole night in bed with my catatonic wife."

Grace reached her hand across the table and rested it on top of his. "She's adjusting to her new meds. Dr. Bob said they'd make her sleepy. And they're quieting the voices in her head while you entertain your houseful of guests across the lawn."

Eddie looked up. "I know, you're right. Do you think she'd mind if I brought Pancho to the other house tonight? Gisela might be disappointed if Gerry goes out with me and doesn't bring her along. The dog could keep her mind off her papa."

"Fine," Grace said, turning back to her puzzle. "Pancho can amuse both of your under-age charges while you take Gerry on a pub crawl through Cincinnati."

She filled in a few squares, then scratched out her markings. "Gaah. I hate these theme puzzles. Everything is in French today. How do you spell Catherine Deneuve's last name? You know, that blonde model in the perfume adverts?"

Eddie sipped his coffee. "Not sure. There's an 'E' and a 'U', but I don't know in what order. What are the words around it?"

Grace reviewed the clues. "Twelve down: Tartuffe playwright."

"That's Moliere," Eddie said. "M-O-L-I-E-R-E."

"Right," Grace said. "So 'E' comes before 'U' in 'Deneuve'."

Eddie put his cup down and rested his head in his hands. "God,

I feel like I'm living in a Moliere sex farce. Who am I supposed to sleep with tonight?"

Grace put the paper down and stood up to make breakfast. "Pancho," she answered. "She can guard your bedroom door."

### Cincinnati, Ohio

"Belle!" the cheerleaders squealed in unison. They dropped their shiny orange pom-poms on the floor and ran to the dance studio's door to envelop Belinda in a group hug.

"I wouldn't mind trading shoes with your squeeze just now," Gerry said to Eddie as he admired the scene.

Eddie leaned against the doorframe and looked on. "You have to give her this moment. The hometown girl who hit the bigtime comes back to her original roots. Let her bask in the glow."

Gerry ogled the long-legged dancer standing closest to him. "What d'ya call a group of Ben-Gals, Eddie? A gaggle? A clutch?"

"I'm not sure," Eddie answered. "Tigers are solitary creatures, but when they get together, I think it's called an 'ambush'."

"Sounds about right," Gerry laughed.

"Everybody, I want you to meet my new boyfriend!" Belinda shouted as she extracted herself from the group. She grabbed Eddie's hand and pulled him forward.

The chorus of squeals grew higher and louder as the cheerleaders surrounded Eddie.

"Hey, I'm a rock star too!" Gerry called out. A few women on the edge of the group straggled away from Eddie and hugged Gerry.

"Ladies, ladies!" shouted the choreographer from across the room. "Let's get back to work. Belinda, come here. I'll find you some pom-poms."

"Group photo first!" yelled another man. "With Belle's new beau!"

Eddie turned towards the voice. "No, I'm on my way just now."

The cheerleaders blocked his path to the door and fashioned a formation around him. Eddie flashed Gerry a hopeless look.

"I should be so lucky!" Gerry shouted to him.

A flash caught Eddie off-guard. He posed for one more photo, then pulled away from the cheerleaders and waved goodbye.

\* \* \*

The waitress topped off Eddie's coffee and turned towards Gerry. "Would you like a re-fill on your Seven-Up?"

"I suppose so," Gerry muttered unenthusiastically.

She nodded and left the two men to their conversation.

Gerry stared at the glowing *Christian Morlein* sign behind the bar and sighed. "It seems such a waste to be downing fizzy drinks in a perfectly nice bar like this."

"Have some coffee," Eddie suggested. "It's a proper grown-up beverage."

"You're hopeless," Gerry replied. "You want me to act like a grown-up, while you carry on like an immature rock star. But you know perfectly well that neither of us is suited to the other role."

The waitress returned to the table with Gerry's drink and two dessert menus.

"No, thank you," Eddie said. "I'm full."

"We still have another hour before we pick up Belinda at the dance studio, and another two before JoJo's shift is done," Gerry reminded his friend. "We might as well eat." He scanned the menu and asked for two servings of chocolate cheesecake.

Eddie amended the order. "Make that a piece of cake for my friend and a bowl of fruit for me."

Gerry watched the waitress' bottom as she walked away. "I wasn't ordering for you," he complained. "I wanted two slices."

"And you called me hopeless?" Eddie laughed.

"Yes I did," Gerry said. "I always used to think you were smart. But seeing you toss away a lovely girl like Jenny has changed my mind. You're either a bigger fool than I am, or you're just blind."

"I know what I'm doing," Eddie said. "I have no business pursuing a girl like her, even if Birdie weren't in the picture. Jenny's young. She has her whole life ahead of her. I want her to embrace a future of endless possibilities, not tie herself down to a middle-aged goat like me."

"But she really digs you. Anyone can see that. Even Belinda can see that. You should have seen the looks she was shooting at Jenny today over brekkie while you were at the farmhouse."

"Jenny would grow tired of me," Eddie countered. "Maybe not right away. But after a few years she'd start to wonder why she threw her youth away on a man old enough to be her father."

"Bollocks!" Gerry shouted. "She's used to being with older people. If she went to university, she'd probably fall for one of her professors."

"Keep your voice down, you pillock," Eddie whispered as the waitress returned with their desserts.

"Thanks, love," Gerry said. "This looks almost as tasty as you."

The waitress giggled and walked away. Eddie slid further down into the booth. "All right, Ger, even assuming that Jenny likes older men, I still have my own scruples to consider. I like her, but I'm also repulsed by the notion of corrupting a minor."

"She's not a minor, Eddie. She's nineteen-going-on-twenty."

"That's still pretty damn young."

Gerry swallowed a mouthful of cheesecake and washed it down with a swig of Seven-Up. "Not by the standards of your peers. You said you wanted to act like a rock star, right? Well, follow their examples. Elvis started dating Priscilla when she was fourteen. Jerry Lee Lewis married his own cousin when she was thirteen. And Bill Wyman, Christ! He was boffing that teenaged Mandy bint and her mother at the same fucking time!"

"And this information is supposed to make me feel better?" Eddie retorted.

Gerry stabbed at his cheesecake. "A lot of entertainers end up in May-December romances," he added. "Look at Bogie and Bacall. Frank Sinatra and Mia Farrow. Cher and her bagel-boy."

Eddie chewed on a piece of melon and offered no reply.

"Belinda's probably fifteen years younger than you," Gerry continued. "But that didn't stop you from shagging *her*."

"Belinda is mature in the ways of the world," Eddie replied.

"You mean she's a slut, while Jenny's still a virgin," Gerry said.

Eddie speared a grape with his fork. "Say it however you want."

"I like Jenny's specs," Gerry mumbled as he downed a mouthful of cake. "They give her a sexy librarian sort of vibe. I somehow always imagined you'd end up with a girl who wore glasses."

Eddie pushed his coffee cup to the middle of the table. "I'm going to the loo. I feel a sudden need to wash myself."

"Be my guest," Gerry said, reaching his fork into Eddie's bowl and piercing a strawberry.

"That's mine," Eddie protested.

"You weren't eatin' it," Gerry replied.

Eddie slid out of the booth and walked away. As soon as he stepped out of sight, Gerry summoned the waitress and held up his glass. "Could you ask the bartender to throw a couple shots of Seagrams in this? But don't put it on the tab, love. Just keep the cash." He winked and handed her a twenty-dollar bill.

### Millcote, Ohio

Eddie stood in front of Belinda's bedroom door and gathered his resolve. *Is this worth it?* he asked himself. *Jenny's already upset. I don't need to rub my cruelty in her face by making a lot of noise just outside her bedroom.*

Pancho ran down the hallway and jumped up against him.

"Down, girl," he commanded her. "You're not invited."

"You don't need to post a guard dog," Belinda teased as she opened her door. "I'm sure JoJo will knock if she wants to come in. Though I imagine she'll spend the night in Gerry's room again."

"I just don't want the dog to get in our way," Eddie said as he stepped into the room.

Belinda closed the door behind them and threw her arms around him. She scratched his back with her tapered fingernails and covered his mouth with kisses. Then she stood back and smiled. "So I've got you to myself tonight?"

Eddie smirked. "Yes. Sorry about last night. My friend Alan started asking me about Jim, and Rosamond Oliver's concert, and what clubs we visited in New York, and the next thing I knew it was three in the morning. I didn't want to bother you."

"You wouldn't have bothered me," she said, raising her hands back to his shoulders. "Did you tell him about our night at the St. Regis?"

"Some details of my trip to the Big Apple will remain under wraps," he replied, leaning down and kissing her again.

She led him to the bed, then released his hand for a moment to pick up a large stack of papers.

"Are those your galley proofs?" Eddie asked.

"Yes," she sighed. "Don't look at them. They're terrible." She laid them on her nightstand.

"No, please," Eddie said. "I want to. I'm impressed, you know. I read English at university. Sorry—I mean, I was an English major in college. It's not every day I get to bed a published author."

"I'm not published yet," Belinda said. "And at this rate, I don't think I'll ever be. My agent wants me to look these pages over, but I don't even know what to do."

Eddie picked up a page and sat down on the bed. "You just mark your edits. You know—correct any typos or grammatical mistakes. And re-write the sentences you're not happy with."

"I'm not happy with *any* of it," she whined, flopping down beside him.

"Well, didn't you write it?" Eddie asked.

She turned her face away. "No. A ghostwriter interviewed me, and he re-wrote my answers into chapters. But he used a lot of his own words. None of this sounds like the way I talk."

Eddie smiled. *I could spend the evening editing this, then leave her bedroom with a clean conscience,* he realized. He put his hand to her chin and gently turned her face towards his. "Would you like some help?"

"Oh God, yes!" she cried out.

Eddie cringed. *I hope Jenny didn't hear that,* he thought. "Give us a pen. Let's see what we can make of this."

\* \* \*

JoJo knocked on the bedroom door and opened it a crack. "Are you alone, Belle?" she asked as she stepped into the room. "I couldn't take Gerry's snoring anymore and thought I might sleep better if—Oh, you're here, Ed! Sorry. I'll leave."

"No," Eddie said, climbing off the bed. "Come in. I'm sure you'll sleep much better without my old drummer snuffling in your ear."

Belinda pouted. "But we aren't done yet!"

"We're at a good stopping point," Eddie countered. He leaned down and gave Belinda a big kiss. *If I have to re-write another paragraph about the merits of exfoliating sponges, I'll surely throttle her,* he thought as he walked to the door.

"We can work on the rest tomorrow," he assured her. "Goodnight, Belle." Eddie kissed JoJo's hand as he left the room, then jogged down the hallway and into his own bedroom.

He unbuttoned his shirt, threw it on the floor and collapsed on his bed. His hand brushed against his hard-on as he reached down to undo his fly. *No sex equals no guilt,* he reminded himself as he slipped his boxers down and reached for his cock. An image of Belinda's soft breasts peeking out of her low-cut blouse while she sat beside him on her bed sprang to his mind. The scratch of Pancho's nails against his door pushed the image away.

*Christ!* he cursed in his head. *This house is too crowded. I can't even wank off without somebody pestering me!* He pulled his trousers back up and opened the door. Pancho and Jenny were both standing in front of him.

"I'm sorry to bother you," Jenny said. "Pancho came into my room while you were, um, well—Pancho was sleeping on my bed this evening while I was reading. But then she heard you going down the hallway and seemed to want to join you instead."

Eddie smiled at her. "Thank you for bringing her to me."

"You're welcome," she replied.

He gazed at Jenny's face fondly. Then he dropped his eyes and noticed her soft breasts were pillowing out of the low lace neckline of her worn flannel gown.

She sensed his gaze and pulled up her dress. "Oops. This is a hand-me-down from Gigi. It's a little bit big on me."

He looked back up and tried to read Jenny's face. He wondered if she felt embarrassed to be standing in front of him in her pajamas, or to be seeing him shirtless.

"Did you have fun today in Cincinnati?" she asked.

"Yes," he fibbed. "It was great. Gerry and I had lunch at that new sports bar overlooking the river. And then the four of us went out for dinner at the Montgomery Inn. What did you do?"

"I played with Gisela and did some drawings. And I took Pancho for a long walk while Gisela was at school."

"Thanks for doing that," Eddie said, smiling and wishing Jenny hadn't pulled her sagging gown back up.

"I see a girl who wants to sleep with Eddie tonight!" bellowed a gruff voice from down the hall.

Eddie turned and watched Gerry walk towards him. Gerry bent down and scratched Pancho's ears. "You want that, don't ya, girl? You wanna sleep in Eddie's room now, I can tell. Such a good girl you are. Yes, I know. You're a good, good doggie."

Pancho lifted her face and licked Gerry's nose.

"So why'd ya give the Graham girls the suite with the private toilet?" Gerry asked Eddie. "You know I always need to take a leak in the middle of the night."

Eddie rolled his eyes, "Shut up and take your leak, Gerry."

"Right," Gerry replied. He stood up and winked at Jenny as he walked away.

Jenny giggled. "He's a goof, isn't he?"

"I can think of a few other words that might describe him better," Eddie said.

"Put a shirt on, Rochester!" Gerry shouted over his shoulder.

Eddie looked back at Jenny and cleared his throat. "So, you said you were reading in bed. Are you still slogging through that GED practice book?"

"No, it's so boring," she confessed. "I've gone back to working my way through your Trollopes."

"That's what everyone seems to be doing these days," Gerry called out from the bathroom doorway.

Eddie brought his hand to his forehead to mask the humiliation in his eyes.

Jenny gave the dog one last pat. "Goodnight, Mr. R. Maybe I'll see you in the morning before you drive back into town."

"I hope so," he answered without realizing what he was saying.

Jenny turned and headed back to her bedroom. After she stepped out of sight, Eddie closed his door and invited Pancho to jump on his mattress.

"So tell me, girl," he said wistfully. "What does it feel like to lie next to Jenny in bed?"

## Chapter Four

"Just look at it falling down, Birdie," Eddie implored, holding back the curtain to reveal the side yard. "Isn't it beautiful? There must be five inches of snow on the ground already."

"It's been falling since midnight," Alan said, opening the newspaper to the weather forecast. "It says here we might get fifteen inches by nightfall."

Eddie took a seat beside Roberta on the sofa and started tuning his guitar. "It's a little early for Christmas carols, but I think this might be an appropriate song for the day." He started playing the opening chords to *Let it Snow*.

Grace walked in from the kitchen and chimed in on the chorus. Birdie continued to sit in silence on the sofa, wrapped in her afghan and barely acknowledging the music.

Eddie called the song to a halt after the second verse and reached out to touch his wife's hand. "Would you rather hear some poetry? I know this one by heart." He cleared his throat and started reciting Frost's *Stopping by Woods on a Snowy Evening*.

Roberta slowly turned around and faced him. She reached out her hand and rested it on the guitar strings.

"Right," Eddie said, putting his fingers back to the frets and forming a 'C' chord. "Do you remember this one, love? From those months we spent in Andermatt?" He strummed a slow 4/4 rhythm and started singing in German.

Roberta watched him sing. Her expression remained dull and inscrutable, but her eyes began to glisten.

Grace took a seat beside Alan and listened to the song. After Eddie finished the last verse, he hummed the final line once more as a slow coda and plucked out an arpeggio.

"That was lovely," Grace said. "What does it mean?"

"It's called *Der Junge mit der Mundharmonika*. In English, 'The Boy with the Harmonica.' It was a huge hit in Germany and Switzerland in 1973. You couldn't escape it if you tried."

"It sounds sad," Grace said.

"It's more wistful," Eddie replied. He touched Roberta's cheek. "You remember that song, don't you, love? We'd sit in your room and listen to the radio while we watched the snow fall outside the window. And sometimes the nurses would come in and switch the dial to that station that played nothing but yodeling songs?"

Roberta turned her head away and looked out the window.

Eddie sighed in frustration, then stood up and placed his guitar back in its case. "I'll take this upstairs before I go."

Alan nudged him with a folded newspaper as he walked past. "Better take this too," he whispered. "Page 2 of the sports section."

Eddie rested his case on the floor and opened the newspaper to the page Alan had mentioned. He saw his own face staring back at him, surrounded by a dozen smiling Ben-Gal cheerleaders. Belinda was hugging him tightly and kissing his cheek. "Bugger," he mumbled under his breath.

He glanced at Roberta. She was staring out the side window, seemingly lost in a daze. *God, what is she thinking?* he wondered. *Will I ever know? Is she as sad as she looks?*

He folded the paper and tucked it under his arm. Then he stole a peek out the front window. Jenny and Gisela were making a snowman in the yard behind the mansion. He walked closer to the window and watched them for a long moment.

"Maybe I'll bring my guitar to the other house," he said, grabbing his coat. "Gisela might like to hear some German songs too. I'll bring Pancho back this afternoon to keep Birdie company."

### Athens, Ohio

John Reed slammed the door of Dick's hotel room. "I've got eight-hundred-and-fifty-dollars—the full amount I promised you! Go ahead and count it."

"I will," Dick said, taking the wad of cash and dividing it into piles by denomination.

"And guess what else I have?" John added with a devious smile.

"Haven't a clue. Tell me," Dick said without looking up from the money.

"Today's *Cincinnati Enquirer.*" He handed Dick the sports section, folded back to reveal the photograph of Eddie with Belinda and the Ben-Gals. "Your brother-in-law seems to have found himself a new girlfriend."

Dick examined the picture and shrugged. "Well, he always did go for the pretty ones. My sister was actually quite a dish when he married her."

John scowled. "Don't you see what this means? This could mark a change in your fortunes!"

Dick tossed the newspaper onto his mattress. "No it won't."

"Didn't you see how Belinda Graham was clinging to him? They're obviously a couple."

"So?" Dick replied.

"So he probably doesn't want her to know that he's still married to your sister. And he certainly doesn't want her to know he once got into a knife fight with your sister. You have information that could hurt him, and I'll bet you anything he'd be willing to pay big bucks to keep it under wraps."

"Not interested," Dick said, slipping the cash into his wallet.

"Seriously? You're not interested?" John challenged. "You'd rather keep running this fly-by-night operation when you could be making thousands of dollars on the side?"

Dick sighed. "If I'm going to blackmail the bastard, I have to be absolutely certain my plan will work. I don't want him to just sic the cops on me. And my gut tells me this Belinda bitch doesn't mean anything to him. Eddie only likes girls who read. He's not going to pay me thousands of dollars in hush money just so he can keep a dimwitted cheerleader like her in the dark."

"She's not just a cheerleader," John pointed out. "She's a *Sports Illustrated* swimsuit model too. She's a genuine catch."

"To you, Johnny," Dick said. "But not to Eddie Rochester. I know the man, and Belinda Graham is not his type. If I want to wield any power over my brother-in-law, I'm going to have to discover his weak spot first. Only then will I strike."

"And how are you going to do that?" John asked.

"I'm watching him," Dick replied. He ran his fingers through his slicked-backed hair and smiled. "That's why I moved to Ohio a few years back. I'm watching him, and waiting for him to slip up."

# Chapter Five

### *Millcote, Ohio*

"Explain this to me again please, Belle," Eddie said, looking up with a bleary expression from the galley proof. "If I don't understand the concept, I can't help you clarify it."

"What don't you understand?" Belinda replied, her voice showing traces of exasperation. "Seasonal color analysis is so simple. It's all about matching your clothes and make-up to the color of your skin, hair and eyes. It's not a difficult concept."

"But why do you keep referring to yourself as a 'Summer' in this section? You wear different clothes in the summer than you do in the winter, don't you?"

Belinda rolled her eyes and started lecturing Eddie on the four dominant skin tones and their seasonal counterparts. Eddie put on a brave face and tried to listen, but his eyes kept wandering away from her to the other occupants of the sitting room. Gerry was losing to Gisela in a game of *Candyland*. Jenny was sketching JoJo's portrait by the window.

"Earth to Ed," Belinda said, waving her hand at his face.

Eddie looked back and forced a laugh. "I'm paying attention, Belle. Really. I was just trying to guess everyone else's season."

"You can't do that properly at a distance," Belinda said. "You need to look closely at the skin's undertones. But if you really want to know, JoJo is a 'Summer' like me. Jenny is an 'Autumn'."

"Really?" Eddie asked, looking back at the window. "I would have pegged her for a 'Spring'."

"She has freckles," Belinda said curtly.

*"Oh Scheiße!"* Gerry cursed. "I'm stuck in Mr. Gloppy's Swamp again!"

"Say 'poop', Papa," Gisela scolded him. "*Scheiße* is naughty. Miss Temple has me that teached."

Eddie laughed at his friend. "You better watch yourself, Ger, or Gisela's kindergarten teacher will come out here and cane you."

"Might not be such a bad prospect," Gerry replied. "Miss Temple looked pretty fit in that class photo Zellie showed me."

Belinda cleared her throat. Eddie looked back at her and squeezed her hand. "Sorry. Got distracted. So—" he released her hand and picked up a galley sheet. "This sentence runs on too long. We need to put a full-stop in here."

"Two reds. I win!" Gisela exclaimed as she slid her token to the final square. "*Noch ein mal!*"

"*Nein!*" Gerry said, standing up from the table and folding the board. "Let's play something else." He gathered the pieces into the box and stopped by the window on his way to the cupboard. "Damn, Jenny, that's a beautiful drawing! You're quite the artist."

"Say 'darn' Papa," Gisela chided.

"Let me see," Belinda said. She stood up from the table and walked to her sister's side. "Wow. This *is* good. That doctor's wife was right, Jenny. You should be in art school, not working here."

Eddie rested the galley sheet on the table and joined the women by the window. *Good lord, she's talented,* he thought as he admired Jenny's sketch. *Why have I been pushing her to read books I want to discuss? I should have been encouraging her to draw. I am such a selfish bastard.*

"That's lovely, Jenny," he said, trying to maintain a nonchalant voice. "I'd like to see your folder of artwork sometime."

"Thanks," Jenny said. She smiled brightly at him.

He smiled back and held her gaze. Belinda tugged at his arm.

"What the hell, Eddie—you've got a Ouija board in here!" Gerry shouted from the corner of the room.

Eddie turned and watched Gerry pull a long game box from the cupboard. "That's Alan's," Eddie called across the room. "After he saw *The Exorcist,* he insisted I remove it from the farmhouse."

"That's a creepy game," JoJo admonished Gerry. "You shouldn't let Gisela play that."

"Nonsense," Gerry scoffed. He took the board out of the box, laid it on the game table, and showed Gisela the heart-shaped planchette. "This game is magic, Zellie. It can tell the future."

She gave him a puzzled look, so he explained the game to her in

German. Her eyes lit up. "I want to play!"

"Thought you might," Gerry said. "Let's ask Mr. Ouija a question, shall we? *Frag auf Englisch.*"

"Let's watch," Belinda said, grabbing Eddie's hand in a firm grip and leading him away from Jenny.

Eddie smiled as he watched Gisela furrow her brow in concentration, then ask in a solemn voice, "Will I a prince marry?"

Gerry showed her how to place her fingertips on the planchette, then gently pushed it to reveal the word 'Yes'.

Gisela squealed in delight. Gerry smiled indulgently.

Eddie laughed. "You smile now, but wait till the royal family stiffs on the wedding bill and sends it to the father of the bride."

"I'll pass it along to my more responsible friend," Gerry said, his eyes fixed squarely on the game. "Ask another question, Zellie."

Gisela turned to the window. "Will Jenny a prince marry?"

"You want to give it a go?" Gerry called across the room.

"No," Jenny replied. "When I was eight years old, Sister Claire made me promise I'd never touch a Ouija board. But Gisela can play for me. I'll watch." She laid her sketchbook on a chair and walked to the game table. JoJo followed her.

Gisela frowned as Gerry nudged the planchette towards the word 'No'.

"Don't be sad, sweetie," Jenny said, ruffling her hair. "I don't want to be a princess."

"But who will Jenny marry?" Gisela asked in an anxious voice.

"Let's find out, *liebchen*," Gerry said. "You say the letters out loud." He guided the planchette to the letter 'L', then swooped it around the board and landed it back on the 'L' once more.

JoJo shook her head. "That doesn't make any sense. What kind of name begins with two 'L's?"

"L.L. Bean," Belinda suggested.

Eddie let go of her hand.

"A llama?" Gisela guessed.

Jenny giggled. "Very good, sweetie," she said, turning towards Eddie. "She learned that from her animal alphabet book."

Eddie shook his head. "No, she learned that from you." He held her gaze while he listened to Gisela recite the letters, 'L-L-Y-W-L-Y-N'. He cringed and turned his face away.

"That word makes no sense," JoJo said. "It's like *Wheel of Fortune.* You need to buy a vowel."

"Is that a Welsh name?" Jenny asked, suppressing a laugh.

"Possibly," Gerry said. He looked up at Eddie, his face a picture of innocence. "Hey, Eddie! Your granddad on your mum's side was Welsh, wasn't he? You want to have a stab at this word?"

"I'll pass," Eddie said. He stared dumbly at the board, but sensed both Jenny's and Belinda's eyes focused on his face.

Belinda cleared her throat. "I have a question for the board. Could I take your place please, Gisela?"

Gisela nodded and slipped out of her chair. Belinda sat down and glowered at Gerry.

He grinned at her. "You want Mr. Ouija to predict your future?"

"No," she replied. "I want Mr. Ouija to spell out *Ed's* future." She rested her fingers on the planchette, and before Gerry could stop her, pushed it towards the letter 'B'.

Gerry frowned and pressed harder against the wood. Each time Belinda tried to push the planchette towards the letter 'E', Gerry nudged it away. "I think you're right, JoJo," he joked. "Mr. Ouija needs to buy a vowel."

"Fine," Belinda said. She quickly guided the planchette to the letters 'L', 'N' and 'D', and smiled in triumph.

"What does that spell?" Gisela asked.

"It's obvious," Gerry said, leaning back in his chair and crossing his arms in front of his chest. "Eddie is going to have his colors done and discover he's a 'Summer,' then dye his hair blonde."

Eddie smirked. "Perhaps it means my future will just be bland."

Belinda stood up from the table and wrapped her arms around Eddie's neck. "I think you know what it means," she said. She stood on her tiptoes and started kissing him.

"Now now, Ed, behave yourself!" Gerry called out in the voice of an angry schoolmaster. "Not in front of the child!"

*Christ, how do I get out of this gracefully?* Eddie wondered as Belinda ran her fingers through his hair and pulled his face down towards hers. He closed his eyes and heard Jenny speak. Her words came out rapidly. Her voice sounded higher than usual.

"It's getting late. I'll put Gisela to bed. Give Papa a goodnight kiss then come with me. C'mon sweetie. It's past your bedtime."

Eddie heard two sets of footsteps scramble up the stairs.

"Get a room, Rochester," Gerry bellowed. "C'mon JoJo. Let's get back to where we once belonged."

Eddie struggled to push back the mounting desire Belinda was arousing within him. He tried to focus his attention on the sound of Gerry and JoJo pulling back their chairs and clomping up the steps.

Belinda continued kissing Eddie until everyone had left, then released him from her embrace and gazed up at him.

"Let's go to bed too," she said.

Eddie looked into her eyes and sighed. He took a step backwards and closed his eyes again. "Belle, I—" he mumbled.

"You heard the nanny, it's bedtime," Belinda continued. "You were listening to her, weren't you? Or were you just looking?"

Her rebuke stung like a slap. "What's that supposed to mean?"

"You know exactly what it means," Belinda said, her voice rising. She backed away from him. "God, Ed, she's still a teenager."

Eddie sucked in a deep breath and forced himself to remain calm. "There is nothing going on between Jenny and me."

"There's not much going on between you and me, either," she replied. "Why did you bring me here? That night in New York, I thought we had something special."

"We did," Eddie said, looking down at his shoes. *Think fast*, he urged himself. *There must be a poem I can quote. That usually works.* He lifted his gaze and sighed.

"You're right, Belle," he said after the awkward silence had stretched to a breaking point. "I do look at Jenny a lot. But it's not what you think."

His voice grew stronger as an excuse took shape in his head. "I see her playing with Gisela and I think, I think—Christ, you know I spent my childhood here at Thornfield. I always thought I'd raise a family here too. And then I imagine me and you together, and I just can't—I just can't picture you living on a farm and being mum to a big brood of Rochesters. I can't see you making posters for the Millcote Elementary PTA bake sale. You're gorgeous, Belle. Bloody gorgeous. But I just don't—I don't see us having a future together."

She put her finger to his lips. "Stop it, Ed. Don't say anything else. You don't get to dump me twice. It's my turn to ditch you."

Eddie's lips curved into a hint of a smile.

She noticed, lowered her hand and smacked his chest. "Don't you dare laugh at me."

"I'm not laughing, Belle, I swear," Eddie said, taking her back in his arms. "I'm just relieved. I think we both know we're not right for each other. You need someone who will bring you excitement, and I need someone who will bring me peace."

She leaned against him and released a long sigh. "Yeah. I know. You're right. Goddammit." She wrapped her arms more tightly around his waist and pressed the side of her face against his chest. She listened to his heartbeat for a long moment, then slowly loosened her grasp. "I'll pack my bags. When do you think the roads out of Thornfield will be plowed?"

Eddie rubbed her back gently. "The snow was tapering off the last time I looked. I'll ask my estate manager to plow the driveway as soon as he can tomorrow morning."

Belinda stepped out of his embrace. "Pity we didn't finish proofing my galleys. Where will I ever find another English major to help me?"

"You will, Belle," Eddie assured her. "Put up an advert on any college bulletin board, and they'll come falling at your feet."

"Right," she said with a sad laugh. "Do you suppose JoJo will want to stick around with Gerry?"

"That probably depends on how loudly he snores tonight," Eddie replied. He walked to the table where they had been working and gathered up her papers. "Where would you like me to drop you off tomorrow? At the dance studio or JoJo's flat?"

"Take us both to JoJo's."

"Okay," Eddie said. He handed her the corrected proofs.

"Take the girl shopping, Ed," Belinda added in a quiet voice. "She has holes in her coat."

"I'll do that," he replied. He watched her back as she walked away. *I underestimated her,* he realized with a pang of regret. *Christ, I am so thick.*

"Jenny would look good in olive, gold or dark purple," Belinda said before stepping onto the staircase. "She's an autumn."

\* \* \*

"I've put your bags in the back of the Cherokee," Eddie said, extending his arm towards Belinda. "Take my hand. It's icy."

He led her through the front door and onto the driveway. "Shite cobblestones," he muttered under his breath. "They look pretty, but they're a bitch to walk on."

She clung to him tightly, tottering on the stiletto heels of her boots. "Shite Manolo Blahniks," she replied. "They look pretty, but they're a bitch to walk in."

Eddie laughed and guided her towards the car. Jenny and Gisela were waiting beside it already, shivering in the cold.

"Wait for us," Gerry called from the mansion's door. He started leading JoJo over the icy path, catching her as she slipped.

Belinda glanced over her shoulder to check on her sister, then looked back at the Cherokee. "Who's that?" she asked, pointing to a car winding its way up the long, freshly plowed driveway.

"Haven't a clue," Eddie replied. He stopped and stared at the mysterious vehicle.

"You expecting visitors?" Gerry asked.

Eddie shook his head. "No, but I left the front gate open so the city could plow the base of the driveway. That was probably a mistake."

The approaching car skidded to a stop in front of the mansion. Its driver opened the door and called out a loud greeting.

"Eddie Rochester! You are just the man I was looking for!" he exclaimed in a clipped British accent. "And what's this? Is that the indestructible Gerry Enis I see with you?"

"Who are you?" Eddie replied coolly.

The uninvited guest started walking towards Eddie, taking small, measured steps to avoid falling on the ice. "I'm Philip Randall from the *London Eyewitness*. Perhaps you've heard of me. I wrote a piece on you not long ago that garnered a considerable bit of attention."

"Get off my property," Eddie said through clenched teeth.

"Your gate was unlocked," Philip pointed out. "So I simply assumed—oh, my! It's Belinda Graham! My dear lady, you're even more beautiful in the flesh than you are in your photographs! I saw that delightful picture of you and Mr. Rochester at your dance rehearsal and—just look—the two of you are still joined at the hip! Can it be? Are you, perchance, an item now?"

Eddie released Belinda and marched towards Philip. "I'm giving you five seconds to get back inside your car. One. Two—"

"Don't leave me, Ed!" Belinda cried out. She stepped forward and fell into a bank of snow.

Eddie took a deep breath and turned around to help Belinda.

"How gallant," Philip said as Eddie pulled her back up. "Now tell me, please, who are these other lovely young ladies?"

"I'm Belinda's sister JoJo!" JoJo called out obligingly. "And that sweet little angel by the car is Gerry's daughter Gisela. Oh, um—and that's her nanny."

Philip gave Jenny, Gisela and JoJo a quick once-over and returned his attention to Eddie. "You may find this surprising, Mr. Rochester, but as much as I'd love to write a piece about you and your little harem, I'm actually here in the interests of science. At the advice of my proofreader, I'm researching a story about crop circles. And I recently learned that you summoned one of the world's leading authorities on the subject to your farm to inspect a mysterious pattern that appeared in one of your corn fields."

Gerry started laughing. "Bugger, Eddie, you never told me you were visited by space aliens!"

Eddie scowled, standing squarely in his place while Belinda clung to him for support.

"Actually, Mr. Enis, I believe the newest scientific theory proposes that crop circles are caused by rare meteorological phenomena," Philip said.

"Actually, Mr. Randall, I believe I've told you twice now to get the hell off my property," Eddie hissed.

"I won't stay long," Philip promised. "It looks as if you and your little party were just about to go out, and I don't want to keep you. Though I couldn't help but find it interesting, Mr. Rochester, that you've not only had a crop circle appear on your property—you've also been struck by lightning this past month!"

Gerry laughed. "Thornfield's just a happenin' sort of place!"

Eddie glared at Gerry to silence him.

"Before I leave, might you do me the favor of posing for a picture?" Philip asked, pulling a camera out of his coat pocket. "I realize your crop circle must be covered by a foot of snow now. But I think my readers might actually prefer that I illustrate my article with a photo of you and your lovely lady-friend."

"Get. The Fuck. Away," Eddie stated in a slow, menacing growl.

Philip began shooting pictures of the assembly from a distance of a few yards.

"Stop it!" Eddie yelled. His voice echoed through the frosted trees and sent several clumps of snow tumbling off the thinnest branches. He let go of Belinda and took another large step towards the journalist.

"Ah-EEE-OOW-EEE!"

The distant cry punctured the air and sent shivers running up Eddie's spine.

"What the hell was that?" Philip asked.

A second cry rang out, louder than the first. Eddie looked towards the farmhouse in a panic.

"Holy fucking Christ!" he cursed. "Gerry, get this bastard off my property. Now!" He abandoned Belinda to the ice and started running as quickly as he could through the snow to the source of the howls.

## Chapter Six

"I'm here!" Eddie shouted, flinging open the door to the farm house and slamming it shut behind him. He surveyed the pile-up at the base of the stairs and shouted again to make his voice heard over his wife's cries and Pancho's barks. "Christ, what happened?"

Grace tried to extricate herself from Roberta's tight grasp. "Thank the lord, son. Give me a hand."

Eddie held out both of his hands. Grace stood up with his assistance and immediately started rubbing her left hip. Roberta was sobbing too hard to respond to Eddie's pleas. He grabbed her by the shoulders and rolled her off of Alan, then guided her to a seat on a lower step. He sat down beside her and wrapped his arms around her. Pancho approached the couple and rested a reassuring paw on Roberta's lap.

"Are you all right, love?" Eddie asked gently. "Are you hurt?"

Roberta collapsed against Eddie's chest and wailed again.

Alan righted himself on his elbows and looked up at his mother. "Are you okay, Mum? Is anything broken?"

Grace rubbed her hip some more, then wiggled her arms and legs. "I think I'm fine. How about you? You took the brunt of the fall."

Alan stood up and walked slowly to his favorite armchair. "Oh hell, I don't know. Should we call a doctor?"

Eddie rocked Roberta back and forth in his arms and looked up at Grace for an explanation.

"We took a tumble," she said as she resumed stroking her sore hip. "Birdie was starting to nod off over brekkie, so I thought I'd take her back to her room. You know how sluggish she's been since—well, since Dr. Bob changed her meds. Alan saw me struggling on the steps, so he walked over to help us. And then, well, like I said, we all took a tumble."

Eddie twisted his finger around a tendril of Roberta's curly hair and kissed the top of her head. She settled down into a soft pattern of hiccoughs and sniffs, and closed her eyes.

"I'll call Dr. Bob and see if can stop by to look at us," Grace offered. "Did Ron finish plowing your driveway yet?"

An unsettling image flashed before Eddie's eyes of the scene he had just fled. *Christ, I hope Gerry can handle everything,* he thought with an encroaching sense of doubt. *The last thing I need is for that bloody reporter to pop in here with his camera.*

Eddie nodded at Grace."Yes, the path's been cleared. I was just about to run some errands. But I'll stay here now. Gerry can take care of everything across the way."

"Take your boots off," Grace admonished him. "You're dripping snow all over the floor."

Eddie looked up at her and frowned. "First things first," he replied. He stood up, scooped Roberta into his arms and carried her to her room.

* * *

Gerry banged on the farmhouse door. "It's just me, by my lonesome!"

Eddie let him in. "What's been happening at the mansion? I've tried ringing you all afternoon, but the line's been engaged."

"Lots of good things," Gerry answered, slipping his coat off and hanging it on the rack by the door. "But you go first. Tell me what happened with this lot."

"Let's talk in the kitchen, so we won't disturb Alan," Eddie said. He led Gerry past the parlor, where Alan was sleeping on the sofa with Roberta's afghan draped over his knees.

Eddie took a seat at the table and gave Gerry a run-down of the accident. "Everyone landed on top of Alan, but I don't think he broke anything. Grace fetched him some Demerol, and now she's having a long soak in the bath. Bob's going to stop by the house this evening, weather permitting, and check on everyone."

"You have Demerol in this house?" Gerry asked, his eyes wide.

Eddie glowered at him.

Gerry shrugged "Hey, I was just curious. Glad to hear everyone's okay. Birdie's scream scared me shitless too, you know.

But now if you're done, I'll share my news. Guess who landed a job?"

Eddie eyed him suspiciously. "It couldn't possibly be you?"

Gerry smiled in triumph. "Jimbo called. As soon as he finishes this session he's doing for Rosamond Oliver, he's flying to L.A. to work on a movie soundtrack, and he arranged for me to fill in for the original drummer."

"A movie soundtrack?" Eddie asked. "That's a change."

Gerry shrugged. "A gig's a gig. And I could use the paycheck."

"What happened to the other drummer?"

"Unfortunate snorkeling accident," Gerry replied. "Poor bloke was attacked by a blue ringed octopus off the coast of Australia. Nearly died. He's recovering in hospital now."

Eddie snorted. "What is it with you percussionists? Don't you ever get injured under normal circumstances?"

"Hey, it's a sad day for drummers everywhere when an octopus' garden is no longer a happy and safe place to swim about!"

Eddie smiled and stood up from the table. "Well, this calls for a celebration. Lord knows I could use a stiff drink after this morning's excitement." He opened the cabinet where Grace kept her liquor and hesitated. "Sorry, almost forgot. I'll make tea."

"You're no fun anymore," Gerry groused.

"Neither are you," Eddie replied. "Octopus anecdotes aside." He turned on the gas flame and grabbed some tea and a china pot from another cupboard. "I don't suppose you'll be taking Gisela with you to California," he said with his back turned to his friend.

"The gig'll just last a few weeks," Gerry said. "I'll come collect her at Christmas, if that's all right."

Eddie closed his eyes and imagined sending Jenny back to the convent. *It's what I've been planning all along,* he reminded himself. *I need to start taking care of Birdie again.*

He pulled two mugs off a shelf and sat down opposite his friend. "Sure, that'll be fine. I'll mind her for another month."

Gerry smiled. "Thought you might."

"So," Eddie continued, tapping his fingers against the table. "I'm assuming you dispatched that arsehole reporter?"

"Wasn't hard," Gerry said. "After you ran off, the wanker walked up to Belinda and offered her his arm. I spied a bag of rock salt on your porch, so I carried it to his car and pried open the petrol cap. I told him he'd better bugger off if he didn't want me to cock up his fuel system. That got him moving."

"Thanks," Eddie laughed. The kettle started whistling and he stood up to make the tea. "So, have you told JoJo you'll be going to Los Angeles?" he asked as he brought the pot to the table.

"I will tonight. It's just as well. I overheard her talking with Belinda about a party the club is throwing for the Ben-Gals after Sunday's game. Belinda snagged JoJo an invite. I should leave before I lose another woman to a footballer. I'll pack her things and bring them to her flat when she gets off her shift tonight."

"Good," Eddie said. "Did you buy Jenny a coat at the mall?"

Gerry nodded. "And a new set of dollhouse toys for Zellie. She lost her old ones somehow. You have any cream for the tea?"

Eddie pushed aside his memory of the toy Birdie had left on his nightstand and opened the refrigerator. A sentimental expression washed over him as he fetched the cream. "I remember making ice cream on days like this when I was small. I wonder if my grandma's old ice cream machine is still in the cellar."

"How can you even think of making ice cream on a day like today?" Gerry asked. "It's colder than a witch's tit outside!"

"Jenny's birthday is coming up," Eddie answered. "It might be a fun way to celebrate."

"Isn't it time you sent that girl back to the convent?" a stern voice called from the kitchen doorway. Eddie looked up and watched Grace walk into the room, her hair wrapped in a towel. She loosened the belt of her dressing gown and sat down.

Eddie held her gaze. "Gerry just landed a gig in Los Angeles, so she'll need to stay here a while longer while he's working."

"He could take Jenny with him to California, and she could watch the child there," Grace pointed out.

"And pull my daughter out of school?" Gerry countered. "Just when she's starting to learn English and make friends? How could you suggest such a thing?"

Grace rolled her eyes. "May I have a spot of tea?"

Eddie fetched her a mug and sat back down. "How's Birdie?"

"She was asleep when I looked in on her, with Pancho curled up at her feet." Grace reached across the table and rested her hand on Eddie's. "When Dr. Bob comes by tonight, I'm going to ask him to change her prescription. She can't go on like this, lost in a state of confusion, too muddled to even climb the stairs by herself."

Eddie hung his head. "I know. I don't like seeing her so drugged up either. But I'm scared." An image of the defaced toy sprang back to his mind. "I don't want her setting any more fires."

Grace lifted her hand and picked up the jug of cream. "I think the best way to keep that from happening is to put everything back to rights. Take away the things that are provoking her, and she'll be her usual self again."

"Right," Eddie sighed. He fell silent as he sipped his tea, then stood up from the table. "I'm going to look for my grandma's old ice cream machine in the cellar."

Grace grimaced. "Lord, Eddie, were you not listening to a word I just said? That girl has to go back to the convent!"

Gerry rested his hand on top of Grace's. "I'll only be in California for a few weeks. Then I'll fly back and take care of everything. Don't you worry. I have a plan."

\* \* \*

*I will tell her,* Eddie vowed as he stood outside the mansion's back door. *I will tell Jenny all about Birdie and be done with it, and then I can look at her without feeling guilty anymore.*

He kicked the snow off his boots, opened the door and let Pancho bound into the house in front of him. Pancho barked and ran up to Jenny. Jenny turned away from the sketch she was working on and started petting the dog.

"Somebody missed you," Eddie said as he watched them.

Jenny looked up and smiled. "Hi, Mr. R. How's Mrs. Poole? I heard she fell down the steps."

Eddie's heart sank. *This is the time,* he realized. *She just set me up for my explanation.* He rested the ice cream machine on the floor, slipped off his coat, and took a seat in his favorite chair.

"She's doing better. My friend Bob looked her over last night. Nothing is broken."

"Good," Jenny replied. "I remember when Sister Gabriel slipped and fell on the stairs leading into the chapel. She broke her hip. I had to call for the ambulance. I was so nervous."

Eddie nodded and summoned his courage. Then he noticed Jenny was flipping her drawing over. "Hey, don't hide that," he said, losing his train of thought. "I'd like to see your work."

"You will," she said, averting her eyes. "But not until I'm done.

So what's that bucket you brought with you?"

He sighed, realizing his opportunity to slip easily into an explanation had passed. "It's my grandma's old ice cream maker. I thought we could pack it with snow and make some ice cream."

"That sounds like fun!" she giggled. "Gisela will love it!"

"I brought it for you," he confessed. "For your birthday. I wanted to take you—you and Gisela—to the Ice Cream Bridge downtown, but it closed after Pogue's merged into L.S. Ayres."

She smiled at him. "You remembered that photo I showed you of my Uncle Henry."

"Of course I did," he replied, holding her gaze. *I remember everything you've said to me,* he wanted to add. *I think about you constantly.*

"Oh," she said, her cheeks blushing. "Thanks."

He closed his eyes for a long moment. *It can wait,* he decided abruptly. *She'll only be here for one more month. There's no reason I can't keep chatting with her like this until then. Nothing is going to happen between us. I'm an arse, but not that big of an arse.*

"I found one of Belinda's galley sheets under that table where you two were working," Jenny said, interrupting his thoughts. "I left it on the desk in your library."

"Thanks," he said. He cleared his throat. "I, um, I hope you weren't too bothered by having the Graham sisters here." He offered her an apologetic half-smile.

She looked out the window. "It's your house. You can invite anyone you want here. Gisela's dad seemed to really like JoJo."

"Yes," Eddie agreed. "He did. Belinda and I, um, well—we had a brief relationship seven years ago. I saw her in New York and thought that maybe we, well, um—I'm not sure what I was thinking. I'm a fool. But it doesn't matter. She's left now."

*That wasn't so hard,* he realized. *And it felt good to get at least one thing off my chest.*

"Are you going to the Bengals game to watch her dance?"

Eddie shook his head. "No, I don't much care for American football. I've never learned the rules."

Jenny faced him again. "Yeah, I don't understand it either. I prefer baseball. I love listening to Reds games."

"Me too," Eddie replied with a smile. "Can't beat spending an evening with Marty and Joe."

Pancho licked Jenny's hand and rolled onto her back. Jenny slid out of her chair and sat down on the floor to pet the dog's belly. "And now I know your secret," she added in a smug voice.

Eddie's stomach lurched. He cut his eyes away from her. "What secret might that be?" he asked, drawing in a deep breath.

"Your middle name is Llywelyn."

He released a loud sigh of relief and smiled. "Ah, yes, the omniscient Mr. Ouija has let the cat out of the bag."

Jenny giggled again.

"And now you can tell me your middle name," he added.

"Nope," Jenny replied. "I read in a book that a woman must always strive to project a certain aura of mystery."

Eddie snorted. "What kind of crap book did you read that in?"

"Belinda's galley sheet," she laughed. "You crossed out one of her lines and wrote that in the margin. So it must be good advice."

\* \* \*

Grace stood up from the dinner table and collected Eddie's dirty dishes. "So did the girl have a nice birthday?" she asked.

"The girl has a name," Eddie replied testily. But then he took a deep breath and composed himself. *It's no use trying to win Grace over to Jenny's side,* he thought. *And why should I even try? I need her to take care of Birdie when I'm not here.*

"I gave her some nice art supplies," he added in a kinder voice. "So she can build a portfolio if she decides to apply to art college."

"Good," Grace said. "She belongs in uni."

Eddied looked into the living room and watched Roberta as she sat transfixed in front of the television set. "So what do you think?" he whispered. "Are the new meds working?"

"She seems a bit more alert," Grace whispered back. "And she's walking much more steadily now too. But she's been awfully quiet. I wish I could tell what's going on in her head."

"I've never been able to tell what's going on in her head," Eddie grumbled. "Though perhaps it's better not to know."

"Go sit with her, son," Grace murmured. "That's why you came over here, isn't it? Or did you just want to chat me up over the remains of the meal?"

Eddie stood up and walked into the parlor. "Hey there, love," he said, taking a seat beside Roberta and kissing her cheek. She offered him a weak smile and lifted her afghan. He tugged half of it over his lap and wrapped his arm around her shoulder. "So what are we watching?" he asked Alan.

"*MacGyver* will be on in a few minutes, once this bloody program ends," Alan replied. He muted the sound, but then a familiar face looked back at him from the screen. "Bugger me, it's our Ger on the telly!" He turned the volume back up.

The manic soundtrack of *Entertainment Tonight* pulsed from the speaker, while an overly-excited newsreader shouted over a looping newsreel of grainy footage:

"It was the Brits versus the Bunnies last night, when a fight broke out at the Playboy mansion in Los Angeles. A witness to the incident claimed two English celebrities were vying for the attention of Miss October Carmella Sanchez and fell into an argument. Several bunnies are said to have ganged up on both men. Police were called to the scene, but no charges were filed. A veritable galaxy of British stars was seen leaving the mansion this morning, including Dudley Moore, John Entwistle, Gerry Enis, Lemmy, and Oliver Reed. Now turning to sports—"

"Holy crap, Gerry didn't waste much time getting back into the thick of things, did he?" Alan laughed, muting the sound again.

Eddie smiled in response. *Gerry might not be ready to pick up Gisela in a few weeks after all,* he realized. He squeezed Roberta a little more tightly.

She looked up at him and smiled. "Zherreez onnteev."

Eddie wrinkled his brow and tried to puzzle out her words. "Did you say you wanted cherries, love? I can ask Grace to look for some the next time she goes to the market, but I don't think they're available this time of year."

Roberta grunted and looked back at the television screen.

### London, England

"I called that doctor Belinda Graham's sister told you about," June said, folding her hand-written notes and offering them to her boss. "He confirmed her story."

Elsie leaned over Philip's desk and smiled at him. "Poor Phil," she taunted. "You went after the wrong Pilot, and ended up missing out on Gerry Enis' barney with the bunnies."

"Never mind that," Philip huffed. "Any cub reporter could have guessed what would happen when that lot of boozers met up at the Playboy mansion. I have bigger fish to fry."

"Well, I'm sorry to tell you this, Phil," June said, pulling her chair a little closer to his desk and offering him a mocking smile that belied her apology. "But you're fishing in the wrong stream. Dr. Robert Carter of Hamilton, Ohio, assured me that the scream of the banshee you claimed to hear at Eddie Rochester's farm was just the sound of an elderly lady crying as she fell down a flight of stairs."

"Eddie Rochester is living with an elderly lady?" Elsie asked.

"No," June said, throwing Elsie an exasperated look. "He lives by himself. But he's given a small house in the back of his estate to his late manager's mother and brother—Grace and Alan Poole. And the old dear slipped on a step and let out a holler when our Phil was snooping around."

"Poor thing! I hope she's okay," Elsie said.

Philip reviewed June's notes and raised an eyebrow. "These notes say that Dr. Carter is a psychologist."

"A psychiatrist," June corrected him. "He's a licensed doctor who made a house call to check on Mrs. Poole after her fall."

"House call?" Philip protested, dropping the note into the pile of papers on his desk. "Doctors don't make house calls anymore!"

"Well, apparently this one does," June retorted. "And why shouldn't he? He's a friend of Eddie and he lives close by. And you told me yourself, Phil, the roads were covered in ice after that blizzard. Why should Eddie risk injuring Mrs. Poole any further by driving her to a casualty, when there was a doctor living a stone's throw away who was willing to stop by and examine her?"

Philip retrieved the paper and re-read June's notes. "There's a story here," he muttered under his breath. "Eddie Rochester is hiding something. I can just taste it. Call it reporter's instinct."

June clucked her tongue. "Your instincts were wrong about Eddie and Belinda Graham. He didn't even go to that football game she was dancing at, or the party afterwards."

"I know," Philip admitted, disappointment creeping into his face and voice. "JoJo Graham told me Belinda left the party with the team's star running back."

"Gold digging tramp," Elsie groused.

"Maybe," Philip said with a shrug. "But at least she has no

trouble attracting men. Unlike you two spinsters."

Elsie and June both scowled at him.

Philip snorted. "Oh, get off your high horses, ladies. You're working women, and we have a job to do."

He leaned back in his chair and gestured towards the door of his office. "Junie, I want you to search the archives for everything you can find about Eddie Rochester from the year his wife died. And Elsie, see if you can dig up a copy of Roberta Rochester's death certificate somewhere. I think it's about time *Randall's Scandals* ran a piece retelling the story of the most tragic romance in the history of rock-n-roll."

# Chapter Seven

### *Millcote, Ohio*

Roberta rolled over and reached her hand across the bed. Eddie was gone, just like he usually was in the morning. She had been surprised he even came to her bed last night to cuddle. He seldom did that anymore.

She sat up and walked to the window. The morning sunlight blinded her when she pulled back the curtain, and she had to close her eyes for several seconds. When she opened them again, the sun reflected so brightly off the dazzling field of snow that it brought tears to her eyes.

She lingered at the window, transfixed by the white patch of earth where the elm tree had once stood, and remembered how she'd watched Eddie the night of the fire. He'd gazed up at her for several electrifying seconds before he grabbed the hose and ran back to the tree. She'd stayed at the window watching him until the firefighters arrived and the clouds opened up, drenching everyone below in torrents of rain.

She had thought Eddie would come to her room and scream at her after the firemen left, but he hadn't. Grace had come instead and made her lie down to await Dr. Bob's arrival. When the doctor came, he gave her a shot. She couldn't remember much after that.

The last few weeks had passed in a blur. Or had it been the last few months? She had no idea. She only knew it was winter now because a blizzard had covered the world in a blanket of snow.

Eddie had never mentioned the fire to her. Or maybe he had, during those weeks when she trudged through the house in a fog of confusion and fatigue. She couldn't be sure. All she knew was that he was being very kind to her now. Clueless, as usual, but kind.

He was always particularly attentive to her when he returned from his vacations. That must be it, she decided. He probably took that girl with the glasses on a vacation, and now he was done with her. Perhaps that's what Grace and Alan were always whispering about when they thought she couldn't hear.

"She's still there," Dick said in a taunting voice. "You know that as well as I do. He's screwing her brains out each time he crosses the yard and leaves you here with the dog."

Roberta turned around. Dick was sitting on the edge of her bed, leering at her.

*Go away,* she told the apparition. *Get out of my room.*

"You should have set his bed on fire, not the tree, you stupid bitch," Dick sneered. "You've lost your touch."

Roberta closed her eyes and willed the vision to disappear. When she opened them, Dick was melting into the shape of her father. His body grew thicker, his face rounder. He screamed in agony as flames engulfed his hair and clothing.

She spun around and put her hands to her ears. Her heart beat rapidly until the howling behind her stopped. When she finally found the courage to look back at the bed, the vision was gone.

She waited for her breath to become steady again, then opened the bedroom door and walked downstairs. Eddie was sitting on the couch in the parlor, strumming his guitar. She sat down beside him. He startled.

"Birdie, I didn't hear you come down!" he exclaimed. He flipped over a sheet of paper on the coffee table that seemed to be covered with handwritten lyrics and chord notations, and leaned over to kiss her. "Good morning, love. How are you feeling today?"

### *London, England*

"Shut the door," Philip said as Elsie stepped into his office.

Elsie shoved Philip's dirty ashtray to the far corner of his desk and sat down next to June. "Better make this quick, Phil, before we all die from smoke inhalation. This room reeks."

"You both read the original article?" Philip asked, ignoring her.

Elsie and June nodded.

Philip leaned forward against his desk. "And did you believe it?"

Elsie rolled her eyes. "What's not to believe? Roberta

Rochester's own brother said she was dead. Why would he lie about a thing like that?"

"Dick Mason didn't use the kindest words to describe his brother-in-law in this story," Phil replied, tapping his fingers against the microfiche printout. "It almost seemed to me like he was accusing Eddie Rochester of contributing to his wife's untimely demise."

"That's nonsense, Phil," June snapped. "Dick never said that. He only suggested that Eddie hadn't been as attentive to his wife as he should have been. But that's the grief talking. Dick Mason had just lost his sister. He was lashing out in pain."

"Read this again," Philip said, pushing the page across the desk and pointing to the section he had marked.

June scanned the long paragraph, then handed the paper to Elsie. "I rest my case, Phil. Dick claims Eddie was too caught up in his own problems to notice his wife had developed a drug habit. But he's just accusing Eddie of being neglectful, not murderous."

Elsie read the page more carefully. "I hate to say this, but I see your point, Phil. Dick Mason is definitely hinting at something in this interview. But he's pretty vague in his accusations. It's almost as if he were challenging Eddie to respond to his remarks."

Philip smiled in triumph. "And he didn't, did he? Eddie Rochester never made a single comment about his wife's death."

"None that I could find in the archives," June agreed begrudgingly. "Though his manager Emmett Poole did issue a statement asking the press to 'please respect Eddie's privacy during this difficult time'."

"You couldn't find a death certificate?" Philip asked Elsie.

"Not yet," she admitted. "Though the Swiss are rather notorious for keeping their records private."

"I didn't ask you to look up a bloody Swiss bank account, I asked you to find a death certificate!" Philip shouted.

Elsie pursed her lips. "I've asked our correspondent in Zurich to look for it. He hasn't gotten back to me yet."

Philip snatched the paper back. "She's alive," he said in a soft voice. "Roberta Rochester is still alive."

"Oh piddle!" June scoffed. "That's rubbish. Our own newspaper broke this story. Are you suggesting *The Eyewitness* didn't check the facts before we ran the article?"

"Rupert Brocklehurst wrote this story," Philip replied smugly.

"That wanker got sacked in 1975 after he ran a piece on Marlon Brando that led to a libel suit. *The Eyewitness* settled out of court. Rupert went on a bender and died in a car crash the next year."

"That was before my time, Phil," Elsie said. "I never met him."

"I was hired to replace him," Philip laughed.

June scowled at her boss. "So what if Roberta Rochester *is* still alive? Why does that matter after all these years?"

"She's a public figure," Philip said. "And the public has a right to know if she's alive or dead."

"Roberta was never a public figure," Elsie argued. "She was just married to one."

"Well, Eddie Rochester's a public figure then," Philip retorted. "And he's been lying to the public for sixteen years."

"That's not true," Elsie countered. "He hasn't lied if he never issued a statement claiming his wife was dead. All he ever did was retire from the music industry and move to Ohio."

Philip met her eye. "I heard her. There's no way that horrifying scream came from a little old lady falling down a flight of steps."

"Why are you so obsessed with Eddie Rochester out of the blue?" June scolded. "A few months ago you didn't even want to run a picture of him with your column. You called him an old fart and mocked him for retiring too young."

"I've changed my mind," Philip said. "Retired or not, his legacy lives on in every insipid soft-rock radio station that's polluting the airways today. He started the whole goddamned, lovey-dovey, weeping poet trend in the early seventies that drove a stake in the heart of rock and roll. I hold him personally responsible for the rise of Dan Fogelberg and Air Supply. And I am going to expose him to the public for the fraud that he is."

Philip picked up a snapshot of Thornfield from the pile of photographs on his desk. "There's a story in this picture. I feel it in my bones. I just haven't found the missing link yet."

Elsie grabbed the photo away from him and examined it. "I'll tell you what I see, Phil. I see Belinda Graham hanging off Eddie Rochester's arm. I see the blur of some other tart running through the snow trying to claim a spot in the picture. I see Gerry Enis snarling at you. And I see a cute little girl holding hands with her nanny. There is nothing else to see in this photograph."

Philip snatched the picture back and pinned it on his wall. "Eddie Rochester is hiding something on his farm, and I intend to find out what it is. Junie, pull some strings and get me the phone number of Eli Deere, the Pilots' old bassist. If I ply that tosspot with enough drink, I'll bet I can get him to talk."

## *Millcote, Ohio*

The sound of Christmas carols enveloped Eddie as he stepped into the farmhouse. He admired the tree that stood in the corner of the living room and offered Roberta a brief kiss.

"Give us a hand here, Eddie?" Alan shouted over the music as he carried a large box of ornaments across the room.

"Just let me talk to your mum for a bit," Eddie answered.

He walked into the kitchen and offered Grace a weak smile. "I see you have an artificial tree this year," he remarked.

She cut her eyes at him. "Are you questioning that decision?"

"No," he sighed. "I just wanted to give you some news before I help Alan and Birdie trim it. Your Christmas wish has come true. Jenny is heading back to the convent. This evening."

Grace put down her mixing bowl and turned to face him. "Really? I thought she was staying until Gerry returned."

Eddie stepped closer to her so he could speak more quietly. "There's been an outbreak of flu at the convent, and Jenny's old German teacher is very ill. Jenny wants to go visit her while she still has the chance. She's packing right now. Sally is going to drive her out to Indiana after Gisela gets home from school."

Grace nodded. "So who will watch Gisela?"

"Yours truly," Eddie said. "Tonight anyway. Gerry is flying back to Cincinnati tomorrow. He's going to stay for the holidays, then take Gisela back to Europe."

"So this is it then?" Grace asked, turning back to her dinner preparations. "Jenny won't be returning to Thornfield?"

Eddie squared his shoulders. "I suppose not," he said. He turned around and joined Alan and Roberta in the other room.

\* \* \*

Gerry knocked on the heavy wooden door of Eddie's bedroom, nudged it open a crack and peered inside. "Can I come in? You're not wrapping my prezzie, are you?"

Eddie snorted. "Stupid me. I thought it would be nice to have one child in the house on Christmas morning. I hadn't counted on having two." He slipped his guitar off his shoulders and rested it on the bed beside him.

Gerry walked into the room and closed the door behind him. "I wanted to show you something." He handed Eddie a sketchbook. "Zellie found this under Jenny's bed. She left it behind."

Eddie tossed it on his mattress. "Fine. I'll make sure she gets it. She left her bike behind too. Alan can drop them both off."

"But give the book a look through first," Gerry said.

"No," Eddie replied. "If she was keeping it under her bed, then she was probably hiding it. Looking through this would be akin to looking through her diary."

"Oh, c'mon," Gerry said. "Just a little peek." He picked up the book and opened it to a random page.

Eddie cast a quick glance at the drawing. "So? She drew a picture of me. She's allowed."

"She drew a whole bloody book of pictures of you!" Gerry leafed through the pages and showed Eddie sketches of his face, eyes, hands and bare torso. "Look at all the detail she put into these. She even drew that funny cluster of moles on your chest."

Eddie stared dumbly at the page. "When did she ever see that?"

"Must have been that night you were chatting her up in the hallway," Gerry suggested. "You were shirtless. I remember."

Eddie frowned. "She couldn't have seen the pattern in that lighting. It's so faint."

"She's been watching you closely," Gerry retorted. "She even got the right number of wrinkles in the crow's feet by your eyes."

"We have no business looking at this," Eddie said, shutting the book with an emphatic thump.

"If you say so," Gerry replied. "Just thought you might want to know how she feels about you."

"She has a crush on me," Eddie said. "An innocent schoolgirl crush. And now she's gone, and we'll never see each other again."

"If you say so, mate," Gerry repeated. He walked out of the room whistling the chorus of the Beatles' old hit *She Loves You*.

Eddie collapsed on his bed and covered his face with his hands. *If I give this back to her, she'll know I saw it*, he realized. *How can I handle this discretely?*

He looked at the sketchbook, hesitated for a long moment, then opened it up again. *It's just a crush,* he tried to convince himself as he paged through the drawings. *I'm the first man she's ever spent any time with. It's only natural that she'd develop a crush on me.*

He slammed the book shut, sat up and reached for his guitar. *She'll get over me sooner than I'll get over her,* he decided. He formed his left hand into a 'C' chord and started humming the melody to the song he was writing about Jenny.

# Chapter Eight

*Lowood, Indiana — 1989*

Eddie's footfalls echoed through the vacant corridor of the convent, shattering the silence. *Why is that woman not making any noise?* he asked himself as he followed a nun through the long hallway. Every step he made seemed to boom like a kettledrum beat. He couldn't remember the last time he'd felt so self-conscious. He took a deep breath to calm his nerves and inhaled a noseful of stale incense.

"She's right there," the nun said, pointing to the cemetery beyond the door. "I'm not wearing a coat, so I'll wait for you here."

*And watch me like a hawk through the window,* Eddie felt like adding. "Thank you, Sister," he said instead.

He stepped into the open field, crunching through a fine surface of packed snow, and focused his gaze on Jenny's back. She was wearing her new olive green coat and a multi-hued crocheted hat he'd never seen before. *I'll bet one of the nuns made it with scraps of old yarn for a Christmas present,* he guessed.

He slackened his pace as he approached the graveyard. Jenny was kneeling in front of a stone. He stood silently a few yards away, not wanting to disturb her, and watched her pray.

The moment stretched on. She kissed her gloved fingers and touched them to the gravestone. Then she stood and turned. Her face lit up the moment saw him. "Mr. R!" she exclaimed. "I was just thinking about you!" She ran out of the cemetery to greet him.

"And I you," Eddie replied. He lowered his voice. "Were you visiting the grave of your German teacher?"

She tossed her head back towards the cemetery. "Oh no, Sister

Waltrude pulled through. I was talking to my friend Eileen."

A small shiver ran up Eddie's spine. *She talks to the dead,* he thought. *Either she is unspeakably lonely, or she actually does come from a galaxy far, far away where magical things are possible.* He took a moment to compose himself, then offered her a gentle smile. "And what did you tell your friend Eileen?"

"I was telling her about yo—you know, working at Thornfield and everything that's happened the past few months," she stammered. "This is the first chance I've had to visit her grave since I got here. The nuns have kept me busy. So why are you here?"

"I have your bike and your sketchbook," Eddie replied.

She winced. "My sketchbook? I left that behind?"

"Sally found it in your room, and wrapped it up so she could mail it to you," he fibbed. "But I figured I'd save her a trip to the post office, since I was coming out here with your bike."

She smiled in relief and rubbed her hands together for warmth. "Oh, thanks. But I thought you'd have Mrs. F or your friend Alan drop it off."

A lump came to his throat as he gazed at her. He wondered if this would be his last memory of her. "Well, I didn't get a chance to say a proper goodbye when you left," he managed to say at length. "So I thought I'd try to remedy that."

"Oh," she said, her face falling. "Yeah, okay."

*Bugger, that was the wrong thing to say,* he realized. Fighting the urge to embrace her, he shoved his hands in his coat pockets and flicked his head toward the small carpark. "C'mon, let's get your things out of my car. You can tell me about your Christmas as we walk."

She fell into pace beside him. "There's not much to tell. I went to Mass in the morning and vespers in the evening, and in between, I sat by Sister Waltrude's side, singing *Stille Nacht* and reading to her from her book of German prayers until my throat went dry. What did you do?"

*I sat by Birdie's side and sang her Christmas carols and read her poetry until my throat went dry,* he considered saying. "I watched Gisela open her presents in the morning, and in the evening, I drove her and Gerry around Hamilton to look at the Christmas lights," he answered instead.

"So he's done with his session in California?" Jenny surmised.

"Yes. And now he's off to England to play some gigs. He's

leaving this weekend."

She giggled. "Don't tell me, another one of his drummer friends got into a dangerous scrap with a weird animal!"

"No, the circumstances were even more surprising," Eddie said, her laughter lifting his mood. "Tony is playing a set of concerts at a new resort in Blackpool, and he invited Gerry to back him up. The two of them had a falling out a few years ago, but Tony figured Gerry deserved a second chance after his stint in the clinic."

"That's kind of him," Jenny said. "So will Gerry be taking Gisela to England with him?"

Eddie fell silent. *That's what I told Gerry to do,* he reminded himself. *Gerry's cousin in Manchester even offered to watch the child for him while he was working.*

Eddie walked towards his Cherokee, watching it grow bigger with each step he took across the field. *I'll return her things and drive home,* he told himself. *This infatuation ends here.*

Then he considered the role Jenny's bike had played in their relationship. She was riding it the day he first met her. A week later, she'd taken him on that long ride to see the crop circle. *I had to fix up my own bike so I could ride alongside her,* he recalled. *The bike I'd hoped to ride alongside Birdie once upon a time. Birdie never wants to leave the farmhouse. The last time she stepped outside the building on her own volition, she—*

A surge of anger consumed him and he came to an abrupt halt. He turned to face Jenny and clasped her hands. "Actually, Gerry was wondering if he could leave Gisela at Thornfield for a few weeks more, so he could focus all his energy on the rehearsals and concerts. I told him that would depend on you—on whether you'd be willing to come back."

Her eyes lit up and her cheeks flushed. "I can do that!" she exclaimed with a smile as wide as her face.

Eddie's heart pounded. A familiar warmth rose in his groin. "That's great! I'll wait in the lobby while you pack your bags."

He started walking her back to the convent's main entrance, holding her hand tightly in his own. The nun who had been watching him through the back window was now standing behind the front window, eyeing him suspiciously. *Christ, if that woman exchanged her habit for a cardigan and tweed skirt, she'd be a dead ringer for Grace,* he thought.

Eddie released Jenny's hand. "Tell you what, I'll just wait in the car for you. Take your time. I'll run the heater if I need to. I have some B.B. King cassettes I can listen to while you pack."

## Millcote, Ohio

Eddie ushered Tony into the private recording studio on the top floor of his mansion and slammed the door shut behind him. "What the fuck are you doing here?" he cursed.

Tony flashed him a toothy grin. "I came to see you, old friend. Gerry gave me the new passcode for your gate."

"Where the hell is he?" Eddie continued, his voice rising. "And what load of bollocks have you been telling Jenny all afternoon?"

"Calm down, mate," Tony replied. "I rang your doorbell and Jenny answered it. I told her I had saved you another trip to Europe by checking Gerry into a clinic myself this time around. That wanker was too plastered to even stand our final night in Blackpool. I had to hire a last-minute replacement from the local M.U. Jenny told me you were in the other house, so I just decided to chat with her for a bit. I wanted to check her out, after everything Gerry has been telling me about her."

He walked away from Eddie and started fiddling with the knobs on a large amplifier. "What groovy gear you have in here! I haven't seen tube amps like this since 1970!"

"That amp was manufactured in 1972," Eddie replied coolly. "Emmett built me a state-of-the art recording studio when he designed this house."

"God rest his soul," Tony said. He opened up a guitar case and slipped a Fender Stratocaster over his shoulder. "Damn, I remember this axe! You played it on our '69 tour."

Eddie glared at Tony. "Stop with the fucking guitar talk. I heard you telling Jenny that she didn't know the real me. What the hell did you say to her?"

"Quiet down, she'll hear you," Tony scolded. "Oh. Wait. Maybe she won't. This room is soundproofed, isn't it?"

Eddie rolled his eyes.

Tony started tuning the strings. "Don't worry, I haven't revealed your big secret. I'll leave that up to you. I just told her a few stories from our touring days, you know? Like the time we played the Ohio State Fair and Emmett arranged for you to milk a cow as a publicity stunt, good old farm boy that you were."

Eddie slowly started to relax. "That's it then?"

"Well, I considered sharing some sordid details of your romantic conquests," Tony admitted. "But the only bird I could remember you fancying was that reporter from *Tiger Beat* who trailed us in the summer of '66. What was her name again? Emma?"

"Emily," Eddie said, the defensive tone creeping back into his voice. "She was a very talented writer who was financing her master's degree in literature by taking any journalism jobs she could land. She quit *Tiger Beat* when *The New York Review of Books* took her on as a proofreader. We kept in touch for a while."

"Is that so?" Tony asked with a suggestive leer.

"Yes. Until she married a novelist in 1968."

Tony slipped the guitar off his shoulder and rested it against a speaker. "Sorry to hear it, mate. I hadn't realized she meant that much to you. But now that we've moved onto the subject of matrimony, I suppose I ought to ask after your missus."

"She's fine," Eddie mumbled without meeting Tony's eye.

Tony walked closer to his friend. "Divorce her, Eddie. Divorce Roberta right now and marry Jenny. She's perfect for you. She's goofy and cute and she obviously adores you. And she's young enough to give you that passel of brats you always used to say you wanted."

Eddie stiffened his back and turned away. "No. I've made a commitment to Birdie. It's too late to back out now. I couldn't live with myself if I deserted her after all these years, just so I could—"

"Just so you could what?" Tony challenged. "Be happy with a woman who suits you better?"

"Jenny and I are not well suited," Eddie countered. "I'm old enough to be her father. She deserves the chance to see the world before she ties herself down to—to an old fart like me who's practically senile. Christ, Tony, I can't even think straight anymore. I'm starting to wonder if I have early onset Alzheimer's."

Tony rested his hand on Eddie's shoulder. "You can't think straight because you're in love," he said gently. "That's one of the symptoms. Don't you remember?"

Eddie covered his eyes and tried to push aside the image of Jenny's smile that kept rushing to his mind every time Tony said her name. "I am not in love with her," Eddie insisted. "I'm just—going through a mid-life crisis, that's all."

"I doubt that," Tony retorted. "But even if you are, that means you still have half your life to live. You might as well spend it with someone whose company you enjoy."

Eddie walked away and stared blankly at a tilted soundboard covered by a dusty sheet. "I haven't told Jenny about Birdie," he confessed. "I should have, I know. But I didn't think there'd be any reason to at first. I figured she'd just be here for a few months until Gerry was able to collect Gisela. I never considered the possibility that we would become close friends, let alone the notion that she would ever mean so much to me. But now—Christ, Tony, how can I tell her about Birdie now?"

"You just sit her down and say, 'Jenny, there's something I have to tell you.' That's how."

Eddie shook his head. "If I did that, she'd hate me for hiding the truth from her while I was playing with her feelings. Or she'd start hating herself for the role she inadvertently played in making me want to leave a sick person who needed me. But in either case, she'd insist we call off whatever tenuous relationship we have. She's made of stronger stuff than I am. Her moral fiber hasn't been corrupted yet."

"You're sure that's how she'd react?" Tony asked. "You've thought this through?"

"I think about it all the time," Eddie confessed. He turned his face to the wall. "I think about *her* all the time."

"Well, damn, then, mate, you're screwed."

Eddie looked back at Tony and scowled. "Thank you for that helpful assessment."

Tony laughed and walked back to the speaker. "Do me a favor, Eddie," he said as he picked up the Stratocaster again. "If you decide to write any amazing love songs for Jenny like you did for Roberta, drop one or two of them in my lap. I could use another hit single. I haven't cracked the Top 40 in almost four years now."

Eddie sighed. "You are the most hopelessly shallow person I've ever known."

"I never pretended to be otherwise," Tony agreed. He handed the Fender to Eddie. "So, Gerry told me he heard you strumming your guitar every night in your bedroom while he was staying here at Christmas. You must be writing something. Play it for me. I want to hear what you're working on."

Eddie slipped the instrument over his shoulder. "Hand me a

cord so I can plug this into one of my state-of-the-art tube amps. I'll give you a listen."

## London, England

June knocked on the door of Philip's office. "I have that copy of the *Blackpool Gazette* you wanted with the review of Tony Wright's show," she said through the wood.

Hearing no response, she opened the door. She found Philip sitting in the dark, slumped over his cluttered desk, his head resting on his hands. She switched on the overhead light.

"Damn it, woman, shut that off!" he cursed.

"Let me guess," she said, leaving the light on. "You're hungover from your lunch date with Eli Deere."

Philip groaned. "Don't ever try to keep pace with an Irishman drinking Jameson."

June laughed. "Words to live by, Phil. So what did Mr. D tell you about Mr. R?"

"Not much," Philip admitted, lifting his head to reveal a pair of bloodshot eyes. "Eli said he felt guilty for having introduced Eddie to Roberta. But he didn't explain why."

"And he didn't enlighten you as to whether or not Roberta Rochester is still alive?"

Philip reached in his pocket and handed June a cardboard coaster with a picture of Shakespeare and the words 'Avon Ale' printed on one side. "I asked him that question point blank, but he grew vague and refused to respond. So I told him to just write his answer on this."

June examined the coaster. "He underscored a quote from *Richard III*: 'Dispute not with her, she is lunatic.' Is that supposed to mean something?"

"Christ, woman, I didn't mean his doodle on the bloody beermat!" Philip cursed. "I meant the words he wrote on the back. Turn the damned thing over!"

June flipped the card and read the handwritten scrawl on the back out loud: "If Eddie says she's dead, then she's dead."

"What do you make of that?" Philip asked.

June tossed the beermat back at Phil and handed him the newspaper. "It means nothing. Eddie has never said she's dead."

"Right," Philip agreed. He closed his eyes and rubbed his

temples. "So now I have to find another person who knows Eddie Rochester and can tell me something I don't already know."

## Chapter Nine

"Don't let go!" Jenny yelled. Her feet slid out from under her, sending her careening rump-first to the ice.

Eddie held out his hand to help her, but as soon as he shifted his weight, he slipped and fell as well. "I need help too," he laughed.

"I know I could skate when I was little," Jenny insisted. "I remember my Uncle Henry taking me to a frozen creek that ran alongside our street."

"Did you ever manage to stand upright by yourself, or did your uncle always hold your hand?"

"I thought I used to skate by myself. But maybe I'm remembering it wrong." She crawled to the edge of the frozen pond on her hands and knees, then grabbed a low lying tree branch and used it to support her weight while she stood.

Eddie got back up, skated cautiously towards Jenny and grabbed the other side of the branch. "I take back every rude remark I ever made about male figure skaters. I have a newfound respect for the athleticism of both of the battling Brians."

Jenny giggled. "What are you talking about?"

"The last Olympics." Eddie said. "Remember Brian Orser of Canada and Brian Boitano of the U.S. duking it out for the gold?"

Jenny shook her head. "The convent's TV set was broken. I haven't watched the Olympics in years."

"You poor kid," Eddie sighed. He let go of the branch and tried to skate to her side, but slipped and fell once more.

"You poor old man," she laughed. She offered him her right hand while she clung to the tree branch with her left. He took hold of it and somehow managed to stand back up again.

"I think that's enough fun for today," he said. They worked

their way off the ice, using the tree for support, and sat down on a large exposed rock to remove their skates.

"Thank you for buying me the skates, anyway," Jenny said as she struggled to undo the laces with her frozen fingers.

Eddie took off his gloves and helped her untie the tangled knot. After he loosened her laces, he held her boot in his hands so she could slide her foot out.

"I feel like Cinderella," she said.

"But Cinderella had help putting her shoes *on*," Eddie reminded her.

Jenny gazed into his eyes and wrapped her gloved hands around his cold, bare fingers. "I know," she whispered. "But I still feel like her."

\* \* \*

"You got a phone call," Sally told Jenny the moment she stepped into the mansion. "A woman named Hannah wants you to call her back right away."

Jenny hung up her coat and waited for her glasses to defog. "That's funny. Hannah never calls me. She only writes letters."

Sally handed her the phone number. "She's calling from Good Samaritan Hospital. This is her room extension."

Jenny's face blanched. She grabbed the paper and ran to the phone in the kitchen.

Eddie watched her scurry off. "Hannah was Jenny's housekeeper when she was a little girl," he explained. "They were very close."

Sally took the two pairs of skates. "I'll put these away for you."

Eddie nodded. He hung up his coat and walked into the sitting room to wait for Jenny.

"Is Hannah okay?" he asked when she came in to join him.

She sat down in a chair opposite him. "Yes, Hannah's fine. But my Aunt Sheila is dying. Her liver is finally going out on her."

Eddie sighed. "Ah, your alcoholic auntie who cast you out of your home when you were twelve. I realize it's customary to express condolences at a time like this, though I don't imagine the world will mourn your Aunt Sheila's passing too greatly."

Jenny shrugged. "Hannah wants me to come to Good Sam right away. She says Sheila's been asking for me. Over and over."

"Maybe she wants to assuage her guilty conscience for the way she mistreated you," he suggested. "And beg for your forgiveness before she goes to meet her maker."

"More likely she just wants to tell me in person that I won't be named in her will," Jenny replied.

"Then don't go," Eddie said. "You have no obligation to her."

Jenny sighed. "Hannah wants me to come."

"Who are you going to listen to, Hannah or me?" Eddie asked.

Jenny squeezed her eyelids shut and blinked back a tear. "I can't say no to Hannah. She's the closest thing I have to a mom."

Eddie rested his hand on top of hers. "Will your cousin John will be at the hospital?"

She flinched and looked away. "I dunno," she said. "Maybe. Probably."

"Then I'll go with you," he said. "I won't have you sitting unprotected in the same room with the bastard who molested you and cut off your hair."

Jenny relaxed her posture. "Thank you," she whispered.

"It's nothing," he said. "Get your coat back on. We'll drive to Good Sam right now and get this over with. Sally can take care of Gisela when she gets back from school."

Jenny looked back at him and smiled. She tried to slip her hand out from under his, but he clasped her fingers tightly with his own and held them for several more seconds.

"Don't worry," he said. "I won't let anyone hurt you again."

### *Cincinnati, Ohio*

Eddie and Jenny followed the nurse down the hospital corridor and into a patient room. Eddie watched Jenny's face light up when she saw a large Black woman sitting by the bed, then freeze when she spied a young man in the opposite corner of the room.

Jenny walked up to her former housekeeper and squeezed her hands. "Hi, Hannah, I came as soon as I could. My boss drove me here."

Eddie nodded at Hannah, then walked over to the young man. "You must be John Reed," he said, placing his hand on John's shoulder. "I'm Jenny's boss. Your mother wants to talk to your cousin in private. I'd like you to come with me."

"What the fuck!" John shouted. "Get your hands off of me!"

"I'm Jenny's boss," Eddie repeated. "And she has told me all about you. Everything. Now please stand up and come with me."

Sheila rolled her head on her pillow and opened her rheumy eyes. She looked at Jenny with an inscrutable gaze and mumbled a few incoherent syllables in a low, breathy voice. Then she closed her eyes, drew in a deep breath from the oxygen tube attached to her nose and whispered, "Go. John. Hannah. Go."

Hannah gave Eddie a quick once over, then turned her attention to John. "You better do what she say," she told John. "We'll leave your cousin and your mama to speak their piece."

She slowly hefted her weight out of her chair, then patted Jenny's hand before she walked to the door. "Thanks for comin', sweetie," she whispered. "I know this is hard for you."

"I'm not leaving my mother's side!" John protested. "I'm calling the nurse!"

Eddie grabbed John by the forearm. "I've brought Jenny here at your mother's request," he said through clenched teeth. "And now you are going to come with me to the waiting room while they talk, and you are going to stay with me until they are done."

"Your cousin's boss don' look like a man you wanna argue with," Hannah added, smiling at Eddie.

"All right, I'm leaving already!" John shouted. "Just stop touching me. What are you, some kind of homo?" He shook off Eddie's hand and left the room.

"The waiting room is *this* way," Eddie said as John started walking to the nurse's station. "Didn't you hear me? I said I'm not letting you out of my sight while Jenny is alone with your mother."

John shrugged and turned around. When he reached the waiting room, he collapsed on top of a large vinyl couch and spread his arms and legs out wide, taking up as much space as he could. Eddie took a seat across from him and cracked his knuckles.

John met Eddie's eyes. "You look familiar," he said, scrunching up his face and scrutinizing Eddie in a long, rude stare.

"Funny, you don't," Eddie replied. He held John's gaze and refused to break eye contact until John looked away in defeat.

John grabbed a copy of *US Weekly* from the table beside him. He opened it to a random page and made a deliberate show of ignoring his companions.

Hannah settled into the seat beside Eddie and rested her hand on his knee. "Thanks for gettin' Jenny here so quick. I know Sheila wanna tell her somthin'. She been askin' for her all day. But she gettin' weaker. I don' know if she gonna make it through the night."

Eddie turned towards Hannah. "I'm happy to help," he said. "I know this is a hard time for everyone in the family."

"Well, some of us been takin' it harder than others," Hannah said, shaking her head disparagingly at John.

John looked up from his magazine and cast Hannah a dirty look, then turned the page loudly and resumed reading.

Eddie glanced at the clock. "I hope the meeting is going well."

John eyed Eddie over the top of his magazine with seeming disinterest. Then he looked back down and turned another page. His eyes grew suddenly wide. He looked back and forth several times between Eddie's face and the periodical in his hands. Then he closed the magazine, rested it on his lap and broke into a nasty smile. "So, you're my cousin Jenny's boss?" he asked.

"I believe I've already told you that I am," Eddie replied.

"So she's working for a rock star now," John said, his lips curling into a sneer. "What exactly do you pay her to do?"

Eddie crossed his arms in front of his chest and scowled. "She's babysitting my friend's daughter while he's in hospital."

John shrugged and rolled the magazine into a tube. "Just curious what she's been up to these days," he added in a flippant tone. "I don't see her much anymore."

"Thank the Lord for small mercies," Eddie said. He glowered at John, but then noticed Jenny walking into the room. He stood up and took her hands in his. "That didn't take long," he said. "How did it go? Did she have anything important to say?"

Jenny shook her head. "She could hardly speak. She looked at me and said 'Jenny' a few times. Then she started mumbling something about my father, but I could barely understand her. After that she closed her eyes and fell asleep."

Eddie saw Jenny cast a nervous glance at John. He wrapped his arms around her in a sheltering embrace. "Well, I'm not sure if it was worth your while coming all this way just for that. But maybe she wanted to make peace with you in her own mysterious way."

He smiled at Jenny as he released her. But then he felt John's eyes upon his back. Eddie turned and saw John staring at him with a disturbing intensity.

Jenny walked towards Hannah. "It's good to see you again

anyway," she said, smiling and offering her a hand.

Hannah stood up with some difficulty, took Jenny's hand and pulled her into a long, warm hug. "It's good t' see you again too, chil'. You grown up all nice now."

"Have you eaten dinner yet, Hannah?" Eddie asked. "I thought I'd take Jenny to Rookwood Pottery for supper. Perhaps you'd be good enough to join us?"

"That'd be real nice," Hannah replied. "I'm sure gettin' tired of eatin' this hospital food day in and day out."

John cleared his throat loudly. "I'm glad you're all taking my mother's imminent death so well."

"By all means, young man, rush back to her side," Eddie said contemptuously. "What's keeping you?"

John held Eddie's gaze. "Oh, I don't know. Maybe I just wanted to gawk at you for a while longer. It's not every day I get to meet a superstar like yourself." He leered at Jenny and said, "See ya cuz," then walked out of the room, holding the rolled up magazine under his arm.

## Chapter Ten

### *Athens, Ohio*

Dick opened the door of his motel room and motioned for John to step inside. "Hey there, Johnny," he said, his voice uncommonly kind. "Sorry to hear about your mom."

John slipped past Dick and threw himself on top of the unmade bed. "Pity you can't afford a proper apartment," he said, tucking his hands behind his head. "There're a lot of transients living in these flea-bag, pay-by-the-week motels. I can't imagine it's the safest place for you to store your stash."

Dick rolled his eyes and returned to his wobbly wooden chair. "I appreciate your concern for my welfare," he replied, his voice testy again. "Though I distinctly remember you expressed an interest in leasing a room in this flea-bag motel not long ago."

"Well, I'm not interested anymore," John said. "I'm about to make a shitload of money. No, I take that back. *We're* about to make a shitload of money."

Dick eyed him suspiciously. "I'm all ears, my boy."

John sat up and flashed him an evil smile. "Our stars have aligned. I have met your brother-in-law Eddie Rochester. And I have uncovered his weak spot."

Dick pulled his chair closer to the bed. "I'm listening."

John let out a derisive hoot. "He's in love—with my cousin Jenny!"

"Are you joking?" Dick laughed. "Are you pulling my leg?"

John tugged the rolled-up copy of *US* out of his coat pocket and opened it to the article about Eddie. "Look at this picture. It was taken last November at his mansion. There's Eddie and Gerry Enis. The hot babe leaning against Eddie is Belinda Graham, the swimsuit model. The chick running away from Gerry is Belinda's sister. Says so in the caption. But check out this girl on the edge of the picture, holding hands with the child. That's my cousin Jenny."

Dick examined the photograph. "You sure that's your cousin? Her face is turned away from the camera."

"Of course it's my cousin! She's living at Eddie's mansion, working as a nanny for Gerry Enis' kid while he's in rehab!"

Dick scowled. "If Eddie is in love with your cousin, then why does he have his arm wrapped around that model?"

John ripped the magazine out of Dick's hands. "This photograph is two months old. Things have changed since then. I saw Jenny and Eddie Rochester together last week at the hospital, and God, what a sight they made. He's old enough to be her father, but that didn't stop him from groping her in the waiting room for everyone to see. Then he took her out to dinner at this fancy restaurant in Mount Adams. But he brought along my maid Hannah to act as a cover."

Dick snorted. "Something tells me you're exaggerating your cousin's relationship with Eddie. But even if you're right, I can't see how we stand to make a shitload of money out of this."

"That movie of yours," John replied. "We can finally use it against Eddie! He wouldn't want my innocent little cousin to see that—especially if we edited it to show only the worst bits. He wouldn't want the magazine reporter who wrote this story to see it either. And he damn sure wouldn't want that same reporter to discover your sister was still alive and has been living in his back yard the whole time he's been screwing my cousin."

Dick grew quiet for a few moments. "If what you're suggesting is true, then we might be able to leverage that movie against him," he agreed. "Though we'd have to play our cards very carefully. Eddie's not stupid. I'll have to think this through before we make any moves."

John kicked off his shoes. "Hey, don't worry!" he laughed. "You have me working with you now! What could possibly go wrong?"

## *Millcote, Ohio*

Eddie carried his dirty breakfast plate to the counter of the mansion's kitchen and returned to the table to finish his coffee.

Jenny stepped into the room just as he was bringing the mug to his lips. She smiled and sat down across from him. "I've discovered your secret."

He winced and brought the mug back to the table with a jerk, spilling several drops of coffee. "And what secret might that be?" he asked, struggling to keep his voice even.

"You always fill your coffee mug to the brim right before Gisela leaves for school, so you'll have an excuse to linger in the kitchen before you go visit the Pooles for the afternoon."

Eddie smiled in relief. *Off the hook again,* he thought. *Well, almost off the hook.* "You're right," he admitted. "I like spending a little time with just you before I face the folks in the other house."

He lowered his eyes and stared into his coffee mug. "I've discovered your secret too. Gisela told me last night when I was reading her a book about Sleeping Beauty. Your middle name is Aurora." He looked up quickly to catch her response.

Jenny blushed. "Yes and no. Actually, I have two middle names. It's Aurora Borealis."

He covered his mouth to hide his smile. "Oh, Christ, I'd forgotten that hint you dropped, that I should 'think hippie'."

She offered no reply.

"It's a lovely name," he said, trying very hard not to chuckle.

"Really? You think so?" she asked in a teasing voice.

"Sajani Aurora Borealis Ayr?" he replied, meeting her eyes and holding her gaze. "It's the most exquisitely original name I've ever heard. And it suits you too. The Aurora Borealis is a magical sight to behold. And I've always thought you possessed a certain magical quality too, right from the first day I met you."

She smirked. "I remember. You confused me with a Jawa."

"Exactly," he agreed, the corners of his eyes crinkling with mirth. "Jawas come from a galaxy far, far away. And the Aurora Borealis comes from—well, hell, I don't know where the Northern Lights come from, but they're up in the night sky, just like stars in the galaxy. Have you ever seen them?"

"No," she replied. "I think you have to go to Canada or Alaska to catch a glimpse. I've never been further north than Indianapolis."

"I saw them once in Norway," Eddie confessed.

Jenny's eyes grew wide. "That's so cool! Did you take pictures?"

"I tried, but they didn't turn out very well."

"Can I see them anyway?"

Eddie thought about the night they had gone stargazing in the back yard and started to smile. But then he remembered how that evening had ended. *If I ever try to do that again, I'll have to take her someplace far away,* he decided on the spot.

He took a last sip of coffee and stood up from the table. "I keep my photo albums in the library. Come with me. I'll see if I can find the right book."

She followed him into the other room and sat down on an over-stuffed couch. He scanned a bookshelf filled with large photo albums, pulled one down and brought it to her. "I think they're in this one," he said, taking a seat beside her and flipping through the pages. "I went on a cruise through the Norwegian fjords, and then took a train ride to the Arctic Circle."

Jenny stared wide-eyed at the photos. "These are beautiful!" she gushed. "You're so lucky to be able to visit places like this!"

"Sometimes I just really need to escape from Ohio," he admitted, biting back a pang of guilt. "Here are some glaciers I saw from the deck of the cruise boat. And this is a shite picture of the Aurora Borealis. I know—it just looks like a blurry patch of green. You'd need a good movie camera to capture the lights properly."

Jenny nodded and turned the page.

"Oh, bugger," Eddie muttered under his breath.

Jenny ran her finger around the edge of a photograph of Eddie with a nearly naked blonde. "I recognize you in this picture. But who is this?"

"Um, that's um—I think her name was Karen," he mumbled. "She was studying polar bears in the Arctic, and I—um, I met her at—well, after the cruise. I took that train ride to the Arctic Circle, like I said, and I stayed at this nice hotel with a sauna and—um, well, we just sort of, kind of—had a date. Or two."

"I see," Jenny said. "Funny, I would have thought a polar bear researcher would wear a few more layers of clothes."

"Well, I'm sure she wears a heavy parka when she's out in the tundra observing wildlife!" Eddie blustered.

"Just not when she's staying at a nice hotel with an even nicer sauna," Jenny replied.

"Right," Eddie agreed. He closed the photo album with a loud thump. "I think it's time I go check in on the folks across the yard.

You need to work on a GED practice test, or your college portfolio."

\* \* \*

Eddie shivered as he stepped into the frosty back yard. He gazed at the farmhouse and felt a horrible ache in the pit of his stomach. He looked back to the spot where the great elm tree had once stood. That made him feel worse. Tiny flakes of snow danced in front of his face and melted as they touched his warm skin.

*I'll tell her everything,* he promised himself, rubbing his nose with his glove. *I will. I must.* He inhaled deeply, filling his lungs with the cold afternoon air, and held his breath until his chest started to hurt. Then he exhaled and watched his breath take shape in front of him. It hung in the air for a second, like a pure, white cloud of shimmering substance. But then it curled up and dissipated into the breeze, as if it had never been there at all.

### Athens, Ohio

John Reed stared at the grainy movie scene projected against the bare wall of Dick's hotel room. "Damn, it's a pity there's no sound. I can read Eddie's lips. I know he's saying, 'you goddamned, fucking bastard.' But it's like watching an old Charlie Chaplin movie. You need subtitles."

"Charlie Chaplin never called anyone a 'goddamned, fucking bastard' in his films," Dick pointed out. "Nor did he hold a knife to the camera and threaten to slice somebody's throat."

"I thought you told me Eddie threatened to castrate you with the knife," John laughed.

Dick grunted. "Some of the details must have slipped my memory. I haven't looked at this movie in years."

John leaned forward and scrutinized the images on the wall. "My friend who lent me this projector said he could edit your footage anyway we'd like, once he's transferred it onto videotape. Maybe he could add the *Psycho* theme song."

"You trust this man at the camera shop?" Dick asked. "I don't want this film falling into the wrong hands."

"He's one of my best customers," John replied. The film came to an abrupt end. John turned the knob on the projector to stop the motor, then rethreaded the film through the sprockets and started rewinding it back onto the original spool. "Pity the movie's so short. It's action-packed, but it's not even three minutes long."

Dick stood up and switched the lights back on in the room. "Eight-millimeter films never ran for more than three minutes. And they never had sound either."

"So what do you propose we do next?" John asked. "Offer this movie to Eddie for a price, or sell it directly to the press?"

"I think it's worth more to Eddie than it would be to any journalist," Dick replied. "But here's the rub. My brother-in-law and I aren't on speaking terms. If I tried to approach him, he'd sic his lawyers on me before I even had a chance to present my case."

"Right," John said. "So let's contact the reporter from *US* who wrote that story."

Dick frowned. "No. All *US* did was quote an article that ran in the *London Eyewitness* last November. We'd be better off approaching that paper or another British rag. American tabloids don't usually pay their sources. They like to pretend they still have journalistic standards. But Fleet Street reporters have no qualms about throwing cash after dirt."

"I'll try to find the name of the reporter from *The Eyewitness* who wrote the original story, and give him a call," John offered.

"Why would he bother taking your call?" Dick asked.

John took the film off the projector and slipped it into its canister. "I'll send him my calling card first. Not the whole movie, mind you. Wouldn't want to blow our horn too loudly. I'll just have my friend record a few seconds of the most scintillating highlights onto a separate tape so we can whet the little slimeball's appetite. And then we'll let him call us."

Dick reached for the canister. "I'll take that. I'm going with you to that camera shop. I'm not letting this film out of my sight."

John shrugged. "Suit yourself."

Dick ran his hands nervously over the edge of the thin metal can. "I have a bad feeling about this, Johnny. This could turn out bad. Spectacularly bad."

"Or not," John retorted. He folded back the arms of the projector so it would fit inside its hard-shell carrying case. "But we'll never know until we try."

## Chapter Eleven

### *Millcote, Ohio*

Eddie stood in the back of the foyer and watched Jenny hand Gisela her lunch box. He sucked in a deep breath and stared at her intently as she blew the child a kiss and said goodbye to Sally. *It's now or never,* he told himself as he watched her close the front door. She turned around to face him. He swallowed hard.

"There's something I have to tell you," he stated bluntly. Waving his right hand, he motioned for her to follow him and walked into the sitting room. He took a seat in his brown leather chair and waited for her, hoping desperately that this conversation would go quickly and somehow end in a happy resolution.

"I'm all ears," she replied, taking a seat on the sofa across from him.

He closed his eyes and summoned his courage. "It's about my wife, Roberta."

Jenny nodded.

"I haven't told you everything about her," he continued.

"You never speak to me about her at all," she agreed.

He looked down at his shoes for a few seconds. "It's very difficult for me to talk about her," he began. He cast a quick, nervous glance at Jenny, then stood up and walked to the window. He stared at the farmhouse for a few seconds and took another deep breath. "Roberta is—"

His voice trailed off and his shoulders slumped. "Jenny, I—I didn't know her very well when I married her. It wasn't until after the wedding that I found out she was—she was—"

He left the words hanging in the air and gazed out the window.

After a few seconds had passed, he heard Jenny's gentle voice breaking the awkward silence. "She died from a drug overdose, didn't she?"

Eddie squared his shoulders. "Actually, Jenny, she didn't die from the drug overdose."

A few more seconds passed. When Jenny finally responded, her voice was cracking with concern. "Oh my God, did you have to make the decision to take her off life support?"

Eddie threw back his head in exasperation. "No, no, it didn't come to that." He turned around and looked directly into Jenny's eyes. Her face appeared ashen. *Why can't I just admit the truth?* he chastised himself. *I am married to a suicidal schizophrenic who hasn't been able to speak to me for the past sixteen years. And I want to leave her now, so I can be with you instead.*

"Was she a drug addict?" Jenny asked.

"No!" Eddie shouted in frustration. He clenched his hands into fists and tried to calm his nerves. "She only took prescription drugs. She—my wife—she suffered from an affliction for which there was no cure. Nothing could have saved her from—"

He swallowed hard and struggled to find the words to finish his sentence. *Save her from what?* he asked himself, his sense of purpose unraveling with each passing second. *From her illness? From herself? From her thick-headed fool of a husband?*

Eddie closed his eyes and took a deep breath. *Just say it!* his conscience goaded him. *Just say 'My wife is still alive, and you and I have no future together.'* He stood silently before Jenny for almost a full minute, hoping she wouldn't hate him after he admitted the truth. But before he could force the words out of his mouth, he heard her footsteps coming towards him and felt her hands resting upon his shoulders. He opened his eyes and saw her face a few inches away from his own.

"It's okay, Mr. R," she whispered, her voice trembling. "You don't have to tell me anything else. I see how hard it is for you to talk about this. But it doesn't matter. Whatever happened all those years ago is over and done with. All that matters is now."

She lifted her hands to his cheeks. "I know I'll never mean to you what she did. You probably think I'm just a silly girl who needs a lot of help. But I know how I feel about you, and there's nothing you can say that will change that. I don't care what happened between you and your wife all those years ago. All I care about is what's happened to me since I came here and met you. I love you.

No matter what secrets you've kept buried inside of you. I love you."

Jenny stood on her tiptoes and kissed him softly on the mouth.

Eddie's mind went blank and his cock grew instantly hard. Every half-formed, self-serving explanation that had occupied his thoughts in the hours preceding this conversation went flying from his head at the touch of her lips. His earnest desire to tell her the truth crumbled to the wayside, like a lop-sided sandcastle in a crashing wave.

He took a deep breath and turned his head, forcing himself not to return her kiss while he fought back the urge to grab her in his arms and carry her to bed. His eyes fell upon the snow-covered farmhouse through the window glass. He immediately turned his face away from it and gazed back at Jenny. The longing inside of him swelled and made him dizzy. He closed his eyes and took a step backwards.

"No, Jenny, no," he mumbled, his voice catching in his throat. "You don't know what you're saying. You don't know me at all. You think I'm a much better person than I really am. We could never—Christ, Jenny—I'm not—We're not—"

A quick sob escaped from her lips. "That's okay," she whispered. "You don't have to say anything else. I'm sorry—I should never have said that, or done that—you don't have to—you don't—I'm just so sorry!"

She broke away from him and fled to her bedroom in tears. He covered his face with his hands and remained by the window, cursing himself while the sound of Jenny's heart-broken sobs echoed down the stairwell.

## Chapter Twelve

### *London, England*

Jim McCudden locked eyes with his former songwriting partner and frowned. "Why the hell are you asking me for advice? I'm the pillock who suggested you boff Belinda Graham a few months ago. Remember how well that went?"

Eddie slumped his shoulders. "I don't know, Jim. I just need to talk to someone who knows a thing or two about handling potentially disastrous romantic relationships."

Jim snorted. "Are you referring to my divorce from hell?"

"Well, yes," Eddie admitted. He turned away from Jim's penetrating stare and gazed at the gold records lining the wall of his friend's posh London townhome. "I mean, I know it was awful the way Pippa dragged you through the courts and tabloids. But you survived somehow. And I want to survive my divorce too."

"You forget," Jim said. "I'm not just Pippa's ex. I'm also Clara's father. And I would not take kindly to any old geezer chatting up my daughter before she reached her twenty-first birthday."

Eddie crossed his arms in front of his chest and stared at Jim defiantly. "Well, Jenny's an orphan, so incurring her father's wrath is the one problem I actually don't have to worry about at the moment."

"Fine," Jim continued, softening his tone a bit. "You just have to worry about the press then. That bloke from *The Eyewitness* is already stalking you. But once this story breaks, the paparazzi will descend upon Thornfield like a plague of locusts. For sixteen years the media has written you off as a tragic romantic hero. But now the world is primed to discover that the woman who inspired your album of beautiful love songs is not only not dead, she's also a psychotic pyromaniac, and you want to divorce her so you can marry an underage kid you've been living with since September."

"Jenny is not underage!" Eddie protested, the veins bulging in his neck and blood rushing to his cheeks. "She's twenty. And I haven't been living with her. I've hardly even kissed her!"

He stood up from his chair and started pacing the floor. A framed portrait of Jim's daughter Clara caught his eye. He stopped walking for a moment to examine the photo. Clara looked a lot like Jim's ex-wife, but her impish grin was a dead ringer for her dad's trademark goofy smile.

*Damn, it's no wonder he's taking me to task,* Eddie reflected. *Jenny's closer in age to Clara than to Birdie.* He took a few short breaths to calm his nerves, then closed his eyes and lowered his voice. "Well, okay, you're partly right. Jenny and I have shared the same roof. But I haven't been sleeping with her."

Jim frowned. "Spin the story any way you like. It doesn't matter. This is going to get ugly." He stood up from his chair and approached his friend, then leaned his back against the wall, blocking Clara's portrait from Eddie's view. He rested his hand on Eddie's shoulder.

"My advice to you is to take Jenny out of the picture before the media feeding frenzy kicks into high gear," he suggested. "Send her someplace out of the way until the worst of the story blows over. Or at least until your divorce papers are filed and you have Roberta safely locked up in a mental hospital."

"My friend Bob is looking into a few places for me," Eddie replied. He looked down at his feet, ashamed to meet his friend's eye. "I mean—places where I can commit Birdie."

"How does she feel about that?" Jim asked. "Do you have any idea?"

"I don't know," Eddie sighed, swallowing back the wave of guilt sloshing in his gut. He backed away from Jim and collapsed in the overstuffed sofa that faced the wall. "I'm sure she'll adjust."

Jim eyed him dubiously. "You'll put her someplace close to Thornfield, right? So you can still visit her?"

"Of course!" Eddie replied. "Or, well, maybe. I don't know. I haven't thought that far in advance yet."

Jim shook his head. "You're just making this up by the seat of your pants, aren't you?"

"I don't know what the hell I'm doing," Eddie admitted, his

voice ragged with frustration. He picked up a decorative pillow and punched it. "I don't know what's right or what's wrong anymore. All I know is that I'm hopelessly in love with Jenny, and that she loves me too. And I have to be with her."

Jim reclaimed his seat and faced his friend. "How much have you told her about Roberta? She understands your peculiar circumstances, doesn't she?"

Eddie threw the pillow on the ground and hung his head. "Next question, please," he mumbled.

Jim glowered at him. "You wanker! Does she even know why you flew to London? What did you tell her?"

Eddie stared at his shoes. "I told her I had to meet with my attorneys to discuss some long-standing legal issues. I didn't elaborate, but that's okay. We had a—well, a rather awkward conversation the day before I left, and she was too embarrassed to even look me in the eye when I said goodbye."

"So you're dead serious about this," Jim said, shaking his head. "You're finally going to get a divorce."

"Yes. I've made up my mind," Eddie insisted. He looked back up at Jim with a hopeful expression. "But Bob said it would be easier for me to have Birdie committed to a hospital while I'm still married to her. I also want to ask my lawyers here in London to restructure some trusts I've set up for her. I want to make sure she'll always be taken care of. And I want to visit that church in Italy where we were married and see about applying for an annulment. Jenny's Catholic, so that might matter to her."

Jim offered Eddie a slim smile of encouragement. "When is Gerry getting out of the clinic? Maybe you could send Jenny to live with him in Munich while you tend to your—long-standing legal issues. The press might not even suspect that Jenny is part of the story if she's safely out of the country, minding her own business and babysitting Gisela in Germany."

A ray of sunlight streamed through a window across the room and fell upon Eddie's feet, offering him a fleeting sense of serenity as he considered Jim's proposition. "Well, maybe," he replied at length. "That might be a good idea. But the last time I pulled Gerry out of treatment early, he fell right back on the bottle. And I'm not sure if Jenny could handle him by herself."

"You might not have a choice but to spring him out early again," Jim said. "The sooner you get Jenny out of Ohio, the better."

"Yes," Eddie agreed. He ran his hands through his hair and wondered if Jenny would need to get a visa if she lived in Germany for more than a few months. *Damn!* he cursed in his head. *She doesn't even have a driver's license! I doubt she has a passport!* He exhaled loudly and tapped his fingers against the armrest of the sofa in frustration. "I'm sure she couldn't handle the paparazzi," he agreed. "They're going to be ruthless, aren't they?"

Jim smiled ruefully. "You could try to deflect them," he proposed. "Why don't you look up Belinda Graham again? Make the papers think she's the one who inspired you to leave Roberta. I somehow imagine she'd welcome the attention."

Eddie covered his face in his hands and sighed. "She might. She actually called me a few days ago and invited me to join her in Capri for a photo shoot. She doesn't want to rekindle our romance, though. She just wants me to finish editing her manuscript."

"That swimsuit model is just using you for your mad grammatical skills," Jim noted, pulling a face that looked just like his daughter's expression in her portrait on the wall.

Eddie looked up and let loose a sad laugh. "God, my life is a joke, isn't it? How did I ever let things get this far out of hand?"

"It's been a long time coming," Jim said. "If you had responded all those years ago when Dick started that lie about Roberta being dead, things might have turned out differently. But your silence seemed to confirm his story. And now you're living a lie."

"But I never meant for that to happen!" Eddie insisted, his voice growing increasingly agitated. "I simply enjoyed the way Dick's lie kept the press at bay. They all assumed I retreated to that little town in Switzerland so I could bask in my grief, and left me alone so they could pursue other stories. Like Watergate, and Princess Anne's wedding, and Uri Geller bending a bloody spoon on the telly, and—God, I can't even remember what other bits of dribble. But Birdie and I became yesterday's news, and we were able to retreat to Ohio with our privacy intact."

"And now your privacy is going to go up in flames like that elm tree in your back yard," Jim noted.

"I know," Eddie mumbled. He stood up from the sofa and grabbed his coat off the back of the chair by the piano.

Jim walked him to the front door of his townhouse. "Well, my old friend, I think you've topped yourself. You always had a singular talent for fucking things up with women, but you've taken that up a notch this time around. Still, I beg you—as a friend—don't rush into things with Jenny like you rushed into your marriage to Roberta. Use your head this time around."

"I'll think about it," Eddie promised as he reached for the doorknob. "If I can even remember how to think anymore."

## Athens, Ohio

John hung up the telephone in Dick's dingy motel room, leaned against the headboard of the lumpy bed, and smiled smugly at his partner-in-crime. "He's interested."

"How interested?" Dick replied, his voice strained with worry.

"He didn't quote a figure, just a range. He wants to talk with you first and see how much information you're willing to share." John tucked his hands behind his head and knocked askew the framed print of a sad-looking beagle on the wall behind him. "He wants a recent photograph of your sister too, that he can run with his column. If he can see her in the flesh, he'll pay more."

Dick drummed his fingers against the surface of the cheap laminate desk in the corner of the room. "This is going to be very tricky to pull off. I can get us onto Eddie's estate, but snapping a picture of Roberta will be a challenge."

"You know the passcode to his entry gate?"

"No, but I've staked the place out. There's an old abandoned road on the edge of Thornfield that you can access from a neighbor's farm. The road dead-ends in a huge cornfield. We can slip through that, then cut through a copse of trees and get right up to Eddie's compound. It's about a mile hike in all."

"How often have you been there?" John asked.

"A few times," Dick said. "There's a huge mansion in the front of the property, a little farmhouse behind it, and a large detached garage off to the side. Eddie keeps my sister locked up in the farmhouse. I've glimpsed her through the window."

"Great," John said. "So if we bring this Philip Randall bastard onto the property through the cornfield and woods, then he can snap your sister's picture through that window."

"If she's in the living room when we arrive."

"We'll take our chances."

Dick closed his eyes and sighed. "A lot of things could go

wrong. It's late winter now, so the corn's all been reaped and the trees in the woods are bare. We won't be able to hide very well. And my sister—" He let his voice trail off.

"Your sister what?" John asked.

"My sister is very unpredictable. She might fly off the handle if she sees me. We didn't exactly part on good terms. And Eddie hates me. He will definitely fly off the handle if he sees me."

"He's in Europe now," John said. "That reporter I was talking to has been following his every move."

Dick fell silent as he considered the situation.

John watched him carefully for several seconds before making a proposal. "I can scope out the farm, if you'd like. I'll check out that road you mentioned, and see how much cover we'll have in the woods. My family's house in Cincinnati hasn't been sold yet, so I can stay there and make practice runs every day. I'll learn the lay of the land and figure out the best time of day to pay our visit."

Dick leaned back against his wooden chair, ran his fingers through his greasy hair and frowned. "How much is this Randall bastard going to pay for my scoop?"

"That all depends on how much of a story you can sell him," John replied. He stood up from the bed and approached the desk.

Dick surveyed the environs of his rented room and noted the peeling wallpaper and well-worn carpeting. "The more I tell him, the more he pays?"

John slapped him on the back. "Hell, yes! And I'm counting on you to tell him a lot!"

### *Millcote, Ohio*

Eddie pulled his car into the long driveway that led up to Thornfield just as the sun was starting to set. He tore his eyes away from the colorful clouds, switched off his radio and practiced reciting the speech he had been crafting in his head all the way home from Europe.

As he approached the mansion, he noticed Jenny crouching beside a forsythia bush in the front yard, its branches awash in an explosion of yellow blossoms. His heart pounded in his chest, and the carefully rehearsed lines flew out of his head. He parked the car but lingered in his seat while he summoned his courage. Then he flung open the door and called out to her.

"Hey, Jenny, I'm back!" he exclaimed, his baritone voice squeaking like a tenor's in nervous excitement.

Jenny cast him a quick glance, then went back to her task without offering a reply. He walked up to her slowly, tucking his hands in his trouser pockets to stop himself from throwing his arms around her.

"What are you doing?" he asked.

"Tomorrow's St. Patrick's Day," she answered without looking up. "I'm hiding some leprechaun coins for Gisela to hunt for in the morning. Mrs. F is tucking her into bed right now. She's probably not asleep yet if you want to drop in and say hello."

"That's all right, I'll see her in the morning," Eddie replied, his voice growing steadier as he watched Jenny work. "I'm more interested in saying hello to you."

"Hello," Jenny whispered, still not meeting his eyes. She placed her last plastic coin by a clump of newly sprung daffodils and turned to face the mansion.

Eddie swallowed hard and took a step closer to her. "Hey, is that anyway to welcome home a weary traveler?" he teased.

"Do you need help with your luggage?" she asked.

"No, I'll get it later," he answered with a sigh. "Come on, let's go sit on that bench over there and talk for a bit. There are a lot of things I want to tell you."

Jenny held her ground. "You don't need to tell me anything. Mrs. F showed me the picture of you and Belinda Graham in the newspaper."

Eddie's heart sank. "There was nothing to that," he insisted. "I just visited her in Italy to help get her book ready for publication."

Jenny stared at her shoes and offered no response.

*Bugger, this conversation is not going the way I planned*, Eddie cursed in his head. He cleared his throat.

"I was only in Italy with Belinda for two days," he reiterated. "I spent a lot more time visiting Gerry. He thinks—we both think—that he might be more inspired to stay off the bottle if he had Gisela living with him. So, we were wondering how you'd feel about going to Germany for a few months, and working as her nanny there?"

"I don't want to be Gisela's nanny anymore," Jenny said, her voice growing bolder but her gaze still focused on her shoes. "I've written my letter of resignation. I want to go back to the convent."

*No, no, no!* Eddie thought. *This is not the script I planned!* He struggled to choke back the desperation from his voice as he asked, "Why?"

"I think you know why," she whispered.

"But—but I don't want you to go," he stammered.

"You just said you wanted me to go to Germany!" she shouted, raising her face to meet his at last.

He stared at her hopelessly. The last few rays of the setting sun cast her face and hair in a golden light. She looked even more beautiful than he remembered. He swallowed hard. "Jenny, I—I don't want you to go. Not to the convent. Not to Germany. I want—I want you to—"

"Do you think this is easy for me?" she asked, cutting him off. "This is the hardest thing I've ever had to do!"

Her nostrils flared and her cheeks flushed red. "I can't just drive away in my sports car or fly off to London when I want to avoid an awkward confrontation," she continued, pointing accusingly at his MG. "I can't fall back in the arms of my last lover to show you how little our friendship means to me. Maybe if I were rich and beautiful, I could make it as hard for you to leave me as it is for me to leave you. But I'm not. I'm poor, plain, little and obscure, and I—I just can't—"

Her voice started cracking and she looked back down at the ground. "I just can't live any place where I might see you again."

The sun sank lower against the horizon, and the pale purple sky began dissolving into a darker shade of indigo. Eddie clasped Jenny's trembling hands in his own. She struggled away from him, so he put his hands to her cheeks and lifted her face up to meet his. "You're not plain, Jenny," he said, gazing directly into her eyes. "You are the loveliest woman I've ever seen."

She threw his hands off her face. "You're teasing me again! You always tease me!"

"I am not teasing you," he insisted. "There is no other face I'd rather see than yours. From the very first day I met you, I've gone to sleep each night imagining what it would be like to see your face lying on the pillow beside me when I woke up."

Jenny's back stiffened. "I don't believe you. You think I'm just a silly little girl. You don't care about me the way you care about Belinda Graham or that—that Scandinavian polar bear lady."

"You're right," Eddie agreed, the confidence returning to his voice. "My feelings for you are entirely different than my feelings for women like that. I only want one thing from those girls, and after I've gotten it, I start counting the minutes until I can leave them. But you, Jenny—I want to spend the rest of my life with you. I want to be with you always. I want to—"

He swallowed hard and reminded himself that he couldn't propose marriage to her yet. He brought his hands back to her face and gently forced her to look directly at him again. The sky was mostly dark now, but the porchlight from the mansion reflected off the tears in Jenny's glistening eyes and made them sparkle.

"I love you, Jenny," he said. "With every ounce of my being, I love you. You are the woman I've been hoping to meet all my life. You are everything I've ever wanted."

She swallowed back a sob. "You're teasing me," she repeated.

Eddie leaned forward and kissed her tenderly on the lips. "I am not teasing you," he promised. "I love you, Jenny, absolutely. And I want to spend the rest of my days loving you."

He lowered his hands and wrapped his arms around her waist. Closing his eyes, he bent down and kissed her—softly at first, but then with an increasing urgency. She broke away briefly and caught her breath, but then wrapped her arms around his neck and drew him back to her mouth to return his kiss.

Eddie melted into her embrace. He kissed her lips, her throat, her cheeks, her lips again. "You make me feel alive again," he murmured between kisses.

She stroked his cheek and rubbed her nose against his. "That's how you make me feel too," she replied, smiling through her tears. "Like I've been rescued after being buried alive for so many years."

He wrapped his arms more tightly around her waist and positioned her head against his chest.

"God forgive me," he whispered, his heart pounding against her cheek. "As I hold you, I will have you. And damned be anyone who tries to stop me."

She raised her eyes and gazed up at him adoringly. "I'm not going to stop you," she assured him. She lifted her face back to his and offered him her lips once more.

He met them with a ravishing kiss, giving in to the hunger that had been building inside him for months, stopping only when he sensed she needed to catch her breath.

"Come to me," he said, grasping both of her hands. He threw a quick glance at the mansion's upstairs windows, then looked back at her and smiled. Her face was radiant was joy. "Come to me entirely now. Make my happiness, and I will make yours."

## Chapter Thirteen

Eddie opened his eyes to the morning light and saw Jenny gazing at him from across the pillow. Her eyes were filled with love. "Good morning, Mr. R," she whispered.

He reached out his hand and stroked her cheek. "Good morning, my love," he whispered back.

She leaned forward and started kissing him.

He wrapped his arms around her and returned her kiss, then released her from his embrace and leaned back on his side of the bed. "There's something I need to tell you, my darling girl," he said, his voice breaking.

"There's something I need to tell you too," she replied.

Eddie sucked in a deep breath and tried to summon the courage to make his confession. He closed his eyes. An image of Jenny taking her clothes off the night before filled his head. *She looked so young—so perfect,* he remembered.

He opened his eyes once more and gazed back at her. *She looks so trusting.* His courage failed him.

"You go first," he proposed.

"Okay," she agreed. She put her hands behind his head and drew him towards her again. "I kissed you once before. That night when you got drunk and I helped you into your bed. I stayed by your side, and kissed you on the lips after you fell asleep."

His heart started pounding in his chest. *Damn, she loved me even then!* he marveled. *What did I ever do to deserve a girl this wonderful?*

He reached out his hand and brushed a lock of hair away from her eyes. "Ah, so Aurora turned the tables and kissed the prince while *he* was sleeping," he murmured.

"But you didn't wake up," she replied. "So maybe you're not a prince from a fairy tale after all."

"I most decidedly am not," he agreed, his heart filling with ache again. He opened his mouth to speak, but was drowned out by the sound of Gisela's cries echoing down the hallway.

"Jenny! *Wo bist du?* Frau Fairfax! Jenny is not *in ihren Bett!*"

"Oh, fuck," Eddie cursed.

Jenny leaned across the pillow and kissed him once more before scooting to the edge of the mattress. "I'll go check on her," she said, grabbing her glasses off the nightstand and her clothing from the floor. "I think I am needed."

Eddie threw off the sheet and embraced her. "Nowhere so much as you're needed right here," he said. He wrapped his arms around her waist and kissed the back of her neck. Cupping her breasts with his warm, strong hands, he gave them one last squeeze before letting her go. "I'll join you downstairs in a minute," he promised. "As soon as I get dressed and wash up."

Jenny glanced at the clock on his nightstand. "You could sleep in if you'd like," she said. "You're probably exhausted from your flight. Why don't you rest until Mrs. F drives Gisela to school? Then I'll come back in here and attack you."

He stroked her hair, then brought her hand to his lips. "You—are—perfect—Jenny—Ayr," he whispered, punctuating each word with a kiss to her fingertips.

"You aren't so bad yourself," she giggled. She leaned down and brushed her lips against the top of his head. "I love you, Mr. R."

"My name is Eddie," he said with a smile.

"I know, Mr. R," she replied.

He gazed at her longingly as she threw on her clothes and ran out the bedroom door. Then he fell back against his pillow and stared vacantly at the ceiling while an overpowering sensation of guilt began encroaching upon him.

*Holy Christ,* he thought. *What the hell am I going to do now?*

\* \* \*

He lay in bed for a quarter hour after Jenny's departure, wrestling with his conscience. But failing to come to any happy solution, he decided to lay his moral quandaries aside for just a little longer and went downstairs to join Jenny for breakfast.

Gisela threw her arms around him the moment he walked into the sitting room. But her initial excitement gave way to a more pensive reaction when Eddie told her she would be joining her father in Germany soon.

"But Papa finds me always *schlechte* nannies!" she complained. "I like Jenny."

"But I like her too," Eddie replied, clasping Jenny's hand. "So she will stay with me."

"But you do not a nanny need," Gisela protested.

"But I do need a Jenny," he said. He brushed Jenny's hair to the side and gently kissed the nape of her neck before repeating, "So she will stay with me."

Gisela's eyes grew wide. "Jenny *ist jetzt meine Tante!*" she squealed.

Eddie frowned. "What do you mean? Jenny is not your aunt."

"Papa always calls my nannies my new *Tanten* after he starts kissing them."

Eddie rolled his eyes. "Your Papa is a deeply confused and troubled man. But he loves you very much, and I'm sure he will find you an excellent nanny after he gets out of the clinic."

"But I will here until then stay?" Gisela asked, her lip trembling.

Eddie rested his free hand on top of Gisela's head. "You can stay here for a little while longer, *liebchen*," he promised.

The back door swung open. Eddie flinched at the sound, then caught his breath while Alan walked into the room.

"I saw your car parked out front, Eddie," Alan said. "Why didn't you stop by to let us know you got back?"

"I was—preoccupied," Eddie answered, casting a nervous smile at Jenny. He squeezed her hand a little tighter.

Jenny blushed and stared at her feet for a long moment, then looked back up at Eddie and smiled.

Eddie looked back at Alan. With one glance at his friend's astonished face, he could tell Alan knew exactly how he had been preoccupied the previous evening.

"Jesus fucking Christ, Eddie! What in God's name are you doing?" Alan blustered.

Eddie let go of Jenny's hand. He fell silent for a long moment while he considered his response. But then a wave of self-righteousness rose up inside him.

*I've supported that bastard for the past fifteen years!* he reminded himself. *Given him free room and board, and spending money to boot! I even paid for his drug counseling to get him off the junk! He's got no right to tell me how to live my life!*

"A fine way to say hello," Eddie snapped. "Whatever happened to, 'Welcome back, Eddie, I'm so very glad to see you again'?"

"You are so in over your head," Alan replied. "What are you even thinking?"

Eddie stared defiantly at Alan. "I'm thinking that I will spend a lovely spring morning with this lovely young lady. I'm thinking I spent far too much time away from home. I'm thinking that none of the tired, old sights of Europe can possibly compare with the beauty that surrounds me right here at Thornfield." He flashed Jenny another grin and wrapped his arm around her shoulder.

Alan threw Eddie a look of disgust, then turned and stormed away. "Do stop by and chat when you have a free moment, *Mr. Rochester*. We have a lot of things to talk about." He slammed the back door behind him.

Eddie sucked in a deep breath, then released it with a sad sigh as his sense of guilt started to return.

"Don't mind him," he said, guiding Jenny into the kitchen. "Alan's always in a foul mood in the morning. Now let's see what sort of wonderful feast my wonderful housekeeper has prepared for me and my wonderful girls."

\* \* \*

Eddie and Jenny stood in the driveway and waved goodbye as Sally drove Gisela off to school. Then Eddie popped the trunk of his car and retrieved his luggage. He handed Jenny the smallest bag and asked her to be very careful with it. She brought it into the house and carried it up to his bedroom. He followed closely at her heels, brooding over the topic he knew he must address as he climbed the long staircase.

As soon as Jenny stepped into his room, she tossed the bag on the floor and wrapped her arms around his neck, startling him out of his reverie.

He gazed into her eyes and melted into her smile. *I'll tell her tomorrow,* he impulsively decided. *I'll give us both one perfect day, then explain everything.*

He ran his fingers through her hair and kissed her passionately. When she stopped to catch her breath, he released her from his embrace and picked up the bag she had thrown on the floor.

"Didn't I tell you to be careful with this?" he teased. "There's something precious in here." He unzipped the bag and pulled out a small box. "I bought this for you last week on the *Ponte Vecchio* in Florence."

He opened the hinge and presented the box to her. She stared at the antique emerald ring nestled inside and caught her breath.

"I was thinking of your gorgeous green eyes while I was crossing the bridge, and then this stone caught the light and flashed at me from a jeweler's stand," he said. "I decided it must be a sign."

He started bending his knee, but stopped himself as a flash of conscience kicked in. *Word this properly!* he urged himself. *You can't ask her to marry you yet!*

Standing squarely on his feet, he took the ring out of the box and slipped it onto her finger. "I want to spend the rest of my life with you, Jenny. No matter what happens. I always want to be with you." He kissed her once more and wrapped his arms around her.

She rested her tear-stained face against his chest and encircled his waist with her arms. "I always want to be with you too," she whispered between sobs. "I love you so much."

He scooped her into his arms and carried her back to bed.

\* \* \*

"Hello there, love," Eddie murmured as Jenny opened her eyes. She yawned and snuggled up more closely against him.

"Was I sleeping long?" she asked.

"No," he said, bringing his index finger to her face and tucking a stray tendril of hair behind her ear. "Just for an hour or so. You must be exhausted. I know for a fact that you didn't sleep at all last night."

"There'll be time for sleeping later," she said, wrapping her legs around his. "I have more important things to do now."

"You're a feisty little wench!" he teased. "Who would have thought an innocent convent school girl like you would have such an insatiable appetite for sex?"

"You would have found out sooner if you'd asked," she replied.

He ran his finger down her torso, then rested his hand on her bottom. "God, do you know how long I've dreamt about holding you like this?"

"What else have you dreamt about doing with me?" she asked.

He sighed and rolled onto his back. "I want to take you somewhere," he answered. "Someplace quiet and private and far, far away."

She repositioned herself on the bed so she could face him. "Isn't Thornfield quiet and private enough?"

"The world is too much with us here," he replied, staring at the ceiling. "I want to take you someplace where we can be completely alone. A tropical island maybe."

"Okay," she giggled. "That sounds like fun."

He fell silent for a long moment while he considered how much time it would take to move Birdie into a nursing home. *Grace and Bob can help her settle in,* he mused. *It will be better that way. Birdie'll be too mad at me for my presence to be required. I'd just be in the way.*

"I'll call my travel agent this afternoon, and see how quickly she can book us a flight to the South Seas," he ventured at length.

Jenny took his hand in hers and kissed the underside of his wrist. "I don't have a passport. Will that be a problem?"

Eddie flinched. "I'll have to think about that."

"Well, while you're thinking about that, how about I do something that I've been dreaming about doing for a long time?" she proposed.

"And what might that be?" Eddie asked, his curiosity piqued.

"I want to draw you naked," she answered, throwing back the sheet. "Stay right there while I grab my sketchbook."

* * *

Eddie topped off Jenny's glass of champagne. "Drink up, love. Twenty is old enough for alcohol in my book. I was actually quite an accomplished boozer by the time I was nineteen."

Jenny took a small sip and rested her glass on the edge of the bathtub. "I don't like the bubbles. They give it a funny taste."

He set the open bottle on the tile floor and picked up his own glass. Then he dipped his index finger into the champagne and ran it over Jenny's lips. "How's that?" he asked.

"I can hardly taste it."

He wet his lips with the drink, then leaned forward and pressed them against hers. "How's that?" he repeated.

"Better," she sighed.

*Am I corrupting her?* he wondered for a fleeting moment. *Because she certainly seems a willing participant in this seduction!*

He took a large drink of champagne and gave himself over to the buzz that was blotting out the vestiges of his conscience. He looked Jenny in the eye and smiled.

"Sit up straight," he commanded her.

She sat up and leaned her back against the edge of the tub. He dipped his fingers into the glass once more, then brought his hand to her breast and traced a circle over her nipple. He leaned forward and licked off the champagne, then leaned back again, sending a small ripple of water splashing against her chest. "How's that?"

"Much better," she said, reaching for his hands and drawing him back to her. He sucked on her neck. She closed her eyes and trembled. He leaned back and took another sip of champagne. Then he encircled her in his arms and whispered in her ear:

*"What a person g'win to do,
When he come a-courtin' you
All a trimbling, through and through?"*

Jenny opened her eyes. "Are those the lyrics to an old song?"

"It's a verse by Paul Laurence Dunbar, a poet from Dayton." Eddie finished off his glass of champagne, then leaned back and recited the rest of the poem for her.

Jenny giggled. "Oh, I get it. You're trying to speak in a Black dialect."

"I'm better at Scots," he admitted.

"Yeah," she agreed. She took another sip of champagne, made a sour face, and put the glass away. "Do you still write poems anymore, or do you just recite other people's work?"

"I've written some for you," he confessed, lowering his gaze.

She leaned forward and kissed him. "Can you recite them for me?" she asked.

"I'd rather sing them for you," he answered. "I've set them to music. Here, let me help you out of the tub." He stood up and offered her his hand.

\* \* \*

"No, move your ring finger," Eddie said. He rested the guitar he was playing on the ground, then sat directly behind Jenny, and positioned his left hand into a 'D' chord on the neck of the instrument she was holding. His face rubbed against her hair, still damp from the bath. "See how easily you can move to an 'A7' from this position?"

Jenny watched his hands switch back and forth between the chords, then attempted to finger them herself. A dissonant thud resulted.

Eddie chuckled. "You have to keep your fingers straight. Don't lean them against the next string." He shaped the two chords again with his left hand and asked her to strum the strings.

"That's good," he said. "Now try to put some bounce into it." He wrapped his right arm around her, completely enveloping both her and the guitar inside his reach, and started strumming the instrument with his right hand. "This is a waltz tempo."

Jenny leaned back against him. "This is better than waltzing."

"I agree," he laughed. He leaned forward to kiss her damp hair.

She attempted to form the chords on the guitar neck again, but when Eddie strummed the instrument, they still sounded awful.

"How about we stop the music lesson?" Jenny proposed. "I'd rather hear you play those songs you wrote for me again."

"But they made you cry," Eddie said.

"They made me happy," Jenny corrected him. "Just like you make me happy. Happier than I've ever been."

He rested the guitar on the floor, scooted in front of her, and smiled. A pleasant buzz still lingered in his head from the champagne, but he felt more sober now. Sober enough to talk, anyway.

"I'm glad I make you happy," Eddie began. "You make me happy too. Happier than I've been in years. Decades really. Ever since that day that Birdie—"

"Shhh," Jenny whispered. "Let's not talk about sad things just now. Make love to me again."

She wrapped her arms around his neck and kissed him. He fell into her embrace and let his conscience slip away once more as he surrendered himself to joy.

\* \* \*

"Gotta go now," Eddie mumbled. He slammed the phone back

in its cradle and smiled at Jenny as she stepped into his bedroom. "Hello again. I missed you."

"I was only gone for an hour," she replied.

"That's too long," he said. He stood up from his chair and drew her into his arms.

She hugged him back, then slipped away. "It took me a while to calm Gisela down. She's upset about leaving Ohio. Do you think you could borrow Pancho from the Pooles for the next few days until her dad comes to pick her up? Playing with the dog might keep her mind off her worries."

"Of course," Eddie said, biting back a sense of dread at the thought of calling the farmhouse. "I'll ring Alan in the morning and ask him to drop her off when he comes to take Gisela to school." He kissed the top of Jenny's head. "Let's go to bed."

She followed him across the room and sat down on the mattress. "Who were you talking to just now?"

He clenched his hands in and out of fists for a short moment while he considered how much he should say.

"Bob Carter," he replied at last. "His family spends a week every summer in the Upper Peninsula of Michigan. Bob says it should be very private this time of year. He gave me the name of the man he rents his cabin from. I think we should go there."

"But why?" Jenny asked, stroking Eddie's thigh. "It's so nice here, with spring just arriving. It's probably still really cold in Northern Michigan."

"I'll keep you warm," Eddie promised, leaning closer against her and nuzzling her neck. "We might be able to see the Northern Lights if we went there right now."

"That would be nice," she replied.

"Yes," Eddie whispered, unbuttoning her blouse. "Very nice."

"Don't you have jetlag?" she asked, untucking her shirt and helping him with the buttons. "I mean, you just spent three weeks in Europe, and since you came home, you've hardly slept a wink. I think you need to relax a little. I'm worried about you."

"Why are you worried about me?" he blustered. "I feel fine. I've never felt better!"

She slipped her arms out of her sleeves and started to undo the buttons on his shirt. "Oh, I don't know. You just seem kind of restless, that's all."

*She knows something's wrong,* he sensed. *I can't keep lying to her. But maybe I could find a way to soften the blow—*

"Would you rather go someplace warmer?" he asked, offering her a weak smile. "Hawaii might be nice. Not Oahu, mind you. But maybe one of the smaller, less touristy islands?"

She pulled off his shirt and undid the button on his jeans. "That sounds nice. But let's wait a week or so. I'm happy just being at Thornfield with you."

Eddie closed his eyes and tried to stop worrying. *We're still safe here*, he reminded himself. *Nobody from the press knows what's going on.*

## Chapter Fourteen

"Cor, they're a pair, all right!" Philip laughed. He adjusted his telephoto lens and snapped a few shots of Jenny and Eddie as they lay kissing on a blanket in the lawn in front of the mansion.

John glared at the couple from his spot by the edge of the garage. "He has weird taste in women."

"He always has," Dick noted sourly. He looked away from his brother-in-law and turned his face towards the farmhouse. "So how are we going to do this?"

"Phil and I will position ourselves by the side window," John said. "The curtain is wide open—I checked. You go to the front door, Dick, and when the old lady opens it, call your sister's name. You don't have to go inside or talk to her. Just make her stand up and start walking towards you. Phil should be able to get a good picture of her through the glass."

"Can't he just take a photo of her through the window without making our presence known?" Dick asked.

"We'll look through the window first," John promised. "If Phil can get a good enough shot, we'll settle for that. But we need a clear picture of her face."

"I'd rather take a picture through the front door," Philip said. "There's a high risk of glare with a window shot."

"There's a high risk of injury looking my sister in the face," Dick countered. "I'd rather stand at the window."

Philip glanced at his watch and turned to John. "Are you sure this Poole fellow will be leaving the building soon? I don't fancy waiting here long, now that Eddie's within running distance of us."

"I'm sure. Alan drives the kid to school on Tuesdays and Thursdays. Look, here he comes." John pointed to the thick-set man exiting the farmhouse with a dog at his side.

Alan crossed the yard and stepped into the back of the mansion. A few minutes later, he came out of the building through the front door, with Gisela and Pancho tagging along behind him.

Dick frowned. "I didn't realize there'd be a dog."

"Oh, c'mon!" John laughed. "It's a golden retriever! If it bothers us, we'll throw tennis balls at it and make it play fetch."

"I didn't bring any tennis balls," Dick replied.

Philip focused his camera lens on Alan and snapped a shot. "Lord, that look on Poole's face when he saw Eddie and Jenny on the blanket was priceless!" he laughed. "He obviously doesn't approve of this romance."

John watched in silence as Gisela hugged Jenny goodbye and climbed into the car parked by the mansion. As soon as the vehicle drove off, he turned towards the farmhouse. "Okay, let's get this over with."

Philip snapped another picture of Eddie and Jenny. Dick's face grew pale as he looked back and forth between the mansion and the farmhouse.

"C'mon," John called to them. "Don't worry, Eddie's not gonna notice us. He's too busy licking my cousin's face."

"What about the dog?" Dick asked.

The three men stood in place for a long moment and watched Pancho nuzzle Jenny. Jenny petted the dog for several seconds, then fell back into Eddie's arms. Pancho wandered off to a sunny patch of grass near the blanket and curled up into a ball.

"That dog doesn't look like it's going anywhere." Philip said. He started walking towards the farmhouse. "All right men, let's go pay a little call on Mrs. Rochester."

* * *

The scream shot through the air like a clap of thunder. Pancho leapt to her feet and took off running.

"What the hell?" Eddie cursed as a cacophony of shouts started emanating from the farmhouse. He disentangled himself from Jenny's arms and stood up. "Stay here!" he commanded her as he ran towards the fracas. "Don't follow me!"

"What's wrong?" Jenny called after him. She stood up from the blanket and walked to the edge of the yard.

When Eddie reached the front of the farmhouse, he saw that

Pancho had already knocked Philip to the ground and was baring her teeth at John. John met Eddie's eyes, then took off running. Pancho raced after him and dug her teeth into his calf.

"Jesus fucking Christ!" John hollered. "Goddamn dog!"

Pancho tugged at the young man's leg until he lost his balance and fell to the ground with a loud crunch. Then she ran to his face, lowered her head and started growling in his ear. John tried to grab her. She sank her teeth into his forearm and bit him again.

Philip tried to stand back up. He reached for the camera he had dropped in the fracas. Pancho ran to his side and nipped at his hand. She backed off a few steps, bared her teeth and snarled menacingly at both men.

"Good dog!" Eddie yelled, his voice barely registering over the clamor inside of the farmhouse. He ran through the doorway and saw Roberta wielding a book the size of a large brick. Lunging at her, he grabbed the book out of her hands and flung it to the floor. She howled in protest and thrust her elbows into his side. He bellowed in pain, but held onto her tightly. They wrestled with each other for several seconds before Eddie finally managed to pin her arms behind her back. She let loose an unearthly wail and thrashed her legs from side to side.

"Calm down Birdie!" he shouted.

She moaned and kicked helplessly at the coffee table, knocking a small pile of books and newspapers to the floor. He tightened his grip on her arms and called out, "Grace! Where are you? What the hell is going on?"

"I'm over here!" she shouted. Eddie turned his head and saw Grace bent over a bleeding man lying on the floor.

"It's Dick!" she yelled. "Birdie saw him at the door and started beating him in the face with that poetry anthology! I think she broke his nose."

Roberta released one last monstrous roar of protest, then collapsed against Eddie's chest like a limp rag doll. She started to sob. Pancho continued barking and snarling in the yard.

Grace slipped a pillow under Dick's head and stood up. "I'll call for an ambulance."

Eddie sensed Roberta's strength fading. He loosened his lock on her arms and held her in a gentler embrace. "It's okay, Birdie. Everything's all right now," he assured her in a calm, steady voice. "We're sending Dick away. Nobody's going to hurt you."

She nestled up against his chest. He wrapped his arms around her and rocked her back and forth until her sobs eased into whimpers. "It's okay, love. It's going to be okay," he murmured.

He bent down to kiss her forehead and offer her an encouraging smile. When he looked up, he saw Jenny staring at him through the open doorway.

## Chapter Fifteen

Eddie leaned against the wall of the hallway and rested his hand on Jenny's bedroom door. He listened for the sound of her sobbing, the sound of her packing, for any sound at all, but was met with only silence.

He sat down on the floor, splayed his fingers and pressed his palm against the door, hoping she might sense his presence through the barrier as keenly as he felt hers. Exquisite memories of the last few days rushed to his head, hurling his emotions into a tumult. But each time he tried to draw comfort from the memories, the image of Jenny standing in the farmhouse door flashed before his eyes, and the joy vanished from his heart.

He didn't notice Sally walking down the hallway until she was standing right over him. "I just got off the phone with Gerry," she said. "He'll be here on Saturday to pick up Gisela."

Eddie offered no reply.

She gazed at his forlorn expression for a long moment, then knelt down beside him and placed her hand on his shoulder. "Why don't you come downstairs?" she suggested. "I'll make you a sandwich. You haven't eaten since breakfast."

He closed his eyes and shook his head.

"She needs her space," Sally urged him. "You should come downstairs and let her rest for the evening."

He swallowed hard and whispered, "No."

Sally sighed and stood back up. "As you wish," she said. "Dr. Carter left a note for you. I put it on the desk in your library."

Eddie nodded and closed his eyes again. He listened to the sound of Sally's footsteps echoing down the hall, then turned his attention back to Jenny.

"Please, let me talk to you," he begged her once more. "You

don't have to let me in the room. I'll talk to you through the door. Please, Jenny, please. Just give me a chance to explain."

He leaned his head against the door and heard her footsteps approaching. Pressing his hand more firmly against the wood, he sensed the weight of her body pressing back against him.

"You're there, Jenny?" he asked. "Knock once if you're there."

A small thud resonated through the wood.

"Okay," Eddie said, repositioning himself on the floor. "You don't have to say a word. Just listen."

He drew a deep breath, and told her everything.

\* \* \*

Pancho licked Eddie's face, then sat down beside him and started to whine. Eddie slowly opened his eyes. She whined again.

"Someone else can take you outside," he grumbled.

She focused her sad, pleading eyes on him and whimpered.

"Okay, girl, okay," he muttered, straightening his back and rubbing at a crick in his neck. "I guess everyone else is asleep."

He stood up from the floor slowly. His legs throbbed with a dull soreness. His chest felt weighted down by the crushing ache in his heart. He cast one last sad glance at Jenny's bedroom door, then followed Pancho down the stairs. The dog headed towards the back door.

"No!" he called out, turning sharply towards the mansion's main entrance. *There's no way in hell I'm going to look at that goddamned farmhouse again tonight!* he thought. Pancho turned around and followed him into the front yard.

While the dog relieved herself, Eddie looked up at the sky, hoping against hope that a meteor might appear out of the darkness like a beacon. He lifted his face and scanned the heavens, but a thick layer of clouds covered everything, masking even the dimmest of wishing stars.

He led Pancho back into the house and up to the top floor. He gazed longingly at Jenny's door for several seconds, wondering if he had any right to open it and peek in on her while she slept.

*It's probably locked,* he decided. He turned away and stepped into his own room. The sheets on his bed lay in rumpled disarray, bearing poignant testimony to his morning tumble with Jenny. He approached the bed with a lump in his throat and pulled up the quilt. Jenny's t-shirt spilled out of a fold in the blanket. He picked it up, cradled it to his heart, and collapsed on the mattress.

\* \* \*

Gisela tugged at Eddie's arm. "*Wach auf,* Herr Rochester! *Wach auf!* Jenny *ist weg!* Wake up!"

Eddie opened his eyes and grabbed the child's shoulders. "What do you mean? When did she go?"

"I don't know!" Gisela cried. She stepped away from the edge of his bed and rubbed her eyes. "Her bike *ist nicht in der Garage.* Her rucksack and jacket are *nicht in irhen Wandschrank!*"

Eddie sprang from his bed and ran to Jenny's room. Gisela followed at his heels. Sally stood in front of the door.

"She must have left before I woke up," she apologized. "I came to check on her at eight and she was gone. She left you a note."

Eddie stepped inside Jenny's room and stared at the folded sheet of paper on top of the eiderdown quilt. He reached for it with a nauseating sense of foreboding. The words stung at his eyes:

*"Don't desert her for my sake. She needs you more."*

He swallowed hard and sank down on the bed.

Sally gave his hand a gentle squeeze, then led Gisela out of the bedroom.

Eddie stared at the abandoned furniture for several seconds, then noticed one of Jenny's sketchbooks on the desk. Her favorite sweater was hanging over her chair. *She can't be gone forever,* he thought with the bleakest of hopes. *She wouldn't have left those things behind if she never intended to come back.*

He read her note once more, then turned his face towards the bedside-table. Jenny's emerald ring was perched on top of a slim book. A sob rose in his throat. He pushed the ring aside and picked up the book. It was the collection of Indian poetry he had given her. His fingers trembling, he pulled back the cover and saw she had marked a poem with a tag. He read the opening lines:

*After the first thousand nights we had to part.*
*The sky was closed in cloud, but not quite,*
*For the wound throbbed sometimes, as lightning flickered,*

*And a long, low moaning perished in the pain*
*Of trying to utter the inexpressible.*

He held back his tears until he reached the final stanza:

*. . . but I, who still have time,*
*Have not a thought, or skill, or choice*
*But to leave you, love, in the hand of God.*

He dropped the book, covered his face with his hands, and wept.

## Chapter Sixteen

Eddie rested his hand on the knob of farmhouse door and took a long, deep breath. *Give me strength,* he prayed in his head. *This is what she wants me to do.*

He opened the door and stepped inside. Alan looked up from the television and appraised Eddie's bedraggled appearance. "Long time, no see," he noted with an air of disapproval.

"Yes, I know," Eddie agreed. "I've been busy."

Roberta kept her eyes fixed on the television screen. Eddie sat down beside her on the sofa. "Hello, Birdie," he whispered.

She continued to stare at the television.

Eddie cleared his throat. "Could you watch the rest of this show on the set in your bedroom, Alan? I want to talk to Birdie."

Alan switched off the television and left the room. Roberta turned her head and stared at the vase of tulips resting on top of an end table.

Eddie pulled a paperback book out of his jacket pocket. "I wanted to read something to you," he said, his voice shaking. "It's from your old collection of Irish poems. This is by Yeats."

He opened the book to the page he had marked and started reading aloud:

*The lover asks forgiveness because of his many moods.*
*If this importunate heart trouble your peace,*
*With words lighter than air,*
*Or hopes that in mere hoping flicker and cease—*

His voice cracked and he fell silent. He closed the book and took another deep breath.

"Oh, Christ, Birdie, I'm such a coward," he said at length. "I can't even apologize in my own words."

She turned her head and faced him.

Eddie gazed into her beautiful hazel eyes. He tried to guess what she was thinking, but came up short. After several awkward seconds of staring at her, a truth revealed itself to him. *It's no wonder I can't read her expression. I haven't looked into her eyes like this for years.*

"Birdie, I—" he began, turning away from her penetrating gaze. "I've been unfaithful to you. I know you know that, but it's about time I acknowledged it to you. I've slept with several women these past seven years when I told you I was just going on holiday. But none of them meant anything to me. Then last September I met a young woman named Jenny. She was quirky and artistic, and somehow both shy and passionate at the same time, just like you were when I first met you. She liked reading old books and taking long bike rides and listening to classic R&B records, and I fell in love with her. But now she's gone, and she's not coming back. And I'm still here. For you, and with you."

He focused his eyes on the blank television screen, too nervous to turn his face and look at her. His skin prickled with a small shock, and he felt Roberta's hand squeezing his. He turned towards her. Her eyes were moist with tears. She was smiling at him.

\* \* \*

Tony pulled a guitar case from the line of instruments stacked against the wall of Eddie's home studio. "C'mon," he said, removing an acoustic guitar from its case and handing it to his friend. "I'll set up the mics and work the boards for you. All you have to do is sing those songs for me one more time."

Eddie leaned the guitar against a tall amp. "No. I can't."

"But they were beautiful!" Tony retorted. "You played them for Jenny, didn't you?"

"Yes," Eddie said, his eyes downcast and his shoulders slumped.

"And what did she think?"

"She cried." Eddie picked up the guitar and started walking towards the empty case.

"Don't put that away," Tony said, grabbing the instrument and slinging it over his own shoulder for safekeeping. "Listen to me first. Music is an outlet for anguished souls, Eddie, and you have to be the most anguished soul on the whole goddamned planet. Record those songs now, while your emotions are still raw. They'll sound fucking amazing! Think about how powerful Lennon's *Plastic Ono Band* album was. You could top that!"

"I don't want to top that," Eddie replied. "I don't even want to think about those songs any more. I can't handle them."

"Eddie, you have to do something to try to lift your spirits. You can't just keep moping around like this for the rest of your life."

"Who says I can't?" Eddie challenged, meeting Tony's eye with a confrontational glare.

"I say so." Tony said, holding Eddie's gaze defiantly. "Just look at yourself. You must have lost two stone since March. Maybe even more. Grey hairs are sprouting out of your head faster than mushrooms after a rainstorm. And those dark shadows under your eyes make you look like an extra from *Night of the Living Dead*. You're a complete cock-up."

Eddie shrugged. "So what?"

"So Roberta looks better than you do! She smiled at me when I stopped by the farmhouse to fetch you, and had a little sparkle in her eyes. But I can't say the same for you anymore, mate. If you let yourself sink much further, you'll knock Keith Richards off the top of the annual 'Rock Star Most Likely to Die' list."

"I'm sure he'll appreciate the respite," Eddie replied.

Tony fell silent for a moment, then changed the subject. "You could still get divorced, you know. Find a nice home for Roberta and move on with your life, only with an honest conscience this time around. Jenny might even take you back if you weren't legally married anymore."

Eddie rolled his eyes. "No. This is what she wanted me to do."

Tony sighed. "This can't be what she had in mind."

"You don't know what she wanted!" Eddie barked. "You hardly even met her!"

Tony slipped the guitar off his shoulders, rested it back against the speaker, and stepped closer to his friend. "I know that she loved you, Eddie. And I know that you loved her with all your heart. And I also know you wrote her some goddamned beautiful love songs. I think you should record them. Right now, right here in your studio—without any back-up singers or violins playing in the background. I want you to sing those songs into the mic the way you sang them for Jenny—pure and simple—just you and your guitar. I'll work the boards and make sure the tapes sound good and clean. And then if you want to release them on a proper album in a couple of months you can. Or you can just file them away in your closet like a box of old love letters. But do this, Eddie. You need to get some of this weight off your chest."

"I can't," Eddie protested. "I don't have it in me anymore."

Tony stepped away from Eddie and started inspecting the recording equipment. "Christ. Would you just look at this old reel-to-reel? I haven't seen one of these machines in years!"

Eddie watched in silence at Tony pulled a dusty sheet off the sound board, then cleared his throat with a scratchy cough. "You're an incorrigible shit."

"Always have been," Tony agreed without looking up from the knobs, buttons and levers. "You've got some blank tapes, right?"

"I wouldn't know," Eddie answered. "I haven't looked through any of this old crap in years."

Tony opened a cabinet, found a stack of fresh tapes, and pulled out a narrow case. "I did an interview with the *London Eyewitness* a few weeks back," he stated casually as he worked. "I spoke with a reporter named June who used to be Philip Randall's personal assistant. She said the old git plans to write a book about you. Though for the time being, he's just selling stories about Diana and Fergie to the tabloids. Personally, I think he's a little gun-shy about resuming his investigation into your personal life, after the police hauled him off your property and tried to link him to Dick's sordid crimes."

"I hope so," Eddie replied. "Though I don't imagine he'll stay gun-shy for long."

"*The Eyewitness* never ran his story," Tony added. "June told me Phil's boss dressed him down in front of the entire news staff for teaming up with pill pushers, then sacked the sorry bugger."

"He won't give up that easy," Eddie said. "He'll let the story sit for a while, but he'll be back."

"I don't think he's going to bother you anytime soon," Tony said as he threaded a slip of blank tape into place on the recording machine. "All right now. Let's do a sound check before you start to sing, just to make sure this old gear still works."

"I'm not going to record those songs I wrote for Jenny," Eddie reiterated.

Tony ignored him and picked up a microphone stand. "I'll set up in the far corner of the room. I like how the ceiling slopes a little there. I'll bet Emmett consulted some world-class acoustics experts when he was having this studio designed. You owe it to him to finally start using the parting gift he left you."

# Chapter Seventeen

### *Lowood, Indiana*

Eddie looked up from the drawing of the covered bridge in his hands and stepped to the right. He crouched down and examined the actual bridge in front of him, then inspected the picture once more.

*This is exactly where she was sitting when she drew this,* he decided. He tried to imagine what had been going through Jenny's mind when she sketched the rustic scene.

Glancing back and forth between the picture and the wooden bridge, he was struck by how accurate Jenny's drawing was. She had captured every last detail—the peeling paint on the bridge's walls; the neglected potholes in the road running through the grass; the gnarled, half-dead branches of the old oak trees jutting out from the background.

*She was sad when she drew this,* he realized as he scrutinized the sketch. *She looked at this perfectly lovely scene, and saw all the melancholy pervading the landscape.*

He closed his eyes and tried to imagine how lonely she must have felt living at the convent. Orphaned. Friendless. Impoverished. Totally cut off from the world of her peers. Wasting the best days of her youth in a cloister filled with pious old women. *God, it's a wonder she didn't attempt suicide,* he marveled.

He turned the pages of the sketchbook and admired the other pictures she had drawn before she came to live at Thornfield. When he reached the sketches she drew of him, he closed his eyes. *This is all I have left of her now,* he thought as he shut the book. *These pictures, and the songs I wrote for her.*

Pancho stood up and started snuffling through a pile of fallen leaves. She discovered a dead mouse and picked it up by its tail.

"No!" Eddie scolded, making the drop sign with his right hand. She followed his directive and padded over to another pile of leaves to continue her rummaging.

Eddie stared at the partially decayed rodent. His heart pounded hard in his chest and an icy chill swept through him. *The police haven't found any bodies in the area that looked like her,* he reminded himself. *She's probably not dead.*

He kicked a small mound of crumbled leaves on top of the dead mouse and looked up at the late afternoon sky. A pale white moon peeked out from a curtain of wispy clouds. Memories of the cold autumn night when he and Jenny had watched the moon rise rushed to his head. He sniffed back a sob.

Pancho returned to his side. He bent down and petted her until his heart stopped racing. Then he clutched Jenny's sketchbook to his chest.

"C'mon, girl," he said. "We'd better get going. It's a long drive home, and Grace is going to make me eat birthday cake tonight."

### *Millcote, Ohio*

The flames on the candles flickered wildly as Grace carried Eddie's birthday cake to the table. "Make a wish!" she exclaimed, the forced gaiety in her voice ringing harshly against his ears.

"Let's just get this over with, shall we?" he replied as she rested the cake in front of him. He blew out the green candles shaped like a '4' and a '6' and promptly pulled them out of the cake. "Get rid of these straight away," he whispered, handing them to Grace.

She wiped the frosting off the candles' bases and handed them back. "Take them with you across the lawn," she replied.

Roberta watched their exchange with a mildly curious expression on her face.

Grace noted her interest and cleared her throat. "Hand me that knife, Alan, so I can cut everyone a piece." She cut the cake and handed out slices.

Roberta held her fork in her usual awkward grip, then rested it on the table when she was done eating. Eddie offered her a weak smile. "You seem to be feeling better these days, Birdie," he said.

"Ahm," she replied. "Andahnno wadyu wunt."

He took her hand and squeezed it, then turned his attention

back to Grace.

"I'll read to Birdie for a little while, but I want to go back to the other house tonight. I'm feeling pretty worn out." He stood up from the table and offered Roberta his hand.

"Don't forget these," Grace said, picking up the candles he had left on the table.

"Put them in my coat pocket," he replied.

Roberta turned and stared at the two candles. She resisted Eddie's efforts to guide her out of the kitchen.

"What's wrong, love?" he asked in a weary voice.

"Ahvaghfft," she said, mouthing the sounds slowly and deliberately. "Firyir burffdah."

Grace stood up from her chair and placed her hand gently on Roberta's shoulder. "You just go in the other room with your fella, lamb, while I tidy up the kitchen. Let's not cause any fuss tonight. It's Eddie's birthday, after all."

Roberta grunted an unintelligible response and stood her ground. Grace shrugged and walked to the coat rack by the door. She slipped the candles into the front pocket of Eddie's jacket and returned to the kitchen.

Roberta looked up at Eddie with a focused gaze. He stared at her, then turned and faced the living room. He glanced at the pile of presents he had just opened, resting amidst a clutter of torn wrapping paper on the floor by the sofa. "Do you want me to start reading you one of my new books tonight?" he guessed.

She pulled away from him, walked to the bookcase by the kitchen door, and plucked a thin volume off the top shelf.

He sighed. *"Sonnets from the Portuguese* again? I don't think I need the text, Birdie. I have those memorized by now."

She started leafing through the pages, then stopped when she reached Sonnet IX and held the book up for him to read. Eddie brought it closer to his eyes and recited the first line:

*"Can it be right to give what I can give?"*

He looked back at her. "Do you want me to read this one to you?"

She grabbed the book away from him, paged ahead and pointed to another poem. Eddie started reciting the lines:

*"And wilt thou have me fashion into speech
The love I bear thee—"*

Roberta quickly covered the top half of the poem with her hand and pointed to the middle section. Eddie looked back at her briefly and tried to catch her eye. She ignored his gaze and pointed repeatedly at the text. He looked at the book and started reciting the words she seemed to be indicating:

*". . . that I should bring thee proof
In words, of love hid in me out of reach.
Nay, let the silence of my womanhood
Commend my woman-love to thy belief . . ."*

She snatched the book from him and clapped it shut. He furrowed his brow. "Are you trying to tell me something, Birdie?" he asked. She shoved the book back on the shelf and walked to the staircase.

Eddie cast a befuddled look at Grace and Alan, then turned and followed his wife up the steps.

Alan chuckled. "Well, I've heard of people using an alphabet board to spell out words. And Helen Keller used to write letters in the palm of her teacher's hand. But leave it to Birdie to try to speak through a book of sappy love poems." He sliced himself another piece of cake and dug into it.

Grace sat back down at the table and picked up her fork. "Birdie wants to give him a gift," she said, trying to interpret Roberta's cryptic message. "A birthday present. But she can't tell him what she wants to give."

"That's 'cause she can't talk, Mum," Alan replied, chewing his food as he spoke.

Grace raised her eyebrow reproachfully. "Don't speak with your mouth full!" she scolded. She stabbed at her own piece of cake and scooped up a morsel. "I wonder what she wants to give him," she said as she brought the fork to her mouth.

Alan washed down his dessert with a large swig of coffee. "Dunno, Mum. But it doesn't really matter, does it? There's only one thing Eddie wants, and that's for Jenny to come back. I'm sure even Birdie knows that by now. But she can't give him that."

"No, she can't," Grace agreed. "And Jenny won't come home

as long as she thinks Eddie ought to be taking care of Birdie."

"Right," Alan said. "Well, I wouldn't waste too much time trying to figure out what Birdie might be thinking. That woman's mind doesn't work the same way ours do."

## Chapter Eighteen

"Don't go in there!" Alan shouted. He threw his arms around Eddie's chest and held him back with all his strength.

Eddie stared at the farmhouse in horror while he struggled to break free of Alan's grasp. Flames inched out of the kitchen window and licked the shutters. Bright flashes of orange light flickered behind one of the windows on the top floor.

"She's mad!" Alan exclaimed, his voice rough from shouting. "She won't come out. Mum and I tried to coax her. I even caught hold of her for a coupl'a seconds, but she bit me and threw her candle at Mum. She's like a demon tonight. Possessed. You can't save her."

"Candle? What candle?" Eddie cried. "I threw them both away!"

"I dunno. Maybe she's kept one hidden since my last birthday."

"Jesus fucking Christ!" Eddie cursed. He broke away from Alan and cast a quick glance at Grace. She was lying on the grass in her nightgown, gasping for air, with Pancho by her side. The glow of the fire bathed them both in pulses of golden light.

"Gimme your shirt!" Eddie ordered Alan.

"What the fuck?" Alan replied.

"Gimme your shirt so I can cover my face when I go get Birdie."

"You're as mad as she is!" Alan scoffed. "The firemen can fetch her! They know what they're doing."

"The firemen aren't here yet," Eddie reminded him.

Alan hesitated for a moment, then pulled off his oversized tee-shirt and threw it at Eddie. "Take my slippers too," he said. "You're fuckin' barefoot!"

"Right," Eddie said. He slipped Alan's leather scuffs over his bare feet and took off towards the farmhouse.

"No, Eddie," Grace called after him weakly.

Eddie hesitated for a few seconds outside the front porch while he summoned his courage, then bunched up Alan's shirt, covered his nose and mouth with the fabric, and entered the building.

Smoke clouded the air and stung his eyes. He brought his free hand to his brow to block out some of the flames' glare.

"Birdie!" he shouted, casting frantic glances to his right and left. "Come to me!"

The living room sofa was ablaze. A pillar of fire engulfed the bookcase by the kitchen. The wallpaper beside it was curling up at its seams, browning from the heat like a sausage in a frying pan.

"Birdie!" he shouted again. "Where are you?"

He heard a wild cry and turned his face towards the sound. Roberta stood up from behind a chair in the sitting room, holding a towel in front of her mouth. Eddie rushed towards her, but she dodged him and dashed up the steps.

*Fuck!* Eddie cursed in his head. *I'll never get out of this house alive if I go upstairs!* He threw a despairing glance at the front door, then turned and followed his wife up the staircase.

"Birdie!" he yelled over the hiss and spit of the crackling flames. "I love you! Let me help you!" He reached the top step, and following his gut instinct, ran to his wife's bedroom.

He pushed the door open and saw her standing beside her bed, clutching a burning pillow over her head.

"Birdie!" he screamed from the doorway. "Come to me now!"

"Nrowoo!" she yelled back at him. "Ah sstaheerr!"

"I love you, Birdie!" he repeated. "Come to me! Please!"

"Ahllfffyuutuu eddeee!" she replied. "Nau gohw!"

Eddie approached her cautiously, holding out his free hand in supplication. "Come on, love!" he shouted through his fabric mask. "Please! Let's get out of here!"

"Gohw!" she hollered back at him, tossing the pillow at his feet. He stepped to the left to dodge it. She grabbed the lithograph they had bought in Germany off her wall and lobbed it at him.

The corner of the metal frame hit him squarely in the chest. He winced in pain. She bolted out of the room.

*Get out of here!* screamed a voice in the back of his head. *She doesn't want to be saved! Save yourself!*

He shut out the voice and ran into the next bedroom. As soon as he entered, he saw Roberta slipping out of a gabled window. Cursing loudly, he followed her onto the roof.

A cold blast of night air smacked him in the face. He threw off his fabric mask and sucked in the oxygen with a deep, greedy breath. Flashes of red light from an approaching fire truck and ambulance rippled across the lawn. Their sirens screamed with increasing, ear-splitting urgency as they pulled up to the farmhouse, then fell silent with a drawn-out, deflated wail. Eddie turned away from the trucks and searched the rooftop for Roberta. He found her standing near the top of the house, facing the fields beyond. He cautiously worked his way up the steep, sloped tiles and stood within an arm's reach of her.

"Birdie!" he yelled, extending his arm. "Take my hand!"

She spun around and faced him. *"NO-OH!"* she screamed. "No murr! Sover frus! Yuuh murree zhennee. Ah goh." She lunged at him and pushed him away.

He lost his balance and fell backwards down the long, slanted rooftop. He grasped at the shingles as he tumbled, frantically searching for any protruding surface he could grab onto to break his fall. His right hand slid past the rain gutter. He clutched at it and held it tight while his body came to a stop at the base of the roof. The red-hot metal seared his skin.

He screamed, pulled back his hand, and rolled onto a patch of smoldering shingles. Tongues of fire escaped from a burned hole in the roof's surface near his head and licked his face.

He lay on his belly and writhed in agony until the pain enveloped him completely and he lost consciousness. A jumble of disparate images started swimming through his mind...

\* \* \*

*Pancho jumped on his chest and panted in his face. Her foul-smelling breath reeked of smoke. He looked away from the dog and saw the magnificent elm tree burning once more—an eighty foot torch of light shining luridly against a black November sky.*

*The fire consumed itself and melted into a shimmering pool of golden embers. The embers rose like fireflies from the dark green grass beneath them and started spinning in a circle around the blackened tree stump. Eddie watched the flecks of colors swirl and take shape, then looked up and gazed into Roberta's vibrant hazel eyes. "It's you," he whispered. "My love."*

"My love is fire," she replied. "And in thy sight I stand transfigured."

\* \* \*

Roberta slid down the slope of the roof and grabbed Eddie's unburnt hand. She pulled his head away from the flames, and cradled his unconscious body in her lap until the firetruck's cherry picker reached the edge of the building. Then with all the strength she could muster, she lifted her husband into a sitting position and held him upright while the fireman in the bucket grabbed him. Once the fireman had pulled Eddie to safety, he extended his free hand towards her. She held his gaze and scooted backwards.

"Come to me!" the fireman commanded her. "Now!"

Roberta stood up and ran away from him. When she reached the top of the building, she turned and locked eyes with the fireman. Her long hair and loose nightgown billowed in the waves of heat. She opened her mouth and let loose a wild cry of release, then threw herself onto a patch of fire that had sprouted from a chasm in the roof, and was swallowed by the flames.

The fireman watched the scene in silence, then lowered his face and ordered his men to pull the crane away from the house.

\* \* \*

The paramedics checked Eddie's vital signs the moment he reached the ground. They strapped his limp body onto a stretcher and rushed him into the waiting ambulance.

Sound waves from the whirling siren reverberated through his gut, summoning him back to consciousness. He opened his eyes, but was met by a blanket of darkness. He felt the sharp edge of a plastic object being pushed against his nose and chin. A rush of cool gas streamed into his nostrils. He sensed a cloth being pressed against his right hand. It felt like a branding iron. He tried to scream into the mask that was covering his mouth, but didn't have the strength. So he surrendered himself instead to the pain. He closed his eyes and welcomed the colorful, dreamlike images back to his drifting mind...

\* \* \*

*Roberta lay strapped to a stretcher beside him, looking exactly as she had the morning he accompanied her to the hospital in Switzerland. Her long raven ringlets were spread messily about her white pillow. Her exquisite face was frozen in its flower of youth.*

\* \* \*

A stabbing pain jolted Eddie out of his dream. He felt a needle puncturing his left arm and a sudden rush of warm liquid coursing through his veins. He opened his eyes, but saw nothing.

A man's deep voice pierced the darkness, offering words of encouragement. "Just hold on now," the voice said. "You're gonna make it. I won't let you die on my watch."

The words sounded achingly familiar. Jumbled memories flooded Eddie's mind and he realized he had spoken those same words to Roberta when he sat by her side in the rear of the ambulance all those years ago. He closed his eyes once more. The sedative took hold and his dream swelled back to life…

\* \* \*

*The ambulance raced through the streets of Zurich. Eddie smoothed back a loose wisp of Roberta's hair. She opened her eyes and looked up at him with a clear and focused gaze.*

*"I love you, Eddie," she said, the gentle lilt of her West Indian accent caressing the words as they eased through her full, sensuous lips. "I love you to the depth and breadth and height my soul can reach."*

*He smiled and lowered his face towards hers. And then, with a warm and tender kiss, he swallowed her final breath and set her tortured spirit free at last.*

# Epilogue

Sally guided Eddie to the folding chair in the lawn behind the mansion, then took a seat beside him. Pancho curled up on the grass by his feet.

"It's a lovely day," Sally said. "There's a bite in the air, but the sun is warm for November."

Eddie settled back in his chair and adjusted his hat to keep the sun's rays from beating on his bandaged face. "Indian summer," he muttered under his breath.

"It's hard to believe everything was covered in snow this time last year," she added. "That awful blizzard."

Memories flashed through Eddie's mind of the mad week he had spent trying to juggle the attention and affections of three separate women. He remembered gazing out the window of the farmhouse and watching Jenny and Gisela build a snowman. *I'm probably sitting right where it stood,* he thought.

*Everything is gone now,* he mused. *The snowman. The farmhouse. Belle. Birdie. Jenny. Everything.*

Sally stood up from her chair. "I'll brew up a pot of coffee," she said. "Unless you'd rather have tea."

"Coffee's fine," Eddie grumbled.

Sally returned to the mansion, leaving Eddie to his thoughts. He heard the back door open and close. A few seconds later he heard a squirrel chirp in the side of the yard. Pancho's tags jingled as she stood up, then jingled once more as she took a step away from the chair.

"Leave it," Eddie said. He signaled the sit command with his left hand. Pancho whined in protest, but curled back up at his feet.

The song of cardinals punctuated the air. Dry leaves rustled in the breeze. Pancho's heavy pants settled into a rhythmic breathing, and then a quiet snore.

*There's too much noise,* Eddie thought. *I can't even mope in peace.*

The dull clap of the front gate opening in the distance set his mind reeling. He listened with increasing irritation as a car puttered up the driveway. Its brakes squeaked. Its humming engine fell silent. Muted voices crept around the corner of the mansion, but he couldn't make them out.

*Christ, I don't need another visitor,* he groused in his head. He heard the front door of the mansion open and shut, and tensed up inside. *Who is it this time?* he wondered glumly. Nobody had called to warn him of a visit.

He waited impatiently for the back door to open. But instead, he heard the car's engine sputter back to life. He listened to the puttering grow quieter as the car drove away, and smiled to himself when he heard the front gate click shut. For a brief, hopeful moment, he believed that Alan, Grace or Sally had dispatched his unwelcome guest, and left him to bask in his loneliness undisturbed.

Then the back door opened. He grimaced. Pancho stood up, barked, and ran to the door, her tags jingling wildly.

"Who the hell is it now?" Eddie cursed.

"Wow, what a greeting," a high-pitched voice replied. "At least Pancho is happy to see me."

Eddie froze. His hair bristled and his breath caught in his throat. A powerful rush of joy washed over him, sweeping aside his dark thoughts in an instant. He leapt to his feet and reached out his hands. "Jenny!" he shouted. He took a step towards the voice and started to tremble. "You're still alive…"

"Yes, I'm still alive," Jenny replied. She walked up to him and clasped his hands. "And so are you, thank God!"

His heart pounded hard in his chest and his breath became rapid. Tears moistened the snug bandages wrapped around his eyes and he felt the sting of his injuries afresh. He squeezed her hands tightly. "It's you, it's you," he whispered, his voice breaking.

"Yes, it's me," she agreed, her voice solid and strong.

He swallowed back a sob. "God, Jenny," he murmured. "My darling, lovely girl."

A memory of her face flashed through his mind. *If only I could see her,* he thought. His voice cracked once more.

"Could I just—could I please—" he stammered. "Could I touch your face? Please?"

She lifted his hands to her cheeks. He gently rubbed the

contours of her face and the earpieces of her glasses. He stroked her chin and her forehead, then ran his fingers through her hair before letting his hands slip down to her shoulders. He drew her towards him and grew silent, taking in the feel of her body, the smell of her hair, the sound of her breathing—trying to convince himself that she wasn't just a dream.

"I can't believe you came back to me," he whispered.

"I'm not alone," she replied. She took a step backwards, then grabbed his hands and guided them down to her abdomen. "Feel this," she said.

Her belly felt strangely distended, like a hard medicine ball. Jenny pressed his fingers more firmly against her shirt. A small jab pressed back at him.

"Did you feel that?" she asked. "Your baby just kicked you!"

"Holy crap," he whispered, tears escaping from his bandaged eyes and running down his cheeks. He lifted his hands back to her face. "You're preggers?"

"You guessed it," Jenny laughed.

"When—when did you—when are you—" he stammered.

"I think you know when I got pregnant!" she replied.

"Christ," Eddie muttered, lowering his head in embarrassment.

"No, this baby is not Christ, though it is due in December," she teased. "It's just a baby. Our baby. C'mon, let's sit down. We have a lot to talk about. Mrs. F is making me some tea to go with your coffee. She said she'd bring out our drinks in a few minutes."

Eddie nodded and took a step back towards his lawn chair. He lost his footing and stretched out his arms for balance. Jenny clasped his scarred right hand and guided him back to his seat. She sat down beside him and examined his fingers.

"What happened here?" she asked gently.

He withdrew his hand. "The doctors had to amputate the tips of my pinkie and ring finger."

"Can you still play guitar?"

He exhaled slowly. "You know, I haven't even thought about that." He took a few deep breaths to quiet his nerves while he considered his reply, then admitted in a shameful voice, "I've been too busy wallowing in regret to do much of anything. But yes, I should still be able to play. I make the chords with my left hand."

"Good," Jenny stated firmly. "So you can play those songs you wrote for me when I'm in labor to calm me down. Unless they make me cry again. Then you can play me Ruth Brown covers instead."

Eddie could hear the smile in her voice. He tried to smile back as a new, bittersweet reality floated over him. *A baby, Christ! I'm going to be a father. A blind, eight-fingered father.*

"I'll play anything for you," he promised, facing her but not seeing her. A fresh set of tears dampened his bandage.

"Can the doctors do anything about your eyes?" she asked.

"I don't know, maybe," Eddie said with a sniff. "There's a surgeon flying up from Miami to see me after Thanksgiving. He runs one of the best eye centers in the country. My doctors called him a miracle worker. Maybe he can help."

"I hope he can," she said. She took both of his hands in hers and drew in a deep breath. "The first thing I have to say to you is that I'm sorry. I'm sorry I left without telling you where I was going. I'm sorry I never got in touch with you after I got there. And I'm really sorry I never told you I was pregnant. That last one has been eating at me. You had a right to know."

He squeezed her hands back. "Apologies accepted, unconditionally. I'm the one who should spend the rest of my life apologizing to you. I've been such a bastard."

"Well, yeah, you're right," she agreed. "Though you always were kind of cranky, so maybe I shouldn't have been surprised."

He lifted his head and laughed for the first time in months. The heavy weight of remorse that had been crushing him down since springtime finally started to slip off his shoulders. "So where did you go?" he asked when he managed to compose himself once more. "And why did you come back?"

Jenny let go of his hands. "It's a long story, and I promise to tell you everything later. But I'll give you a quick rundown now. I followed in my mother's footsteps and went to California. Only I didn't hitchhike like she did. I took a Greyhound bus."

Memories of the horrible day she had left rushed back to his head. "You took your bike," he corrected her.

"Yeah. I hid it in an abandoned barn a few miles from the convent, near this crossroads where I'd seen Greyhound buses stop before. It took me a couple of days to get to the West Coast. But I eventually found my way to San Diego."

"San Diego?" Eddie repeated. "Why did you go to San Diego?"

"I told you—I was following in my mother's footsteps," Jenny answered. "I had the letter she sent my uncle along with that picture I showed you, and her address was on the envelope. But I had a hard time finding her old house. It was in the desert, outside of the city. And it's not an ashram anymore. It's a Catholic mission house run by an order of nuns who serve Mexican immigrants."

Eddie tried to picture the scene. Images of the convent in Lowood sprang to his mind. "You went and lived with nuns again."

"That's right," she said, gently stroking his knee. "And I fit right in, at least at first. But I was afraid you'd try to find me, so I made up a new name for myself and said I was from Illinois. And when my stomach got too big for me to hide being pregnant, I invented an imaginary boyfriend from Chicago, and told the nuns he left me for a rich girl whose family gave me money to go away. And after a while, I got so caught up in the lies I was telling them, I didn't even know how to speak the truth anymore."

"God, this sounds achingly familiar," he said, his voice growing sad once more. "You learned your craft from a master."

"We're an awful lot alike," she agreed.

She squeezed his hands again. Her skin felt cool against his.

"You're cold," he said. "We should go inside. I don't think Sally is going to bring us out our drinks."

"In a minute," she replied. "Let me just finish my story. So last week Sister Inez drove me to a clinic for a check-up. And there was a crazy, fierce wind blowing across the desert."

"The Santa Anas," Eddie said, remembering the howl of the wind outside a Los Angeles hotel room where he had once stayed. He pictured palm fronds flying through the air and piling up against fences. "I've felt them."

"They're kind of scary!" Jenny agreed. "But anyway, as I was getting out of the car, I heard your voice on the wind. It took me a few beats to realize it was actually your voice on a car radio in the parking lot, but it freaked me out. Then in the waiting room, I picked up a copy of *People*. I saw a story about you and your wife and the fire, and I started crying so hard, the doctor had to give me something to calm me down. When I finally stopped sobbing, I told him and Sister Inez everything. It felt so good to be honest again. Then the doctor bought me a ticket to Cincinnati so I could be with you. He told me he and his wife danced to *Dreaming Tonight* at their wedding. It was their song."

Eddie opened his mouth in slack-jawed amazement. "Okay. Wow. That's a weird twist."

Jenny tickled the palm of his left hand. "It gets even weirder. Guess what I found in the attic of the mission house?"

"I haven't a clue," Eddie chuckled. "A missionary, perhaps?"

"No, something even better—a box filled with junk the hippies had left behind! I found my mom's old sketchbook, with pictures of me as a baby and a lot of drawings of my dad in the nude! And tucked in the back of the book was my dad's old draft card, all covered in rude doodles!"

Eddie laughed deeper. "How rude?"

"Pretty disgusting," she said. "I was almost tempted to burn the card so the nuns wouldn't see it. But the coolest thing was, I learned that my father's name wasn't really 'Ayr'. That was just an alias he used after he dodged the draft. His real last name was 'Earhart', like Amelia. So I share a name with a pilot. I can join your band now!"

Eddie sighed and gave her hands another squeeze. "And here I was, hoping you would want to change your name to Rochester."

Jenny stood up from her chair. She lifted Eddie's hands up high. He stood up as directed. She wrapped her arms around his neck and kissed him hard on the lips.

"Ow," he said. "That hurt. My face is still burnt."

"Sorry," she replied. She kissed a finger on his left hand and lifted it gently to his lips. "Does that make it feel better?"

Eddie nodded.

"I love you, Eddie," she said.

He broke into a wide smile.

"You called me 'Eddie'!" he laughed. "Not 'Mr. R'!"

"Yes," she agreed. "You're not my cranky old boss anymore. I quit my job. Remember?"

"How could I ever forget?" he replied. He wrapped her into his arms and held her steady, breathing in her scent and feeling the weight of their child against his abdomen.

The quiet peace of the farm enveloped them as they held one another. Then Eddie lowered his head and kissed her brow.

"Jenny," he whispered. "My beloved Sajani. You are my hope, my heart. My life."

*fin*

# Author's Note

Reader, I thank you!

I truly appreciate your taking the time to read this book. I hope you enjoyed it. It's been a long time in the making.

I started writing this novel in 2007, after my childhood friend Mary died of breast cancer. It was Mary who first told me the story of *Jane Eyre* when we were traveling by bus to Canada on a high school class trip. My first draft (entitled *A Wing and a Prayer,* for the Pilot and the convent school girl) was basically a re-write of *Jane Eyre*, told from Jenny's point-of-view. After I finished it, I started writing sequels, plopping Eddie's bandmates Tony, Gerry and Jim into the other novels by the Brontë sisters. I took a lot more liberties with the plots of those books.

But *Jane Eyre* was always my favorite of the Brontë novels, and I kept coming back to *A Wing and a Prayer*. I rewrote it in third-person point-of-view, chopped Jenny's tortured childhood into a single opening chapter, and started fleshing out Eddie's character, making him less like the original Mr. Rochester and more of a kind-hearted (though often clueless) poet. I still wasn't happy with the book, however, especially now that I'd written three sequels with a pop star as the central character. *A Wing and a Prayer* didn't really fit in the series I'd created.

So in 2010, I threw the whole book out, rewrote it from Eddie's point of view, and retitled my new novel *Mr. R*. While I miss some of the characters I created for *A Wing and a Prayer,* especially Jenny's childhood friend Eileen Burns (who was modeled after my friend Mary), I loved developing the characters in Eddie's life, particularly his bandmates, Grace Poole, and Roberta. I tried to make Birdie a woman who could inspire not only an album of great love songs, but a life-long love as well. I hope I succeeded.

Since finishing my first draft of *Mr. R*, I've fought my own battle with breast cancer. I'm in remission now. But I still think about Mary a lot, and wonder how she would have liked what I did with the story she told me on that long, dark bus trip from Cincinnati to Montreal.

If you liked this book, please tell your friends about it. Share it with your book club. Review it on Amazon. And if you'd like to read the sequels, please check them out! I've published one already (*Restless Spirits*, a mash-up of *Wuthering Heights* and *Agnes Grey*), and am presently getting a third book ready for publication (*Wildfell Summer*, a magical mystery trip through the pages of *The Tenant of Wildfell Hall*).

Please drop me a line if you'd like to contact me. You can reach me at tracyneis@aol.com, on my Facebook page (Mr. R by Tracy Neis), or through my blog:

https://mrrarockrollromance.wordpress.com/

~Tracy Neis

# Many Thanks

I find myself once again drawn to the inimitable prose of Charlotte Brontë, who wrote in the preface to the second edition of *Jane Eyre* that the publication of a book by an "unknown and unrecommended author...demands a few words both of acknowledgement and miscellaneous remark."

First of all, I would like to thank Cat and Gineve at Mischievous Muse for taking a chance on me, and for all of their help in guiding me through the process of developing and editing this story.

Many thanks are also due to:

My husband Mike—for his endless love and support in not just this literary undertaking, but in all of my other endeavors.

My daughters Emily, Karen, Laura and Maria—my very first readers, and the source of so much inspiration. Eddie's mistresses would also like to thank you for lending them your names.

My other "first" readers (of both this book and its many other previous drafts and attempted sequels)—Louanne Bachner, Warren Brown, Jennie Brown Hakim, Merrijoy Buist, Patricia Cooper Courtney, Mercy Hume, Paula Roth, Megan Roxberry, and Jack Wessling. Thank you for all of your time and input.

Louise Fallon Brown—for your help translating my English dialog into German. *Danke viel mal!*

Tessa O'Shea—for helping me with English slang.

Laura Neis—for leading me through the self-publishing process.

Karen Neis—for your beautiful artwork.

Ron Cree—You had *one thing to do!* And you did it brilliantly. May flights of angels sing you to your rest.

My many English teachers who encouraged me over the years to write—especially Jane Hutchins, Chris Modrill, James Robinson and Thomas Jermelity.

The California Writers Club (Orange County Branch)—for providing so many helpful tips at your monthly meetings.

Stevie T of Moptops Tours—for chauffeuring my daughter and me to Haworth to see the Brontë Parsonage.

And, of course, my gratitude rests on the shoulders of Charlotte Brontë, who wrote a truly magnificent novel in 1847 which has continued to inspire readers, writers and lovers ever since.

# Acknowledgments

The author wishes to thank the estate of Buddhadeva Bose for its kind permission to quote Mr. Bose's poem "A Parting" in this novel. The poem first appeared in print in the United States in *Green and Gold, a Bengali Anthology*, edited by Humayan Kabir and published by New Directions (Norfolk, CT) in 1958.

*The following works were quoted or paraphrased in this book:*

*Jane Eyre*, by Charlotte Brontë (published in 1847)

"Elegy XIX: To His Mistress Going to Bed," by John Donne (1654)
"Goblin Market," by Christina Rossetti (1862)
"In a Gondola" (1842) and "Rabbi ben Ezra" (1864), by Robert Browning
"Love and Sleep," by Algernon Charles Swinburne (1866)
"The Lover Asks Forgiveness Because of his Many Moods," by William Butler Yeats (1899)
"The Love Song of J. Alfred Prufrock," by T.S. Elliot (1915)
"Love's Philosophy" (1820) and "The Indian Serenade" (1822), by Percy Bysshe Shelley
"A Plea," by Paul Lawrence Dunbar (1896)
*Richard III* (circa 1592), *Venus and Adonis* (circa 1592), *Romeo and Juliet* (circa 1595), *A Midsummer Night's Dream* (circa 1595), *Macbeth* (circa 1603 to 1607), and *Sonnets 18 and 147* (circa 1609), by William Shakespeare
*Sense and Sensibility*, by Jane Austen (1811)
*Sonnets from the Portuguese*, by Elizabeth Barrett Browning (1855)
"To a Mouse, on Turning Her Up in Her Nest with the Plough" (1785), "Auld Lang Syne" (1788), and "My Love is Like a Red, Red Rose" (1794), by Robert Burns
"To Celia," by Ben Johnson (1616)
"Who Ever Loved," by Christopher Marlowe (1598)
"The World is Too Much With Us Here," by William Wordsworth (1807)

Book Two in the *Rock and Roll Brontë Series*

# Restless Spirits

Bad luck happens in threes.

Or so it would seem for British Invasion-era keyboardist Jim McCudden. First his car conks out on him in a desolate patch of Northern Ohio farmland. Then he suffers a crippling injury while seeking shelter in a seemingly abandoned cottage. But Jim's troubles really begin when he meets the cottage's proprietors — an ethereal hippie chick named Cathy and her bad-tempered ex-boyfriend Cliff.

Meanwhile, across the pond, English piano teacher Maggie Grayson finds herself hosting more visitors than she can handle when she opens her home to three uninvited guests—Jim's two children and the disembodied spirit of a garrulous governess named Agnes.

This rock-and-roll romp through *Wuthering Heights* and *Agnes Grey* brings together the plots and characters from Emily and Anne Brontë's classic novels in a toe-tapping ghost story that will set your heart racing and your spirit soaring.

"I loved the merging of two very different storylines and the spin Neis puts on it. Reader, I really enjoyed this one, and I actually think it's better than "Mr. R."

*—Nicola Friar, author of*
**The Brontë Babe Blog**

*Coming Soon...*

# Wildfell Summer

It's 1967—the Summer of Love—and the Pilots are touring America. But much to his bandmates' surprise, drummer Gerry Enis is skipping the after-show parties every night and curling up with a novel in his hotel room instead.

The hard-drinking percussionist, however, is not just *reading* his book. He's found a way to go tripping into the pages of Anne Brontë's tour de force *The Tenant of Wildfell Hall,* so he can party alongside the notorious Arthur Huntington, one of the most dissolute characters in all of English literature.

Can Gerry's bandmates and manager find a way to tear their friend away from his fictional foil? Or is Gerry destined to become the first rock star in history to succumb to the dangers of laudanum addiction and Victorian-style debauchery?

Roll up, roll up to *Wildfell Summer.* It's dying to take you away...

# About the Author

Since earning her degree in English from the University of Notre Dame, Tracy Neis has written for numerous publications, including *Cincinnati Magazine*, *Goldmine*, and *Beatlefan*. She is the author of the Rock and Roll Brontë series of novels—*Mr. R: A Rock and Roll Romance* and *Restless Spirits*—and the young adult collective biography *Extraordinary African-American Poets* (Enslow). She also publishes Beatles-themed fan fiction on her blog, cremetangerine.video.blog, and under the name CremeTangerine on fanfiction.net and archiveofourown.org. A proud Ohio native, Tracy currently lives in Southern California with her husband and four daughters.

Made in the USA
Las Vegas, NV
01 October 2023

78395474R00208